THE COUNCILLOR

THE COUNCILLOR

E. J. Beaton

DAW BOOKS, INC.

DONALD A. WOLLHEIM, FOUNDER

1745 Broadway, New York, NY 10019

ELIZABETH R. WOLLHEIM
SHEILA E. GILBERT
PUBLISHERS

www.dawbooks.com

First Printing, March 2021
1 2 3 4 5 6 7 8 9

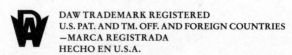

DAW TRADEMARK REGISTERED
U.S. PAT. AND TM. OFF. AND FOREIGN COUNTRIES
—MARCA REGISTRADA
HECHO EN U.S.A.

PRINTED IN THE U.S.A.

For John—
my first reader
my biggest supporter
my other half.

You are in everything I do.

One

The shape of a crown stood out in the emerald wax of the seal, and Lysande glanced at it once before looking away, staring at anything but that envelope. She raised her vial and drank. Gold tinged the room, spreading from the corners, glossing the piles of manuscripts and slipping across the bedsheets; she felt it transmute her insides, moving from her chest to her abdomen. The clink of glass dripped luster, and through it all, she struggled against a surging wish to let the effects spread and spread.

"Signore Prior!"

Calm settled upon her. The vial felt newly cool, as if it truly had been purified; as if it had never contained a spoonful of chimera scale, nor any ingredients that might mix and, if swiftly consumed, permeate the bloodstream. She did not need to think about the composition of the drug. She certainly did not need to think about the envelope.

"If you please, Signore Prior, the queen would see you."

The ball of emotion in her chest had begun to soften. How easy it would be to let it dissolve, under the same force that had gilded her vision. The old chant repeated in her mind: *restrain, constrain, subdue.*

When the messenger shouted through the door again, she pushed against her ease and forced her fingers to trade the vial for an empty basin. Slowly, she withdrew a small piece of hardened resin from her desk drawer and watched the surface of the stone glitter in the candlelight. After staring at it for a long time, she drew a swift breath and placed the night-quartz on her tongue. The reaction worked through her, and she bent over and retched; her hands gripped the edges of the basin until everything was expurgated. In the middle of the blue liquid, her own eyes shone, and she glimpsed something that was almost desperation.

Words drifted through the door. As Lysande threw on a pair of trousers, she anchored herself to the messenger's phrase: *the queen would see you.*

Gathering her keys, she put on her best doublet, a thick garment in the royal green, with only a smattering of ink-spots. She took the envelope with the emerald seal from her desk and paused, staring at it for a long time, turning it over in her fingers before slipping it into her pocket.

The physicians were leaving the royal suite as she arrived, carrying baskets of tools; only Surrick lingered in the corridor, wiping her hands on her robe. She nodded to Lysande, who nodded back slowly.

Lysande turned away from the chief physician and approached the suite. Her stomach swirled, but she kept her back straight and her hands from trembling.

Through the antechamber, trying not to look at the points of the swords in the brackets, she kept up a stiff gait. In the bedchamber, she threw up a hand to shield her eyes. Sunlight embossed the shelves on the wall. She watched an aureole form around a silver chalice, illuminating the words *Sarelin Brey—Unifier, Warrior, Conqueror—the Hand that Held Back the White Tide and Saved Elira*. Lysande shook her head and, after a moment, ran her finger over the edge of the envelope in her pocket.

"Sarelin?" Her voice resounded in the chamber.

She walked to the bed. The robe on the sheets drew her gaze, mottled with blood.

"Sarelin? Are you awake?"

"I hope so," a woman's voice said. "If this is the next life, it's lacking a bottle of red."

She felt the weight of Sarelin's presence, even before a figure emerged from behind the dressing-screen. Lysande was certain that the queen had not only chosen this position to show off the daggers at her left hip, nor the sword at her right, for at this angle, sunbeams struck the dent in her armor, turning it into a gleaming scar.

"Thank Cognita!" Lysande said.

"You can thank those damned physicians." Sarelin strode over and clapped her on the shoulder until her teeth knocked. "If they don't stop hectoring me, I'll tip the ghastly potion down their throats."

"Armor after an injury, though? Is that your wisest idea?"

"Surrick says I'm healed enough for it."

"And did you perhaps order Surrick to tell you that?" Lysande said.

"You want to watch that you're not too clever before breakfast. You can't enjoy a tart if you're full of a retort." As Sarelin clanked over to her table and poured herself a goblet of vivantica, Lysande noted the absence of a flush in her cheeks. The queen was not the wan figure she had been a few days ago when two women in armor carried her into the palace, shouting about a panther attack, but she still looked drawn, Lysande thought: too drawn by far.

She tested the words she had planned in her head.

"Ugh." Sarelin eyed the rose-pink liquid, swirling it in the cup. "Here, Trichard, Trichard!" A ball of golden fur leaped up from one of the chairs into Sarelin's hand. "You did a good job finding this little fellow."

"Call it an investment in the realm." Lysande tried to conjure a smile, hoping it would not crack.

"He lives up to his namesake." Sarelin tickled the tiny monkey. "Father could never shut his mouth, either."

The monkey chattered, as if on cue. It took a sip of the medicine and smacked its lips, and the two women laughed as one, Lysande's smile softening.

"Surrick's been bleating at me since I woke, telling me to use your little taster every time I drink. Claims your monkey can sniff out poison in seconds." Sarelin gave the animal another stroke. "Maybe she's got a point. With the whole realm thinking I'm about to collapse, there's some who'd like me to collapse faster."

Some moments arrived like a break in a song: pauses between beats that were not prearranged but opened up of their own accord, when the musicians drew breath. Lysande was looking at Sarelin, and then, in the space between words, she was aware of everything that she had agonized over since the hunt returned: all the possibilities, suspicions, and doubts, culminating in last night's reading. Sentences needled her mind.

She should at least say something. A hint about the panther. The animal was not the problem, but as for the associations that her research had thrown up . . . there was a certain name that you did not say, if you were wise, and Lysande was already bargaining with herself. When Sarelin was well enough to bark a greeting at the guards; when Sarelin was slamming the door of her suite and making the swords trembling in their brackets; when the queen's cheeks were flushed, then, she would bring up the possibility that the panther's attack had not been a coincidence.

Sarelin downed the goblet of vivantica in one go, shuddering, and reached underneath one of the platters. "I know it's late, but take this as the second half as your gift-day present."

"Sarelin, you cannot—"

"How dare you tell a queen what she cannot do?" Sarelin thrust a box under Lysande's nose, her face half-split with a smile.

Lysande opened the lid. The feather dazzled her eyes. Every barb was star-bright; the stem shone, painted gold and whittled to a point. She lifted the quill out of the box.

The first half of the present had been a gold dagger, presented a week ago, on the day that marked twenty-two years since she was found. She had never understood how the silverbloods expected her to celebrate that day, as if her childhood were a play with a magnificent ending. The problem with nobles was that they could not imagine a genre aside from heroic drama. What kind of story was it if your parents had abandoned you in a carpenter's shop during the war, a naked child in a room of blazing wood—tragicomedy? Or farce?

But the dagger. That was worth celebrating. Sarelin's present had carved straw enemies in the target range. Lysande turned her gaze to the quill now. Squinting, she made out her own face in the surface of the feather. The frown and the straggling mane of hair glimmered in reflection; she really should have combed her hair this morning, but at least the glinting, deathstruck lock was hidden beneath the other strands.

"You're spoiling me," she said.

"It's an exchange. You're going to copy out the news of my recovery."

"Ah. Of course I am."

"Anyway . . . there's no better scholar. Haven't I said it enough times? You're the girl who translated the Silver Songs, Lys. The girl with the quill."

Those were the same words Sarelin had spoken the day she had visited the schoolroom of the orphanage, the day that she had questioned each child about the history of Elira. *I'll take the girl with the quill*, she had said. Lysande swallowed. She placed the quill back in its hollow. In the pit of her stomach, unsaid things circled around and around and kicked, and every warning she had rehearsed in the last two days strained to get out.

"And you're taking care of the envelope for me," Sarelin said slowly, holding Lysande's gaze. "That deserves a reward."

It would not help, to run her hand over the envelope again. It would not aid her one jot to take it out and gaze at it—if overthinking could have made her feel confident, she would already be a worriless scholar. Lysande hugged Sarelin, her fingers interlacing behind the silver breastplate. There were too many chalices and plates on the wall, she thought; too many gleaming things from which her own countenance could gaze back.

She left the target range in the quiet before dusk. Once the door to her chamber was shut, she removed the jar from her drawer, unscrewed the lid, and dipped the spoon in, taking care not to let her hand tremble as she tipped a spoonful of shredded scale into the vial. Blue. Still the same stock, the same hue shining; maybe in a year or so, the smugglers would source their product from different chimera remains. Then she would be spooning out purple scale, or green. The properties of a long-dead beast were likely to transmogrify . . . with each different stock, new risks blossomed . . . Charice's warnings repeated themselves to her, but she could smell the scale wafting up in dozens of different notes.

Spiced wine, grass after heavy rain, and the scent of old books when the covers had begun to wear; sometimes, like today, the chimera scale smelled of the things she enjoyed. At other times, she caught the scent of things she had tried to forget, like the rotten wood of the floorboards at the orphanage, and pipe-smoke: a thick tang from a particular herb which she had breathed all too recently.

Lysande held the vial over the fireplace until the heat nipped at her fingers. She poured the shredded scale into the goblet, tipped in a spoon of sugar from a jar on her desk, then added two spoons of water from another goblet.

The mixture began to fizz. It shivered and melted, leaving behind a liquid the color of lake water in the early morning, and Lysande drank until the goblet was half-empty. Her heartbeat began to hammer with the force of an angry blacksmith, but she ignored it; if she had pressed a hand to her forehead, she knew that she would have felt a fiery swathe of skin. Her stomach writhed. She told herself to push through the symptoms, one by one; to hold on to the thought of the reward. The calm spread through her next: it might not be pleasure that coursed through her veins, exactly, but she could see everything without frustration. The world around her, from the papers on her desk to the light streaming through the window and the wood of the bedposts—it all felt golden. The worries within her melted away and a purity imposed itself onto the room.

Had she really been thinking about the panther all afternoon? Had she truly been considering telling Sarelin what she had discovered, weighing it against the risk of the queen storming through the palace, forgoing medicine and rest? Had she really been imagining the way that rage dug trenches on Sarelin's brow—the way that Sarelin's voice smoked with fury when she swore revenge on one particular woman?

She tilted the goblet. Another drop of the concoction landed on her tongue. The hammer-blows of her heartbeat began to land faster and faster.

How familiar the practice of avoidance could be, and how sweet. There would be no need for night-quartz this time. She took the new quill from its box and traced a few shapes in the air, snaking the tip around.

Her hand flew over the pages of her notes, tracing tables of siege campaigns and checking officers' names sprinkled in brown ink. It was easy to forget about her distress when she was unearthing details, picking out the fine points from the stories and records that immersed her in another time. The tasks had changed, slowly. In her early years in the palace, she had compiled and translated as much of the realm's political history as she could, leafing through fat manuscripts in the queen's private library that had promised tales of assassinations, old stories of chimera attacks, and newer, mud-spattered accounts of rebellions. She had summarized trade deals, cross-referencing them with foreign alliances, noting whether they were achieved with arms or ink. Only when she had felt confident enough in her knowledge of history had she begun to search for patterns, analyzing the strategies that Elira's queens and kings had used against invaders, and classifying the tactics that city-rulers had employed to defend or expand their territory. It had taken many false starts with a quill before she had written the first words of her own treatise, the title pricked out boldly in rare violet ink: *An Ideal Queen.*

Today, she could not write for long. No matter what approach she tried to take, the prose came out in ungainly lumps. Sarelin's confident smile appeared in her mind, undercutting every sentence.

She opened her map-book, turning to the pages at the back. After surveying the diagrams of the White War for a moment, she touched the golden quill to the paper.

The final battle came out quickly; the Mud Field bloomed with legions and captains on her page, the Pyrrhan clash appearing on the White Army's left flank and the archers on the right. She covered the field with thin lines, marking the movements of the battalions.

There remained one thing to add, after the White Queen's advance: Sarelin's last charge. Her quill hovered above the page. Somehow, she could not touch it to the map.

Beneath her flow of thought ran a stream of a deeper source, an augury within the flesh that she had never felt before. The rhythm in her body warned her that something terrible—perhaps something terrible and great at once—was coming over the horizon toward her.

That night, she did not dream of a panther and rivulets flowing wine-dark down Sarelin's sides, as she had since the queen's injury. When she closed her eyes, her fingers gripped the top of a scratched desk, and she fell into the flow of recitation, evading the stares of the other children.

Sarelin's hand grasped her own and shook it, just as they had first shaken hands all those years ago. The touch seared her. She had been

so busy naming the five monarchs of the Steelsong Era, in the orphanage, that she had not noticed the royal gloves coming off. That palm
felt so warm . . . and then the queen was pointing to her, signaling to
the headmistress . . .

But now the nature of that pointing changed; they were walking in
the forest, and Sarelin was jabbing at Lysande's chest, shouting. Although she could not hear the accusation, she knew that she had said
something to rile Sarelin—another argument over the execution policy? Her boots squelched in the wet soil. She drew a blanket from her
saddle bag, flung it over the soft mud in front of the queen, and watched
pleasure spread over Sarelin's face like a new dawn, the two of them
gazing at the crown woven into the cloth for a moment. They stood
side by side until the wrath of the northerly sent the blanket flying.
Lysande watched as Sarelin flailed, the earth giving way beneath her
boots, a dark gash opening and widening.

She rushed to the edge of the hole and flung herself down. Shouting
the queen's name, she reached out. Sarelin's strong fingers grabbed her
own, and she pulled, straining every sinew in her body to haul her up,
because whatever happened, she must not let go of Sarelin's hand . . .

Yet you could not hold what you had never possessed, even if you
tried with every particle of your being. Lysande wanted to dive and
grab Sarelin, but the soles of her feet would not obey. She remained
rooted to the ground as the queen tumbled into the darkness.

She opened her eyes and a shower of light greeted her. Despite the
glow, she shivered.

The golden quill awaited on her desk, and she forced herself to pick
it up, focusing on her phrasing as she spelled out Sarelin's news; once
she had sped through her writing, she combed her hair quickly in front
of the mirror, pausing, for a second, to finger the deathstruck strands
on the left side of her part. The lock of silver hair evaded understanding, even to her. The longer she looked, the more clearly she could see
that it was not silvered by natural age but by a queer and sharp flecking
of radiance, like the glitter of angry stars. Was it a failure of her own
scholarship that, after all this time, she could not confirm whether a
heightened color or a bleaching of the strands made the hair shine?

"Be proud of your mark," Sarelin had told her, a few years ago, when she had visited Lysande's room to escort her to the jubilee, stopping in front of the small mirror. "Be proud of the bold and curious thing that sets you apart."

"Easy to say when you bear the scars of battle, and the realm loves you for it." Lysande had put a finger to her hair. "You charged through a fire—I merely survived one."

"Other children survived the blazes of the White War. All manner of little brats from the Addischild family seem to have lived through them, though the goddesses know it would have been cheaper for the crown if they hadn't had a lake to dive into back then." Sarelin pointed a finger at Lysande's hair. "But you, only you, bear this glorious mark."

"You know it looks . . . queer. It makes people feel unsettled." And not from admiration, Lysande wanted to add.

"Well, I have to work very hard to make people feel unsettled. You should be pleased."

She had looked down with a dutiful smile, avoiding Sarelin's stare, fearing to find a hint of pity in it, but when she had looked up again, Sarelin had been gazing at her hair with a pensive expression. "Perhaps it is not the hair itself that matters, Lys. Perhaps you were always going to stand out. The hair is just a reminder."

The words sounded in her head with the clarity of a silver bell.

Carefully, she tucked the deathstruck lock beneath other strands and smoothed her ordinary, red hair over it, until it was entirely concealed.

She descended from the staff tower and strode through the hedges and fountains of the grounds. Light ribboned the walls, just sufficient for Axium Palace to glow a pale, cold, glistening silver, turning the twenty-four spires atop its buildings into needles. Their gleam reminded Lysande of the dent in Sarelin's armor, the mark that had become more famous than the crown since the war; a dent that she had once seen a captain kneel to kiss. Lysande had sketched the scene, later, inside the back cover of her own book. For a moment, she had been tempted to draw a smile on Sarelin's face. But on reflection, she found that she preferred the expression she had seen: a grim look, tinged with determination. Some women would have worn the evidence of the White Queen's blow as if it was a badge of talent, the mark that sealed a permanent victory. Sarelin had never made that mistake.

Lysande crossed the lawn, now, passed the target range, and entered the library. Columns of hard-bound tomes shone in the slivers of dawn that pierced the windows, throwing out a light brighter than that of the oil lamps. It comforted her to smell the leather and to feel the presence of so many books around her. She could never be alone in a realm of shelves, where characters from ancient stories might speak to her in smooth metaphors and pleasantly gnarled phrases, and places she had never seen might spring into life, painted in the full range of hues that her imagination supplied, offering a pale green forest, a mountain daubed with gray limestone, or an ocean splintered by the dying sun. Making her way to the volumes on the far side of the chamber, she selected a book whose cover bore the words *A Study of Northern Flora and Fauna* and sequestered herself in the quietest corner, focusing her attention on the pages.

Her finger traversed the entry on panthers. A map of the habitat, a list of suggestions for hunting, a picture with anatomical notes . . . and at last, the characteristics of Elira's common panther . . . she sped through the list and stopped at the words *green eyes*. Her breath quickened. She tried to calm it in vain.

After she had signed three books out of the library, she walked into the courtyard with her head down, still contemplating the same phrase, and nearly crashed into a wall of silver armor.

Captain Raden Hartleigh halted, his "sorry, sorry, Lys" washing over her. Raden was not a short man, but nor did he possess Lysande's commanding height; for all that, he seemed to take up more space than the average Axiumite, the breadth of his shoulders giving him the presence of a well-plated bull.

"Becalm yourself, Raden. My bones are not noble enough to be fragile."

"What were you doing, galloping along without looking up?" Raden said.

"Thinking."

He returned her smile. "I've done enough of that for a year. Thought I'd never get rid of that pair." He jerked his head at two nobles watching them from an archway. "The silverbloods are all riled about the appointment of a new Councillor. I must've told them twenty times that even if I had the envelope, I wouldn't give it to them."

Lysande tried not to look at her doublet pocket, where a flat piece of paper lay. "You'd think they'd be pleased to keep out of it."

"They think they've got the right to rip the thing open and scrawl their own names. I warned them, plain enough: as Her Majesty lives, there's no need to put a city-ruler on the throne, and no need for a Councillor to choose one." Raden's look darkened.

She tried to stop the surge of memory, but it was no good: again she saw the pillows emblazoned with the Axium crown, and Sarelin perched atop them, her hawkish gaze softening as Lysande sat down beside her. Blood crusted the queen's robe. Lysande had placed her fingers carefully below the stain and peeled back the silk to reveal three pink gashes, one of the cuts slicing so deep that she glimpsed intestine.

"I know this isn't an easy time for you." Raden's voice sounded distant. "All this talk of an heirless monarch . . ."

Lysande felt something ripple within her. She clasped the books to her chest.

No, she thought. She can't be inked into some sealed account.

"Let's speak of something else, then," she said. "Like this heinous panther. Are you sure about what you told me last night?"

"Couldn't miss it. The thing looked right at me, before it lunged at her. Thought I was going half-mad. Seeing coins in midair, or something. Of all the colors, *yellow* eyes . . ."

Lysande fell silent. They walked together back across the grounds, with the ease of those who have shared many silences. In her mind's eye, Lysande picked up the four bunches of nectar roses that had arrived at the palace and considered the thorns poking out from each stem.

"Did you notice the prince of Rhime's gift, Raden?"

"A hundred cadres' worth of nectar roses? I think even the stable-hands noticed."

"I was thinking more of how quickly he sent them." Sarelin had once declared that the only weakness she would discuss with the prince of Rhime was his own, and Lysande did not think the queen had mellowed just because she was injured. All of the other flowers had been sent by Axiumite nobles. How had the prince of the eastern city learned so quickly of the queen's hunting accident?

"It's not those flowers I'm worried about," Raden said.

She was aware of his glance. "I know the paucity of viva-flowers in the royal medicine-garden as well as you do, Raden."

"Fortituda save her," Raden muttered. She stopped and faced him. Without a word, she embraced him, and he held her too, stepping back after a second and giving her the customary brusque pat on the shoulder to finish, the nearest thing to an Axiumite consolation. Raden was never one to overstep a customary line.

He peeled off to greet a group of guards at the stables, and Lysande returned to her chamber, poring over *A Study of Northern Flora and Fauna* at her desk. She was nursing Haxley's *Guide to Eliran Wild Beasts*, ignoring the cramp in her neck, by the time the first mist of evening blanketed the palace. She did not douse the candles until her fingers had stiffened.

The same dream woke her, swelling in the half-dark before dawn, and she embraced her fear, using it to drive her work, forcing herself to finish the statement about Sarelin's recovery. She reached the royal suite at a stride in the mid-morning. After several knocks, a man padded out, nodding slightly to the guards before hastening down the corridor. Lysande noticed that the laces on his doublet were half done-up.

When the queen finally emerged, her silver cape billowed.

"Don't give me that look." Sarelin beckoned Lysande in.

"I wasn't giving you any look," Lysande said, as the doors slammed behind them. "I'm merely concerned for your health. Are you sure you should exert yourself?"

"He did all the exerting." Sarelin was smiling as she lifted the cover from a platter of hazelnut tarts. "And I won't be lectured by you about late mornings. I still remember the day I found you curled up with that Lyrian harpist after the jubilee."

Lysande looked away, as if that would hide the roses blossoming in her cheeks. She saw Sarelin hold a tart out to Trichard, then pick up her crown. Every time the queen put the ornament on, it seemed to speak to Lysande of battle, with its silver cut thickly, inlaid with diamonds that glittered and gave out shards of light; yet for all the solemnity of it, Sarelin's eyes danced. After a sip of vivantica, she rose and kissed Lysande on the brow. She walked to the end of the room and threw open the double doors to the private garden.

Lysande took her arm and walked into the grove. The roses were blooming here, unfurling like wounds on the skin of the earth. Their fragrant scent filled the air, and silence reigned, except for the sound of Trichard chattering to himself.

"It means a lot to me, you know. To be sure that you'll help things get sorted when the day eventually comes," Sarelin said.

"I hope it never comes."

"Don't be a stubborn ass. That's my job." Sarelin smiled. "You've heard them, going on about the envelope, as if it carried pure gold cadres instead of a Councillor's name."

They walked on, their elbows linked like chain mail, through the patch of verdant green. Lysande's tall frame cast a slightly longer shadow than Sarelin's, though she noticed, as always, the breadth of Sarelin's shoulders. She opened her mouth and shut it again.

She could feel the shape of the envelope in her pocket. Her mind churned up memories of afternoons sitting in the library while motes of dust pirouetted in the thin beam of gold from the oil-lamp, copying out the history of Elira's succession, shaking her head at some of the less suitable people to be invested with the crown. And there was a niggling memory, too, in which she argued about the "unconscionable brutality" of Sarelin's policy of execution, quoting the anti-Conquest philosopher Perfault to justify her thoughts. Sarelin had pointed a finger and told Lysande to stop being "a damned plugged-ear idealist."

Magic. Ethics. They had argued these topics until the sun dwindled to a red ember in the sky.

"Listen, Sarelin." She waited until the queen was looking at her. "Do you remember the night you came home from the hunt?"

"If I couldn't, my ribs would damned well remind me."

"I watched you bleeding onto the bed. You can't imagine what it was like, watching the life drip out of you, minute by minute, hour by hour. I stared at those gashes in your side until the sun was rising. I expect you'll chide me for being an over-thinker again, but I noticed that when you reached out in your sleep, it wasn't to touch the fresh wounds. It was to stroke the battle-scars on your jaw." Lysande faced her directly. "And when you moaned something in your sleep, it was a word I recognized."

"Not something about the treasury, I hope."

"It was *Mea*."

Sarelin paused, one of her hands touching the head of a rose. Lysande did not drop her gaze. She was conscious that she did not need to speak of the day that Sarelin had ridden into the flames, feeling the fire disappear around her, and staring at her unburnt mare, before combing the enemy lines and finding no trace of the White Queen who had terrorized the land.

Sarelin could make all the jokes she liked. They were only gauze atop a wound.

"Promise me something. In return for making me keep the envelope. Don't go hunting. Not for a while," Lysande said. She was not going to falter at that snort. "If you're going to keep the chopping block and the executioner for elementals, at least ready yourself for what may come after. It's just as you said when they were lifting you out of the carriage—everyone in the Three Lands will know you're injured—and if you ride out again, someone could—"

"Could what?"

"Loose something with teeth or claws on you."

"And who is this 'someone,' then?"

"I think you know." Lysande's fingers tensed. "Or at least, when you sleep, your tongue knows her name."

Sun glanced off Sarelin's crown. A breeze tickled the flowers around them.

"You know I listen to your advice," Sarelin said. "You tell me to get more guards, I get more guards. You tell me to stay in bed and heal, I stay in bed. You tell me not to drink before meeting those fool advisors, I put down the bottle. You, and only you, my singular friend, can buy a taster monkey worth its weight in gold and have the Treasurer pay later." Sarelin's arm uncurled itself from hers. "But ask yourself. Would you hack off your own limb? Hunting's a part of me. I fight, I feast, I slay brutes. That's what the Iron Queen does."

"She also conquers her enemies, and remains in one piece." Lysande knew she was walking on shaky ground, but she kept her balance, holding on to the thought. "Look, it's strategy. I've thought it over. Here, you're surrounded by dozens of personal guards. If you ride out into Axium Forest again, do you think you will be as lucky the second time, if Mea Tacitus sets something on you?"

The silence that followed the name was so dense, Lysande felt it cleave to her.

"Go on," Sarelin said, at last.

Lysande gathered every shred of her tenacity. "It's the panther. I know you don't want to hear about those 'dull as weak wine' books, but science is clear on it—the eyes—they're not native to the realm. I've been researching it in Lady Haxley's *Guide to Eliran Wild Beasts*. They should have been green eyes, not yellow." The fear swelled, and she pushed it down, forced it into retreat. "Haxley writes that there are panthers people can train and lead, outside of Elira. I think someone waited until you were stalking game, with your armor off, and set that panther on you. I think they knew that was the only moment you would be unprotected. I think—" She became vaguely aware that the garden had gone quiet. "Where's Trichard?"

Sarelin shrugged. "In the roses, I expect, munching on my best heart-petals. What's this about the panther?"

Lysande's mind was full of yellow eyes and the words in the *Guide*, but when Sarelin's words clicked into place in her mind, she ran along the length of the flower-beds, looking for a flash of gold. "Trichard! Here, Trichard, Trichard!"

No reply came. She dropped to her knees and began to crawl, pushing the leaves back as she searched among the bushes, until the thorns pricked her fingers and drew blood.

"Trichard!" she shouted. "Trichard!"

She saw it at last—the patch of orange-gold among the dark green leaves. The monkey was lying under a rose bush. Almost before she laid hands upon the body, she knew what she would find, but she pressed her fingers to the throat and the tiny chest anyway, searching for a pulse.

How? she thought, staring into Trichard's frozen eyes. How did you die?

There was no obvious sign of blood. No paralysis. No trace of poison at all; but the closed eyes and the lifeless body told their own story.

"What is it, Lys?"

She ignored the question, turning the animal over and combing through the fur with her nails. No manifest marks or swelling. Yet the monkey's skin was somehow already cold.

The sound of Sarelin's voice pierced her thoughts. *Sarelin.* If the monkey was dead . . .

She turned just as the queen fell, grabbing at a branch but failing to gain purchase and tumbling onto the grass. Sarelin's black eyes clouded with confusion. For a second her lips opened wordlessly, then she convulsed, gasping for air.

"Fortituda judge me," she gasped. "Vindictus . . . strike my enemies . . ."

"No!" Lysande dropped Trichard and sprinted over.

Sarelin scrabbled at her bodice. The spasms wracked her body and she roared and lashed out. One of her arms struck Lysande as she clutched at her throat, clawing the skin.

The physicians were gone. Lysande screamed for the guards and heard the door opening, boots slapping the floor. A woman in armor reached her first, stopping when she saw Sarelin, the man behind nearly smacking into her.

"Don't stand there gawping." Sarelin's shout tapered into a rasp. "Get Hartleigh. Tell him to skewer the bastard who did this!"

Lysande stared after the guards as they hurried out. She could run out with them, but by the time she returned . . . she stared at Trichard, lying stiff and cold on the ground.

"Listen to me," she said, grabbing hold of Sarelin's shoulders, as the jerking ceded to a stiff twitching. "I can go, too. I can get Surrick—anyone—"

Sarelin's fingers closed around her wrist. "No use," she managed. Another shudder ran through her.

The skin against her hand was already turning cold. Lysande felt tears welling up behind her eyes and fought the urge to curse, to hurl her anger at the sky.

"No use . . . don't leave . . . Lys . . . don't forget . . . to open . . ."

One of Sarelin's fingers twitched in the direction of Lysande's pocket. Lysande glanced down and saw the corner of the envelope poking out.

Sarelin strained for air, and Lysande leaned closer, crouching until their noses were almost touching. She could feel Sarelin's nails biting into her skin.

"Find the Shadows. Tell them." Sarelin's voice had turned into a croak. "Tell them they were right—"

But the rest of the words never came out. Another breath strained, barely making it from her lips. The queen gave a shudder, hacked out one last cough, and lay still.

The silver cape had spread out around her and the crown winked, its diamonds sharp and bright against the grass. Points of light danced in her hair. Lysande took in her stillness and felt a stone settle inside her.

She stood up. She heard the door of the royal suite banging, and Raden came running through the bedchamber and out into the garden. *Too late*, she wanted to shout. The words stuck in her throat.

The captain's boots trampled a rose bush as he hurried to her side. Lysande heard his cry, sob-raw. "She was nearly recovered!"

"Poison." Lysande's lips seemed to be moving of their own accord, as if her mind had severed its connection with her flesh. She picked up the little monkey's body and held it before Raden. "The animal tasted it first. But the queen's tasters . . ."

"Alive. As far as I know."

Something tinkling into a goblet. Sarelin pouring rose-pink liquid. The tasters would have tested everything from the kitchen, but they would not have wasted vivantica, surely, with so few viva-flowers to replace it. If someone else had known of the scarcity of the only life-restoring medicine, then the route for a poisoning would have been obvious.

She had to keep thinking, keep analyzing, keep deducing. She could not allow herself to look into those black eyes.

"I've sent the guards to search the palace," Raden said.

He knelt and inspected Sarelin's mouth and ears, his hands skimming over her body. Lysande knew he would find nothing. Ignoring the memories of mocking remarks thrown at her across the staff table as she read, she returned to the medical manuals she had pored over, flipping through them in her mind. All the scientific books she had absorbed in twenty-two years told her that if it was an ordinary poison, there would have been stiffening of the muscles and coughing up of blood. Poor Trichard had not detected anything.

Her mind was racing. The weight of what had happened—the huge, heavy reality of Sarelin's still body—had to be held back, until she knew how this had come to pass. Sarelin deserved that. She moved closer to the queen, the flow of thoughts coming so fast that it was hard to fish the details from the stream.

She turned Sarelin gently onto her front and pushed her dark hair to one side. Below the hairline and just above the cloth, there was a small purplish mark, about the size of a fingernail, a little darker than an ordinary bruise. Lysande rubbed the spot, tracing its edge. "Chimera blood only leaves one mark, on the nape of the neck."

Raden's gaze locked on hers for a long moment. He did not speak.

"It takes several minutes, then kills in a quick stroke. I watched her die, Raden. Right here. And the medical texts say the body goes cold at once—feel her skin!"

For the first time in her life, she would have been happy to know less about anatomy.

Raden placed his hand on Sarelin's neck. He held it there for a few seconds. Slowly, he removed his hand and rolled Sarelin onto her back, before rising to his feet.

"It's impossible," he said. "It hasn't been used for a hundred years. You know all the gold in Lyria couldn't buy a vial."

Rare. Like a panther with yellow eyes. A panther that couldn't have been born in Elira. Lysande's throat tightened.

"It must have been in the medicine," she said. The words came out half-choked.

"I'll round up the physicians. There's a cell under the palace where they can rot," Raden said. "My women and men are trained to be persuasive."

"There was a man. This morning. Coming out of her chamber. Very fit; black hair."

"Lord Brackton. Her latest. I'll get him, too."

"And the Rhimese envoy." Nectar roses, bristling with thorns, were hard to forget.

"I'll prepare a chamber. The best we can do is hold her in the staff tower, unless we want a spat with Rhime. Or another poisoning."

Lysande gazed ahead. Panther. Poison. It was all part of the same picture. She kept her gaze trained on Raden's face. It was easier to look at him than to gaze down at Sarelin, her face dappled with light from her crown, all the color drained from her cheeks. She had the odd feeling that she had stepped into another world. Just moments ago, they had been walking arm in arm. There could be no reality where Sarelin's arm did not link with hers again, no realm where Sarelin did not clap her on the shoulder, surely.

"I'll have to get the damned steward to call the court at once. But without a Councillor . . . if only she had named somebody," Raden said.

Lysande pulled the envelope from her pocket and felt the emerald wax of the seal, a thick daub. Her head felt heavy as she looked at it. It was strange: she had glanced at that envelope many times, turned it over in her fingers, and positioned it in her eyeline while she worked on her treatise. In all those moments, she had resented that green seal. She had never asked for the responsibility of keeping it. Now that she had to let it go, however, she found that her fingers did not want to part with it.

"She gave me this." Somehow, she forced the words out. "It was to be opened after her death. She insisted I take it, after the hunt returned, when she was bleeding onto her bed. There was so much blood, and she kept ranting about the future of the realm . . ."

Raden's hand reached for the envelope. He jerked it back just as quickly. For a moment, he hesitated. "No, she gave it to you. And if you're charged with it, you have to open it." He gave a short laugh. "Whichever silverblood's got the job, they won't like getting their news from the palace scholar. Maybe that was her last joke."

Lysande only nodded. It felt like a deception, seeing Sarelin lying there on the ground, still and cold; she did not want to think about the realm, or anything other than Sarelin. Her mind was too numb to feel pain. Yet Raden's stare reminded her that she did not have the luxury of waiting, and she forced herself to move, pushing her body into motion. Had not Sarelin said—on that endless first night—that Lysande would need to open it immediately?

Her fingers fumbled as she tore the envelope. The slip of paper inside had been folded many times, but it bore Sarelin's scrawl, recognizable anywhere. Her stomach gave a lurch.

"In the event of my death, I appoint a Councillor to choose between the city-rulers of Valderos, Lyria, Pyrrha and Rhime. I invest in the Councillor the power to judge these rulers fairly, and to bestow on one of them the honor of ruling Elira. I ask the Councillor to make their choice in the best interests of the realm."

"Go on," Raden said.

"I hereby name as Councillor . . ."

But she could not finish. She stared at the paper, unable to digest the words.

"Who? Not that leech, Pelory, is it?"

Her hands were trembling. There was no way to make sense of it. It was like some horrible illusion, only the words did not shimmer and melt away. And yet she had known—had she not guessed, somewhere shadowed inside her, once Sarelin handed her the envelope?

Raden snatched the page from her and held it up.

"I hereby name as Councillor: Lysande Prior, the scholar of Axium Palace," he read.

There was no sound but the wind whipping through the garden and shaking the heads of flowers. A gust caught the rose bush beside them, and red petals rained down on the soil.

In her mind, Lysande saw her dream: her own hand reaching for Sarelin's, straining to pull, and Sarelin slipping from her grasp, flailing, tumbling deeper into the quiet earth.

Two

She was rushing through bracken. Her soles leaped. The melody billowed around her: the fluting of the swallows in the tops of blackfoot trees, the chirrups of finches among clumps of paradisiac and northern heather, the cicada-song floating up from a carpet of jadeheart moss, and the calls of harpmouths dripping from hidden boughs. Deer flitted in and out of shadows. Over the birdsong she heard the whipping of her own steel, a rhythm punctuating the tune.

This was far from the Axium pavell, where nobles kept their distance from each other through the dancing, stepping around each other's boots. This was a dance with blades, with bodies lunging. She kept her eyes on the glint of armor as she hastened to reach Sarelin again. A gap would open, and if she charged, she could try a thrust, or even a full swing of her sword.

An arm blocked her path. Sarelin's great boom of a laugh rang out.

"You don't need to worry," Sarelin shouted. "What you need is to *be* the sword. If you're steel, can you be worried?"

"I'm not a blade. I'm a woman. I have a brain, and it worries." Lysande lifted her sword.

"Then you must forget how to be a woman. Listen to me, Lys. When you run, are you worried about your legs?"

"I suppose not."

"Because you trust your feet not to trip."

"They're part of my body. Of course I trust them."

"So are your hands. And they grip the sword." Sarelin took advantage of her limp posture, charging in and grinning. "Try."

And she had tried: entered the flow, for a moment. The moment became a little longer each time, until she could beat the queen back enough to defend her dignity.

"Councillor?" Lysande heard someone say.

She could still hear the trill of a harpmouth and see the raindrops gleaming on Sarelin's shoulder.

"Councillor, the ceremony is complete." The birdsong faded. Lysande opened her eyes. The chafing of the sword-hilt against her palm receded and the forest melted into a hall ringed with flickering torches. It took several seconds for her to recognize the heavy, orbed staff made of silver, while her memory retreated, but she realized at last where she was, and why she was standing on the stage. The stones inside her chest multiplied.

At the row of priests bordering the stage, she knelt, taking the tokens one by one from the attendant. She deposited the elder-oak branch at the feet of the woman dressed as Cognita, though it seemed a dry offering for the goddess of wisdom. The second priest, clasping the longsword of the goddess of justice, accepted Lysande's rose thorns. As the third priest pushed back the hood of her mantle, she wore a carefully blank expression; once Lysande drew close, a sneer spread over the woman's face.

You listened to my instructions for the blessing of the jubilee parade, Your Beatitude, Lysande thought. *Two years ago, in the city prayer-house. You did not speak, but your eyes said plenty when they wandered over my sleeves, finding the ink spots there: the marks of my employment. Do you remember that I conveyed Sarelin's thanks to you, Your Beatitude? Because I remember how your face scrunched when you had to acknowledge me, as if someone had pricked you.*

Everything in its place. She almost heard the Axium motto, spoken in the other woman's gaze.

A surge of rebellious vigor moved through her. It took all of her effort to push it down, with the help of the chant that she usually reserved for the force of her addiction: *restrain, constrain, subdue.* She had become so good at following the rules of self-discipline in the orphanage that she had never stopped to consider whether they offered the right lessons for a low-born woman.

She placed the winterberries for Crudelis, goddess of love, at the third woman's boots, ignoring the renewed sneer.

Two sprigs of holly separated easily, for the last priest. She hardly needed a kiss on the brow from Fortituda, in return, but she would have taken a blow, for Sarelin's sake.

Whispers carved through the audience, and as she took the staff from the steward, she could see ruffled sleeves and breeches of starched cloth, doublets trimmed with silver thread, and stoles of deep emerald draped over their wearers. Descending to the courtroom floor, she was pulling a great weight, each step the hauling of a boulder. Black faces, white faces, brown faces, and other shades still: with all of them pressing around her, she returned to the same observation she had made several times in this room: that Elira's trade history seemed painted in the skin of its oldest families. Whatever the origins of each courtier, they moved with the same high assurance, not only a confidence to *do* but a confidence to *be*, each footstep and each sweep of an arm guided by birthright. Nobles' eyes raked her as they made their pleasantries.

At the end, beyond the last bench, Raden waited. Lysande came to his side. The sight of the dark oak benches and the portraits of queens and kings around the walls could do nothing to allay the pain inside her, yet she could not weep, either. As she looked around, Sarelin's voice echoed in her head, telling her to keep her back straight, like Queen Brettelin riding over the battlefield toward the elemental rebels. *Never quaver, never yield.*

"Tell me you have some news, please." She spoke softly.

"After all the tricks my guards've tried, I hoped . . . but Brackton says nothing. And the physicians won't break." Raden shook his head. "Even Surrick claims she's innocent, and we can't keep holding her. She's no use if her hands are mangled."

Lysande stared past his shoulder, and he followed her direction, turning to face the map of the Three Lands and the Periclean States, a vast network of black lines that the royal cartographer had painted on the wall for Sarelin's twenty-year jubilee. Lysande's eyes followed the outline of a long territory pressed between two much wider neighbors, bordered by a round sea to the north and an expanse of ocean to the south.

She darted a glance at the thick wall snaking along Elira's western border, then her gaze flicked to the encampments that dotted the eastern periphery. Lines were not only made in ink, of course.

Royam. Bastillón. The kind of friends you keep your sword unsheathed around, Sarelin had remarked to Lysande, when they were sitting in the garden beside the palace orchard, talking about a skirmish on the eastern border, while a man in a half-open doublet plucked gently at a lute and batted his long lashes at Sarelin.

Lysande had thought in broad brushstrokes, back then: rulers, treaties, and wars had formed her preoccupations. Since that day, she had added finer strokes to her understanding of the Three Lands, from import taxes to prisoner exchanges, feuds over shipments of grain, and the abrogation of hunting laws, and her estimation of Elira's popularity made her frown deeply now.

"I cornered the envoys this morning," Raden said. "Nothing from the Royamese, of course. Condolences from Queen Persephora in Bastillón, but no apology for peppering an Eliran trader with arrows last week and making off with the woman's load."

"Sarelin didn't trust the Bastillonians, either."

"I don't trust a pack of curs, whether they come snarling from the east or the west. But I wouldn't launch a war on them over one scrap." Raden sighed. "We're still the jewel of trade, in their eyes. They want our wine more than they want our crown."

"Good thing we have four royal hunting-dogs of our own to snap at it."

"Oh, I see." Raden shot her a close look. "You did take a look at those nicely wrapped bribes."

The display-table in the foyer had just managed to fit all the tributes from the city-rulers: spiced perfume from Lyria, a ceremonial sword from Pyrrha, a wolf pelt from Valderos, and a second round of nectar roses (sporting more thorns than blooms) from Rhime. Lysande had tried not to stare too obviously at the long, thin bundle beside the roses, but looking at Raden's faintly amused countenance now, she suspected that she might not have succeeded.

Cutting across the foyer, she had reached for the bundle. She had felt the cloth and held it up before her face, examining what could only be Lyrian summersilk, its delicacy evident at once compared to the thicker fabrics of the capital. Without knowing why, she felt drawn to this gift; its lustrous wrapping seemed to stir a desire inside her, a sharp and shifting thing that she could not name.

Curiosity wrestled with a reluctance to unwrap something this finely decorated, but curiosity won quickly, and she untied the bundle. Black petals greeted her, swirling in layers around a central point which eluded the eye. The stem of the flower bristled with thorns, like the nectar roses on the table, yet this flower was black where it should have been red or green: stem and thorns and petals, all black.

A piece of paper fell from the summersilk. Lysande unfolded it. The message took up only a little of the page:

For the palace scholar.

L.F.

A colorless flower and a note without so much as a name attached. Fortunately, Lysande recalled the full name of the prince of Rhime, shouted once by Sarelin in her presence. Prince Luca Fontaine was certainly bursting with charm, to send such a present.

Summersilk . . . she had turned the idea over for days, blotting out the thought of Sarelin's body with that one, thin word. If Prince Fontaine was sending a rose from Rhime, with all the royal fabrics of his city at his disposal, why not use his own cloth to wrap it? The irregularity niggled at Lysande; yet she should really be wondering why a prince she had never met was including anything for her at all.

Her thoughts had been mercifully occupied as she considered the rose. Now, she stared out at the crowd, not hearing the noise.

"All the gifts in the world cannot make up for . . ." She did not need to finish the sentence to know that Raden could hear the ending.

The last two weeks had slipped by. She felt the weight inside her, the same force she had endured through the funeral and now the swearing-in ceremony. It was as if the waves of sorrow had ceased pounding her, leaving a raw edge where they had struck.

"I miss her just as much," Raden said, quietly.

"You know we can't talk about what happened." Lysande dropped her voice. "If you finish cleaning up the capital, I'll owe you a barrel of red from Queen Brettelin's store."

"I'd have done it for a goblet. Have to warn you, though, it's not a merry show out there. Not everyone believes the story that Queen Sarelin died of her hunting wound."

They love her, Lysande reflected. She had known it as a child, and she had learned it anew yesterday, when Raden's women and men had returned from their ride through Axium. There had been looting over the past fortnight, but yesterday there had also been doors kicked in, people dragged into the street and blamed for the Iron Queen's death. Raden had reported mutterings about the Old Signs—about cairns, ivy, and carvings on bark. Yet although Lysande had ordered the Axium Guards to take tempero handcuffs when they rode out, they had not found any magical rebels to use them on. She was not sure if she should feel guilty or pleased. Was it wiser to feel remorseful about failing to catch any criminals, or glad about avoiding any wrongful captures?

Tempero controls them, but only a blade ends them, Sarelin had said.

If she had pushed harder, if she had persuaded Sarelin to reach out to elementals, maybe the queen would still be alive. Even as Lysande permitted the thought, she recognized it as fantasy. Sarelin had once chopped the hands off an elemental woman who had used her firepower to burn an effigy of the queen. *I didn't save my throne so they could slash away at its base*, Sarelin had declared, that night.

"You might need company, to spread the word," Lysande said, turning slightly toward Raden.

"Five legions of guards is more than enough company," Raden said, glancing at her staff. "The steward keeps nagging me to tell you that the advisors will meet you at midday."

The women and men closest to the crown. They would be sitting upstairs, talking to her in the Oval. If everything had not turned into a gray morass in her mind since Sarelin's death, she might have been nervous. But she could keep moving, working through the list of things that needed to be done. It was when she sat still that grief crept up.

Lysande passed the Councillor's staff to Raden, trying not to look at Lady Scarbrook, who was staring at her with the intensity of a falcon circling a mouse.

"Skewer the bastard who did this," she said. "Those were Sarelin's words, as she lay choking. I may not be much of a skewerer, but I know how to investigate when no one else bothers. She trained me to research in old manuscripts. All I need is a morning in Axium."

"What shall I tell the advisors?"

"That I look forward to hearing their best ideas for the realm, at midday." She patted him on the gauntlet.

"Lysande." He kept his voice low. "Take care to look over your shoulder. Some of the populace do not mind who is cut down, right now, so long as they never get up."

The road between the palace and the capital could be traversed in half an hour, and Lysande was not stopping for anything today. The wind buffeted her hair as she rode, and as she galloped into Axium the bells were ringing, four chimes on the hour: one for each of the goddesses, a toll that reminded every citizen of the queen's passing. It echoed inside her, a dirge of blood and memory.

Prayer-houses across the capital bustled with queues that extended into the street, and Lysande slowed her pace at last, skirting around the crowds. After tethering her horse to one of the few vacant posts, she fastened the hood of her cloak. She had half a mind to stride through the group of people in velvet doublets that was thronging around a bust of Sarelin, casting off her cloak as she did so. *Queen's foundling* or *gutter-born*, their looks would say; perhaps even *traitor*, today, if they had decided on a goat for the scaping.

Instead, she wove through a mass of women and men in rags, keeping her eyes fixed on the other side of the square. She knew, through long practice, how to focus on one goal, as she had learned to focus on the translation of a phrase or the conjugation of a verb.

The hawkers shouted their prices at her as she arrived at Abacus Street, and though she had a hankering to hear the current cost of grain and leather, to pick out ordinary details that would make the extraordinary more bearable, she elbowed her way across and into the first laneway. There, she passed merchants' premises with spiderwebbed windows. Every second or third pane had splintered, and some shops had been painted with a black E for *elemental*. It did not feel like justice. At last she found the mouth of an unmarked lane and slipped through. A sign outside a shop declared FOREIGN AND EXOTIC BEASTS—FOR HIRE OR PURCHASE. She stepped into the interior, blinking.

Lamps around the room gave out globs of gold, just enough to illuminate the cages lining the walls; some of these pens shimmered with masses of dark fur, while others held horns, or teeth that seemed to float in the gloom. Spearfish from the Lyrian delta shared a tank with a puffing-snake, swimming among shining pebbles. Lysande tiptoed down the right wall. She could feel dozens of eyes watching her from the cages, and heard a growl emanate from further along, yet she could only think that the last time she had been here, Sarelin had been alive.

She heard a smash from the street, followed by a tinkle of glass. Clutching her saddle bag, she hurried along.

One eel's description promised "pleasingly quick paralysis," and at the back of the room, a sign proclaimed "panther: Pyrrhan, with lethal bite and excellent speed." She drew closer to the cage. The animal stalked up and down behind the bars, pausing to regard her, narrow eyes glittering in its black fur like chips of emerald sewn on velvet.

"Interested?" a voice at her side ventured. "A rare animal, for a swearing-in jubilee, perhaps? That one's a hundred cadres, forty mettles, and twenty-six rackets."

Lysande nearly bumped into a man in a brown merchant's doublet as she turned. She steadied herself and began to unfasten her hood. "It's your colleague I've come to see, Signore Perch."

While Perch disappeared into the back room, Lysande watched a spearfish goring something vigorously at the bottom of its bowl. The merchant returned bearing a ring of keys, and Lysande followed him into a chamber overflowing with paper. His knock on the far door brought a woman's head out. It was set with a sharp chin and eyes that were shadowed; the rest of the woman followed, in a doublet almost as ink-flecked as Lysande's own.

"Signore Owl," Charice said. "Still quick-thinking."

"Signore Fox," Lysande said. "Still quick to bite."

"My favorite palace-dwelling, carriage-riding scholar. Come to ask for something, I assume."

"Just a horse, not a carriage, today." Lysande smiled. "As for asking, you can always deny me, you know."

"If only that were true."

They clasped each other by both hands, with wrists crossed—the movement easier now that it was chosen, not enforced by the orphanage headmistress—and Lysande's tongue loosened at last, giving Charice the news of the funeral and the swearing-in ceremony. A tide of pain rose inside her, lapping higher and higher. She circulated through the little room, picking up new scrolls and running a thumb over gem-imbued parchment, asking about the price of violet ink and the availability of silverfowl quills. Details helped, in the absence of scale. The fine points of facts kept the big picture away.

That Charice was tenser than usual, Lysande noticed at once, mapping the lines on her friend's brow. Charice had never asked for help in all the years they had been acquainted. The two of them had revealed enough of their secrets to know how the other coped with life's most incisive darts; how each managed when the world rested upon her shoulders. You could share a bed with someone, as the two of them had done, lips speaking without words, but the real intimacy came when you saw your lover crying at the news of an execution, stifling sobs with their palm, or shaking and retching over a basin until the last of a bad dose was gone.

Seeing her frown, Lysande knew that Charice would have burned her sprigs of heather today. Glass tinkled in the street again. They both pretended not to hear it.

Lysande navigated Charice's questions about Sarelin, steering them away from anything that touched on grief, aware of the pricks of recent memories under her skin. She was well aware, too, that she had less than an hour to ask her real question.

A silence fell between them, and Charice took Perch's ring of keys and rolled up the hanging of Sarelin on the wall, revealing a small door. Lysande caught Charice's look and nodded.

The hidden chamber seemed colder than usual. Perhaps it was the glass of all those vials and bottles, or perhaps it was the unlit fireplace, but Lysande found herself clutching her upper arms as they entered through the little door. Colored powders on the left shelf sparkled in their vials. She knew each hue of that rainbow: blackseed, snakeseed, seed of bliss. She did not like to recall why she remembered each drug so clearly.

Beside the powders, she recognized bottles of gold liquid, stoppered with blackfoot oak. *Down it after nights spent in intimate company*, Sarelin had instructed her, a long time ago. *With men, I mean. You won't need it with women.* Lysande had wondered how Sarelin had known that she had moved through a few lovers, both female and male.

Best not to think of Sarelin, now.

"The usual?" Charice said.

Lysande nodded again. Her eyes picked out pale green dragongrass, suspended in a jar, and the uncomely burnt-hazel powder of second-century gryphon talon, collected in a thin bottle.

Dragons and gryphons. Echoes of another time . . . all those marvels of nature wiped out by non-magical people as they waged war on elemental rulers, and then the chimeras, feared for their strangeness as well as their power: snuffed out. A waste, she had always thought. She had known not to voice her opinion, however, except in this chamber.

She watched Charice open a box with a key and take out a jar, holding it up to the glow of the torch on the wall. The sight of the blue flakes should have had less effect. *Like bottling up the sky*, Haxley had written, but even that did not capture what she felt when a new batch of scale lay before her, its sheen promising stimulus to the body and calm to the mind. Lysande handed over ten silver mettles. Her fingers brushed Charice's, cold against the other woman's warmth.

"Two more jars," Lysande said. The tremor in her hand almost subsided.

When Charice shut the box, Lysande could not resist a glance at the large drawing of a chimera on the right wall, taking in the curvature of the horns, the elegant shape of the lioness' head, the point where fur gave way to scaly hindquarters, soft and smooth textures melding into the dragon-like wings, preceding the almost-calligraphic line of the tail. She resisted the urge to walk over to the artwork, yet as always, something moved inside her at the sight of it; something that she felt should have stayed still.

"Do you really think you should be displaying a magical beast?" she said.

"Do you really think *you* should be buying a magical drug and strolling straight into Axium Palace with it?"

Lysande inclined her head. "I should know better than to question the orphanage wit."

"Tread carefully. That's all I suggest."

"Shredded chimera scale is not a drug, you know. Some priests use it in ceremonies, for prayer," Lysande said, twisting her sleeve into a finely scrunched pattern.

"You're not exactly a convincing worshipper." Charice's voice was not jovial. "Don't take it awry. Even in the old days, I could never have kept you from yourself. I would warn you about a cumulative effect— about what happens when one spoonful of any drug becomes two, or three, or five—but I don't think a lack of understanding has ever been your problem." Charice's stare passed over the jars. "Have you thought about how you will explain . . . this, when someone catches you?"

Lysande looked across at the drawing, as if she suddenly found the arc of the chimera's back fascinating. "A scholar may study anything, in theory. You should take care, Signore Fox." She returned her gaze to Charice. "I can only clean up the riots, not change the law, with the whole court set against elementals."

"There are people one can seek out. Adaptation is a necessity, for some of us."

They looked at each other for a moment.

Lysande was sensible, in the pause that followed, that she owed more to the woman who had swum through the seas of adolescence with her. Their trip into the countryside with the orphanage class returned, so clearly that it could have been illuminated in the book of her mind: the dense forest of beeches, in which she and Charice had lost their way, and that night under the stars . . .

But she had not come here to reminisce. Nor had she convinced herself, despite her best efforts, that this was purely a visit of acquisition.

Looking at the drawing again, she crossed the room and ran a finger along the animal's body, tracing her way to where fur met scales.

"What you said to me, once, about the scarcity of chimera blood . . . it still holds?"

Not even a flicker passed over Charice's face as she nodded.

"Could there be more stock? A vial here, a bottle there, unaccounted for?" Lysande pressed.

"Perhaps. But the only vials I've ever seen were headed north, a long time ago. And merchants . . . my kind of merchants . . . we talk among ourselves. Certain goods attract gossip more quickly than a bankrupt noble," Charice said.

Lysande thanked her, feeling the cogs and pulleys in her mind already moving. She was halfway to making her farewell bow when she saw the look on Charice's face change. "What is it?"

"They're going to come for us, you know. All of them. The bakers, the smiths, the millers who smile at us as we pass, the cobblers who chat with us while they hand over our boots; the people we're supposed to feel on an equal footing with. They're already looking around to see who's different—who they can blame. The queen is dead and their whole world is wobbling, so they can't seem to find a stable place to stand. And that, my *dear* friend, is where the danger lies. They will put our bodies in the ground, and they will stand on us."

"You don't know that," Lysande said.

"I know people."

"So do I."

Charice laughed. "You're an owl on a perch. A fox runs on the ground."

Lysande's tongue darted over her lip, dispelling some of the dryness. "Well, I won't be running anywhere. If I stay in the palace, maybe I can work to change public opinion. Someone has to try."

"How long do you think that will take, amidst a sea of silverbloods vying for place?" Charice's voice rose. "Do you think the ladies and lords of Axium's finest manors will care what happens to an elemental merchant and a drug-addled scholar who was once an orphan?"

"Still an orphan," Lysande said.

"You could have fooled me."

Lysande walked back into the main shop, where two green lights shone in the gloom. The panther lunged toward the bars of its cage, growling at the bag in her hand. She did not hear Charice call after her, and she did not turn to check if Charice was watching her leave.

Every footstep rang like judgment. The points Charice had made dwelled in her mind, until she made a concerted effort to put them aside, for a time when she could turn them over.

As she walked through a labyrinth of lanes to her horse, her thoughts turned to her next task. Perfault had written that negotiation with silverbloods required confidence . . . "that high self-assurance" . . . and had she not read that chapter enough times when considering the qualities of an ideal ruler?

The trick was not to move naturally, she thought, directing her observation to Sarelin. It was to appear to do so. Not to actually dance, like one of the earnest young men who had twirled ribbons for the queen, but to look as if you were leaping with such poise.

White roses surrounded the base of the staff tower, their pale carpet sprinkled here and there with crimson buds. The spiral staircase seemed steeper than usual. Navigating her way through the piles of papers in her chamber, Lysande stepped between stacks of mathematical proofs and toppled the *Guide to Eliran Wild Beasts*. She paused at her desk, breathing in deeply.

Language and translation. Those could soothe the most fractious thoughts, the poet Inara suggested. She reached for the thin vase she had borrowed from the kitchens, sliding it from the corner of her desk to right in front of her, examining the single black flower within. There were five names for a pure black rose, she was fairly sure, since each city had a different term: evenrose in Valderos, midnight's bloom in Rhime, blacksalt rose in Axium, corpse-petal in Pyrrha, and inkflower in Lyria. Something about those names seemed significant. Her skill in selecting useful information, honed from years of assessing scrolls and books for Sarelin, was stirring into life, yet it only sent a vague and uncomfortable tingle through her.

Lyrian silk. Just ostentatious enough to stand out, like the key to a puzzle, if you were looking for one. She counted them out again, the five names for a black rose, coming finally to inkflower—the name only used in Lyria—the kind of thing that only a scholar would know. Perhaps the Lyrian silk meant that Prince Fontaine wanted her to think of his gift as an inkflower . . .

But why?

She almost laughed out loud as she drew a line between the dots. It was hard not to appreciate the simplicity of it. *For the palace scholar,* the note had said, and if there was one thing scholars were renowned for, it was toiling with ink.

Was this a test? To check if the new Councillor was really clever, by setting her a puzzle and inviting her to guess why the flower was sent to her? The whole thing spoke of arrogance, or at the very best, a supercilious toying with someone who this Prince Fontaine thought should be honored by his attention.

She tried to recall any details about the prince of Rhime that Sarelin might have scattered into a conversation, but all she could remember were Sarelin's remarks about the latest examples of Rhimese cunning, delivered amidst a cascade of insults. The thought of Sarelin's vividly creative phrases hurt so much that she clutched at her chair, breathing deeply for a moment. She took the three jars of chimera scale out of her bag and held them up.

No. It would not do. She would not be herself if she imbibed before the meeting.

A crunch of wheels sounded outside the eastern gate, as a cart trundled to a halt. Lysande moved to her window. Something inside her recoiled as a woman in a hooded robe dismounted and trudged across the grass.

Hunched on the back of the cart, four prisoners gazed up at the palace, their faces streaked with grime; the fat missing from their cheeks gave them the aspect of ghosts, and they shivered, their hands cuffed. The executioner tapped her foot.

Of course, Lysande thought. Of course, Sarelin was not alive to give her permission. The fact was still not quite real, like a phrase from a story in another world.

She hurried down the stairs and crossed the lawn. By the time she arrived, a noblewoman in an emerald doublet was standing at the gate, conversing with the executioner. Lysande edged toward the speakers.

She made out the prisoners through the bars of the fence, noting how the elementals in the middle of the cart huddled together. Something wrenched inside of her.

The painting in the eastern corridor showed magical people flying over villages on chimeras, but the elementals in that scene sat proudly upright in their armor—they looked down with the contempt of the mighty, like the elemental rulers in the ancient histories. All of the surviving accounts suggested that at the time of the Conquest, those who could move the elements were powerful beyond measure. Tempero handcuffs had put a stop to that, as Lysande had heard Raden remind his guards last night.

She knew this, and yet something twisted within her at this sight, all the same.

Drawing her gaze away from the prisoners, she felt heat surge under her skin, and recognized the guilt at last. The executioner unwrapped an axe from a sackcloth cover.

"You can put that back," the woman in the doublet said, staring at the executioner as if she were a fly. "You know how Her Majesty did these things. She would want the next one to look them in the eyes."

"Where can she take them?" Lysande said quickly.

The woman in the doublet turned. Her gaze passed up over Lysande's tall person, lingering on her unkempt hair, taking in the lock of deathstruck silver among the red strands.

"Back to jail," she said. "We can't have them burning houses and flooding the streets like savages." She surveyed the frayed edges of Lysande's coat. "Good day."

She gave a tight smile. The velvet of her garments shone as she walked away. Lysande turned back to the gate and watched the cart jolt its way down the road until the faces of the prisoners on the back were nothing more than dots.

Sarelin would not have executed anyone without reason, she thought. Yet she saw the queen's two bodies: the armor-clad warrior who was the realm, who brought down a gauntleted fist on elementals; and the woman who drank, laughed, and debated philosophical texts with her into the evening. Perhaps she was to blame for not winning the former over.

High above her, the midday bells began to roll their clangor into the palace.

The staircase to the fourth floor curved around in a long arc, its walls lined with portraits of Axiumites of note, and the ascent dampened her spirits, the pictures seeming to sneer at her as she passed. She shook off her melancholy to greet a portrait at the top. Shining in a silver frame, it stretched almost from ceiling to floor, showing Sarelin in her armor, clutching a dagger in her left hand and a tapestry in her right, the pale steel blazing against her skin.

Lysande felt something strain inside her, as if her very flesh was trying to shift from her bones. Her body wanted to throw itself into the frame. It was a flat image. She knew that. And yet knowing that made no difference; the ghost of past joy was standing in front of her.

She stood before the frame for a long time, staring into Sarelin's face. Those black eyes gazed back at her. She traced the metaphor with a finger—Elira, the tapestry of many colors, climates and cities, sewn together by one leader.

At the expense of a certain type of people, her conscience added.

When she walked on, her boots rang against the floor of the corridor, steady as a knell.

The palace's oldest meeting-chamber bore the name of its table, a long construction of dark wood that dated back to the first century, whose ovular shape dominated a room entirely without windows. The sound of voices carried to her ears. She pressed her eye to the crack where the oak doors hung ajar. The Oval's ambience reminded Lysande of a tomb, and today, more than ever, the candles nestling in apertures on the walls seemed to invite her in, with a votive light that she knew was not hers to enjoy. As she looked around, she discerned six people in emerald robes, five of them leaning over something on the table's surface.

She knew that this was the highest she had ever risen; that facing a room of advisors alone would have been unthinkable, before she was Councillor. No matter what aspersions Charice might cast, this was a moment for everyone who had been flattened under two unpolished words: *the populace.* This was a moment for craftswomen, chamber-lains, millers, blacksmiths, fathers at home, and, yes, even scholars . . . for the populace she knew, and did not know. It would probably have felt better if her hands had not been trembling.

She strained her eyes to pick out details in the candlelight, focusing on the six figures around the table and listening. The murmur of conversation gave way to a single voice.

"The Rhimese will be the ones ready to act. And bargain. I say her death is a piece of luck," a woman declared.

Three

~

Her breath hitched, as if someone had yanked a stitch out in the middle of sewing. Although her feet wanted to carry her to the stairs, she forced herself to let the figure in the painting go. She concentrated on the crack between the doors.

"You all know as well as I do that no one could get the warrior-brute to do a thing she didn't want," the same cold voice said.

Lysande had never heard anyone refer to Sarelin as a "warrior-brute" before. She felt a spurt of anger. The speaker looked up from the table, and with a start she recognized the noblewoman who had fended off the executioner at the palace gate.

"If you were thinking tactically, instead of ferreting around for a promotion, you'd be looking to replenish our treasury," another woman said, her cadaverous figure swamped by the folds of her robe.

"And I suppose you think placing a Lyrian prince on the throne is a bright idea," the cold-voiced woman said. "They don't conserve their gold, unless you count slathering it all over their palace."

"What about Valderos?" a young man cut in.

The discussion flowed without a pause. The advisors all bargained as if the city-rulers were pieces to be moved around a tactos-board: indeed, the cold-voiced woman spoke as if the choice of monarch was a mere formality. Anger rattled through her. The five people leaning over the table compared armies, munitions, and coffers like merchants weighing up splitgrain and summer-rice.

Lysande thought of what Sarelin might say, if she could hear them, and swallowed something that was warm and painful at once.

"I trust the Rhimese with a crown like I trust a snake with a rabbit," the young man said.

"I'm not entirely sure snakes eat rabbits, Addischild. Did you borrow that from a tavern song?"

"A Rhimese snake would sink its fangs in and suck the poor thing dry."

At the far end of the table, a man that Lysande had never seen reached for a piece of fruitcake from one of the many platters. His brown hair was sprinkled with a few strands of gray, but she put him in his mid-forties, around the same age as Sarelin, though less beaten by the elements. His robe came up to his neck and his sleeves were neatly brushed. In the pause that opened up, he put the cake down, coughed once, and looked around the table with an earnest expression.

"Go on, then, Derset," the cold-voiced woman said.

"I don't suppose any of you have considered the Councillor?" Derset, whoever he was, ran a hand through his graying hair. "I hear that she was picked out as palace scholar at the age of eight, when Her Majesty took the cleverest pupil from an orphanage. The queen made the girl her particular companion. This Lysande Prior translated the Silver Songs into modern Eliran when she was twelve. Perhaps, if she has aptitude, she has formed an opinion."

"Could have guessed you'd support Her Majesty's choice." A burly woman made the remark. Several of the others snickered.

"We all remain loyal to our queen," Derset said.

"We didn't all carry her sword around, though," the burly woman said, smirking.

"Never mind that. I would sooner have our leader chosen by a silverblood than by the whelp of some farmer or cloth-peddler," the cadaverous woman put in, her lip curling. "These are not times for muddying the palette."

Lysande did not mean to enter, but as she leaned forward to catch their words, she moved a little too keenly, and her shoulder pressed against the wood. The doors swung open. The advisors scrambled to make their bows; there were cries of "Good morning, Councillor" as they recognized the orbed staff in her hand. It would almost have been comical if Lysande had not felt the heat rising in her cheeks. Forcing a smile onto her face, she took a few steps forward, trying to give off the air of one who had deliberately burst in on a group of nobles.

"Please, do not trouble yourselves for me." She raised a hand, motioning them to sit, and as she readied herself to join them, she saw the object on the table. The last time she had seen it, she had been standing over the greatest woman in the realm, looking at her stiff body. She had engraved the sight of it into that moment. It was almost a dream, seeing it here, but there was no mistaking the hard glitter of those diamonds.

She held the crown up just long enough to observe their reactions. The Treasurer, the Master of Works, and the two envoys to the cities: Lysande ticked some of the positions off. They were not roles Sarelin had pronounced with a smile. Nor were their bearers smiling now.

"I believe we have not met," Lysande said, facing the cold-voiced woman.

"Lady Pelory." Her tone did not warm at all. "Mistress of Laws."

Pelory folded one hand over the other. A ring protruded from the forefinger on top. Taking in the emerald in its center, Lysande noted the small but coveted line of rainbow heartstone inside the gem and estimated the ring's worth at more than fifty chests of gold.

Swallowing, she looked along the table. All of the advisors were staring at the crown, except the sixth: the man with the sober manner met her gaze as he bowed from the neck. "Henrey Derset, Councillor. I serve as the crown's envoy to foreign lands. I rode back from Llara in Bastillón last month with an offer to purchase more Eliran steel. Happiness sped me onwards, but I see that sorrow was waiting to meet me. I offer you my condolences, Councillor Prior—to you, I expect, Queen Sarelin was more than just our ruler."

The sentiment struck Lysande, and her reply caught in her throat. No one aside from Raden had seemed to spare a thought for her feelings. She was certain that the nobles in the courtroom had not. "Thank you, Lord Derset," she managed, after a moment.

Derset sat down again, and Lysande busied herself with looking around the room. The candles burned steadily, thanks to the unseen hands that had lit them before the meeting; the apertures were clear of dust, and the table was so polished that the grain in the Conquest-era oak stood out. The faces surrounding her looked proud, disgruntled, even skeptical.

She listened to her breath: in and out. In and out. There was nothing but that sound.

"As you are aware, no doubt, the city-rulers will be here in less than a day."

"I, for one, will be ready to judge them." The burly woman, Lady Tuchester, who Lysande recognized as a former captain, thrust her chest out.

The young Master of Works, Lord Addischild, twisted his sleeve so that the silver embroidery caught the light. "Some of us have already determined our choice."

"You mistake my meaning. I am asking you to oversee preparations for their arrival."

Glances darted around the table. Silence followed. Pelory was the first to look her in the eyes. "And what of our duty to help you select the new monarch, Councillor Prior?"

"I expect you will be busy with the duties of greeting, lodging, and welcome," Lysande said. She could feel a rasp at the back of her throat, a scratching of something very like the quill-tip of grief, and she strained to keep it out of her voice.

The advisors began babbling about their successful inter-city missions, their experience with investiture, and the quality of their strategies; Lady Bowbray, the Treasurer, made her voice the loudest, arguing over the top of the others' anecdotes. Lysande had expected this. As the talk continued, she looked to Henrey Derset. He had one hand in his hair, rubbing his scalp. She studied him for a moment, observing the lines cleaving his brow.

"Will you not argue your merits, Lord Derset?" she said.

Derset shook his head. "If you would make this decision alone, then it is your right."

She wanted me, Lysande thought. Not an envoy, or a treasurer. "I think—"

A voice cut her off, Tuchester's complaint ringing through the Oval, and Lysande felt a spark ignite inside her, the tiniest of flames, barely nascent, but accompanied by a reminder that Sarelin would not have borne this.

"I will take one of you to advise me," she said, "and only one. Lord Derset, stand up."

The talk died. Derset rose, his eyebrows rising with him.

"I name you as my sole advisor, to work with me as long as I am Councillor." Lysande looked around the table. "The rest of you may return to your work."

"This honor weighs greatly upon me, Councillor." Derset bowed his head.

It did not take long: Bowbray, Tuchester, and the other envoy, Lord Chackery, made their exits in a swirl of emerald green. Lord Addischild followed them at a more leisurely pace. Lysande heard their voices echoing in the corridor, then a door slamming.

Pelory was last to leave. She stopped a few inches from Lysande before departing and looked her over. "Good luck, Councillor," she said, clipping each word.

Lysande might have slumped into a chair, were it not for the cough behind her. She turned. Derset's eyes fixed on her with something like sympathy. "I expect you have had little privacy, Councillor," he said. "If you desire it, I could show you a place where you might mourn."

Lysande hesitated for a moment. "Meet me on the sixth floor of the staff tower, Lord Derset, when the light is fading."

The crown felt cool, its silver heavy in her hands as she took it. She walked out, holding it before her. In the corridor, she nodded to Derset and, with considerable strain, managed a smile before turning in the direction of the palace vault. Her stiff bearing seemed to startle the guards and attendants into silence as she passed; it would have startled her, too, if she had not recognized a stirring, beginning somewhere deep within herself, and growing.

Splinters littered the streets of Axium. Urging her horse through the debris, she found the alley empty of looters; Raden's latest report of a surge in rioting was real to her at last, in a way that even his riven brow had not conveyed. She had missed the storm, but Charice's words about the fear and anger of ordinary people fell upon her like midwinter rain, the kind of angry patter that sluices topsoil from graves.

In Charice's first room, the quills lay among shards of glass on the floor, their feathers trampled or snapped, and the majority of the ink and paper had vanished. Breath rose, hot in her lungs, mingling with anger.

The hanging of Sarelin had gone too. It was a curious devotion, avenging the queen and purloining her image at the same time, but Lysande had no time for reflection, her cheeks still reddened from the ride. The door to the back chamber stood open on its hinge.

No smashed glass lay inside; no powders dyed the floor purple or red. Bare walls sparkled on all sides. The hook that Charice had used to hold the drawing of the chimera had disappeared. She sniffed the wall where it had hung and caught the scent of lemon soap: few elementals fleeing a mob had time to clean their storeroom.

The thought cheered her somewhat, but anger lingered beneath it. It went deeper than a feeling of obligation, with Charice. They had both stood outside the window of Axiumite society, looking in.

She had first purchased a jar of blue flakes from Charice when her friend had been taken on as apprentice to an apothecary. One evening, after a particularly savage snipe at her from some of the palace staff, who had made it clear what they thought of an orphan rising to the rank of the queen's personal companion, Lysande had ridden out to join her friend. Guiding her horse between clumps of crushed paradisiac in the light of the winter moon, with the flowers' sharp scent rising around her, she had determined to do what she had been thinking about for months.

Once ensconced in Charice's chamber, she had taken two spoonfuls of blue flakes, heated them, mixed them with the amounts of sugar and water specified in the old physicians' records. A scent of old books had wafted up to her—the particular smell of her favorite histories and compendiums of stories from the library, the ones with well-thumbed pages and worn covers—and as she brought the goblet closer to her, the scent mingled with the fruity notes of spiced wine, compounding her desire. The heating of her cheeks and forehead as blood surged up beneath her skin; the writhing of her stomach; the quickening of her heartbeat until it knocked at her ribcage: she felt the symptoms as she drank, and chose to endure. Charice had watched her down the chimera scale, not saying a word.

By then, it had become clear to Lysande why Charice was good at keeping secrets, and why she never spoke when others were discussing magic. Amidst the fear and furtiveness, they had rolled together, like the glass balls that wealthy children played with, until the duties of work parted them. On certain nights, they found their way back to each other, each reflecting the other's light. Lysande had studied many poems, but she knew the poetry of Charice's body best of all: the meter of her breathing; the ever-twisting metaphors of her tongue; the syncopated rhythm of her fingers, which wandered along well-worn routes and then veered onto new paths without warning.

They had not begun with skin. Skin had simply become a part of the flowing thing between them, after one of their card-games, when Lysande had approached, amidst a cloud of Charice's thick and fragrant pipe-smoke, and discovered that Charice did not mind her hungry eyes at all. In fact, Charice welcomed the hunt, when Lysande was the one encroaching.

Sometimes, she found Charice's door locked. Sometimes, she found an ocean of paper covering the table, and Charice tidying it away, the pages whisked into a box before Lysande could glimpse more than a word. Sometimes, she found a stranger leaving, always different and always pretty; Charice greeted her, on those nights, with a look that dared her to object.

All this, and she still had not guaranteed Charice's safety.

The empty room confronted her. She was on her way out when, treading on a floorboard, she heard a creak. She squatted down and tapped three boards. The one in the middle replied with a higher sound.

She loosened it with her dagger and removed the slat to reveal a hollow. Picking up the box in the hole, she brushed off the wood-dust. A chimera stood rampant on the lid, wings spread, horned head lifted proudly.

It took all her strength to lift the chest, but there was no need to search for a key. Her breath shortened when she saw the contents. She sat down unsteadily on the floor, staring. Did forty-four jars of shredded chimera scale mean jail, or execution, if you were caught?

She pried out the paper wedged between the bottles and the back of the chest.

For L.—a gift I pray you will discard.
Sorry that I could not say goodbye.

Until we meet in some happier place,

C.

For a long time, she stared at those lines, reading them over and over, gripping the page by the top corner, until she realized that she had torn the paper.

When she reached Axium Palace, she galloped to the stables, where Raden was removing his saddle from his stallion. "Tell the steward that there will be no more executions," she said.

The thud of the saddle dropping went unremarked by both of them.

He was staring at her face, and she knew that he would be reading the infusion of red, the naissance of a flush, but she did not care. Emotion did not stop her from digging deep and finding a handful of logic. "There is a precedent. In the *Legilium,* Volume Three. I intend to transcribe it freshly, write it in calligraphy on silver-edged paper, and have a copy of the new order slipped under every courtier's door."

"But Queen Sarelin . . ."

"Is the woman I love most in the world." Her voice did not waver. "Now that she has left it, that is still so. But I am in charge, and while I am, I do not intend to sever necks."

Raden could not be made to understand about Charice. The words of Perfault and other philosophers on ethics would do little here, she knew. But there was one thing that Raden cared about very much indeed.

"The army answers to me," she said, "by Queen Montfolk's Decree of Velvet and Steel. I am Councillor, and a Councillor holds military authority until the monarch is chosen." A shudder ran through her. The words had sounded . . . like sunlight refracting off a gauntlet. "I want the Axium Guards to halt the executions. Tell no one. Wait until they ask, and only then let them know what I have decided."

Again, sun and steel rang in her voice. It felt very new, and she did not dislike it. After a few seconds, he nodded, still staring at her, and she returned the nod without bowing.

In the mid-afternoon, she wound her way through a lesser-known grove in the region of the grounds that was farthest from the palace, searching among the beds of blooms—cultivated and maintained beds, since wildflowers were only allowed to grow so much on the palace grounds. Her fingers brushed the heads of sugar-poppies and heather flowers until at last she sighted a pale yellow bloom sitting atop a tall stem, its petals tapering to a point. Seeing it up close and noting the even size of the petals, she knew that her idea was worth pursuing; the species was a terrible gift for a friend, but as for the prince of Rhime . . .

She plucked the flower out with a single motion. Back in her chamber, she halted, one hand on the small cabinet, allowing herself a moment's misgiving before she pushed her qualm aside: it was a particularly clever puzzle, if she thought so herself. She had every reason to be satisfied.

The flower wrapped up well in a piece of emerald cloth. The ribbon she chose was long enough to tie in a quadruple knot; she had to practice the ancient tying techniques several times before getting it right, but it was a distraction she had needed, even yearned for, amidst the pain. When she walked through corridors now empty of Sarelin, she had to make a concerted effort to breathe deeply. Far better to focus on tying a complicated knot and preparing a reply, even if it was a slightly too-bold reply. She could not guess whether Prince Fontaine would like her puzzle or consider it an act of effrontery, but something inside her wanted to find out.

Once the flower was wrapped, she mixed a goblet of scale from the jar in her drawer, the other jars stowed beneath her bed. Her stomach writhed long after the mixture had gone down, but she ignored its spasms, letting the golden afterglow wash through the room.

The possibility of needing more scale in the future could not be dismissed. Forty-four jars would take care of the foreseeable future, however. There was no need to cloud her mind.

She added a paragraph to *An Ideal Queen* before abandoning her treatise, perusing the chart of the White Queen's tactics during the five years of the White War instead. She was aware, even as the calm spread through her, that something required her attention.

"Two strikes," she said, to the air. The words had been Sarelin's once.

Derset's knock came just as the sun was lowering itself beyond the forest. He waited outside until she was ready. They descended the tower, and her new advisor said nothing as they walked on. The main building of Axium Palace boasted many capacious chambers and masterworks of sculpture; they passed the statue of a chimera being slain by a warrior with a lance, entitled *The Winged Horror*, the jaws of the horned creature opened wide as if to roar. Lysande always felt an urge to stop and stare at it. Tonight, Derset guided her to a staircase she had rarely used, and she put all thoughts of ancient beasts behind her.

They descended several flights until she guessed they were down among the cells. Instead of prison bars, a narrow corridor greeted her, stretching as far as she could see.

"Have you ever been to the crypt before, Councillor?"

She had been eight, and still reeling, on her first tour of the palace. "Once."

"I know you were close to Queen Sarelin." Derset glanced at her. "I thought you might like to say goodbye."

Lysande did not trust herself to speak, but gripped his forearm.

Down, down, into the bowels of the palace; the royal crypt was buried deeper than the cells, and the air felt icy against her neck. The unadorned walls led to a single door whose hinges protested shrilly. They passed into a long room with a low ceiling, its silver stone almost entirely hidden behind slabs of white marble: hundreds of squares lined the floor and walls, engraved with capital letters. Lysande recognized the names of advisors and envoys through the ages, a chronicle of the appointments of the women and men who had worked for each monarch. Some of them had helped leaders to rise, while others had been instrumental in their falls.

Dynasty after flowering dynasty. It was thanks to their trading advantages that Elira had never been invaded by the Royamese or the Bastillonians, Sarelin had said once. Meditations on history had been rare from the Iron Queen, and Lysande had copied that one down in her notes.

On the right side of the chamber, fourteen white tombs stood in a line, spaced apart, each several times the size of a commoner's grave and fashioned of thick marble. Statues loomed from the headstones. A hawk swooped above Queen Ann Montfolk's tomb, its wings spread and talons outstretched, the stern eyes and cruel beak as intimidating as Queen Ann had reputedly been. The lion atop King Aydul's tomb was missing its left paw as well as a large piece from its tail. Lysande remembered Sarelin saying that a visiting Rhimese noblewoman had sneaked into the crypt and attacked the stone with a mallet after King Aydul imposed sanctions on the Rhimese for stealing carts of grain.

Standing before the tombs, she felt very close and yet very far from them.

Axium to Rhime. Valderos to Lyria. Pyrrha to Valderos, and back to Axium again. Monarchs had died heirless enough times for the crown to pass from city to city; how forward-thinking Elira was, the silverbloods claimed. How equitable. Of course, they preferred not to mention that you could only tilt at the crown if you were a city-ruler, that only those of a certain lineage could expect to serve in court, and that the crown itself sat on the head of the monarch like a thornbush curling inward.

She wondered what Sarelin had thought of this room: if she would rather have been buried on the battlefield, in living earth, instead of in dead stone.

"This is Queen Illora's tomb." She ran a hand over the first headstone, whose lioness monument cast a shadow over the inscription. "This room . . . it must date back to the construction of the palace."

"It is old indeed. The bones of all the queens of Elira lie here, and our few kings', too." Derset was looking closely at her. "It is also a place where a servant of the crown might speak without being over-heard, if he were commanded to, my lady."

"I am no lady, Lord Derset. I have no blood claim."

"Yet I know that you were the queen's companion. The woman I knew as the Iron Queen wasted no affection on those she found un-worthy. Lysande Prior, she said to me once, is like the goddess Cognita mixed with Queen Brettelin—the right combination of wisdom and strength. I suspected years ago that she was training her scholar for something more. You do not fawn on your advisors, but nor do you insult those who resist you, or fly into a rage."

Henrey Derset had a manner of ancient courtesy about him, but it did not disarm her. "If you have advice about my task, I would hear it now."

"You must know, my lady, that Queen Sarelin was very dear to me. What station I have, I owe to her. And as Her Majesty trusted, so do I."

She thought again of the remarks about his devotion to Sarelin, and of the way that the others had snickered in the Oval, as if remembering some past incident. "I have heard it said that you carried her sword."

The words came out before she could stop them. Derset colored slightly. "Once, my lady, when the King of Bastillón was visiting, she permitted me to bear her sword for her, during the hunt in Axium Forest."

"I see." And she could see it, too . . . the Axium Guards, following their queen through the trees, the captains milling around the royal party; the Bastillonian and Eliran nobles walking behind; the advisors up front, and Derset, with an emerald-studded scabbard and a leather belt in his hands, falling into step behind Sarelin. She had seen it in person, with a different young man holding the weapon each time. The silverbloods used to joke that the man who carried the Iron Queen's sword by day would feel her strokes at night.

Derset had been envoy to the foreign lands. He had come and gone from Sarelin's side for years. He must have known how her interest changed, surely.

"Her Majesty did love to have a man trailing her," Derset said, as if he had guessed her train of thought.

"It was in her nature to be followed," Lysande said, carefully.

"As a bear's nature is to be obeyed." Derset's voice did not sound resentful.

She noticed the flush in his cheeks again. She considered telling him that she had heard him defend her appointment in the Oval, but felt that admitting to eavesdropping would not be a good way to repay his trust. She could see that he was still struggling to contain a pressing sentiment.

"I must say this now, or I will forever regret it. You are going to be dining with these four rulers and entertaining them. For two days, you will be surrounded by the ice-bear, the cobra, the spearfish, and the leopard. What do the four emblems of the cities have in common, my lady?" Derset said.

"They are all beautiful. Animals of royal grace."

"Beautiful, yes, but more than that. They can all kill."

The animals surrounding the crown on the Eliran crest swam into her mind. They were displayed on flags, cushions, and tapestries; yet everything she knew of the cities felt distant, filtered through the pages of books or passed on through Sarelin's anecdotes.

She could see the queen lying on the grass. Points of light from her crown danced in her hair.

"These are dangerous people, my lady," Derset said. "Who do you think gains from Queen Sarelin's death? Who profits, in the realm, by the queen dying without an heir?"

She did not need to reply. Had she not dwelled on that very thought last night, unable to sleep? Once the word of Sarelin's hunting accident spread across the country, the city-rulers had had an opportunity ripe for the taking, and one of them might well have taken it. This was a time to shake off her feeling of inadequacy. This was a time to scrutinize. She pushed down the grief inside her and compressed it into something hard, something like a weapon.

"A few drops of poison . . . it could have been done while the physicians slept. Even those at work grow drowsy after a time. And there are assassins who know the ways of silence, my lady."

Lysande hesitated for a moment. She thought of Sarelin's words in the carriage when she had returned from the hunt bleeding. *All of Elira is thinking about my death right now. Not just Axium. Valderos, and Lyria, and Pyrrha and Rhime.*

"Wait until the queen is injured, and suddenly the palace is in chaos. Physicians are coming and going, and orders are flying back and forth," she said.

"Indeed. Everyone busies themselves with trying to help."

"Two strikes," Lysande murmured.

She recalled, again, the chart of the White Queen's tactics she had made, each pair of attacks laid out after the other. Panther and poison. *Two strikes.* Sarelin had observed it first, of course. Sarelin had told her how the White Queen could wait until a battalion was limping, bleeding, struggling to draw breath, then spring out with flames or steel, never hesitating.

For another long moment she looked at the same infusion of color in Derset's cheeks. She could imagine him in Sarelin's chamber, years ago, when his bloom of youth was fresh. Sarelin had always been able to pick unusually beautiful men from the court and its milieu; she would bring not only athletes and hunters to sit at her table, but poets, dancers, and merchants, too, in an ever-changing pageant of companions. Derset was not what silverbloods called a "high beauty." His features lacked the delicacy and softness which made some men widely coveted. He would have been honored by the queen's favor, eager to please, and that, Lysande thought, would have held a different kind of appeal.

"You must have known the queen well, my lord."

"Not as well as she knew me. I would have followed her into the flames, though, if she had asked me to."

They met each other's gaze in the noiseless crypt. "Lord Derset," she said, "there is something I must tell you, too. Queen Sarelin did not die from her wound."

They slipped out of her, then: all the events of that horrible afternoon, from the monkey capering among the bushes to Sarelin pouring a goblet from the jug of pink vivantica. The effort of sharing stripped away a little of the pain inside her. Yet something had to be kept back, to ensure a layer of protection. She left out Sarelin's last words about the Shadows—those had been meant for her alone, she was sure. Derset listened in silence. When she had finished telling him of Raden's efforts to extract a confession, she saw him shake his head. "I doubt the physicians are to blame."

She nodded. "A physician's salary is more like a drabble of coin than the river needed to buy a rare poison. I had a conversation, once, with a friend, who heard rumors that the last vials of chimera blood were purchased a long time ago." It was important to tread lightly, here.

"Is your friend an envoy, by some chance?"

"A merchant from Rhime." The truth could be a little malleable, surely, in some circumstances. "She heard smugglers saying that the last vials of chimera blood found their way to someone who dwells in the Periclean States, across the North Sea."

"Excuse me, my lady, but I fail to catch your meaning."

"Mea Tacitus crawled through the frozen northlands, toward the sea."

The words had sounded like an oath on Sarelin's lips. They came out like a whisper on hers.

The room felt very still, all of a sudden, as something settled upon the two of them. Lysande recalled the hours spent copying out Queen Illora's Precept, inking the wording of the ban on discussing elemental magic. It was not the writing of those words that changed things, but what came after—the moderating of what you said, the learning of what not to say.

"They never found proof that she died." There was more that she could add. But she did not know him well enough for that kind of confidence, and could only judge him by the color in his cheeks. "Consider our situation. The White Queen may be dead or broken in spirit. The question is, can we afford to assume that she is vanquished, at a time when no monarch sits on the throne?"

Her question echoed in the crypt. It was hard to forget what she had warned Sarelin of, just weeks ago, in the garden of the royal suite: the counter-effect of injustice.

"There is no reason we could not both be right," Derset said, slowly.

Their eyes met. "You think one of the city-rulers may be working as a spy for the White Queen," Lysande said.

"It is possible. When an heirless monarch dies suddenly, from a poison of great rarity, one must open one's mind to possibilities."

Lysande remained silent. She thought of Sarelin jerking on the ground in the rose-garden, and remembered the famous story she had been made to recite in the orphanage—about the queen riding into the flames, her hair burning, as the power of the most terrible elemental died—the legend of the Iron Queen whose will alone had brought down her enemy.

The poets had claimed that Sarelin charged out of death's grasp. But death came back for her, in the end.

Sarelin had told her once that she had not expected the fire to fail; that she had led the Axium Guards toward it thinking that they would all burn. When they did not, she never stopped to thank Fortituda. She had slashed, hacked, and thrown daggers, watering the ground with the White Army's blood, but in the moment of the fire's failing, Elira's future had flipped like a dagger in flight. That was history, Lysande thought: a series of dagger throws.

There would have been a comfort in asking Derset for advice about the blade spinning toward them now.

"I will have the steward order a watch on your door—a double watch," Derset said. "Forgive me, my lady, but I have served as an envoy. City-rulers do not merit trust."

Lysande did not say anything, but she watched him and saw no sign of a façade. She had opened her mouth to reply when a knock sounded at the door. As Derset bowed his head and left her, the knock came again.

"Come in," she called.

She recognized a wiry page-girl who had sat beside her a few times in the staff dining hall. They had never spoken, until two of the senior guards, Oxbury and Risset, had asked Lysande about her day's duties as "queen's pet." The wiry girl had glowered at them. She had pushed their hands back when they made to snatch Lysande's goblet of wine. Lysande had liked the girl for that.

"How may I greet you?" she had asked, at the time. "Litany," the girl had muttered.

Now, she looked at the page standing in the doorway, a statue in green livery.

"The steward, Signore—Councillor Prior—he asks to see you."

"Some goodbyes must be said slowly, Litany."

The girl tiptoed out.

Lysande turned to the line of white monuments and walked slowly past the resting-places, while the statues cast shadows on the wall: an elder-oak tree for Queen Jebel, the first monarch to establish a library; a sculpture of three crowns for Queen Alighiero, who had been famous for burning the Royamese envoy at the stake after a deal with the west soured; a shield adorning Queen Brettelin's thick headstone, carved with her motto: ALWAYS MIGHT. A poem stretched below King Ramsar's name, covering most of the marble. Lysande smiled as she spotted the reference to the young lord that Ramsar had famously wooed. She had never thought she would stand beside monarchs in a place like this, a girl of no breeding among the crowned dead. Stopping for a moment, she soaked up the silence.

There was a quality to a silence like this. Once you noticed it, you could not ignore it. It was as if the thoughts that you could not voice had leaked into the air and were brewing.

The tomb at the far end of the crypt led her further down the chamber. Dust had not yet settled on its surface. She could see a stone dagger mounted on the headstone, pointing at the ceiling. Although she knew whose name she would find, she knelt beside it anyway.

Sarelin's headstone bore no verses, nor any engravings of flowers. Only four words carved out a phrase beneath her name: SAVIOR OF THE REALM.

The inscription was still raw at the edges.

Something wet fell on Lysande's cheek. The tears flowed out now, faster for having been checked, and she leaned down to press her lips to the cold marble.

"Help me, Sarelin," she whispered. "If you're in the halls below . . . if there *are* halls below, as you always said, then guide me through this. You gave me this task."

There was no answer from the tomb.

"Please. Don't be so damned selfish, Sarelin. I love you." The words echoed off stone. She was talking to silent bones, and waiting for a reply.

When she left the crypt, the door swung shut with a bang, oak ringing on stone, and a symphony of echoes followed her into the corridor.
Litany averted her eyes from Lysande's damp face. The air grew warmer
with each step they climbed, yet the chill of the marble slabs in the
vault still lingered, and she felt it in her flesh after she had left the tower.

Give me strength, she thought, as she climbed into bed that night.
Just let me do what Sarelin wanted and get the right ruler on the throne,
before swords are drawn.

This time, she slept without dreams. Her body softened until it was
almost weightless; an autumn gust carried her beyond mist and vapor
into the upland of peaks, and she floated in the empty air, like a feather
that had never been used as a quill. All the cares that had borne her
down were gliding away to somewhere out of sight, until she was pas-
sionless, drifting on a current without sorrow or pain.

When she woke, it was to the sound of horns.

Four

"If they had to shake the walls with their damned blasts, the least they could have done was wait until midday. But you try telling a pack of Valderrans to turn around."

"I value my head." Surrick laughed. "Did you hear the stable-hands? Poor things had to wake up a dozen horses and move them early. One of them got a kick in the face."

"My attendant claims the Pyrrhan lot rode in on thirty mares. Look at this, she says, calling me to the window: there's a bunch of Pyrrhans threatening to throw punches if they don't squeeze through."

"I shouldn't like to catch a Pyrrhan punch," Surrick said.

Shifting further into the shade of blackfoot branches, Lysande watched as the two women conversed, noting how the second physician grinned, dipping her fingers in the fountain. "You know why I was really looking, anyway."

"And is the Lyrian prince as pretty as they say?"

"Didn't get a glimpse. His carriage nearly blinded me. The thing's adorned with solid gold."

"Well, I'd sooner have gold than something feral." Lysande could hear a note of relish in Surrick's voice. "I heard that Prince Fontaine has brought an animal in a basket and given orders for it to be handled only by him, in case it snaps off the hand of an attendant."

"Best hope he doesn't bring it near this one." Surrick's friend tapped her own hand. "There's at least a dozen things I need my right hand for, this morning."

"And then there's surgery. You use it for that, too."

Surrick's friend laughed. The two physicians moved away from the fountain and began to meander across the eastern lawn. Lysande waited until they had moved some distance before leaving the bench under the blackfoot tree.

It had all gone well enough, then. The advisors had done their job, and the city-rulers should all be relaxing in their suites while their retinue ran about. She had even dispatched her gift for Prince Fontaine, with the help of a page who had darted into his suite and left the flower on his desk. So why did she feel no contentment?

She resumed her progress along the path. At the target range, only straw women waited. It took a moment for her to realize that she did not need permission from the steward to practice.

She drew the daggers from her belt, one by one, placing them on the table. Five blades and five blank hilts. The hilts were only blank, of course, if you were used to seeing family insignia there. If you had never seen an eagle, a bear, or a pair of twined snakes on a dagger-hilt, then perhaps the smooth metal was normal.

Her first blade carved the air, soaring past a straw woman. The next dagger struck the shoulder, but as she found the flow of her practice, she hit the neck, stomach, heart, and lungs marked on the target, reusing her four steel blades. Her hand hovered over the hilt of the gold dagger, but she could not quite bring herself to pick it up. Derset joined her as she was pulling a blade out of the target's heart.

"Preparing for our royal company?"

"Perhaps." She yanked the dagger free, sending the target wobbling on its stand.

"The red streaks in your eyes tell me something else."

"It still feels like she'll walk up behind me and guide my aim." She dropped her voice. "My lord, I keep thinking about what you said to me in the crypt. What if I pick . . ."

"The city-ruler who might have organized the poisoning?"

Lysande said nothing, but nodded. He watched her slide the gold dagger into its sheath on her belt. "If I may, I would suggest that you get to know each leader and linger with them beyond the dinner. Some would say it is customary to provide entertainment. Why not use tomorrow morning's festivities for your own ends?"

Of course. The only event in Axium where you could hack people to pieces for money and claim that it was sacred. Kill someone in an alley, and you were a criminal; kill them in front of a crowd, and you were honoring the goddesses. She had forgotten about the prize-fighters' tournament that was scheduled for tomorrow, what with losing her best friend, becoming Councillor, dealing with the advisors, calming the capital, and turning over the circumstances of Sarelin's death . . . but that was no excuse. Details were not supposed to slip by her.

"If I sit with the city-rulers in the box . . ." Yes. She could observe them more closely while they watched the fight. "You have a talent for quick thinking, Lord Derset."

"So Her Majesty said, once." He gazed into the distance. Lysande studied him for the second time since they had met, noticing the focus in his gaze and wondering what it was that he was imagining. He turned his face away, slightly, after a few seconds. Though she was tempted to cough to bring his attention back, she refrained from doing so.

She knew how it felt to have grief sneak up on you. One moment, you were going about your work, and the next, you were clutching your stomach, wondering what had hit you and when exactly you had doubled over. Derset deserved a moment to breathe. She counted to twenty, pausing between the numbers.

"Perhaps we should discuss that briefing, Lord Derset," she said, gently.

"My lady." He held out a scroll. "I came on that very matter."

She took in his face. He had veiled the pain quickly, she thought, the Axiumite way. "You were able to procure it, then?"

"They may not have been exactly . . . eager, but at short notice, Lady Tuchester and Lord Chackery have compiled statements for you on the four city-rulers."

She read through the comments in silence, moving from name to name down the page. The longer she read, the more anxiety threatened to flow from her. The First Sword of Valderos had defended the north during the Ice-Rose Campaign against Periclean raiders, Lord Chackery's brusque phrases explained. The Irriqi of Pyrrha had brought her city out of internal warfare "and into a certain prosperity," which Lysande suspected was a deliberate understatement on Chackery's part. The prince of Lyria was the youngest ever city-ruler; and no matter what aspersions Lady Tuchester cast on the prince of Rhime, it was noted that he had amassed a following of loyal supporters, in a city known for anything but "the standard of fidelity we Axiumites uphold."

She tried to dwell on the report, yet she found herself thinking of the black rose Prince Fontaine had sent her—and the flower she had prepared in reply, tying its wrapping with a complicated knot, accompanied by a message. *For the palace guest.* She had thought it rather witty, a reply to match his own, doubling as a warning that she would not be easily manipulated; but now she wondered what his reaction would be, especially if he managed to decode her flower-puzzle the way she had decoded his. She had not sent him the politest of challenges, after all.

If a prince doled out a public reproach to the palace scholar, would anyone intervene? Or would the nobility of Axium look on in approval?

More to the point, why did she keep focusing on Prince Fontaine? Something about the audacity of the black rose and the message kept tugging at her mind, and she did not like it—did not enjoy the way that he had slithered into her consciousness and coiled in her mind, refusing to remove his words.

He was not her only concern, of course. Four rulers. All of them accomplished; all of them, surely, practiced in the ways of court.

Gather yourself, like a star-plant, she told herself. Bind yourself to a wooden stake and stay upright, so that your branches do not spread. This was no time to feel inadequate.

She listened while Derset expanded upon the background of each city-ruler, and she ran through her prepared questions: the state of each ruler's army, their personality, any known alliances. Derset leaned against one of the straw targets while he answered, absorbed, at one point, in an account of the last five decades of enmity between Valderos and Lyria. She suspected that he could tell she was mentally taking notes on the details of Lyrian smallsword maneuvers in the Southern Skirmish, for he finished with a smile. "Scholarship is the noblest pleasure of the mind, I have always thought."

"Noble or not, I appreciate the gift." She matched his smile.

Once they had parted, with a brief bow from Derset this time, she took herself further away from the staff tower, to a place where she could sink onto grass and look out at the branches that dangled from a row of slim copper trunks, the dragon-willows kissing their twins in the water.

A spot of white moved on the lake. It glided around the side and came near to where she sat, and she saw the visor of black atop the beak, the bird shaking its feathers, rising up, feet skimming water marbled by sun. She had watched swans bathe here plenty of times, usually while eating a hastily packed repast, but today something was different, and the way this one puffed out its chest reminded her of someone.

She felt her throat tighten. The bird landed with a splash. A silver spray arced over the water, shining dagger-bright, and she looked out at the surface of the lake until warmth touched her cheeks.

These people, she told Sarelin, holding the page up before her. I am not enough for them. When I meet them, I will be a sheet of thin paper, the kind made cheaply for the populace; and they will be torches, in whose light my veins and flecks will show.

A movement caught her eye. Beside her boot, a purple flower swayed, its petals cast into relief against the leather. She cupped it in her hand.

A queensflower, growing wildly and alone. She had not seen such a thing in the palace grounds for many weeks.

It was hard to pull herself away from the lake, but she managed. Back in her chamber, she halted beside the window. As if it were yesterday, she was walking in here for the first time, flinging open the curtains and declaring that this was the chamber she wanted—the one on the sixth floor, farthest from everyone—and Sarelin laughed, loud enough for all the tower to hear. "You're a gem, all right," the queen said. "An odd gem." Then she was bobbing atop a horse, Sarelin's strong hands curling around her waist, holding her in place as they trotted through Axium Forest. The queen barked words of encouragement in her ear. And then she was laughing at a play in the capital, but not as hard as Sarelin, whose hand slapped her own knee hard enough to produce a sound: *bap, bap, bap,* while one of the players struck down another with a wooden sword, pouring red juice over his chest.

Lysande opened her eyes again. Her fingers reached into her drawer and brushed the cold glass of the jar. She mixed a dose of scale into the vial, heated it, prepared a goblet, and drank half the mixture so quickly that her stomach fizzed and bubbled. Instantly, her heartbeat battered against her ribs, and for a moment she felt that they might break: that she might split from the middle like a wineskin that has been squeezed too hard, spilling its contents on the floor.

This time, she smelled rotten floorboards, as she had not done for weeks, and with it a hint of sour sweat: the tang of too many children packed into one room. It was not enough to stop her from downing the rest of the mixture.

The violence of the reaction surprised her. She had not thought it possible for her heart to hammer even faster. It was one spoon of scale, exactly, therefore it could not be harmful; Charice's lecture already sounded far distant, fading.

Her hands found their way to the jar again. Somehow, she was measuring an extra half-spoon. Surely, if she was more distressed, more remedy was required? Yes. That made sense. The night-quartz lay there, waiting beside the jar, just in case. She mixed the flakes and downed the concoction without pausing, ignoring the smell of the orphanage.

This was not irregular. This was a necessity under the circumstances.

She was a Councillor, now, and responsible. The burden of emotion was weighted with cause. She could pretend that it was not grief, that insurmountable pain you were meant to climb over like a few pebbles. She had public, political problems now; the kind of problems that everyone treated as real; problems that could justify a scholar mixing something special, something she had labored to learn the production of.

She packed the drug away and closed the drawer. When a knock came at the door, she opened it to find Litany holding a stack of clothing and jewelry.

"The steward says I'm to dress you for the banquet. And I'm to wait on you at all times while you're Councillor—to be your personal attendant."

The girl stepped in, depositing her bundle on the bed and laying out each garment and ornament on top of the cover. Lysande eyed the green velvet doublet, the shirt and trousers, and the gleaming pins. Tiny emeralds had been studded onto the neck and shoulders of the doublet. It could have been worse, she told herself. *Sarelin could have seen me trussed up in this.*

"I will see to it that you are paid well. But if you would rather serve a silverblood, you should not feel bound to this duty," she said, hearing the stiffness in her voice.

"I've never had the chance to serve a woman of the crown before."

A woman of the crown. She almost chuckled. *What would Charice have said about that?* "You must know that I am new to this station, Litany, and my position is temporary. I should not like you to miss an opportunity elsewhere."

"If you please, Councillor, that makes two of us." Litany gazed at the floor. "I've been working as a page and training in the skills of wardrobe. The steward saw fit to offer me this promotion after you were given the orbed staff. So you see, Councillor, I am new to my station too. I should be honored to dress you."

Lysande moved to stand against the bed. She tried to let go of thoughts of city-rulers, poison, and the White Queen, and let her mind be still. It was a very curious feeling, having another person strip her clothes off and dress her again. She knew that this was what ladies and lords did every morning, standing like statues so that others could lace their boots, but it was all an uncomfortable fuss. The girl insisted on plaiting her hair and fixing it with little crown pins, weaving and pinning the deathstruck strands among the others, as if the queer, glittering silver were no different from any of her red locks; she held a small mirror up for Lysande's benefit. Only when Lysande asked for her hair to be rearranged did Litany agree to tuck the silver strands beneath others. Finally, Litany guided her into a stiff posture, and Lysande realized that she had been slouching.

"You must think me ridiculous," she said, as her new attendant took a green ribbon and fixed a bow in Lysande's hair, which now, thankfully, showed only red. "A Councillor who doesn't know how to stand formally."

"I think you've got better things to do than stand about. From what

I hear, you translated the Silver Songs in full when you were twelve—did you not?"

Lysande stared at her. Litany dropped her gaze.

"Someone else's words," Lysande said, at last. "I merely moved them from an old language to a new one. I did not write them."

"But before you did, I had never heard of work by a low-born—by a girl of little means, that is—being taken on by a monarch and distributed."

If her voice had not been so soft, the remark could have been deemed impertinent. After a moment of silence, Litany returned to powdering Lysande's hands. In doing so, she ran a fingernail under Lysande's sleeve, and Lysande noticed the detail, filing away in her mind that it seemed a strange way of sizing up fabric. Despite Litany's compliment, she felt the distance between them, the gulf that even a childhood among the populace could not bridge.

The Great Hall was buzzing when they arrived, and her stomach prickled, a resurgence of the nerves that had been dulled by loss and scale. She had never seen the room so packed. The four long tables surrounded a walkway: captains, senior guards, priests, merchants, and artists of note chatted to each other on the left, while on the right side of the hall, the members of the royal court murmured. Beyond the long tables, four smaller tables awaited. Silver tablecloths bore the emblems of the horned ice-bear, the snarling leopard, the reared-up cobra, and the slender yet fatally swift spearfish.

Come and fill your goblet in the Hall, tonight, Sarelin had said, once, when the city-rulers arrived for a ball. Lysande had caught glimpses of silk and fur in the corridors, carried by chattering attendants, and when she had imagined the stares fixed on her, she had felt something inside her cringe and curl itself up. She had sent her apology.

She could feel those eyes upon her now. Just a day ago, she had managed to give orders to the royal advisors, she reminded herself; she was aware, even as she did so, that this was something bigger than a meeting in the Oval, and that she stood out here, exposed not by her clothes but by the unpolished surface of her name. It was not the Axiumite way to encourage those without silver blood to rise through the court, she had long observed—it did not need to be decreed for everyone to know it. There was a reason that grocers and goldsmiths taught their children the Axium motto, just as noble children were required to copy it out for their tutors on thick paper, tracing those four words that she had seen on hangings all over the capital. *Everything in its place.*

Do you call that a philosophy, she had once asked Sarelin, or do you call that a threat? Sarelin had become very busy with cleaning her hunting-knife and had said nothing.

Another step, and then she was staring at the table looming at the end of the hall, a thick, oak structure with high-backed chairs, furnished with plates and goblets of solid silver and cutlery embellished with little diamonds. On the upraised platform, six seats stood.

"Oh!" Litany said, her eyes shining. Lysande followed the girl's gaze.

In cages on either side of the high table, green and silver birds twittered, their fluty song weaving through the hum of talk, a shower of glittering dust falling occasionally from their wings. *Gilding-doves*, Lysande recognized, from another of Haxley's entries. Should she really be surprised that the steward had chosen the most expensive birds in the capital to display to their guests? The Axium flag fluttered at the back of the room, and a great portrait of Sarelin in her armor hung on the right wall, dwarfing the other portraits. Lysande stared at the painting as she walked. From each angle, Sarelin's gaze seemed to fall on her.

I never asked for this, she told the picture. She had to address Sarelin; it was the only way to manage their separation, talking *to* the departed instead of about her. I hope I don't make a complete ass of myself, trying to stand and talk like you, she added.

Making her way down between the benches, she noticed the five brocaded shapes dangling from the back of every chair, the crown-shaped decorations stuffed much larger than the cities' emblems. A familiar group waited at the end of the aisle. "We are your guard of honor, it seems," Lady Pelory said, her eyes following Lysande.

"I have scarcely met such honorable ladies and lords."

"What a fine party we shall make." Pelory gave a knife-like smile.

Raden and Derset walked up to her. The spotless surface of Raden's breastplate told her that he had cleaned it since he finished securing the

capital, and burnished it this morning. The sight of Derset's sober attire reassured Lysande, somehow, and she noticed he had parted his
hair to the side, revealing streaks of deep silver that lent him a handsome maturity. Natural silver, Lysande thought: not hard and glittering silver. Respectable hair.

"Are you nervous, my lady?" he said, taking his place on her right.

"Of course not."

"If you were not nervous, I might think something amiss."

She shifted on the spot and dared to glance across at him. Once her
smile broke out, his did too, and they both looked quickly away.

A single trumpet note sounded. Hundreds of eyes turned upon her.
It was impossible not to be aware that the great oak doors at the end of
the hall would open at any minute and reveal the city-rulers, yet with
Raden on her left and Derset on her right, she faced the crowd with her
best blank countenance. She stole a glance at the painting of Sarelin
again.

This was not only about diamonds, gilding-doves, and silver tablecloths. She knew the opposing opinions of the north and the south—
their divergences on the punishment of magic, and the reasons for their
bloody history, fueled by the rivalry of leaders past—and thanks to a
study of court opinion over the years, she knew that the silverbloods
worried a meeting of their delegations could be a spark to the kindling.
What a way to be remembered, if she made a misstep today: she would
be the Councillor who set the realm ablaze.

A fanfare of trumpets drowned out the chatter and the doors opened
at last, pushed by two heralds who sported emerald jackets embroidered with the silver crown.

What if I can't think of anything to say? she asked herself. Imperative. Be imperative. Say *I shall*, not *I might*.

Heads turned across the hall as a troupe of musicians marched in,
blowing trumpets, plucking strings, and beating drums. The sound
billowed in a harmony that spoke of silver and gold and treasures from
places Lysande had read about. Her fingers tingled.

I'm doing this for you, Sarelin, she thought. Don't let me fall on
my face.

She gripped the staff tightly, her hands wrapped around the orb. As the trumpets died away, a herald strode down the middle. "I now present, from our fair city on the delta," the woman shouted, "the jewel of the south, and the true son of the desert . . ."

"Son of a rich philanderer, more like," Raden whispered.

". . . and most radiant Prince of all Lyria, Jale Chamboise!"

Lysande felt her breath speeding. For a moment, it felt like she was staring into the sun. Jewelry adorned every figure that entered the room: sapphire earrings and necklaces, rings of solid gold, pendants in the shape of fish, and headpieces set with a rainbow of jewels shone in the candlelight. The thin shirts, fine trousers, and transparent overlays looked like they might slip off their wearers and pool on the floor, so light was their gauze.

The party of Lyrians shimmered down the hall, drawing many disapproving glances and just as many thinly concealed stares of interest. One Lyrian woman stopped beside a chair and stared at the brocaded ice-bear dangling from the back. She picked up the decoration and drew her smallsword.

Lysande's whole body tightened for a moment, readying to stop the insult, but before she could take more than a few steps forward, one of the other Lyrians snapped at the woman, and she put the ice-bear decoration down.

"They're southerners, all right," Raden muttered.

Southerners, Lysande thought. With a desire to poke holes in the north. It did not bode well for cordiality. Some of the Lyrians shivered, looking around with less than pleased expressions. As they drew nearer, Lysande saw that dark kohl lined the women's eyes, while the eyelids of the men glimmered with a sheen to match their overlays; their gait reminded her of descriptions of the famous Lyrian dancers from the histories.

Yet none of them moved as gracefully as the boy who walked at their head, a long, gauzy cape trailing from his shoulders. His blond hair and blue eyes recalled a portrait of the warrior Abattre, but there the similarity ended, for where Abattre's glare had been reputed to cut through legions like a bread knife, this prince looked more likely to butter them up.

He approached with soft steps, wisps of hair falling across his forehead. A sapphire ring shone on his hand in the candlelight, sending beams of blue across his features. He could not have been more than twenty, yet he carried himself upright, breaking into a smile as he neared the end of the walkway.

"Councillor, how charming to meet you." Prince Jale Chamboise stopped, his guards halting behind him in perfect alignment. "The last time I was in Axium Palace, it was as gloomy as your Lady Bowbray." Lysande guessed that Bowbray was grimacing somewhere behind her. "Still, there's nothing like a dash of decoration to brighten a room up."

From anyone less cheerful, such a remark might have seemed like arrogance, but the prince's smile disarmed her. "We welcome you to the capital, Your Highness," she said.

"Jale, please. And I daresay you're the first person to welcome a Lyrian in fifty years. My mother had a habit of stealing people's consorts." He shook his head. "I always wondered why she didn't get invited to more feasts, until I learned she had sampled more than just the fare. That's all behind us, I hope." He dropped his voice. "My envoy tells me that executions have halted in the capital. A prince of Lyria can have no opinion on the subject, but if he could, he should say: congratulations, Councillor."

She bowed. "I am endeavoring to reconfigure the situation."

"You have my condolences, too. Though I know that nothing must seem a balm, right now . . . it is not long since my mother died, and the more I remember her flaws, the keener I feel her absence."

Bowing with a flourish, he walked on, leading his party to their table. A warm current of emotion surged through Lysande; she was aware that Jale had not been obligated to share something personal with her, and that he had done so deliberately—and quickly, too, as if he knew the awkwardness that Axiumites exhibited when they grieved. She watched him take his seat. After a moment, she noticed that others were watching him with expressions that suggested a less formal interest. Several noblewomen were leaning across their seats to look at Jale, and one young lord looked to be straining his neck for a better view of Jale's profile.

Whispers broke out everywhere amongst the Axiumites as the southerners took their seats, and Lysande noticed many of her guards place their hands on their hilts. It was not hard to see why the capital's precision and the southerners' looseness sat uneasily together, especially when the old rivalry between Lyria and Valderos might yet bring disorder to the hall. She should be alert. She certainly should not be distracted by the rush of gratitude that Jale's approval had brought.

She leaned over to Derset. "Sarelin said that Prince Chamboise assumed his throne a short time ago."

"Just three years ago, my lady. When he was seventeen."

Lysande thought that if Jale Chamboise had held the biggest city in Elira securely since he was seventeen, he had already achieved a lot. Another fanfare of trumpets blared through the hall.

"From the snow of the north, I present the son of Raina, slayer of wolves and warriors, and First Sword of Valderos: Dante Dalgëreth!" the herald shouted.

She focused her attention on the aisle. The Valderrans moved with heavy steps, longswords hanging at their hips. With strong jaws and dark brown hair, the women and men stood a head taller than most Axiumites, and the fur trim on their coats only seemed to increase their size. Their expressions were so resolute that Lysande wondered if they ever smiled, or if they reserved that for one occasion per year: a private gift-day dinner, perhaps, when they might express their levity in total solitude.

Raden caught her eye and nodded toward the Lyrian table. Lysande was conscious of the swords in the Valderrans' sheaths and felt a flicker of concern that she had not taken enough precaution. She turned back to the man coming down the aisle.

As Dante Dalgëreth entered the hall, she saw the nobles at the back lean away from the walkway, muttering. The First Sword of Valderos walked taller than any of his guards, his hand on the pommel of his longsword. His solemn stare swept the hall. Judging by the whispers, Axium's nobility had not failed to notice the powerful figure encased in a brown doublet and trousers, exposed every so often by the flapping of his fur cloak, yet Dante Dalgëreth did not spare them another glance. His eyes fixed on something at the Lyrian table.

Two banner-bearers knelt before Lysande, carrying the gray ice-bear of Valderos on brown cloth, and Dante stopped behind them, shifting his attention to Lysande. "The north grieves with you, Councillor."

"I thank you, Your Highness."

"Valderos does not change its loyalties for profit, you will find." As he said it, his eyes darted again to the Lyrian table. It was as if he wanted to look over there, Lysande thought, but was attempting restraint.

He bowed and marched on, and the pack of Valderrans followed. Lysande surveyed the hall. Half the room was talking loudly and pointing at the Valderrans, while the other half were craning their necks for a better view of the Lyrians. She watched some of the Valderrans settling themselves beside the slender southerners. The two princes' parties glared at each other with an intensity that did not diminish. A wave of concern washed through her mind. Sarelin's dying moments in the garden still hung over her, and she could feel her own shoulders on edge, her body taut, awake.

She was studying one of the Lyrians when she felt pain seize her head. The room blurred, and she gripped the orb of her staff.

"My lady?" Derset turned a solicitous gaze on her.

It was as if her skull was being pressed from both sides, threatening to cave in.

"It's nothing." She took a deep breath.

"I've never seen 'nothing' have such an impact," Raden said.

"I could call for a physician," Derset suggested.

She shook her head. There was some sense to what he said—headaches were normally splitting pains, not this strange crushing sensation, yet she was aware of Chackery and Tuchester watching her from one side and Pelory looking from the other.

"That will not be necessary," she said, straightening up. "It is a passing pain."

Once the words left her lips, they came curiously true. The crushing sensation at both temples ceased, and her head cleared. No time to contemplate her relief, for the herald reached the middle of the hall and began reading from a piece of parchment.

"From the jungle beyond the mountains, where leopards prowl . . ."

"Here we go," Raden whispered. "More titles than a Rhimese library."

"I present the supreme leader of the west, tamer of leopards, and mistress of the purple hills . . . venerated from Suhai to Neiran, the breaker of bones and winner of fifty-eight tournaments in the Hungry Pit, where warriors fear to tread . . ."

Lysande put a hand gingerly to her temple. No pain sang through the skin.

". . . the first lady of mist and steam, ordained by the goddesses themselves . . . the Irriqi of Pyrrha, Cassia Ahl-Hafir!"

The doors rattled. Guests sat up straight. The northerners and southerners stopped trading stares. The rattling came again.

Someone's locked the Pyrrhans out, Lysande thought.

She could see Pelory smirking. A hot feeling crept through her cheeks. Everyone was waiting; they were probably all gloating over the clumsiness of the palace scholar.

Then the doors burst open with a crash, and a mass of people thundered through. There were so many of them that the procession seemed never-ending; walking five by five, they could barely fit across the walkway. The crowd leaned back to let them pass. Lysande forced herself not to stare at the lightly muscled arms and the billowing pants the color of ripe plums, though she could not help glancing across as a man with a curved sword walked past.

"Goddesses below," Raden said. "If I could get my hands on a hook-sword . . ."

"Don't think about trying to steal the Irriqi's," Pelory put in. "I hear she killed a man at fifty paces in the Pyrrhan court."

"Why do we continue to parrot 'Irriqi'?" Tuchester said, in a whisper that Lysande suspected to have reached all the nearest tables.

The envoy was looking at her. Would Tuchester have spoken so to one of her own rank? She suspected she knew the answer already.

"I believe Queen Sarelin reminded you on more than one occasion that the Pyrrhans keep those allies who recognize their traditional titles," she said.

She was a little pleased with how sharply the words came out. The tone did not invite reply. *Never quaver, never yield.*

The woman at the front and center of the guards strode through the tables. Two long hilts protruded at her left hip and another three jutted up at her right. Her purple cape swept the floor as she walked, and her forehead shone with a silver band shaped in an upward V that bore an egg-like amethyst surrounded by many smaller purple stones. Lysande thought that the Pyrrhan leopard on her trousers, gleaming in white thread against the dark cloth, seemed a particularly apt emblem; she could not help remembering, too, that a great cat had attacked the queen. Pulling herself straighter, she squared her shoulders, trying to face the Irriqi like Sarelin would have—signaling respect, but no fear.

The Irriqi was not smiling as she approached. The women and men on either side of her wore equally unimpressed looks. Lysande suddenly felt very glad that she had covered her deathstruck lock of hair before entering the hall.

"So you are the Councillor," Cassia said.

"I am, Irriqi. Welcome to our fine capital." Lysande bowed.

"You were close to the queen. I did not see eye to eye with Sarelin Brey, as everyone knows, but I respected her."

"Perhaps you will respect her Councillor, too."

The words slipped out of her mouth before she could check herself. For a moment she was sure that she would be rebuked, yet the ruler of Pyrrha gave her a cursory glance.

"We shall all know each other better soon," she said.

She led her guards onward, and the Pyrrhans settled themselves beside the Lyrians. Lysande felt the room simmering once more as the third party settled in. "Well done, my lady," Derset said.

"I'm surprised I did not pay for my cheek."

"A little vigor is what the Pyrrhans prefer."

"Hard to tell the difference between vigor and a good deal of insolence, sometimes," Raden said, grinning.

As she seated herself, Cassia Ahl-Hafir shot a contemptuous look at Jale Chamboise. He turned his back to her and began polishing his ring. Behind them, Lysande saw a group of kohl-eyed southerners pointing at one of the Valderrans, and one of them drew a smallsword from his sheath and began to finger the blade. She did not like the look of that, and she was about to command her guards to move closer when she was interrupted by the herald. "Excuse me, Councillor." Lysande motioned her to speak on. "It's the Rhimese party. They're not here.

They were meant to arrange themselves in the first chamber while the Pyrrhans made their entrance."

Raden and Derset were both looking at her. "Go and search the grounds for them," she told the herald. "Send a group of guards, if you must."

The crowd began to stir. Many of them cast glances at the front of the Great Hall. Lysande glanced to her right and saw Pelory watching her, her gray eyes as cold as ever.

"I'm sure they'll be here in a moment," Derset said.

The seconds dragged on. In the cavernous hall, the walkway drew all stares, and the wait was threatening to transform the whispering to whipped-out blades; Pelory looked on the verge of making a remark when a chair scraped at the front of the room.

A Valderran woman rose, holding something up. "Take this back to the desert waste you came from!"

A man in blue and gold got to his feet beside her. "Stay your tongue, runt. Or I'll cut it out for you," he shouted, gripping his sword-hilt.

The Valderran woman let out a stream of curses. Lysande stiffened. The pot was boiling over, and she was about to see the mixture scald everything in its path. Her hand reached for a dagger before she remembered her position.

The pair of quarrellers moved closer to each other, their cheeks flushed. It was impossible to hear every word, but Lysande caught something about skinning ice-bears and an utterance about gutting southerners in their fancy frocks before the Valderran noble thrust out her hand, waving the object again at the southern man. The spot of bright purple at the end of a stalk told Lysande that it was a queens-flower, freshly cut.

Dead royalty, she thought.

Five other Lyrians rose and drew their swords. "You dare leave the Old Signs at our table?" the Valderran shouted. "You dare support el-ementals? Delta scum!"

Lysande stepped forward, catching Raden's eye, and pointed at the woman and man in turn. Her heart galloped.

The Axium Guards reached the Valderran woman just as she lunged. They gripped the sword-arms of other Valderrans and pushed the Lyrians back, leaving Raden and an officer to steer each participant back to their seat. The Valderran woman shoved the Axiumites back, then flung the queensflower at the Lyrians before taking her chair. At another gesture from Lysande, Raden rattled off orders, bringing more guards running.

The Lyrian man held forth for another minute, making a few gestures with his hands that required no translation. At last, however, his shouts subsided, and the barrier of boots, swords, and armor dissolved. An officer nodded to Lysande once it was over, her armor gleaming in the torchlight, and Lysande exhaled.

The crowd's testiness had disappeared. For a few minutes, the hall hummed with a spirited exchange of views on whether there might be a brawl. It was all a game to them, Lysande thought. A pleasant diversion, if you had a castle to lock yourself up inside should things turn sour.

Raden returned to her side, wearing a tired smile. "Well, that livened up the occasion." He held out the queensflower and Lysande turned it over in her hand, running a finger over the stem, the bulge that bristled with sharp green leaves, and the crown of needle-thin purple petals at the top. There was no hiding the symbolism of a cut queen.

She knew well what kind of people might have placed it there. From circlets of ivy placed on doorsteps to sprigs of heather nailed to pillars, and cairns of waterstone erected in the street, reports of the Old Signs abounded in the capital. Since Sarelin's death, she had found herself taking out the banned copy of *A History of Elementals and Their Habits*, and returning to one part: the claim that the Old Signs represented the stealthy justice of the elemental people as well as their powers.

Perhaps it was as simple as that: gloating over the end of a reign.

Don't let this be the first blood-spattered banquet in years, she pleaded to Sarelin, glancing at the portrait on the wall.

The boom of the doors rang out again. "Ladies, lords, and signore, I thank you for your patience. I present to you the crown prince of our eastern city, master of science and steel, and ruler of all Rhime . . . Prince Luca Fontaine!" the herald shouted.

The tables fell silent. Even the Valderran who had brandished her sword peered toward the doors. A surge of curiosity made Lysande lean forward. It was the same curiosity that had surged through her ever since she received a black rose wrapped in summersilk, and it had not been tempered by her sending a puzzle in reply. She had tried to imagine this moment, more often than she liked, while gazing at the rose in its vase.

The Rhimese party flowed into the hall in black doublets, a stream of ink. As the Rhimese guards and nobles approached, Lysande noticed that some of the captains carried long, curved bows and quivers of silver arrows, while others gripped sword-hilts emblazoned with cobras. They did not pause to show their weapons to advantage but walked on to their seats, and despite the ease of their entrance, intuition warned Lysande that this was the party most likely to make her draw her dagger.

The first group of Rhimese cast disdainful glances at the twittering birds as they filed past. Lysande saw one of the captains shoot her a stare, and she felt the woman's attention keenly.

"Which one of them is Prince Fontaine?" she said to Derset.

"None of them, my lady."

"I'm sorry?"

"He is not marching in the first group." Derset's eyes scanned the faces. "I do not see him in the second, either."

The third group did not yield the prince of Rhime. Nor did the fourth cluster. Lysande felt unease stir in her stomach. By the time the seventh group of Rhimese had entered the hall, the crowd was talking over the band and pointing at each party as they passed, and Lysande was beginning to suspect that the flower she had sent—wrapped in cloth, tied with a quadruple knot, and weighted with a particular meaning—might really have offended the prince.

"This is his plan, isn't it?" Raden scowled as another wave of black flowed by them. "He's going to turn up late so that everyone'll be in a frenzy."

The sound rose to almost a roar, and as the doors opened again, it scarcely diminished. Lysande tried to stop her breathing from speeding up.

"Finally," Bowbray remarked, with a sideways glance at Lysande.

She barely noticed the jibe. Her attention was fixed on the figure coming through the great doors, moving slowly down the walkway.

Luca Fontaine wore only a simple black cloak over a black tunic and trousers, his collar fastened with a single ruby that glittered as he walked. Aside from the stone, there was no other adornment upon him, and his attire allowed all the attention to fall on his face. Fine-boned, with luxuriant black hair and skin that bore no traces of battle-scars, he reminded Lysande of a plant that had grown away from the sun; and there was something very discomfiting about his dark eyes, which seemed to sift through her thoughts. He did not spare a glance for the nobles seated along the aisle, fixing his gaze ahead.

Something moved on his left shoulder, a rippling, like a banner stirring in the wind. Lysande stared but could not discern it.

This was the man who had taken his commoner mother's last name and cast aside that of his silverblood father, Prince Marcio Sovrano. This was also the man who had sent four bunches of untrimmed nectar roses to Sarelin after her injury, and later, an inkflower *for the palace scholar.* He moved with easy strides down the length of the hall. On either side of the walkway, the crowd seemed torn between shying away from their new guest and staring openly.

Luca did not acknowledge the attention. A half-smile played on his lips.

"You will forgive me my tardiness," he said, as he drew to a stop. "I've been looking forward to meeting you, Councillor."

The words rang out in Old Rhimese.

Lysande stared at him, identifying the language and trying to comprehend that she was hearing it in the Great Hall. While she formulated a response, he gazed back at her.

After a pause, she replied in the same tongue: "It is a pleasure to welcome you to the capital, Your Highness."

Luca's left eyebrow lifted. "So you do speak Old Rhimese. I had heard you were fluent in all the old tongues . . . there's nothing like seeing for oneself, though." This time, he spoke in Ancient Pyrrhan, his voice lilting. Something on his shoulder seemed to move again.

Another challenge, Lysande thought.

"Clearly, you are a scholar of languages yourself, Your Highness."

Lysande shifted into Ancient Lyrian. "And clearly, you take an exceptional interest in a mere commoner, to research her background."

She noted the way he carried himself, without the hint of a slouch. Yet there was no tension in his posture, either. One corner of his mouth curled up, and her body betrayed her, leaning toward him before she realized it.

"I wouldn't say it was common to translate the Silver Songs at the age of twelve, would you?" He pronounced the Lyrian *e* with a flawless accent; short and soft. "I take it you liked my gift?"

"It was certainly . . . complicated."

"But then, I received a most complicated gift from you. I must have walked around my suite for a good quarter-hour before it struck me: the meaning of it. Five names, for that flower: starchling, stiff-neck daisy, evenpetal, tall poppy, line-bloom. The latter is only used in Axium. Not even a novice in scholarship could miss that." His smile twisted slightly. "And I did not miss the Axiumite cloth you used to wrap it."

"I congratulate you."

"Congratulations are usually offered when one finishes something, I believe."

"My apologies. I had theorised that a prince would speak directly." Why was it so easy to throw a rejoinder back at him, each time? She could not help herself. Surely, she should be nodding, smiling, or bowing . . . instead of returning his volley.

"I match my speech to the subject," Luca said. "And some scholars are about as direct as a labyrinth, if the gift I received this afternoon is any indication. I recognized the quadruple knot on your package; difficult to tie, and even more difficult to learn about. I suppose you thought it clever to choose a style that was used in the Pre-Classical Era, when the old tongues were spoken. Shall I congratulate you, Councillor, for almost managing to hide a clue?" His smile twisted a little more. "If I had not been a reader myself, I might never have discerned the second part of your puzzle. In the Old Axium tongue, the name for a line-bloom is 'the flower of manners.' I should thank you for the compliment."

"Not quite. I thought it was a flower you could use."

The smile turned to a flinch, the prince's jaw tightening, before settling into a pretense of polity. "Perhaps my gift will prove useful to you, too, in time."

"It was a clever puzzle. Cleverness is often the prettiest ruse. Though I confess, I did not have a guest suite to stroll in as I picked it apart," Lysande said.

"No; I see you are wanting for space in Axium Palace."

Aware of the soaring ceiling above her, Lysande bit back a swift reply. She considered Luca Fontaine for a moment. It was hard to ignore the soft elegance of his skin where his neck was exposed above the top of his doublet, though she had a feeling that nothing beneath his exterior would prove soft. "Some would have dwelled on the politeness of choosing an inkflower," she said, at last. "I found myself more interested in why you sent a gift to the palace scholar."

"Word of your talent reaches even princes."

"I should have thought that princes were more concerned with the queen's health." Why was she studying the lock of black hair that had fallen across his brow?

"You should be pleased, Councillor Prior. I recognized the flair in your manuscript of the Silver Songs when I first read it. Your reputation precedes you."

"As does yours, Your Highness."

She realized, a moment later, that such a remark might be horribly unwise to a bastard son. Derset had told her that the whole realm knew about the prince of Rhime having a palace attendant for a mother. She felt her insensitivity keenly. But there was no petty anger in Luca Fontaine's expression, only a kind of intense interest as his eyes bored into her.

"Indeed," he said, when the pause had stretched for some time, "one is far more resourceful as a second child. A first child is hauled up the ladder, step by step, but a second child finds their own way." He glanced at the high table. "Now, Councillor, I hope you won't mind if I bring a friend to dinner. He has been so looking forward to your banquet."

"Perhaps he might take a seat at the Rhimese table," Derset said.

"Oh, Tiberus needs no chair."

The prince lifted the right side of his cloak back with one hand, and there on his shoulder, a pile of smooth, black muscle shifted and bunched. Lysande did not recognize it at first. It was not until the creature reared its head that she felt fear catch in her throat. Two eyes like drops of blood narrowed, watching her. A pink tongue flicked out and drew back in.

"Is something the matter, Councillor?" Luca inquired.

"Your friend is a cobra." She spoke more calmly than she felt.

"I see your powers of observation are as sharp as the Iron Queen's grindstone. You needn't worry about Tiberus, though; he doesn't eat much."

The advisors edged back from the snake, leaving Lysande and Derset standing alone. The crowd erupted into a babble of competing voices as they realized what Luca was carrying. Some of the Pyrrhans drew their weapons from their sheaths, including several of the hooked swords, and her Axiumite guards moved closer. Lysande felt her nerves kicking violently and she wrestled with a rising panic.

"Can you keep the snake in check?" she said.

"Of course." Luca stroked the snake's head. "He is a spitting cobra, but he never spits on the floor, which is more than can be said of the Valderrans." Several of the Rhimese ladies and lords smirked.

Luca's eyes remained fixed on her, but she matched his gaze in strength. Without further comment, he walked onward and joined the Rhimese table, where his party had left a seat in the very middle of their ranks.

To let the most powerful man in Rhime bring a snake to a feast seemed like some kind of madness—and Lysande was aware of the Axium Guards surrounding her, their hands on their hilts. She was also aware of the queensflower in her pocket, cut off at the stem, and of the looks flying back and forth between the Lyrians and Valderrans, who had not calmed since the queensflower incident.

She was keeping an eye on Luca's elegant figure, too, though not necessarily for a purpose.

Lysande took a deep breath, stepped forward, and raised the Councillor's staff. "Ladies and lords, we make the city-rulers welcome in the capital. There will be five courses tonight: a taste of our land's tapestry."

The crowd applauded dutifully, though many people were still star-ing at Luca and his cobra. The musicians struck up a regal air and the four city-rulers got up from their seats, whilst Lysande and Derset led the way to the high table. For a moment, there was nothing but bus-tling.

As Derset pulled out Lysande's chair for her, he leaned down by her ear. "Remember, my lady, the hand behind Queen Sarelin's murder may be at this table."

Lysande watched as the city-rulers seated themselves around her. Dante Dalgëreth's frame looked even larger in a high-backed chair. Jale Chamboise's ring glittered in the candlelight, and Cassia Ahl-Hafir had one hand on her sword-hilt, while Luca Fontaine's cobra nestled into his neck, rubbing its head against his skin. She took her seat slowly.

The first course turned out to be a traditional Axium pie, coated in flaky pastry and decorated with swirls of dark butter-sauce, far more extravagant than anything she had eaten as palace scholar. As the attendants put down dishes of honeyed carrots and began to serve, Lysande wondered if she should make a speech. She had been too busy staring at Luca, taking in his easy confidence, to find the right words. Sarelin had told her once that it was better to let your guests start a conversation, so that you could figure out what they wanted before you spoke. She had not said whether that applied to royal banquets. Maybe there was some kind of ritual Lysande should have looked up; some custom to observe.

The problem was solved for her when Dante leaned across the table to Jale and began speaking. The young prince laughed, closing the gap between them. His face glowed, and not only thanks to the torches, Lysande thought: all the briefings in the world could not prepare you for a moment like this. The two princes' geniality seemed to thaw something in the hall, and the rest of the guests began to eat. A few Axium Guards drew closer to the high table, and Lysande glanced at them, acutely aware of their movement.

She leaned over to Derset, leaving a gap for an attendant to spoon some carrots onto her plate. "I thought the north and south were ill friends."

"Mostly. We all know how it's been for centuries. And after Ariane

Chamboise nearly started a war with Raina Dalgëreth, a decade ago, the envoys say bad blood spread anew . . . but despite their parents' grudges and the feelings of their own people, these two seem to keep a peace," Derset said.

Interesting, she thought, watching Dante cut Jale a slice of pie. A softness had swept over the First Sword's face for the first time since he had entered the Great Hall, yet she did not have the impression that anyone else had noticed. Dante's whole person had turned toward his younger colleague like an ice-rose growing toward the sun.

Before long, Derset was pulled into conversation with Cassia Ahl-Hafir, voicing his interest in Pyrrhan wrestling, and Lysande had no desire to be left alone in conversation with Luca Fontaine, whose black eyes were making her neck prickle. She was well aware that she had not raised the matter of the brief detention of the Rhimese envoy after Sarelin's death, and that for all the talk of flowers and languages, the prince might be expecting an apology. Or perhaps he thought she was too timid to address the table. As she darted a glance at him, he met her stare again. Lysande felt a swirling sensation in her stomach and told herself that it was merely indecision.

Summoning her courage, she took her spoon and tapped the side of her goblet, gaining the attention of the city-rulers while the rest of the room feasted on. She felt the burn of their eyes upon her skin, and swallowed.

"You all know why you are here," she said, with the slightest tremor in her voice, "so I will not attempt to dress the matter in silver cloth. Queen Sarelin left no heir behind. In the event of her tragic death, it has fallen to me to choose between the four of you for the crown."

"A tragic death, indeed," Luca remarked.

They turned to look at him. The Rhimese prince only wrapped his long fingers around a goblet and gazed back.

"Do you mean to imply something, Fontaine?" Dante said.

"I merely think it unlikely that the woman who defeated the White Army would suddenly expire from an animal's scratch."

"And why not?" Cassia demanded. "Was she not mortal, like the rest of us?"

Luca looked at them with indifference. "Sarelin Brey took three blows during the White War. She was stabbed through the ribs with a longsword on the Mud Field, ripping her side open like a hunted stag. Elemental flames scalded her neck as she charged into the White Queen's fire, and as Axiumites never cease to remind us, the fire died around her. A battle-wound to the jaw—she survived that, too. The populace chose her nickname well. One has to admire the sheer stubbornness of iron when it is reforged." Luca glanced around the table. "Ask yourself: if the whole White Army could not finish her, do you really think a panther could?"

There was silence as they all considered this, and Lysande met Luca's gaze. *He knows,* she thought. *Whether he killed her or not, he knows it was poison.*

"If the queen did not die from a wound," Dante Dalgëreth said, slowly, "then she might have been murdered."

"Excellent reasoning, for a northerner. I had every confidence you would get there."

"Very well," Lysande said, quickly, for Dante looked as if he would like to answer Luca with his sword, "I think we have speculated enough. Forgive me, Your Highnesses, but Sarelin wanted a queen or king on the throne immediately after she died. Rather than trading words like grain-sellers over the manner of her death, we should be thinking of the realm."

"Hear, hear," said Jale, with a reproachful look at Luca.

Cassia Ahl-Hafir raised her goblet. "To the realm," she said.

"And to Queen Sarelin," Dante added.

Lysande felt a tightness in her throat. "Yes," she said. "To Sarelin."

They had scarcely downed their wine before the second course arrived: great tureens of stew, containing something which looked suspiciously like tree-bark but which Dante insisted was a northern delicacy. As it was being ladled out, Cassia leaned over to Lysande.

"Do you care much for weapons, Councillor Prior?" she said.

"I can throw daggers in the Axium style, Irriqi, and do a little with a longsword." She attempted to chew a piece of the bark-like substance but, after a moment, spat it into her hand. "Sarelin always said my quill was my sword."

"We have three royal armories in Pyrrha, each the size of this hall."

Cassia gestured at the room. "If you ever come west of the hills and into the jungle, there is an ancient longsword from Hiraz that would suit you well."

Lysande met the Irriqi's assured stare. She stammered out her thanks, conscious that she had never been given a gift by any of the Axium nobles, and reminded herself of her purpose here. As Cassia called for another goblet of wine, she felt a nudge at her elbow.

"That is what we call a handsome bribe, my lady." Derset was wearing a wry smile. "Come, now, do not look so surprised."

Her glance at Cassia's face told her little. It was a face of royalty hard-won, not softened by years of cushioned chairs. She let her gaze wander to each of the city-rulers.

It was not difficult to gain Jale's attention while the Lyrian course came out, for he struck up a conversation about dancing while they waited for the food to cool—the plates of pale yellow noodles, garnished with little red flakes, were still steaming from the griddle—yet they had not been talking long about the Lyrian sapphire waltz when Jale turned and whistled to the Lyrian party.

A pair of men, their shirts almost transparent in the candlelight, set a golden box down beside Lysande. It thudded on the table. Peering down, she saw that its sides were encrusted with dozens of sapphires.

"For you, Councillor," Jale said. "A little token of Lyria's support."

She opened the box. Slabs of gold winked at her—at least twenty bars, gleaming.

"Your Highness, I cannot accept this." There was more gold in that box than all the coin she had possessed in her life. The thought of touching it made her quail. "To give away something so rare, to one who only holds a short office . . ."

"Rare in Axium, perhaps. But not on the delta." His pretty smile turned catlike.

She gave the slightest nod and returned the lid to its position. She thought of Charice, and of everyone whose name did not sparkle, all the rag-and-polish children and the ink-trade women and men, who would never hold a chest of gold bars in their hands, nor sit at a high table like this one. The schoolroom of the orphanage appeared in her mind.

It was too easy to compare this gift with the chest of plain, brittle, meager sweets that had served as the students' monthly reward.

But before she could reflect on what Sarelin could have done to even out the two situations, Dante Dalgëreth engaged her in conversation. While the First Sword might seem like a silent warrior, Lysande saw that Dante could rise to the same heights of eloquence as the others when he spoke of quarrying in the northern mines. His tale of a blizzard that covered Valderos in a shroud of pure white fascinated her, and she thought what scholarly interest a collection of his anecdotes might make.

So little was written about the north; were there not aspects of the weather she might note down, for military strategy? Could she not add them to the string-bound booklet of notes she had begun on the cities, next to the compilation on Bastillón and Royam? There were pages of quotes, dates, and illustrations, but there were still so many pages to fill.

"If I may ask, First Sword: does the summer in Valderos last long enough to counter the extremities of winter?" she said, noticing out of the corner of her eye that Jale was watching her.

"We claim to have a summer. In truth, it is as if the peaks of our mountains are given just long enough to thaw before the bitterness creeps back. A week, or two at best."

She had been wrong: Jale's gaze was directed at Dante, and he was drinking in the sight of the First Sword as if he could not slake his thirst. That was interesting. Lysande remembered that she was meant to be replying to Dante. "Your people must possess real fortitude from enduring such harsh conditions."

"Queen Sarelin put it slightly differently. But yes. They are no easy targets."

Lysande, who had heard Sarelin putting it differently on more than one occasion, repressed a smile. "Tell me, how do you diversify your crops, with so little warmth?"

"You ask more questions in a minute than anyone I have ever met, Councillor." Dante poured them each some wine. "It is largely thanks to our resourcefulness in growing vegetables beneath the ground, you see, and our skill with salt preservation. . . ."

When the Rhimese course was brought to the table, however, Lysande put aside her interest in Valderos. An oval dish in the middle bore a wheel of flat bread topped with tomatoes, baked cheese, pumpkin, and all kinds of herbs. Around it, a ring of smaller dishes held cheeses streaked with blue veins or crusted with red rind. The final ring of dishes, filled with gleaming black balls, made her gasp.

"Rhimese olives!" she cried, picking up one of the little dishes.

"These are prodigiously rare," Luca said, looking at her over his wine.

I tried them, once, she thought. With Sarelin. On my sixteenth gift-day. It hurt to even think of sharing the memory of Sarelin tossing the olives toward her mouth; there were certain pieces of a person that you wanted to keep, greedily, to yourself.

"If Rhime traded more freely, the Rhimese would not make so much profit," Dante said, with a glare at Luca.

"Making next to no profit is Valderos' specialty." Luca stroked Tiberus' head. "I shouldn't like to tread on your territory."

"You're a clever man, Fontaine."

"From you, I suppose, that's an insult."

Dante turned away. As the buzz of conversation resumed, he addressed Lysande. "Do you know why the commoners call Fontaine the 'red prince,' Councillor?"

"I don't believe so."

The dislike engraved on Dante's face made Lysande aware once more of the risk of having four city-rulers at one table—and of how much Sarelin had juggled, dealing with them. They were like children in a schoolyard, only armed with weapons and soldiers.

"Luca Fontaine murdered his brother. The whole realm knows. It is said that he stabbed him so hard that the blood spurted from his body, painting Fontaine's chest and hands. When his father found him, he looked like he was wearing a red shirt." Dante's voice gave the word *red* a deep resonance. "Do you really want a man like Fontaine on the throne?"

"That depends." She studied Dante. "How do you describe 'a man like Fontaine'?"

"Unnatural. That's how I describe him." Dante's eyes spat fire. "He spends half his time locked up in his castle in Rhime, inventing things and looking at formulas . . . all sorts of queer habits, our envoys say. Keeps a huge library for himself, like a damned scholar—begging your pardon, of course, Councillor—but he doesn't hunt or ride out like a prince should. Any man who carries a snake around cannot be well in the head."

Across the table, she saw Luca feed an olive to Tiberus from the palm of his hand. As he looked up, his gaze sliced through her again. Something about it made her skin tingle.

"May Cognita guide your choice," Dante said, bowing his head slightly. "But I promise that if the task should fall on me, you will never have cause to regret it."

"I thank you, Your Highness."

A northerner's word held true, she had heard Sarelin say, once, and she reflected on the adage as the attendants began to clear away the dishes. Certainly, Sarelin had never forgotten how quickly Valderos committed their troops when the White War began. But there were so many other factors to consider in making her choice of ruler. Some could not be mentioned to anyone in the palace. Even now, Lysande required vigilance to keep her thoughts on elementals guarded; she craved the solace of blue flakes to calm the torrent inside her mind.

Derset caught her eye, and she was relieved to have her attention pulled away. He did not speak, and for the first time, she remembered that he, too, must feel himself a small star beside the brightness of all this royalty. When Dante had leaned over to address Jale again, Derset shifted closer to her, and they spoke in lowered voices of the city-rulers. There was something in the way that she and Derset moved around each other that was unlike her movement with any other Axiumite; it was as if the stiffness of the motto *everything in its place* melted, a little, when they sat together or stood side by side.

The next course arrived in a stream of dishes, and whispers flew around the Axiumite tables. Had there been a mistake? Why were twenty plates dotted across the tabletops? Lysande remembered Sarelin telling her that a traditional Pyrrhan dessert was served in many small pieces, each of which was to be swapped from place to place before it was uncovered, much to Sarelin's discontent. She saw that none of the city-rulers appeared to object.

"We must all trade plates," Cassia ordered, pushing a plate to Derset. "My neighbor who shares my food pledges unity."

"How fitting," Luca said. "We are such a united party."

He was looking at Lysande, and something in his gaze was inviting her, but to what, she could not be certain. There was no action, only a kind of waiting.

She had never felt such interest in another person before, driven by something in his posture, his deliberate stillness. Her fingertips tingled again as he shifted his body to face her. Perhaps he was noticing her height, her posture, or the glinting lock of hair that had always marked her out to the palace as Lysande Prior, foundling scholar and queen's companion, colored by a queerness that seemed, to others, at least, to infuse her entire life . . . but she had the feeling that this regard went beyond surfaces.

Meeting his stare, Lysande pushed her plate over to him. Soon they were all sending plates back and forth. Her own dessert turned out to be a slice of yellow cake soaked in wine. She could smell sweets swimming in rose water and pastries drizzled with honey. There was nothing but chewing for a minute as they devoured the food.

She was nearly ready to take a second plate and set to work on a truffle when Cassia began to cough.

The Irriqi rose, spluttering so loudly that heads turned in her direction.

Lysande put down her fork. "Are you ill, Irriqi?"

Cassia was making gargling noises now. She strained for air. The Pyrrhans were standing up, staring at their leader—yet they hesitated, as if they did not dare to touch her.

Lysande did not pause to consider propriety. She rushed to wrap her hands around Cassia's body and heaved her upward under her ribs, as she had once seen a huntswoman do to a stable-woman who was choking on a bone. Cassia's chest convulsed under her hands. The Irriqi gripped the table, pulling at the silver cloth—time seemed to stop as she hacked and spluttered, and Lysande wondered if she might well die in her arms.

Then Cassia shuddered—gave one final hack—and spat out something into her palm.

The others rushed to the end of the table, all shouting over each other, clustering around the Pyrrhan ruler. Lysande's spine felt rigid, her entire body tightening.

"Goddesses save us," Dante was saying. "You could have died."

"It'd be awful timing, dying in the middle of dessert." Jale sounded concerned, though not quite as much as Dante.

People were standing up, staring in the direction of the high table. The Pyrrhans rushed to the Irriqi, surrounding her, and the Axiumite guards moved in as well. Hands flew to sword-hilts and voices thrummed in the hall. Lysande was watching Cassia's chest rise and fall. She had an urge to grasp Cassia again and embrace her until they were both calm.

"Someone is baking with money, it seems." Cassia held out her palm and Lysande squinted at the little piece of metal. It was so small that it had easily fit inside the cake, and she made out an even tinier carving on the surface.

Behind them, the Axium Guards moved a few paces closer.

"It's not a coin," Lysande said. "There's no Eliran crest. Only a picture."

Her whole body seemed to have tensed. They all bent their heads to look at it, but only Luca spoke. "A silent sword."

"A what?" Cassia said.

"A silent sword. A little piece of metal to be slipped into the food of one's enemy: just small enough that they will swallow it, but large enough to make them choke. Clever, no? They were named after the group of trained assassins—the Silent Swords of the Steelsong Era—because they kill so swiftly and leave no sign on the body."

Lysande sifted through the information in her mind. For some reason, she felt annoyed that Luca had recognized the weapon before she did. Their gazes met, and she suspected that he knew what she was thinking. "Of course. Rhime and Axium used to use them, before the unification of Elira," she said. She recalled the arms chapter in the *History of the Conquest*, with its fine-line diagrams of the many weapons devised to be employed against elementals. "I've read that they are carved with the symbol of the ruler that made them. Elaborate work, according to the historians. A crown for Axium, and a cobra for Rhime, to show the killer's loyalty."

"Seems rather stupid," Jale said.

"Stupid?" Luca shook his head. "Not quite on the mark. A silent sword is left for those clever enough to check for it. It's a warning. A message of intimidation from the killer."

They all leaned down to peer at Cassia's palm. The picture on the silent sword was just discernible on the metal. It showed a beast with horns, a body topped by a pair of wings, and a tail trailing behind: not a lioness, nor a goat, nor a dragon, but something composed of all three.

There had been a picture of an animal like that in the *History of the Conquest*, too, beside the description of the worst massacre in Eliran history. But Lysande had read on the same page that there had been no such beasts for four hundred years. The traditional omen of death . . . "winged horror" . . . "half-beast" . . . "symbolic herald of magic," and "the most potent creature of the elements" . . . fragments of sentences rose in her mind. A visceral dread, coupled with fascination, worked its way through her as she looked at the disc.

"Who uses a silent sword with a chimera on it?" Cassia said, taking the piece of metal between her thumb and finger.

No one answered. The word *chimera* seemed to hang in the air.

"I am afraid I know." They all looked up at Luca. This time, there was no trace of amusement in his mouth. His black eyes were fixed on the silent sword.

"One such piece was used to kill a captain in Rhime, twenty-three years ago. They dug it out of her body with a knife and took it to my dear father," Luca said. "He never found the killer, but he kept the silent sword in his private vault. He was convinced that if an enemy kept records and files of evidence, we should too."

"No one would willingly take a chimera as their symbol," Jale said.

"One would." Luca looked back at him. "The woman who styled

herself as leader of the elementals and wanted Sarelin Brey lying under the soil."

They came upon Lysande in a flood: memory after memory, all of them surging along the fibers that wove through her, because in all of them, Sarelin was present. Tales returned from nights when they were drinking into the silver hours. Why had she not analyzed those bloody descriptions earlier? But she knew the answer, even as she asked herself the question.

"Mea Tacitus," she said, meeting Luca's eyes. "The White Queen."

A story Sarelin had told her of the White War surged above the rest. Two weeks after declaring war, the White Queen brought her army to a town east of Axium called Sacton, where she stood outside the ramparts and shouted for the lady and lord to surrender. A messenger from Sacton rode out and was given a scroll bearing the White Army's promise of terms. *Mercy and liberty, in exchange for safe passage.* Lysande remembered the way Sarelin had spat out those words.

When she entered the town, Mea Tacitus showed the nobles a certain kind of mercy. They did not live to see soldiers run through their streets, pillaging, slitting the necks of guards who tried to stand in their way. The White Queen roasted them alive with a jet of flame from her palm.

One little boy was left to decorate the archway of a prayer-house after the soldiers had riddled him with arrows. Reports held that the White Queen took a throwing axe from one of her captains—an old weapon, and small—and placed it between the child's teeth.

"An iron gift," she announced, to the two citizens of Sacton left standing. "Send it to your Iron Queen."

The Axium Guards who reached the town later that day had halted, staring at the masterpiece in red, a creature composed of wings, fur, scales and elongated talons, carved into the boy's chest. No soldier had needed to speak the word *chimera*.

Lysande remembered the dark fury on Sarelin's face when she had repeated the story, and how it had made her shiver, even beside the fire in the queen's suite. The Pyrrhan historian Lady Tariq had argued that in obliterating Sacton, the White Queen inspired the surrender of

many other towns; that after the infamy of Sacton, the outposts began
to fall to the White Army with speed.

A famous slaughter demands resources, Tariq wrote. *It is a risk in
the short term, though some less scrupulous souls than I would call it a
wise expenditure in the long term.*

A vibration carried through her bones, the same rhythm she had
felt when the city bells pealed. Something aside from grief was causing it.

A grudge between two women who made the world tremble would
end only when one of them expired, she had always believed. If the
White Queen was attacking the Council, Sarelin's death had not finished the carnage. This was part of a much bigger game. One that had
been designed for something more than revenge.

She had never felt smaller, standing on the platform, beside the high
table in the candlelit hall. But she had never known herself so hungry,
either; so ready for the silent possibilities that swirled around her; so
prepared to risk her ease. While she knew that it was partly because of
Sarelin, she also knew that it was not entirely for that reason. Something had moved inside her when she gave an order to Raden, and the
same thing moved with a ravening quickness whenever she inked and
sealed a decision in her mind.

She heard a song of steel inside her, and let her breath march to it.

One of these rulers is helping her play.

Beside her, Cassia dropped the silent sword on the table. The chimera spun and spun, and landed face-up, gleaming in the light.

Five

The carriage stopped, and upon climbing out, she felt them shuffling toward her, dragging their feet over the bare ground: the pairs of duelers with collars of dried blood around their necks; the swordswomen whose biceps resembled knotted rope; the pages who had merely been standing in the wrong place when an arrowhead landed vein-deep; the squires whose livery was now carved in pieces; the splintered archers and broken knights; all of them singing and howling, caterwauling and snickering, crying out in death as they had not in life. Although she could not see them, she made out their incorporeal presence. It was easy to picture the dead when you had heard their stories, and Lysande had listened, in the royal suite, over many years, soaking up tales, until she could see this place groaning with ghosts.

A footstep: Derset climbed out of the carriage behind her, then Litany. She was waylaid by her attendant fussing over her hair and smoothing down the velvet of her doublet. Lysande let the specters fade from her imagination. She was already staring ahead at the wall curving before them, so tall and wide that it dominated the very sky.

"I heard Sarelin speak of this place many times."

"It has seen more duels than the Plateau in Valderos, my lady," Derset said. "The Canduccis and Malsantes of Rhime fought each other here, after the calendar was made—"

"—at the Conquest. In the Pre-Classical Era."

"I see there is no need to explain." Derset smiled.

Was it her fault that she imagined ghosts, in a place like this? Her eyes followed the circular wall, stark and bone-white against the gray of the clouds. Behind it lay a ring of sand—the oldest fighting ring in Elira. If she recalled the clashes and duels from Sarelin's stories, she could hear Sarelin's voice again, and that was what mattered: some warriors fought in the Arena for honor, Sarelin had said, others for duty, but most frequently, prize-fighters came there searching for gold.

"I did not expect it to look so beautiful," she said.

"All theaters of death are beautiful, my lady." Derset's smile had turned wry. "That is the tragedy of them."

The sound of voices carried, muffled slightly by the stone, a wave of shouts and cries that did not issue from spectral throats this time. With every step they took down the path, the noise grew louder. By the time they reached the base of the Arena, the clamor had built to a roar. Lysande hesitated before the door.

"The audience arrived some half-hour ago," Derset said, placing a hand on her shoulder. "They are not accustomed to waiting."

Gathering her spirits, she gave the door a push. The sound on the other side hit her so hard that she stood gaping. Twenty tiers of white stone loomed, packed with so many people that it looked as if the railings might burst and spill them out onto the sand—members of the populace, judging by their dilapidated cloaks. They jostled and pointed at the ring. Lysande remembered a phrase from an old poem: *baying for blood.* The scale she had consumed so hungrily in the weak light of the dawn had calmed her mind a little, but as the sound of the crowd increased threefold, she wished for another dose.

On the other side of the sand she could see the city-rulers, sitting in a stone box halfway up the tiers, their followers behind them. The bright purple and white of the Pyrrhans shone, embroidered beside the blue and gold of Lyria, then the softer gray and brown of Valderos, and finally, the black and red of Rhime. A patch of silver and emerald told her that a party of Axium Guards waited for her. It was a relief, in some small measure, to see the blaze of their armor. And yet she felt, somehow, that she should be sitting in the crowd, amongst those threadbare cloaks.

"Did I ever tell you that I am a third child, my lady?" Derset asked, as she stood, gazing across the sandy circle of the ring.

"I don't believe so."

"No one in my family expected much of me. Honors were bestowed upon my sister and brother—she was the Chief of Arms in our family, he the Protector of Bonds—but I had to work my way up in the service of the crown. There was no one to teach me how to face a room full of nobles. So I taught myself." He placed a hand upon her shoulder again and gave her another gentle smile. "You can learn to stand before crowds, Lysande. Even to like it."

It was the first time he had used her name. She met his gaze, and felt his hand slip down to rest against hers. His palm exerted the slightest pressure and she allowed herself to linger in the sensation for a moment, before pressing back and letting go. There was something soft about his demeanor, almost as if he lacked the edges of the other royal advisors, and Lysande liked the way it felt.

It was not the distance that daunted her as she stepped onto the sand, nor even the crowd. It was the sight of the figures dotted around the arena—the steel-clad warriors as large as Dante Dalgëreth, in helms that came down to their shoulders, leaving only a slit for the eyes. Some of the helms sported horns, or beaks of solid steel like vultures. Their wearers stood with legs apart, dangling swords and maces at their sides. A weapon was nothing compared to its potentiality, and with each one, she saw the phantom form of a blade slicing through her neck; she imagined the spikes of the mace splitting her skull into fragments from an angle she had never predicted, possibilities layering like topsoil over clay.

"These must be the prize-fighters," she said, wrenching her eyes from a mace. "Sarelin once said that it was dishonorable to cover your face in a duel." How well she remembered that discussion, Sarelin waving her goblet, arguing about the importance of rules and the need for Axium's code of conduct to apply nationwide, claiming that her anger had nothing to do with the fact that a Rhimese soldier had just won the capital's biggest tournament while wearing a mask.

"They are mercenaries, my lady. They serve no princess or prince." Derset gazed out at the competitors. "Many of these women and men will die in front of us, slain by their opponents. I do not pretend to understand why they risk it. But I know that the winner today will take home a sack of gold."

Of course, for a noble, to conceive of putting one's neck in the path of a spiked mace for something as commonplace as money was a feat of imagination. Lysande had less trouble understanding it.

The sound of the crowd raged louder around them. It seemed an age before they reached the far end, but at last, Lysande set one foot on the stairs that led up to the box.

Halfway up, Litany turned aside to join the crowd. "Up here!" Lysande called.

Litany hesitated, one boot on the next stair. "In the box, Councillor Prior?"

"Certainly, in the box. If I must have an attendant, I will at least see her enjoy the view. And you may call me Lysande."

Litany regarded her for longer than was appropriate, she thought. The girl must have realized it, for she looked hastily away. When Lysande proffered a hand, however, Litany took it. They climbed the rest of the way together, puffing up the stairs. The girl gripped her palm with a singular strength, and it was enough to surprise her; she reminded herself that Litany unscrewed storage jars and carried stacks of linen on a daily basis.

The city-rulers met her by the railing at the top, arrayed in almost as much finery as last night. Jale was glowing, seemingly wearing half of the Lyrian treasury and sporting a long jacket of gold cloth. Dante leaned forward beside him, draped in gray fur, and Cassia waited in her white doublet and cape, two hooked swords at her hips.

Yet next to all this display, Luca Fontaine wore the same plain black cloak as last night, with the single ruby nestled at his collar, and he watched her from the far end of the railing. Lysande was relieved to see no scales glinting on his shoulder. A cobra in close confinement was the last thing she needed now.

As she led Derset and Litany into the box, Derset moved to shield her. A woman was stepping forward, blocking their path. "Ellice Flocke, Councillor. Keeper of the Arena." She bowed, her doublet sparkling with jeweled pins. "We have been blessed with an even bigger crowd than usual." The Keeper gestured out at the packed tiers.

"Nothing like a bit of blood to get a good turnout," Jale said cheerfully.

"Indeed, Your Highness. There will be four rounds today, to honor each of the goddesses. And for the subsequent entertainment, we have only the fiercest of wolves."

Religion and bloodshed, Lysande thought, looking down at the mercenaries in their helms and the covered cage where the wolves were no doubt chained up, waiting for the attendant to wave an emerald cloth. No wonder Sarelin had liked tournaments so much.

She could see members of the audience waving paper designs of Fortituda fastened to sticks; the stands teemed with images of the goddess of valor, Sarelin's favorite, but every so often, she spotted a design of Cognita, Crudelis, or Vindictus, bobbing above the heads.

Divinity is a draught for the masses, Perfault had written. Would Charice have agreed? More to the point, would they ever discuss philosophical texts in her chamber again? A moment came back to her, brief and glittering as the flap of a butterfly's wings: she was sitting with legs folded, side by side with Charice, bent over a copy of a rare text from one of the old southern scholars, while they absorbed the theory of the "middle space." In addition to a realm of certain things and a realm of emptiness, the scholar Severelle claimed, there was a middle space, a place between being and non-being, where anything was possible.

An ambiguous enough concept, without Charice muddling it further. They had argued over points, definitions, and examples, sometimes reaching an agreement; the idea of a place between absolutes, between certainties, had fascinated Lysande, and she had been unwilling to believe that Charice could see it as purely metaphorical, a dream that defied crystallization.

For the first time, she wondered why Charice had left. She had been aware, for some time, of a creeping doubt in the back of her mind.

"We have clear rules in the capital," Flocke continued, with an unctuous smile. "Fighters must compete one on one. They must both use the same weapon—a sword against a sword, and a bow against a bow, and so on. You see our timekeeper in the next tier?" Flocke pointed to a woman in an emerald jacket holding an enormous timepiece with two hands fashioned out of silver, and Lysande felt a burst of pride as she gazed at Axium's first device to rival Rhimese invention. She glanced at Luca.

Intrigue had etched itself on his face, adding a furrow to his brow that somehow increased the natural beauty of his complexion, but when he looked across and caught her stare, his expression transformed to indifference. Lysande raised an eyebrow, as if to suggest that she had glimpsed his interest in the timepiece. The cool glance she received in return made her smile.

"The fighter who kills their opponent in the quickest time today will take home the prize: some two hundred gold cadres," Flocke said.

"I would not let the crowd make such a noise in Pyrrha," Cassia said, glaring at a pair of fathers below them, who were shouting louder than their daughter.

"Our prize-fighters are accustomed to the pressure, Irriqi." Flocke's mouth curved.

Pressure. That was it. If she could put pressure on the city-rulers, somehow, the traitor might make another move, and if they did not, she would at least have the benefit of distinguishing between their fighting skills. Her time as Councillor was dripping away. She looked down at the ring, her mind working furiously.

"There will be a change of plans," she said, cutting across Flocke.

The city-rulers turned to her. Even Derset raised an eyebrow.

"Don't tell me you're going to cancel the tournament, Councillor," Dante said.

"No, the tournament will go ahead. But you will be doing the fighting."

Be imperative. Stand tall. Speak as if your blood runs silver. Had she managed it?

The silence lasted for longer than even she had anticipated. It seemed to permeate the box and enter her very flesh. Lysande was wondering what she would do if they refused, when Luca laughed. "What a marvelous idea," he said. "We can put Dante in the ring. I've always wondered if he can swing that sword he likes so much."

"You will be fighting too, Prince Fontaine." Lysande looked around the group, taking in the confused expressions, willing her countenance to stay serene. "All of you. Whoever receives the crown of Elira should be able to defend herself—or himself—in battle."

If there was anywhere the city-rulers would feel pressure, it was in the middle of that sand below. Would Sarelin have agreed? She thought so. With a weapon in their hand, the traitor among them might see an opportunity to strike. Even though they weren't fighting each other, the opportunity for sabotage might prove too tempting to ignore; a chink in the armor here, a sprinkle of snake venom there. *Seize your chances while the sun gifts you light enough to sink your blade.* She had written that in *An Ideal Queen.*

"We can't fight each other, surely," Jale said, glancing quickly at Dante.

"You would fight a mercenary, Your Highness. Each with the same favored weapon. You would be allowed to yield, of course," Lysande said.

Nobody spoke. For a moment, the sound of the crowd grew even greater, doubled by the silence inside the box. Lysande kept her back very straight.

"Yielding is for children," Dante said. "I will be happy to take up arms in the ring."

Jale did not protest, and the Irriqi smiled wolfishly. Lysande turned to Luca, who shrugged. "Far be it from me to refuse," he said. "I don't often get a chance to outscore Valderos, Lyria, and Pyrrha in the same morning."

"The matter resolves," Lysande said. "Let the preparations begin."

Flocke sent a messenger running for a bag and sticks, and they drew lots; Dante seized the first, followed by Jale, Cassia, and finally Luca. As the messengers ran around the tiers of seats, spreading the word, the crowd's roar swelled. "You should have charged them double," Jale said, eyeing Flocke. "They're getting royalty into the bargain."

Dante went over to the Valderran party to put on his armor. Litany seated herself on Lysande's left, smiling nervously, but before Derset could take the chair on her right, Luca approached. As he sat down, she was conscious of the proximity between them; of the way that he studied her from inches away. The ruby drew her gaze to his throat.

The jewel shimmered, but it did not seem half so sleek as his skin. The smooth expanse above his collar caught the morning sun, and Lysande pulled her gaze away from his neck with difficulty. She could not help noticing that his flesh looked soft to the touch.

"You surprise me, Prior," he said.

"Call me Lysande, please."

"I must confess, Prior, that when I heard that the queen's Councillor was the palace scholar, I thought you might be . . ."

"Low-born?"

"Impractical. Highly intelligent, but with no notion of applying that intelligence to anything outside a book. I see that I was wrong."

She looked at his throat again, then glanced quickly out at the crowd. "You find me lacking in wits, Your Highness?"

"On the contrary. I think that you have applied your wits very well. You would have us believe that you intend to judge our fighting skills, but you really mean to put weapons in our hands and see if we turn fair or cruel. Anyone might dip a sword in poison or sneak an extra dagger in beneath an arm-guard. And then, there is always the chance to set a trap."

Lysande returned his gaze with all the equanimity she could muster.

"I wonder why you choose to sit beside me, Fontaine. If you mean to win me over, you may find it difficult; I may be of little means, but I do not sell my allegiance for a gilded gift."

"Have I brought a box of gold bars, perhaps? Or do I have an ancient sword to offer from my armory?" He smirked. "That would be inelegant and, more importantly, ineffective. I do not take you for the kind of scholar who is flattered by baubles and trinkets."

"There are many kinds of scholar?"

"Oh, an infinite number, Prior. Some quite ordinary, and others layered, like a starfruit. You have to peel back the hard skin to get to the flesh inside."

"It is the same with princes, I suspect."

Dante had climbed down into the arena, to thunderous applause. Lysande saw his armor glinting, a thick suit of steel plates with a shield that could have stopped a battering ram. His powerful frame appeared even bigger in the plating.

"Do you know why the White Queen is so dangerous, Prior?" Luca said, quietly.

"I fear we are close to violating Queen Illora's Precept." It was a challenge, to keep her voice light.

"And I would have thought a woman who transcribed the Classical philosophers would contest censorship. There is no harm in the talking, nor in the thinking—"

"—only in the doing. Volerus, Book Two." She looked at him. A lock of his black hair had fallen over his brow. His queer, piercing stare gave nothing away.

It came to her, then, the thought of running a hand down his torso, tracing its shape, then pressing two fingers against his throat, watching his reaction. Why it occurred to her, she did not know. The idea seemed to arrive like wood catching flame.

She had felt this before, with a woman she had been kissing in the palace orangery: the woman had flinched at Lysande's sudden interest in the pulse points of her neck. If Lysande was honest with herself, she had been too eager, too ready to take the first sign of interest as encouragement. It was one thing to prompt rejection, quite another to inspire . . . well, she remembered how the woman had looked at her, and the shame she had felt as her lover had recoiled.

No matter how firmly she put it down to scientific research, the flipping of pages on anatomy did not explain what stimulated it. Something inside her had been called to the beating of the pulse beneath the skin, a darkening force from somewhere beyond reason.

To that desire, too, she had learned to apply the lesson of the orphanage. *Restrain, constrain, subdue.*

"I said . . . do you know why the White Queen is so dangerous, Prior?"

"Because she can move one of the elements, I suppose," she said.

"You mean fire, or water, or wind? Those are mere physical forces." Luca leaned slightly closer to her. The lazy elegance of his posture drew him very near her side, close enough for her to be unsure if he knew the effect his proximity had on her. "Fire can be quenched with water, and water can be stopped with stone; even wind can be held back when a fortress is strong enough. And once you clap tempero cuffs on an elemental, those powers are trapped, as Sarelin Brey knew. But there are other powers, Prior. You may be perturbed to hear it, but some magical people are born with what they call powers of the mind."

"If I hadn't heard of the ability to read thoughts, or the power to read dreams, I would be a poor scholar of the Songs."

Luca regarded her for a long moment.

"Even the most assiduous scholar might be surprised to hear that the White Queen has a rarer talent yet," he said. "Did Sarelin Brey tell you? But I suppose that with no time for talking to elementals, she had no chance to find out." He paused just long enough for the barb to prick. "The White Queen can control the minds of others—rule their thoughts, so to speak. At a close range, my sources suggest, or I dare say we would all be dead by now . . . but nonetheless, it puts her beyond compare."

Lysande's mind moved to a tale Sarelin had told her about a captain who slew herself in a public theater. The woman had defeated a number of the White Queen's captains outside a little eastern town, during the war, and had survived the conflict. She had married and raised two daughters after the war, with a comfortable estate and a loving husband; indeed, she had seemed to have been blessed with every possible felicity. No one had ever understood why she fell on her own sword. Lysande found the story less thrilling, now.

"That would be power beyond measure, Fontaine," she said, keeping her voice as low as she could manage. "To control another's wishes."

"Indeed. The mind is the most valuable thing we have. To yield your mind is to lose the very thing that makes you . . . yourself."

One of Derset's remarks before the banquet came back to her. *The prince of Rhime has a love of scholarship. They say he keeps a library of ten thousand volumes.*

"Do you know the motto of Rhime, Prior?"

The crest of the eastern city was a red cobra on black . . . she had seen it in the histories, often enough, with three words written at the bottom. "Strength without swords."

"How does one conquer without a sword? Without a weapon?"

"The real leader conquers with her mind. Princess Santieri's phrase, second century, was it not?"

"Quite." He ignored her triumphant expression. "My brother and I were taught her principles before we could grip our little training swords. A bow or a dagger can be useful, but only so far. To truly outmaneuver an opponent, you must use this." He tapped the side of his head. "If the White Queen is allowed to storm Elira, she will take that power from everyone who opposes her, and there will be no mercy for those she captures. I am sure you are aware she has a precedent."

Lysande knew he meant the Conquest. She did not think it wise to respond.

"You know, some say she was motivated by a much more personal cause in the war. That Sarelin Brey met her, as a girl, and wronged her."

"I try to weight my opinion on the side of evidence."

Below them, Dante had pulled out a longsword. His opponent strode across the ring: a woman in an eagle-head helm who seemed to be made of nothing but muscle.

"If you have any doubt about your choice," Luca said, his lips close to her ear, "better to choose no one at all."

She gave the slightest of nods, her eyes fixed on the ring.

The crowd roared again: Flocke had raised her hand to give the signal and was retreating. Dante held his sword out. The mercenary in the eagle helm lunged forward first, slashing at Dante's ribs, but Dante brought his weapon up. Steel sang against steel, echoing.

Lysande chanced another glance at Luca and caught him watching her. She felt the power of his gaze. He should wear an ice-diamond, she thought; not a ruby. Everything about him is cold and sharp.

She wanted to touch his neck, just as on that day in the orangery, she had felt the urge to place her hand on the most vulnerable part of the woman's skin.

"Lysande," Litany said, turning away from the railing. "Do you think the First Sword will lose?"

Lysande realized how far her thoughts had drifted. "I hope he'll triumph."

"He fights with honor," Jale said, with a hint of pride.

"Oh, Dante Dalgëreth is the most honorable man in the Three Lands, so long as you do not enrage him." A smile curled Luca's mouth.

The tier below them erupted into a cheer, drowning them out. The two figures on the sand were moving again. Swinging with enough force to break a lesser shield in two, the mercenary battered her sword against Dante's; the ringing of the blow was enough to bring Jale to the rail of the box. The two fighters parried and thrusted for a moment. Dante's brows knitted, the muscles in his jaw clenching and unclenching. Every time the mercenary moved forward, the Valderran leader pushed the big woman back.

"Why does he not finish her off?" Litany said, looking across at Lysande.

"I don't know." She watched Dante beat the woman back again.

Valderran doggedness seemed to be paying off, as the mercenary was thrusting loosely now. The woman stumbled as she tripped on a clump of sand. An angry yell; there was enough time for Dante to rush forward and strike above the breastplate; yet still he did not. He doesn't want to kill her, Lysande realized. He wants the mercenary to yield.

"How valiant," Jale breathed.

"If he keeps this going much longer," Luca said, settling back in his chair, "he may stumble and fall on his valiant face."

Below them, the mercenary pulled something short and bright from her sheath. She threw it at Dante's chest. The weapon veered to the left.

"Cheat!" somebody shouted below them. "No second swords allowed!"

Dante's eyes narrowed, and a chill ran through Lysande. The Valderran circled around his opponent for an instant, then charged, his longsword whipping through the air. Blow after blow rained down so hard that the eagle-helmed warrior lost her footing, stumbling again in dry sand.

Just as he reached his target, Dante swerved, his right arm arcing around toward his opponent's neck. The blade carved cleanly through the flesh. Blood rained down on the sand. The woman's head flew through the air, spinning—encased in the helm like a boiled egg in its shell—and landed in the lap of a spectator in the bottom tier.

The catcher held the severed head with a stunned expression. All of the Arena seemed to hold its breath.

There was a kind of silence that widened, opening a space where fear mingled with approval, while people looked around for a sign as to which emotion would triumph, waiting for a pact to be formed: for the numbers to add up a particular way. Fear or approval. Lysande thought that she was watching that decision being made now. At last, cheering burst from the tiers as a bottle of wine comes uncorked, spilling its vintage freely.

She found herself applauding, falling into place with the others as the sound washed over her, yet she could not quite believe what she had seen. Even after Sarelin's grisly stories of tournaments and duels, this was too much. She had examined the queen's wounds, but that was different from seeing a blade carve through a body. Under the pretense of checking her sleeves, she glanced from side to side. Cassia and Jale were clapping, and in response, Dante made a bow in the direction of the box, the sun lighting up his breastplate. Lysande could make out a rainbow of jewels where Flocke was waving.

"I believe that's for me," Jale said, turning to look at them. "Wish me luck, won't you, Councillor?"

Lysande worked to find a smile. "Good luck, Your Highness."

"I daresay I'll be quicker than Dante." He grinned. "Clap loudly."

As Jale left, Dante rejoined them, prompting a flood of congratulations from every quarter and an analysis of the fight from the Valderrans. The headless corpse in the Arena was still being dragged away, leaving a trail on the ground, which Lysande watched, wishing she could look away. The dead of the Arena must be hungry for company, she thought, after all these years.

A pain struck her so forcefully that she leaned forward; it was the same crushing force that had overwhelmed her in the Great Hall, but magnified several times. Surely even chimera scale could not do this. Surely this agony was another level, beyond quotidian aches. She reached out to grasp the railing, almost blind to the Arena, and breathing hard, she listened to the rise and fall of her chest and gritted her teeth; it took a long time for the pain to fade, and when she looked up, Luca was watching her.

"Are you often troubled by headaches?"

"Not at all." Did twice count as often? Blue flakes glittered in her mind. "It is a fleeting pain."

"Indeed." But this time, he did not throw out a quip, only regarded her a moment longer before turning to speak with one of the Rhimese nobles. Lysande wondered if he too had a copy of the third-century physicians' records that mentioned experiments with chimera scale.

She tried to imagine what a vial of chimera scale would smell like to Luca . . . what sensory form desire would take if he breathed it in.

An aftershock ran through her, and she pressed a hand to her right temple.

Below them, Jale entered the ring, his armor sending beams of gold up to the tiers. He was clad in a breastplate over a shirt of mail, while on the lower half he wore a skirt-like garment and a pair of sandals with sapphires in the heels. All of it blazed with gold, including his smallsword, which he whipped around.

"He's no fighter," she heard one of the commoners below her mutter.

"Go back to Lyria!" a woman shouted, pointing south. "Kill the spearfish!"

This last was presumably directed to the mercenary who was walking across the sand: a man carrying a smallsword to match Jale's but far exceeding him in stature. His horned helm gave him the aspect of a demon. Some of the crowd applauded him, throwing tiny bronze rackets at him as he swaggered forward. Jale was busy waving to someone in the box.

Lysande's stomach roiled. "Perhaps we should call off the bout," she said, turning to Derset. "What if Prince Chamboise is killed?"

"It would be a circumstance to be lamented, I am sure, but the rules cannot be changed once the tournament begins. The fighting code is—"

"Axium law." She nodded, glumly. "The *Legilium* should allow mercy." She knew it better than almost anyone. Did she not still recall how the slap of her boots had reverberated through the stones of the eastern corridor as she hurried to the library, and how she had flipped through the illuminated manuscript, on the day that Sarelin had asked her to copy out the book of laws? She had not anticipated the transcriptions of other legal documents that would follow, nor the access to rare political tracts, nor, indeed, her growing skepticism.

Below, Jale gave a deep bow to a group of Valderrans who were shouting insults at him.

"If I were you, Prior, I'd be betting on Jale Chamboise," Luca said into her ear. "Surely you know that he was trained in the style of his mother, one of the most famous fighters in Lyrian history."

"He looks scarcely of age."

"Appearances can be false friends. You, of all people, should know that."

She had no time to query his meaning. Flocke raised her arm and the roar of the crowd swept over them again as the horned man advanced toward Jale, swinging his sword loosely. Lysande watched as the mercenary raised his blade and lunged. Jale stepped backward, as gracefully as if he were dancing. As the man swung again, Jale's legs wove behind each other to sidestep the man's thrust.

His opponent was left hacking at empty air. Some of the crowd shouted in anger, but a few were cheering the prince. "He has agility," Derset said, shaking his head.

"Prince Chamboise could slay the best fighters in the realm, in the southern style. Trained himself to meet his mother's standard." Dante drew himself up proudly. "No soldier in Lyria can match him."

Lysande's concerns about her head pains were soon forgotten. She was curious about the First Sword's tone, which sat at odds with that of the other northerners. As they watched the southern prince, the rest of the Valderrans looked close to snarling. Dante ignored them, a smile burgeoning on his face as he watched the ring.

Lysande remembered how Jale had watched Dante at the banquet, as if he had needed to drink in the sight of him. She fancied that something of the sort was happening now, with the roles reversed.

Jale moved with such speed that the horned man was forced to pivot dumbly, trying to keep up. The young prince circled around, then changed directions, darting left and right. The mercenary seemed encouraged by this display, for he charged after Jale, lumbering.

Only when the man was almost upon him did Jale move, ducking under his sword arm, weaving around and leaping into the air, a blur of gold, clinging to the man's back and wrapping his legs around his waist. It would be the work of a moment to press the tip of his sword to the big man's neck, Lysande thought, but Jale did not drive it in. He was saying something. Within seconds, Jale climbed off, and the big man fell to his knees and groveled.

"A yield!" Flocke declared.

Jale dusted off the sides of his armor and grinned at the crowd. A stunned silence had fallen over the Arena. For a few seconds, no one moved in the tiers; then Dante stood up and began to clap.

Behind him, the Valderrans rose and joined the applause. The sound brought the rest of the audience to their senses, and they rose too, breaking into a roar so loud that Litany's cheers were drowned out, her mouth seeming to move like a puppet in a show. Lysande felt a wave of relief.

"Amazing!" she cried, standing up too. "Power and mercy!"

"Well, he's beaten Dante's time, that's for sure," Luca said. "Best news of the day." Yet Dante was cheering as loudly as any of them, beaming.

"How noble of the First Sword to applaud," Litany said as they sat down again.

"Noble, or foolish." Cassia leaned across from her other side. "An ice-bear should eat a fish, not befriend it. But alliances have made fools of wiser leaders. When a northerner and a southerner let tales of romance be peddled . . . well, they sew up their own shrouds."

Halfway to questioning her meaning, Lysande looked into Cassia's face. In that moment, she became keenly aware of things she had never touched: the cool metal of throne-arms, the glimmering weave of cloth-of-gold, and the impracticably heavy hilt of a gem-studded sword. Instinct held her back. If you had lived as copper or brass, you could not pitch yourself into the world of silver lineage; you could not speak with the thoughtless confidence of those who shone.

"Everyone knows the story about how the First Sword of Valderos saved Jale Chamboise from a blizzard on his first trip north. They have been as sworn brothers since," Cassia added, sniffing, as if the idea of fraternity were risible. "All pageantry."

Jale returned to the box just as Cassia finished speaking, and Dante strode over to greet him, clapping him on the back. Lysande could not share the Irriqi's judgment; she felt that there was something genuinely warm about the bond between the two princes, expressed in that embrace. Dante's hand lingered on Jale's shoulder for a few seconds longer than a customary royal greeting, and as Dante whispered something to Jale, he leaned in slightly closer than was usual among those of high rank, almost touching his lips to Jale's ear.

"I hear the wolves that you Axiumites put out to fight afterward are extremely savage," Cassia said, leaning over again.

"Well, I should hope they aren't too violent—"

"My guards have been looking forward to it all week. They want to see if the beasts in this part of Elira draw blood like ours do, you know? From the jugular." Cassia tapped her neck. "I hope your baiter can shake that banner hard."

Lysande could not find a suitable reply. Her eyes settled on a young man in a shirt that had seen better years, let alone better days, standing beside the cage.

"That must be my signal," Cassia said, looking down at the ring. "You will excuse me, Lysande."

"Good luck, Irriqi."

"Perhaps we will share a bottle of Pyrrhan white when this tournament is over. You saved my life, after all." Cassia was smiling, as much as she seemed capable. She departed to receive her armor, and Lysande tried to keep her face impassive, despite the frothing of pride and honor inside her.

Lysande. It was best to focus on Cassia's use of her first name; not to dwell on the word *jugular*, nor on the threadbare young man by the cage, holding a bolt of cloth.

Dante and Jale had settled down side by side, she could not help noticing; Jale's hair was rumpled, his cheeks slightly flushed, and he looked pleased and flustered in equal amounts. Dante was whispering something to him again.

Cries of "western scum" followed the Irriqi as she descended into the ring, but Cassia did not respond, striding across to the center. She moved in her bronze armor as if it were featherweight. Upon reaching Flocke, she waved a weapon in a curved sheath at the Keeper.

"She can't fight with a Pyrrhan sword," Jale said, sounding more than a little smug. "No mercenary will know how to use one."

As they watched, Cassia gave her hooked sword to a waiting attendant with a glare and exchanged it for an ordinary blade.

"She'll do something clever with it anyway," Luca remarked. "If you've usurped the Qamaras, you can fight with a lot more than just brute force."

Flocke raised her hand, and the whole box leaned forward. Lysande was aware of hard ropes of tension in her shoulders, the same ropes she had felt pulling inside her many times since Sarelin's death. Derset's words from the crypt echoed in her head: *Beautiful, yes, but more than that. They can all kill.*

The fighters raised their swords. Cassia took a few paces to the left, watching her opponent. The mercenary wore a spiked helm fashioned of thick bronze, its points honed so that it was practically a weapon itself, and he advanced on Cassia with his blade high. The Irriqi swatted the man away. There was a certain thrill in watching her move.

The next slash came at her ribs, and Cassia pushed the mercenary back with a parry. The mercenary retreated, sword raised. Lysande recognized the quarter-beat maneuver, traced the positions of Cassia's steps, as if she were following the diagram in ink again. The movement created the impression of being out of reach: she had studied it, among other tactics, in a book of tournament advice, a tangent from many hours of attempting to learn battle strategies, the fruits of which she had added to her own political treatise.

Cassia was illustrating the theory, as if teaching everyone how to keep an eye on your opponent from a vantage point. You could sense the skill of attack even when it was not being used, Lysande thought. The essence of it seeped into your skin, your hair, the spit beneath your tongue.

"She has no stomach for a fight," Jale declared.

"I think she's waiting for something," Lysande said, watching Cassia circle.

As the mercenary lunged at Cassia a third time, both hands on his sword, the Irriqi's arm dropped low. With a flick of her wrist, she sent the sword slicing through the air, flying toward the man's legs, quick and bright in the sun.

"You can't *throw* a sword!" Jale cried.

But as they watched, the blade landed swiftly in the mercenary's right thigh. He bent over, screaming.

"Apparently, you can," Luca said.

The mercenary made a hopeless lurch at Cassia. Cassia did not bother to finish the man off; only deflected his clumsy blow and shouted at him. The mercenary knelt on one leg.

The crowd exploded with noise, this time not pausing to confer. Some of them applauded, while others were jeering Cassia and calling out insults. "That was at least a minute faster than you," Dante shouted at Jale above the roar, grinning.

"Oh, wonderful," Jale said. "She'll be so gracious about it, I know."

As Cassia climbed back up, the Pyrrhans maintained a furor of clapping and shouting. Watching Cassia move with sure steps, leopard-fierce, reminded Lysande of the woman she had admired most. No wonder she felt an affinity for the Irriqi. She could not help but find sketchwork everywhere when she held Sarelin's portrait in her mind.

The Keeper was waving from the sand. Luca got to his feet.

"I believe that is my cue," he said.

He had been sitting beside her for so long that she had almost forgotten he would be competing. Her gaze returned to his throat. It lingered too long, she realized.

Looking up again, she found him watching her and saw not the repulsion she expected, but a faint hint of interest in his features—not quite concealed—and then it was gone. Had he seen the direction of her gaze? Or was he just wondering why she was staring, curious about her attitude?

"Tread with care, Your Highness," she said.

"I always tread with care around people in helms."

"You seem very confident. Are you aware that your opponent could cut your throat?"

"I grew up in the court of Rhime, Prior. Throat-cutting is commonplace before repast, along with backstabbing and shooting through the neck. We salt our bread with conspiracy."

They looked at each other for a moment. The single ruby at the collar of his cloak glistened in the light.

"Tell me, did you really kill your brother, Fontaine, or is that just a rumor?"

He smiled, but with no mirth this time. "The most dangerous rumors are fashioned out of truth. Or so Volerus wrote. You should know."

I should know? She wanted to echo the remark. But he was still watching her closely.

"I was forgetting. I am just an inkflower."

"Oh, I don't think you are *just* anything, Prior."

He left the box and made to join the Rhimese party. Lysande did not notice the movement beside her until she found Derset standing at her shoulder.

It was a relief to have him beside her again. Taking her cue to sit, Derset settled himself and looked from side to side. The others were all occupied with chatting or pointing at people in the crowd, but he hesitated; his glance searched her face, and she had the impression that he knew exactly why she had changed their entertainment.

"Whoever killed Queen Sarelin is clever . . . and careful," Derset said.

Lysande looked out at the stone tiers for a moment. If there was anyone to ask, it was her advisor, who had served her with nothing but faithfulness. She caught the thought as it landed. As she examined her reasoning, she felt the touch of the hand of grief, and knew that it was not only Derset's encouragement that had bought her trust but the things he had not said—that welling of emotion she had detected in his features every time she spoke of Sarelin.

There were some tasks you could not delegate. One problem had been weighing on her mind since that day in the royal suite, but Sarelin's dying words had been entrusted to her alone, and whatever the sympathies of your advisor, Lysande thought, you could not weigh the words of those you loved, parceling them out with paper and twine; you could not spread the burden to others. If she had found no trace of the Shadows in any book in the library, then it was a warning to search harder.

"I wish I could say we had pinned her down by now." Derset's voice was soft. Lysande found herself going over a previous exchange in her head—doves sent to his contacts in the Periclean States—no credible hint of Mea Tacitus' location. She remembered how they had brainstormed, clutching cups of sweet red tea as they leaned over their papers in the Oval, crossing out ideas. Derset's posture had relaxed more with each minute they spent together. He had even spoken about Sarelin without blushing, twice.

"What of our neighbors, my lord?"

"Captain Hartleigh is investigating the sinking of one of our ships. Apparently, the reports of a Bastillonian captain attacking our vessel persist."

She thought of the shape of the Three Lands on the map, with Elira squeezed in the middle between Royam and Bastillón, yet unmolested. "They lack our climates, they lack our peoples, and so they lack our goods. Sarelin said that to me, once, about the Bastillonians. Most of all, she told me, the easterners lack steel and tempero. Why would they risk a trade war now?"

"I know not how they mean to benefit by this."

She could not help frowning. "And then there is the tactical outlook. All wrong."

"My lady?"

"The Bastillonians are subtle. The Royamese are direct. Two hundred years of historical and political records attest to the fact." She was aware that she sounded irritable. "Yet we are supposed to absorb that the Bastillonians are attacking us on the open seas, without provocation." When words in scrolls and books did not match envoys' claims, the whole situation felt dangerous.

Derset was looking at her with an interest she had begun to like. She could not ignore her propensity to indulge it, to feel the glow of his respect and admiration whenever she explained her reasoning, yet she was sensible of the dangers of this new egotism: of its allure.

"Here comes the prince," Litany interjected, leaning toward them.

Luca wore a black suit of armor with a few silver cobras on the armguards; like his robe, Lysande thought, the plates set off his hair and eyes, lending him a startling beauty. But when he moved, he slipped between definitions, something beyond a prince or a man; his body became a river, each step flowing into the next, unmaking itself, yet promising a flood.

All around the stone tiers, women and men went quiet. There were no jibes or curses this time, nor applause. The prince carried a bow in his hands, a sleek, silver instrument, and his quiver boasted arrows with stems far longer than any Lysande had seen; their ends looked sharp enough to cut diamonds.

"The crowd must like him," Litany said, turning to Lysande. "They seem quiet."

Silence in an arena meant something different than silence in a courtroom, Lysande observed. She stared at the figure on the sand. There was no chance of thinking of their neighbors, now.

Luca examined his arrows, running a finger along the edge of one shaft. He did not spare a single glance for the crowd, nor for his opponent, a hulk of a woman, bigger than all of the other three opponents so far; the mercenary was nearly bursting out of her armor, and she wore a helm with thick horns. If the two ever got close enough to drop their bows and trade blows, Lysande did not like the prince of Rhime's chances.

Yet something about Luca's movement warned her that he was looking ahead, into moves and counter-moves, seeing all the shifting possibilities and readying himself to shift around them. Lysande guessed that he knew the exact shape and condition of the arrow he was holding. Taking his time, he gave the impression that he had not even noticed the huge mercenary standing opposite him.

The Rhimese fight with their intellect. Sarelin's tone had not been complimentary when she said that, crouched next to a wounded Axium captain.

"In Lyria, we say a bow is a coward's weapon," Jale said, looking over at Lysande. "You just stand back at twenty paces, and—thwing!"

Twenty paces was a very attractive distance indeed, but fifty would not be too much, with an opponent like this mercenary. The woman appeared built of stone.

Flocke raised her hand. The two fighters nocked arrows to their bows and stood still, while the crowd gawked, waiting for a shaft to fly.

Yet Luca did not fire at his opponent. He tilted his bow upward, toward the sky, and sent an arrow whizzing into the clouds. The crowd raised their heads as one, craning for a glimpse of the shaft. So did the mercenary, tilting her thick neck to watch the arrow soar.

The angle of the woman's chin exposed the gap between her helm and her breastplate: a crack about a half-inch wide, barely visible to the naked eye, but visible nonetheless.

Luca did not miss.

Lysande watched the second arrow fly from his bow and sink into the sliver of flesh. Gasps sounded around the tiers as the huge woman crashed forward in the dust, blood dribbling from her neck, before she had fired a shaft.

A few people in the bottom tier began to applaud, but the rest of the crowd waited. After a moment, Flocke smiled and clapped, and slowly, the rest of the audience joined in, building to a smattering of applause. Lysande caught a mention of the "red prince."

"Well," said Derset, faintly, "I think we have a winning time."

Lysande was still staring at the dead mercenary. Behind the corpse, Luca turned to face the box and made a little, ironic bow, looking at her.

"Excuse me, my lady," Derset added, "but I think Flocke wants something."

The Keeper was hurrying up the stairs, all the way to the box. "Councillor! We would be honored if you would present the prize." Flocke was wearing her oily smile as she blinked up at Lysande. "It was thanks to you that we had four such colorful bouts, after all."

Lysande did not very much desire to descend into the ring, but Litany was beaming at her and Derset leaned over to pat her on the back. Looking at their faces, she drew a breath, and she rose and shook her head at the Axium Guards. Appearing before the people alone would look much better than appearing with a train of soldiers bristling with weapons; if she was to respect ordinary people, she could not appear before them like a woman warding off beasts. Perfault's famous political tract, *On Queens and Commoners*, suggested as much.

Confidence before the nobility. Humility before the people. Books had a strange way of making themselves useful in your life, words sprouting up when you least expected them.

Halfway down the stairs, she felt the noise of the crowd roll over her in a thundering wave, but she remembered Derset's remark. *You can learn to stand before crowds. Even to like it.* This was her own style; her own choice. She put another foot down on the stair below.

Flocke was waiting for her at the bottom, holding out a cloth sack. The gold inside felt like lead. In front of her, Luca had returned to the center of the ring and was looking at his bow, as if he did not hear the spectators shouting.

"You need only walk over and present this to Prince Fontaine," Flocke said. "Make sure that you shake his right hand firmly."

"Is it not the custom to shake with one's weaker hand?"

"Prince Fontaine is left-handed, Councillor."

Of course he was. The right hand would have been too ordinary for him. Foot after foot, she moved slowly over the sand, keeping her eyes fixed on Luca. It helped to focus on one figure instead of the hundreds of shouting and pointing people in the tiers. The body of the horned mercenary had been removed from the ring, but a lake of red dyed the sand where she had lain, and Luca stood behind it, his bow dangling from one hand.

She came to a stop opposite him. In the corner of her eye, a purple scarf fluttered as a woman leaned over a rail to cheer. It reminded her of queensflower petals.

"Congratulations, Your Highness," she said, holding out the bag of gold. "You must be very proud."

"Eminently so." As he reached out to take the sack, his hand gripped hers. "Remember what I said to you, Prior. If you put the White Queen's agent on the throne, we may all die. Do not mistake this for a game of tactos." His voice had dropped to a whisper. "If you lose this game, you do not get to play again."

He stepped back and pulled the sack with him, holding up his prize. The crowd broke into applause. Luca started to walk the champion's circuit of the sand, following the circle of the stands. Lysande left him to it. This was his moment, after all, and he deserved his victory, even if he had won it in a demonstrably Rhimese way. She was halfway across the sand when she heard the growl.

It came from in front of her: a low and ominous sound, like a rumble before a storm. The creature burst from the door of the wolf cage and bounded into the ring, a mass of dark fur and sharp yellow teeth.

It was speeding over the sand now, taking in several feet at a bound. The forest wolves Sarelin had killed had never run like this. How in Cognita's name did it get unchained?

She wondered how her mind had time to pick at details at a moment like this; yet skills could not be wished away. She could not halt the workings of deduction. Not even if mortality was bearing down upon her.

The wolf's slavering mouth opened as it pounded toward her. It was seconds away. It was going to rip her to shreds in front of half of Axium.

This is the end, she thought. Maybe she would see Sarelin again.

Lysande could not say for sure that nothing awaited her, even if she had failed to worship in prayer-houses or stare at relics. For a second, she surrendered to hope.

At the last moment, the coil of her arm unsprung. She drew her dagger and advanced on the wolf. The animal shied and swerved around her, so close that she could see the drool on its jaw. A second too late, she realized where it was going.

"Fontaine!" she shouted. The animal barrelled at him, snarling. The prince of Rhime snatched up an arrow and fitted it to his bowstring. Rays of sun threw a sheen over his black armor as he pulled the arrow taut, lined up the point, and fired.

The wolf stopped, paws scrabbling, jaws snapping at the air.

It landed with a thump at Luca's feet. The shaft of the arrow protruded from its neck. The Arena held its breath; all around the tiers, the crowd stared.

After a few seconds, Flocke laughed nervously and began to applaud. "Congratulations, Prince Fontaine," she called, pointing to Luca. "Our champion triumphs again!"

Relief spread slowly around the audience, the crowd smiling and clapping along with Flocke. Some of them even cheered. Lysande took in the jubilant faces.

The prostrate body of the wolf lay on the sand, and over the top of it, she met Luca's eyes. "We must leave," he said.

The other city-rulers were already departing the box, too far away for her to make out their reactions. She cast a last glance at the wolf, its jaws still open in death. "Whoever loosed that wolf may unlock the cage again and set its furry companion free." Luca came to her side. "We're a prime meal, standing here."

Slowly, she walked with him across the ring, away from the body of the animal and the patch of bloodied sand. *Panther. Poison.* Two strikes. *Silent sword. Wolf.* Another two.

Her eyes found the wolf cage, now surrounded by guards who were interrogating the young man in ragged clothes holding a bolt of emerald cloth, his eyes wide with fear. The boy had never received the chance to wave his bait. And why, in Cognita's name, did Axiumites send one of the populace out to dangle a piece of fabric in front of wolves? Who had established this "custom"? Lysande rummaged in her mental notes, finding nothing. She noted how densely packed the tier behind the cage was. The door had been allowed to come unlocked, under so many eyes. The guards were all defending the box, she realized. It hurt, to realize that she was the one who should have anticipated this: a simple mistake, but one which had steered her to within an inch of disaster.

When they were nearly at the door in the stone, she turned and faced Luca, aware of hundreds of people watching them. "Are you all right, Fontaine?"

He studied her face for a moment.

"Quite all right, Prior," he said. "But when my hosts set their dogs on me, I generally find it is time to leave."

A ceiling of branches sheltered her in a cool, dark world. The fruit drooped around her, so ripe that it burdened the orange and lemon trees and bent the plum bushes to the ground, and scents of bell-flowers and sacharia buds perfumed the breeze. Lysande paced among the blossoms and leaves, turning at the end of the orchard.

An orange plopped at her feet. She stooped to pick it up, examining the swollen exterior, the dark color of the skin.

The guards and the spectators at the Arena had been questioned, but no answers had emerged. If the wolf had been set on herself and Luca, then maybe the silent sword had been meant for one of them, too. In all the swapping of plates, it might have ended up in front of Cassia by accident. But if that was so, Luca might not be the traitor.

He had scattered words like Rhimese rubies at her feet, each one resplendent with facets of knowledge, glimmering all the more when they rolled from shadow into light. He had sought to purchase her trust with rumors, disbursing them while they sat together: here, a clump of the White Queen's powers; there, a clump of Sarelin's veiled past. A more prosaic speaker would have sought to fill in every detail, but Luca had left gaps. There, she thought, lay the danger. You could pick apart a lie, but your imagination would brick up spaces.

Who was she to put on the throne? One of the three city-rulers who might have killed Sarelin and might now be trying to murder Luca Fontaine—or Luca himself: cobra-keeping linguist, bastard prince, fratricide? It was the kind of choice that Fortituda, goddess of valor, gave to seekers in the ancient stories, but she had never asked for a choice, and she was on no quest.

Scholars did not get invited on them. Only if you wielded a sword could you be declared a heroine, if the Silver Songs were to be believed.

As she paced back and forth, Luca's words echoed in her mind. *If you have any doubt about your choice, better to choose no one at all.*

She would like nothing better than to pick none of them and pass the crown to some deserving Axiumite soldier, like Raden, but long years in Axium Palace had taught her how the silverblood families would react to that.

And then there was the matter of how her choice would relate to elementals. The bodies on the cart swam into her mind, and Charice's face . . . always Charice, speaking.

They had never spoken of their first time, since it happened, but Lysande had written it into her memory with careful strokes, recording how she had woken to the irradiance of moonlight from the window, the silver painting Charice's limbs, the two of them no longer entwined but facing each other on the bedsheet. She had listened to the other woman breathing softly. After the encounter, she had lain there, relishing the memory of skin against skin, reliving the warm trail of Charice's lips along her inner thigh, a prelude of kisses that left a pleasant burn, like the aftertaste of spirits. Sometimes you knew that a moment was precious; you were sure that no matter how long it lasted, it would need to live longer, for some day in the future when you would call it up again.

Now, she was glad that she had distilled it and stored it away. She was even glad that they had not referred to that night, during any of the times they had lain together since. Every detail could be stoppered.

Her thoughts shifted from Charice to the wolf bounding at her, and the tiny carving of the chimera on the silent sword. Were they not tied together, though—Charice and this decision? It would be so much simpler to convince herself that elementals were only dipped in this mess insofar as the White Queen was involved.

And then there was the assumption she had made; the very reckless assumption that Charice had left because of the riots, and not for some other reason.

Better to choose no one at all.

Leaves rustled behind her, and Litany's wiry form emerged from the trees. "Are you ready, Councillor—I mean, Lysande?"

"Surely the time isn't up?"

"Lord Derset sent me to bring you back, if you please."

They moved through the trunks and overhanging branches in the stillness of the orchard. The last tree was laden with fruit, four apples jostling for space on a single bough. Lysande tossed the orange in her hand and caught it again, looking at the four ripe balls.

She fell into step beside her new attendant. The perfume of the fruit trees drifted into her lungs, heady and thick. It seemed to waft into her mind.

The Pavilion glimmered today, its pointed roof strung with dozens of little candles of silvery wax, flickering in rows. A split mirror to the side of the door showed Lysande two tall women, their hair straggling over their shoulders, smiling rather unconvincingly. She raised a hand, and both women raised their hands in reply. On the doorstep, she smoothed her collar and straightened her locks, covering the single tress of silver with red strands and refastening her pins, until she had entirely concealed the hard glitter of the deathstruck hair.

The city-rulers greeted her from a circular table piled with platters of sun-fruit, winternut bread, and dragoncherry cake. Goblets clustered around jugs of red wine, waiting to be filled. Derset stood at the back of the room, his high-necked robe impeccable and his hands folded over his stomach, an assortment of guards stationed beside him. He gave her a tiny nod as she walked in.

Lysande took her seat at the table. Every pair of eyes fixed upon her. She could hear Dante's fingers tapping the wood. One more time, she ran through the analysis of each culture's qualities in the poet Inara's *Scroll of the Cities*, retracing the notes she had made for her treatise, weighing them. Recalling texts felt like speaking a familiar language.

"I will be brief with Your Highnesses." She looked around. "I am required by the law of Elira, set down in the *Legilium*, to choose our next ruler. Last night and this morning have shown me a little of who you are. And your talents."

"Are you giving the crown to the winner?" Cassia was watching her closely.

Perhaps she should have taken more scale. And yet she knew, somehow, that she could do this; the choice to alter the tournament had set something burning inside her, something that she had not known was capable of igniting.

"Prince Fontaine has won a tournament, but I watched you all fight bravely in the ring. It is clear that you all know how to defend yourselves. And the realm."

"What is it to be, then, Councillor?" Jale asked. "Shall we pass the crown from person to person? One of us has it at the beginning of the week, and another at the end? Perhaps we can draw up a plan."

They all laughed—some a little too quickly—and Lysande shook her head.

"There will be no need for swapping, Your Highnesses. I have decided." She paused, and drew a deep breath. Imperative. Sarelin would be imperative. A phrase from the *Scroll of the Cities* hung in her mind, yielded from her own transcription: *The best ruler may not take the shape you think.*

"I am appointing you all to work together as the very first Council of Elira."

She could have heard a needle strike the floor in the silence.

"What?" Cassia said.

"You will rule together until the White Queen is dead or imprisoned and Elira is secure." Lysande looked around the table. "You will share the duties—managing coin and works within the realm, dealing with our neighbors, and overseeing the armies. The selection of a monarch must be postponed until the most urgent danger has passed, at which time you will all vote on it together. Of course, in the meantime, you will each need to appoint someone to take care of your city in your stead."

"No need," Dante said. "Valderos has four successors named in line: one for each goddess. I drew up my list a year ago." He thrust his jaw out.

"Whereas Rhime has around twenty successors, self-appointed, with arrows trained on my neck," Luca said. "They will be so pleased to have an excuse to fire."

"I am confident that you are all capable of choosing the best steward of your own city, and keeping a tight grip on them, for the realm."

Several of the guards looked at each other. *Never quaver, never yield,* Lysande thought. The words sounded in her head in Sarelin's voice. She clung to the memory of the queen in her armor, smiling and presenting Lysande with the quill, the sun striking the dent in her breastplate. She could almost feel the calluses on Sarelin's palms as those hands brushed hers.

Yet her memory of the queen was more complicated of late. Sarelin exhaled a forceful breath, beside her, those broad shoulders still spattered with the aftermath of an execution.

She looked across the table at Luca. Of all the city-rulers, he was the only one watching her without surprise.

"This could be a good thing," Dante said, slowly. "It could be our first chance to bind the cities together since the war."

"Sharing power means shedding blood," Cassia said. "Such an alliance will split the realm."

"Not if we rule well," Jale said.

Luca did not say a word, but she noted the half-smile on his lips.

"What do you think of this, Lord Derset?" Dante asked.

The advisor stepped forward. "Matters of such gravity are for Your Highnesses to approve. Still . . . I would say that our Councillor has worked to bring us the best resolution, at a time when the realm is tied together by the thin ribbon of good intent." Lysande hoped her smile was enough to convey her gratitude.

"Spoken like a true diplomat," Luca said. "But you leave one city out, Lord Derset."

The other city-rulers exchanged glances. Lysande waited.

"The capital. We cannot have a council of Elira without Axium, surely," Luca said, smoothly. "If we are to represent the realm, we must have a member from each of its fine cities."

"You have someone in mind?" Cassia said.

"Perhaps."

Lysande was aware of the inscrutability of his gaze. "Who?" she said.

He turned to face her. "You."

She wanted to laugh, for the idea was so impossible that it was almost ridiculous. But the others were nodding instead of scoffing. Her disbelief turned to disquiet. Ever since she had taken up the Councillor's staff, she had felt that she was wobbling on a frayed rope, above a gulf whose depths she could not discern. Step by step, she had inched along it. At first, she had tiptoed, but as the last two days had passed she had taken bolder steps, learning how to interact with city-rulers, challenging them, even daring them to prove their worth. Yet she had not prepared for the possibility of reaching the other side and walking further amidst royalty, amidst silver and jewels . . . amidst cakes laced with metal.

You could not plan for something that you could not imagine. Only now did she see that she had finished crossing the rope, and a ladder awaited, stretching up.

They were all looking at her, Luca, Jale, Cassia, and Dante, and she focused on this moment. She took a deep breath and exhaled slowly.

"A commoner cannot make decisions for the realm, surely. There has never been such an appointment," she said.

"Five minutes ago, there had never been a council, either," Luca replied.

"You are the only Councillor among us." Jale grinned. "So really, you're the most practiced for the job."

"You jest well, Your Highness, but you cannot be serious. The silverblood families will never accept this." You had to feel your way, slowly, when you were climbing a ladder in darkness. You had to test every rung with your feet.

"*I* am quite serious," Luca said. "Who better than a scholar to apply her scrutiny to the realm? Your lack of breeding is immaterial when we consider Queen Sarelin's esteem for your wits. For an orphan, you are better read than many ladies. And you seem to have no hesitation in dealing with royalty."

The look he gave her was much cooler than his praise. If Luca Fontaine wanted her to share in the rule, it was not out of charity: she was sure of that much.

"I do not often agree with the prince of Rhime, but I cannot fault him on this," Dante put in. "I move that we add Lysande Prior to the Council of Elira."

"I have no objection." Jale nodded.

Cassia sighed, and laid her hands on the table. "If I must share the crown, it makes no difference if it is with three people or four. It is all dishonor in Pyrrha."

Lysande's insides were churning. Books flapped before her in memory, speaking their warnings about city-rulers, scolding her with long-dried ink. She held them at bay. There would be a time for insecurities. This was the time to reach up: to grasp the next rung.

"There we are." Luca raised his wine, with a half-smile. "To dishonor."

"To the Council," Dante said, glaring at Luca.

"Indeed. To the Council," Cassia said.

Lysande raised her goblet with a trembling hand, scarcely able to look at the others. A surge of something powerful was running through her. Ever since she had opened the envelope after Sarelin's death, fear and grief had followed her—and both were still there, but joined by another emotion. It was not just the voice of duty or the deep echo of her sorrow but something more like brushwood, kindling within her.

There could be no complacency, she knew. She would have to watch her back and her food. It would be folly to close her eyes for a second around these rulers, or let herself believe for a moment that any of them was worthy of her trust. But this must be it. Her quill was her sword. If she worked with all her effort, surely she could wield it for the woman who had trained her; for the woman who had plucked her from a narrow world and immersed her in a realm of leather-bound books, debates about epic poetry, trips in a carriage to the Axium theaters, hedges sprinkled with white bellflower blossoms, and laughter at ribald jokes.

And yet this extended beyond Sarelin. This was about the shop fronts smashed in the capital; the elementals of skin and bone huddled on the back of the executioner's cart. It was about Charice, and the empty room where they had once spent hours together, hours that became days, days that became achingly beautiful nights. It was about the young man in ragged clothes who had been tasked with baiting wolves with only a bolt of cloth, and all the people who would never hold a chest of gold bars in their hands.

Sarelin was a part of her, but the girl with the quill could see things that the Iron Queen had not. If she could reach around her and touch the populace, perhaps she could weave the threads of their lives together in a way that Mea Tacitus could not, too.

Thinking of her decision to halt executions, she remembered how her words had sounded like sunlight on steel as she issued the order.

The opportunity had been temporary. She had been Councillor for a few weeks, and she had fitted her ambition to that timeframe; as her role had been fleeting, so she had curtailed her desires. But now she could see a way ahead. For the first time, a ladder was hers to climb, its rungs not woven of fibers but fashioned of smooth and unbending metal. Who knew where she might scale it to?

Restrain, constrain, subdue. This time, she labored to push the chant away.

She looked across the room and saw Derset behind the table, a slight furrow between his eyes, and guessed that he was checking himself from showing more concern. Once she spoke the words, there could be no going back.

Steadying her hand, she brought the goblet to her lips.

"To the Council," she said, and drank deeply.

Six

Her quill scratched across the page as the sound of laughter rang out in the wintry air; tails and loops of letters poured onto the fine paper, her hand moving to the rhythm of her thinking, the formulation of phrases so well practiced that to an observer it would have appeared as pure instinct. The scent of ink wafted up to her nostrils, and minutes slipped by before she paused to peer out of her window.

The guests having moved on from the garden below, Lysande felt the new silence. She still remembered how, on the morning she had first been led into Charice's back room, a silence had fallen over her like thick cloth. She had run her finger along the bottles full of liquids and powders, taking in substances transformed by magic or tinctured by foreign ingredients. Some had been familiar to her from a need that it was better not to describe.

Where Charice was now, she did not like to think.

It seemed wrong, to imagine Charice poor or desperate. Far better to recall the night Charice had knelt between her legs, stripped of all her clothes, Lysande still sporting a doublet and nothing else, wrapping her boots around Charice's neck. That was not an easy night to forget. When they had moved to the bed, Lysande had lain pressed to Charice's back and slid her hands around Charice's warm waist, before the two of them had slipped into a state of blissed-out repose, finishing their entanglement slowly.

After recovering, they had taken up their dialogue on Severelle again, Charice blowing smoke-rings toward the window.

"It is metaphorical. It is markedly, unambiguously metaphorical." Charice had waved her pipe.

"Can you not find space among all the sums and measurements in your head for a little imagination?" Lysande had been well aware that she was goading. "Suppose that the middle space is real and you can step into it, as you might escape this world through . . . I don't know, a magic doorway."

"I can suppose no such thing."

"But imagine. Imagine you could." She had poked at one of Charice's smoke rings.

"Not everyone has the luxury of imagining escape."

"If you cannot imagine it, you can never make it real. Just think, Charice. A whole world where there are no rules hammered into your mind, and you may go around and make your own, or none at all."

"Severelle never wrote of such a thing."

"Well, I am writing it now. On your chest." She had pressed her lips to the tops of Charice's breasts, quickly, one after the other. "There. It is inked."

Charice's smile had widened, even as she shook her head. Lysande tried to paint it into her memory with fresh strokes as she closed her window now.

She put down the golden quill and held up the briefing for a moment. The last sentence stared back at her, blotted twice: *The Council shall rule until the White Queen's defeat.* In the two days that had passed since the tournament, she had considered specifying exactly what "defeat" meant: laying out a clear condition for the end of the Council.

A victory in combat? The capture of the White Queen? Her death? Having heard the city-rulers raise all three possibilities, Lysande had decided on the prudence of a general term, which might be interpreted and reinterpreted as one wished, while she kept a precise definition in reserve.

She examined the briefing carefully. It occurred to her, with a twist of understanding, that she had no one to hand it to for approval.

Raden stomped in with an armful of chests and placed them in the only space on the floor. "Your attendant said these were all to be checked. Garments, shoes, weapons, more garments, medicines, and your scholarly things."

"*Six* chests?" Lysande said.

He shrugged. "You can have your clothes washed in Rhime, since you're all dashing to get there for this meeting. And in case the Rhimese make trouble, there's enough there for a few weeks."

Lysande did not have the heart to tell him that six chests would last her for a few months, not a few weeks. She remembered telling Litany that new clothes were unnecessary and jewels out of the question, but her attendant had had a shifty look on her face as she agreed, and Lysande suspected that there were several sets of emeralds and diamonds packed carefully away in lined boxes. The girl was devoted to detail, no doubt.

"I've picked someone to lead your traveling guards. Captain Chidney will be useful if anyone causes trouble—or looks like they're thinking about causing trouble."

"I trust your choice." Lysande, who had seen Chidney's muscles, felt she had reason to.

"You might need her. The range-riders went scouting yesterday and found tracks. Large prints. Like a bear. Some of them swear that they smelled an animal lingering near the trees—and I don't mean a Rhimese scout."

Lysande frowned. "Then I hope Chidney is as dangerous with a sword as you are."

Trying to give the impression that she was checking the luggage, she let her eyes linger for a moment on a chest, half-draped in an old blanket, closer to the foot of her bed. From the ratty covering, she hoped it was hard to tell that the contents included two jars of scale, a spoon, a piece of purple night-quartz, and a vial, each polished and wrapped in its own cloth.

It was not as if she had a problem with the substance. It was a way of coping. If she wanted to, she could throw the chimera scale away at any time, though why anyone would do so when it was packed so neatly . . .

As Raden's boots echoed down the stairwell, Lady Pelory approached the doorway. Lysande adjusted her doublet quickly, brushed down her sleeves, then walked to her desk and picked up a stack of papers, leafing through them casually just as Pelory stepped inside.

"A pleasure to see you, Mistress of Laws." Lysande looked up. "The

Master of Works' figures seem clear, and I am content with the envoys' notes. Yet the Treasurer's report . . ."

"I am agog to hear what you have found," Pelory said.

Lysande kept her posture firm as she walked toward Pelory. "Lady Bowbray has omitted a few expenses. Put simply, her calculations appear imprecise, in regards to funding my jail." The words came out just as she had practiced in front of the mirror—casual, but not so casual as to let the listener forget that an order hung in the vicinity.

"Well, I expected it." Pelory pursed her lips. "Building a jail for elementals is a complicated undertaking."

"True. But we are not building one. We are restoring the Prexleys' disused castle."

It was no longer an idea, but a real solution. After halting the executions of the elementals, she had begun taking notes of the current state of fortune of each of the great families, investigating their known properties, in addition to their coin, art, and jewels; looking into where money pooled and where it disappeared; finding old castles that some families could not afford to keep. Hand the crown your second estate, and the crown will absolve your debts, her overtures had implied. She was not managing the laws like Sarelin but as herself, a girl who had grown up spattered with ink, who had learned to research, to observe, and to take detailed notes. *Surprise the rich*, Perfault claimed, *and you may steal a march on them before the sun rises on their silver.*

She was beginning to see how her scholarship could be used in these dealings.

Pelory hesitated, and Lysande saw her teeter. "Still, an intricate business. One that requires time and calculation," Pelory said at last.

"That is why we must make sure it is adequately funded." She looked into those gray eyes. "I would have you go over Lady Bowbray's books and find out exactly what she is spending the crown's cadres on. As Mistress of Laws, you have the authority to examine the Treasury, do you not? You will bring the results to me in Rhime." She liked the way it sounded. *You will.* The time for dancing with maybes and mights had passed.

Pelory's mouth had opened, but the last word made her pause. "Rhime, Councillor?"

"Lord Derset tells me your husband has long wanted to purchase Rhimese perfumes, rubies, and embroidered cloaks. I recall that Queen Sarelin would not grant you permission to travel out of Axium while she needed you here. Procure the Treasurer's accounts for me, and Lord Clifferd will have his trip."

"He admires the eastern fashions greatly." Pelory allowed her a thin smile. "I shall see you in Rhime, Councillor. Travel safely."

Perhaps I'll need to, Lysande thought. How many people did it take to subdue a bear?

She felt a spark of satisfaction as she watched Pelory leave. Only when the spark faded did she feel the emptiness of the room: the huge, dolorous emptiness that had filled every chamber in the palace since Sarelin died. She gazed out the window, looking for a figure that would not be there, and searching for a crown that had already been stored in the vault.

"I have to go, Sarelin," she said, quietly, drawing a key engraved with a crown out of her pocket. "But first, forgive my intrusion."

The royal suite had not been cleaned since the death of its occupant, and though Lysande did not much believe the Axiumite idea that the dead must be allowed to walk in their chambers for a month with the windows closed, until they were calm, she respected Sarelin's devotion to custom. She found the bedchamber shrouded in dust, lit by a single torch. Leaving the door ajar, she listened as the footsteps of the guard retreated.

The few papers scattered on the table did not help her: treasury bills for hundreds of cadres and mettles, a draft of a letter to King Ferago of Bastillón about trade on the Cordonna River, and a smattering of orders to the envoys, expressed with Sarelin's characteristic tact ("Tell the Royamese to go and jump in their lagoon"). Her pulse sped. She was not sure what she had expected—a stack of papers sealed with emerald wax, or letters secreted away—but she could find nothing mentioning or even hinting at any "Shadows." Sarelin croaked those last words at her again, in memory, her translucent body writhing on the grass.

She left the bedchamber and moved into the study, where the sight of a tactos-board made her stop and swallow. Here, where they had spent so many hours together sliding their stone guards, nobles, city-rulers, queens, kings, and chimeras back and forth, she slipped back to the last time they had played the game, sitting by the lake with chalices of wine on Sarelin's gift-day, the red vintage sloshing near the rim whenever the queen took a piece. It was the same game they had played more than a hundred times: Sarelin leading the attack; Lysande calculating her moves to retreat across the board, bringing herself to lose so gradually that the queen would believe it had been her own doing. Guffawing, Sarelin had slapped her knee after Lysande ceded her chimera, red drops spraying over the tactos pieces.

Lysande turned determinedly to the desk and began to search it. Sarelin had once said that writing was for people who could not think with their sword, and most of the documents that had been stuffed into the drawers were maps of military movements. A list of ideas for a jubilee parade languished in the top drawer. She gazed at the page, taking in the familiar scrawl, until a scrap of paper in the fireplace caught her eye. Only a blank corner had survived the flames, and it gave off a smell of rose-oil as she picked it up: not an Axiumite scent, but the kind of perfume that tinged paper from eastern Elira.

It had struck her as odd, as a child, how often Sarelin burned papers. If you had made your fame by riding into a wall of fire, expecting to wither to ash, it would make sense to keep away from flames for the rest of your life. But she had seen over the years that Sarelin was quick to light a fire on a hunt and did not hesitate to set her fireplace ablaze. The charge that might have seen Sarelin die seemed to have only made her stronger and brighter—a smoking brand in a sea of dry birches.

A knock sounded at the door to the suite. "Come in," she called.

Looking up, she found Derset crossing the room.

"Excuse me, my lady." He bowed. "The steward thought you might want to decide what to do about the Rhimese archers. They have broken two statues of Queen Illora."

Lysande dropped the paper back into the fireplace. Derset was studying her in what he must have thought was a surreptitious manner. The ropes of tension pulled taut in her shoulders again, and she thought of the strange look that had flitted across his face, yesterday, when she had discussed her plan to fund a jail for elementals instead of returning to Sarelin's law. She read questions in his face, now. But he was not going to ask them, and she thought of Charice's empty chamber, and the night the two of them had spent talking under the stars in the forest, so many years ago.

For the briefest of moments, she felt a fervent desire to tell him about Charice—how her friend had always kept a drawing of a chimera on her wall. How Lysande had guessed what it symbolized. How she had learned later, from Charice's own lips, that what seemed an omen of death to some was in fact a source of pride to others. She looked at Derset, again, and faltered.

As they left the royal suite, she could still smell the faintest hint of rose-oil. The scent lingered in her nostrils long after she had returned to her work. It accompanied her still when she lay down to sleep, her mind swirling, and she chased scraps of paper and half-finished notes in her dreams, watched by a figure whose dented armor glittered in the half-light.

The mare whinnied into the breeze, stamping its hooves. "Come, now," she said, stroking its muzzle. "If I am to endure this, so are you."

The tall animal, splotched black and white, stood out among the sleek chestnut horses of the royal team. It nuzzled her hand, and she passed it a handful of nuts, guiding it to the front of the palace.

She spotted Cassia through the mass of riders and tried to brush her hair into a more tameable state as she approached the Irriqi, changing the angle of her hand a little too late to make the gesture into a natural wave. Cassia hailed her over the heads of the Pyrrhan guards, standing up in the saddle. "I suppose you've traveled the Scarlet Road before, my friend?"

"Not at all." Lysande's only acquaintance with the winding path from Axium to Rhime had been in reading of the famous stabbings that had taken place upon it. "I wish I had ventured beyond Axium's territory."

"They are all olive-pickers and wine merchants down there. Not a patch of jungle in the east," said Cassia, sniffing. "You could not stalk a tiger if you tried."

"That is certainly a great disadvantage."

"Olives . . ." Cassia muttered. "You are welcome to share my cook's offerings when we make camp, Lysande. A friend must eat real food."

If only you could excavate a word with your hands, burrowing with fingernails to break through layer after layer, to find the real meaning buried beneath the surface. *Friend* was an opportunity, in the world of royalty. Lysande did not trust that she would find something she liked, but she yearned to dig into the word's core all the same, to feel her way to the chambers and spaces within Cassia's lexicon and understand what resided there.

Guards swarmed around the nobles in front of the palace; range-riders, bodyguards for the Council, ordinary scouts, captains, officers, and special fighters mustered to ride in front and behind, and to flank the party. The captain of Lysande's traveling guards wove between the Axiumites, checking saddles, handing out a few spare swords, and somehow maneuvering her muscular form between two horses that had developed a mutual dislike.

Lysande had seen Captain Chidney reporting to Sarelin before, and when the woman bowed at last to give her the all-clear, she was ready for the sight of six feet of armored soldier bending before her. Yet she was ill prepared for the realization that she was the one who needed protection. This time, it was not Sarelin that the guards would be circling.

"You really need to go all the way to Rhime, just to make a decision about the armies?" Raden said, coming up beside her.

"You know I have no choice. We must meet the Bastillonian ambassador sometime next week. So, we go to the closest city to the border for this meeting. A halfway mark, the Irriqi calls it."

"Some say the White Queen will hunt the Council down."

"Well, some of the silverbloods said that the White Queen had an army of demons during the war. You can't always rely on their assessment," Lysande said.

"She's dangerous, Lysande. And not just because of her magic."

It was impossible not to catch the note of anxiety in his voice. She was getting better, though, at painting on her façade, that layer of assurance all silverbloods seemed to wear. You could not wear the truth on your face, could you? She had considered the dangers of riding, even under heavy guard, with trepidation, but she had committed to making her choices for those who wore rags or evaded the executioner's cart; or so she told herself. Was it better to ignore risk, or to ignore the reasons you were braving it?

"The people must be satisfied we are governing for the whole realm, and we can't do that by sitting in Axium Palace," she said.

"It sounds more like a traveling show than a Council." He allowed her a smile.

"The more I learn about the business of rule, the more it does seem like a show. Only the players are not very heroic, the story changes without warning, and the audience prefers the spilling of entrails to a happy end."

Raden's smile waned as she climbed onto the piebald mare. Glancing down at her saddle, she was aware of the silver trimming, and the design with her initials that attendants had sewn; and she was sure that he was aware of them too. They were both silent for a moment.

"I can work where I won't be seen. Fix things quietly," he said. "Make sure none of them rips up the law. Axium will run like a well-shod horse until you return."

"I know it will. I've seen you shoe a stallion." She saw the sharp edge of his expression. "What is it, Raden?"

"It's only a simple captain's thought."

"I don't see a simple captain anywhere."

He inclined his head, without cheer. "I was thinking that power sits like an ill-tied cloak on some people. They take years just to learn how to wear it. Others tie it on like a mantle, and it fits over their shoulders without a crease . . . and you wonder, is that newly added, or was it always there? Am I only noticing it now?"

She looked him in the eye. A forest cuckoo trilled, somewhere above them. She placed a hand on his shoulder, for a second, before turning her horse around.

The sun spread fingers of pale gold over the rooftops, and once the riders were out of the capital, the chill of the northern breeze receded; they could have been a hundred miles from the capital, trotting through the lanes of Axium's outlying towns. Elsington's thatched rooves hid shops full of silverware, riding leathers, and bodices of heavy velvet, and farmers sold their grain and vegetables in the street. Lysande wished they could dismount long enough to greet the people who waved at them. She noted the brightening smiles and the eyes that seemed to light up when they saw the entourage, and tried to tell herself that it was not about her; that Sarelin would have received a welcome like this, too.

A girl with braided hair ran toward her, shouting something, two syllables, repeating it twice. It took her a moment to realize that the word was *Prior.*

She sat, quite still, listening to the sound. It thickened and hardened.

Perfault called this the mirror of one's majesty. Was that not an apt term? It sounded foreign, hearing her name from the girl's lips. She felt that she was hearing some other, well-known leader's name, yet she wanted to hear it again and again.

A woman in a blacksmith's apron and thick boots ran to the girl and gathered her up, red-cheeked, looking as if she were about to call her twenty names; a man ran to join them, taking the girl and holding her gently. Neither parent spoke. Watching them, Lysande realized that she had inspired this distance; that her presence had spread a blanket of stillness.

"Prior!" the girl shouted again.

They stared at each other. The world shivered, rearranging its pieces.

Hoofbeats: a guard joined her, at last, wearing an inquisitive look, and Lysande remembered to wave to the crowd. She heard the blacksmith call out a blessing, which she returned with a brief nod; she heard well-wishes from the other townspeople, and did not hear them, for in that moment, something had changed within her, something fragmenting and reforming. *Prior.*

At Wiltingford she was aware of a glimmer of movement as she entered the town—a blur somewhere to her right that she could not catch. She shook her head. The extra half-spoonful of scale she had

heated and mixed might have been too much. You could never be
certain of the amount when your measurements were always a little
heaped.

They passed through an autumn festival where orange and brown
strips of cloth fluttered on poles along the main street, and young boys
threw handfuls of dry leaves at girls who led them onward. Lysande
stopped the wagons at Wiltingford Bridge, and a movement drew her
body to the left—not just her gaze but all of her responding—ready for
something, she knew not what. Her muscles clenched and tightened.
Be the blade. There was nothing to strike, however; no animal lurking.

She gave orders and while the horses were rested and watered, she
gazed at the schools of circling trout. A pensive figure looked back at
her from the water, more a woman than a girl. Thanks to her height,
she took up a swathe of the river's surface, blotting out the lily pads.

"This is the furthest I have been from Axium."

"Were your parents from the capital?" Derset asked, bringing his
gray stallion up.

"No one can be certain. A group of guards found me in a carpenter's shop that was burning in the outskirts of Axium during the war.
If the shop hadn't been so near the orphanage, I might have been as
charred as the wood." She remembered sitting on a bench, in the palace
grounds, the day Sarelin had asked her what she knew about her finding. Sarelin's face had been taut with focus. There had been little Lysande could tell her, the headmistress' words doled out to her in clumps
over the years; she had recounted the same story about the knock on
the orphanage door, the hurried words of soldiers, and the bundle of
stubborn life, swaddled in rags and blinking.

"Like many children of the White War, I expect." Derset looked
ahead at a swathe of green fields. "I am sorry, my lady. At least you will
have a chance to see more of Elira now. I still remember my first ride
to Rhime, on an errand for my mother. I stared at that tapestry of wide
fields, narrow streams, and groves of olive trees that might have been
stitched on . . . and I kept staring. I thought: it is magnificent, but not
like Axium. It has its own magnificence. A glory of ripening things,
like a garden of plums which refuse to wither. Once we get through the
hills and onto the Scarlet Road, the land will be more fertile than the

capital. The traders say that if you could bottle up the Rhimese sun, you would make your fortune in gold."

"No doubt Luca Fontaine would oversee the selling." She smiled. "And make the deals in Old Rhimese." The thought of Luca in his black armor distracted her and she pictured the lines of his body, his shoulders tightening as he fired. It was too easy to imagine the fluidity of his movement. She shook her head to dispel the images.

They saw no vineyards for the first few miles, only trees whose leaves formed a queer, vertical shape, spreading slightly out at the bottom like very thin pears. Oxen ruminated in clusters, small farmhouses sat surrounded by bales of hay, and cottages with flower gardens studded the fields between the last of Axium's towns and the first of Rhime's. No manors appeared, but Lysande noticed a smattering of commoners' houses among the gentle hills and dales, merging with the fields as seamlessly as if they had grown there.

At the next fork in the road, Derset pointed out the dark green lumps on the horizon. "I thought you would like to savor your first glimpse of the Emeralds."

The bunch of little semicircles on her map of Rhimese territory had looked a lot less imposing than the real hills. From their sheen and deep color, she had no difficulty guessing why the Rhimese had chosen their name. The Axiumites broke off to take the scenic route. This was no time to fall prey to baseless fears, she told herself, still glancing to either side as she rode. Halfway up the first hill, the grass proved so smooth that the horses struggled, and only Chidney's shouts of encouragement and swift leaps in front of the pack kept them going. Lysande was forced to cling to the saddle as her piebald mare scrambled up, and when the horse stumbled over a loose stone, she thought she might be about to make a very quick fall. The sight at the top was worth the ascent, for a mile of rolling green hills unfolded so softly that the edges seemed to form a single blanket over the land.

The Emeralds basked in the sun, studded here and there with little dark bushes. Lysande had the sudden desire to ride at full speed into them, as she had once done with Sarelin on a slope in Axium Forest, the two of them cackling at the queen's joke about beautiful men and their jousting-lances, meeting the full breeze with aching cheeks.

There was no jocosity now, of course; no bellowing mirth from a woman better known for facing down an army. Since Derset was too dignified for racing, Lysande set off with Litany at a gallop. Her attendant cantered beside her, and when she looked across, she saw that the girl was watching her from her saddle, only half-attending to the slope ahead.

"I find this very disappointing, Litany."

"Councillor?"

"This canter. If you keep it up, how will I ever know if you can beat me to the top?"

A smile brightened Litany's face; it dimmed for a moment, but as the girl checked Lysande's expression, it spread. "When do we begin the race?"

Lysande gave her mare a quick tap on the neck and gripped the animal harder as it began to gallop. "Catch up when you have the fortitude," she said.

Soon they were laughing into the wind, Lysande's fingers curled into her mare's mane, the two of them shouting Axium proverbs at each other as they raced, twisting and mangling the old phrases. Litany proved singularly adept with her horse, and they raced higher, until they reached the top of the last hill together and gazed out on a quilt of color.

Dark squares of vineyards and fields of little red flowers checkered the ground, bordered by lines of the conical trees and interspersed with houses, yet it was the landscape beyond the town that caught Lysande's eye, a canvas of green and yellow fields painted in shades brighter than any she had seen, the ground shimmering, iridescent in the sun. The territory had none of Axium's northern quietude; this land seemed to pulse with a warm rhythm, birds, rabbits, and deer moving here and there among the trees.

"I think we have stumbled upon some paradise." Her imagination leaped to Cicera's ancient poem about a hidden realm, untouched by frost, where the sun always shone. It had always sounded too sublime, too full of mythic qualities to have ever existed. She had imagined it, all the same, lying in bed with the Silver Songs propped on her chest.

"This is no arcadia. Only Spelato, my lady." Derset brought his horse up beside hers, casting a slightly reproachful look at Litany.

"We can spare a half-hour to eat." She heard the command in her voice, unfamiliar.

They could easily meet the others past Ferizia, where the Scarlet Road began, she told herself a little guiltily. She was just about to nudge her horse over the edge of the hilltop when she saw a flash of movement at the very edge of Spelato's vineyards. A figure atop a horse sped between two trees.

From behind the trunk where the horse had disappeared, a head poked out, the face obscured by the top of a hooded cloak.

"Did you see that?"

Derset looked across at her. "See what, my lady?"

The trees offered nothing but leaves and branches. Lysande found no trace of either horse or rider. She scrutinized the trunks for a half-minute more, her mind turning over images of silent swords and poison. "It may have been a fancy," she said.

Derset stared across the vineyards for a long time, leading his horse forward a few steps and peering at the treeline, checking every visible part of it before turning back to Lysande with a somewhat apologetic look on his face. "There are many traders and messengers coming back and forth from the cities."

"Do traders in the east wear hooded cloaks?"

"I should think not. Prince Fontaine forbids any rider to hide their face in his territory, they say, since the Petrioglio sisters sent four hired swords after him last year."

Unease stirred in Lysande's stomach, but she gave Derset a relaxed smile. If her advisor had known that she had taken one and a half spoonfuls of scale, and that those spoonfuls had worked with a new violence inside her, he might have dismissed her concern. The scouts rode off toward the trees and returned with nothing to report. Yet her unease stayed with her as they cantered down the hill and made their way slowly along the vineyards, stopping in one of the powder-blue fields near Spelato to spread out their blankets, and she checked the road every few minutes.

Litany unpacked the palace cook's basket of cheese pies, sun-fruit quiches, hazelnut tarts, and hard ginger sweets, along with several bottles of wine. With Lysande's permission, all the attendants ate and drank to satiety, stuffing their pockets with handfuls of sweets. The guards sat in a cluster, talking of famous Rhimese ambushes with an interest that bordered on relish; Chidney kept them in order, but she looked across every so often, too, and Lysande had the distinct impression that her captain was gazing at Litany.

Lysande engaged Litany on the subject of attendants' etiquette, fishing for clues about how the girl had come to work as a page and why she had trained in the skills of wardrobe. Midway through a discussion of the hierarchy of stable-hands, she reached to fill Litany's goblet. They seized the bottle by chance at the same time. She felt the strength of those hands, which seemed to exceed the promise of the girl's wiry frame.

"I believe Captain Chidney is looking at you." It was hard to resist the opportunity to show off her observation.

Litany shot a glance at Chidney, then immediately stared at her own knees. "I beg your pardon, Councillor, but the captain is a noble-woman. I am the daughter of a stable-hand . . . and possibly a baker. Captain Chidney has no reason to look in my direction."

"I don't think it is your birthright she finds compelling."

Risking a glance above knee-height, Litany caught Chidney's eye and blushed a memorable shade of pink.

The road brought them out of the town, through hills and dales gentler than the Emeralds, dotted with fig and lemon trees. They trotted along slowly, heavy with food, and from time to time Lysande thought she caught a stir of movement on the periphery of her vision—though it was hard to say if it was a tangible presence. Had not Signore Montefizzi written in her *Manual of Rhimese Science* that the mind, once stimulated, could produce iterations of its own distress? That a fleeting fear, if left to grow, could turn into an agitation that consumed the whole brain? And besides that, no physician had ever specified, precisely, what chimera scale could do to one's system . . . physical stimulus, mental calm, if the symptoms were to be believed . . . but that was her own deduction.

She sent the range-riders and the guards to check around them once more. No sign of movement, but one guard reported seeing water-stones piled up in stacks, studding a patch of ground. Lysande followed the woman to find cairns covering most of a slope. The blue head of each pile of stones was bared to the sky, as if daring the sun to set it agleam.

"Charice would like that," Lysande murmured.

"Councillor?"

Some argue that the so-called "chimera cairn" represents the stealth and power of the elemental people. the historian Kephir had claimed. *When the cairn is erected during a time of persecution, it appears to represent an act of protest.*

Sarelin would not have approved, of course.

"Councillor, what did you say?"

"Nothing." Lysande turned away from the slope.

The first time they had discussed the Old Signs, Charice had argued passionately that they were symbols of life, not death. It was the first time Lysande understood that some elementals did not support the White Queen. Funny, how subtly awareness could build—how week by week, day by day, she became conscious that references to ordinary elemental people were absent from the histories; that they appeared as tyrants or rebels to the throne, or not at all.

Charice's visage floated before her, conjured up like the ghosts at the Arena, and she found herself apologizing, telling Charice that she should have petitioned Sarelin for . . . something. A small change. An end to the executions, at least. She had taken the solace of Charice's fingers and tongue, not to mention her time and conversation over the years, and had offered nothing substantial in return. Now, she had the uncomfortable realization that she could have tried to bring about a political shift. Living in Axium Palace had a way of making you feel insignificant, but Charice would have called it a blessed worthlessness, a higher rank than the populace . . .

At the next turning they found a stone town preserved since the Classical Era; clusters of houses surrounded a little square in which a statue of a cobra reared up. Looking at it, Lysande thought of Tiberus shifting on Luca's shoulder.

"This must be Ferizia," she said. "Might we walk through the town?" They would be less obvious targets among the buildings, surely, and with Lysande's height and Chidney's muscle standing out at the best of times, it could not hurt to dismount.

"Certainly, my lady, if you wish it." Derset looked dubiously at the cobra statue.

Few people were strolling the streets of Ferizia in the afternoon sun, and from the square, the olive groves around the town could be glimpsed through an arch. The results of the farmers' toil glistened in the windows along the next street, where jars of olive spread, butter, and greenish-yellow oil shone beside mounds of olives on platters. Leading her mare past, Lysande put a hand to her head. Just as she had been hoping the pain had disappeared . . . she winced.

It was temporary. She would give up the scale, eventually.

A flash of something, to the right. She stiffened.

Only a falcon met her gaze, however; no cloak, but feathered wings, beating the air.

Ferizia's shops brimmed with books and puzzles, tactos-boards made of black marble, and medical guides as thick as small bricks. Lysande spotted a tapestry of an archer slaying a fire-breathing chimera. In the glass of the window she saw Derset staring at something further down the street. "Perhaps we should take another route, my lady."

"What is it?"

"Nothing of note. We should make for the town's edge."

She heard the concern in his voice and led her mare to the end of the street. From a distance, it looked as if a small crowd had formed around a display of some kind, where three dolls dangled from an arch, but as she came nearer, the dolls turned into people and the thick ropes of the nooses became clear. A crusting of red covered the sides of the bodies. Her stomach flipped as she caught the stench of the wounds.

Were they hung first, or stabbed to death? The blood had gushed out onto silk shirts and velvet doublets. Judging by the bare fingers of the victims, they had already been stripped of their gold. The symbol of a deer could be made out on each breast, embroidered.

"You've got to be mad to pilfer from Riscetti's shop," she heard a woman say.

"Are there rocks in that sweet head of yours?" Her companion, a woman in a tunic riddled with holes, chuckled as Lysande dismounted. "Look at their hands."

Lysande squinted over the heads and spotted the red mark on the back of each hand: a curved line carved into the flesh. It looked like a C.

"You'd think we'd be running out of conspirators," the first woman said. She clasped her wife, their matching rings visible for a moment, each shaped decorated with the Rhimese commitment-symbol of interwoven thorns.

Somewhere in Lysande's mind, a comment Sarelin had made resounded: that there had been more poisonings, stabbings, and attempts at usurpation in Rhime than in all the other four cities combined. Luca Fontaine's father, Prince Marcio Sovrano, had hanged eight nobles for trying to sneak nightroot into the palace kitchens, according to one of Sarelin's stories. The Rhimese grew conspiracies as well as they grew olives, Sarelin had said. Looking at the grizzled woman and the two tall men swinging in the breeze, she formed a slightly better idea of how and why Luca could face the city-rulers with such a cool façade.

"I think the prince's caught himself three Canduccis this time." The second speaker pronounced the words with relish. "I see deer on those doublets, under the blood."

As the crowd edged forward to examine Luca's punishment up close, Lysande found herself jostled and elbowed to the side. Before she knew it, she was out of reach of Derset, with hands pushing her and fingernails grazing her, and someone pressing up behind her, a stubbled cheek brushing against her neck.

"I will arrive at night, Councillor Prior," a rough voice muttered. "Be ready."

She whipped around. The bystanders were all looking ahead, eyes fixed on the bodies.

"My lady," Derset cried, grabbing her wrist, "you must not go off alone."

Suddenly Chidney was upon her too, a wealth of muscle blocking her from the crowd, yet without touching her. She had not appreciated until now how gentle Chidney chose to be.

"Someone spoke into my ear."

"Did you see them?"

Lysande looked around sharply. "They knew my—"

One of the bodies swung in a gust of wind, sending a bag of silver mettles tumbling out of a hidden pocket that even the looters had not found. The crowd surged forward, one beast with many legs, scrambling under the arch and dropping to their knees.

Lysande accepted Derset's arm and hurried out of the throng just in time to avoid being knocked to the ground, pulling her mare behind her. As she ran from the street, the last thing she saw was some four dozen women and men scrabbling with their hands, all shoving each other as they searched for silver that had been pocketed, knees rubbing until they were soiled by muddy stone.

The Scarlet Road was not scarlet in hue, nor was it really wide enough to be a road. A pale brown ribbon ran from the end of Ferizia into the eastern country, following the river down to Rhime by way of Ardua and Castelaggio. With room for just five riders abreast, the city-rulers' parties stretched out in a rainbow of banners, coloring the land as they moved, their guards making a shield around them. Despite the peacefulness of the ride, Lysande barely noticed the countryside around her, decorated with the estates of the noble families of Rhime, brown-and-white manors with family banners flying from balconies and Conquest-era blackfoot trees growing in copses. Her mind dwelled on the rough voice in the crowd.

It was the closeness that unsettled her. If the speaker had been further away, calling over the throng, she might have felt more secure—but he had maneuvered himself close enough for his stubble to scrape her neck, and he had warned her to be ready. Why do that, if he meant her harm? Well, she had given Chidney very firm instructions about shadowing her. There was no point dwelling on a danger she could do no more to prepare for, so she forced herself to glance around at the countryside and her fellow riders. She let her eyes linger on Luca's figure occasionally; for observational purposes, she told herself.

As they neared Ardua, a Pyrrhan guard approached Lysande. She permitted the Axium soldiers to part.

"The princes are making camp ahead, Councillor. Night is near."
The Pyrrhan woman looked Lysande over. "The Irriqi invites you and
Lord Derset to dine with the rest of the Council in the comfort of her
tent." She glanced at Chidney's thickset form. "Guards are forbidden."

A dinner surrounded by city-rulers, without a sword to defend me.
Still, she did not wish to refuse Cassia's hospitality, now that she was a
"friend." She had not known, until she heard the word from the Irriqi's
own lips, what it felt like to have a friendship formally declared, the
glow expanding in her chest, yet accompanied by an ever-present sliver
of cold doubt.

"I accept," she said. "On the condition that I may bring my attendant."

As the guard galloped away, Litany smiled at her with a new warmth.
A lifetime of Axiumite decorum told her to turn away or even issue an
order, but she thought of the two of them racing each other up the hill,
shredding proverbs on the way, and she returned the smile.

Walking through the tents that evening, she felt a foreigner among
the many hues of livery and armor. It was one thing to study and mem-
orize the crests of the cities at your desk. It was another thing to walk
among them, and to realize that you did not belong under any banner—
not even the one with the Axium crown sewn on emerald cloth—for
she possessed no Axium birthright, not even one parent's name from
which to fabricate a tie to a great family. What rights she had, she had
received from adoption. And without Sarelin, the crown was just a
diadem, anyway; a piece of silver hollowed out, bereft of life.

At any rate, she should not be contemplating colors and symbols. A
dark shape was her real concern. Groups of soldiers yielded no hooded
figure, though she stared into every cluster, trying to make sure. As she
checked her surroundings, she listened to some of the Lyrians playing
lutes and summerharps, a few raising their voices to sing.

"D'you hear that racket?" The Valderran voice that spoke was not
cheerful. Lysande located its owner, a big soldier who was fingering
her sword-hilt.

Her companions paused their conversation for a moment, and as
the Lyrian song drifted through the tents, Lysande recognized the
melody.

Come all you desert daughters
And sons of the scorching sand
We'll run them through their frozen hearts
Where the southern star-trees stand

For the land of gold and blue—hey!
For the land of gold and blue!

As the voices rose to a raucous pitch, Lysande stiffened, remembering one of the girls in the orphanage humming the song. What she had learned from books—that Jale's mother, Ariane Chamboise, had nearly come to blows with Dante's mother, Raina Dalgëreth—did not matter. The fray that broke out between the orphans of northern and southern heritage had taught her the significance of "The Land of Gold and Blue" much more vividly.

"I've a good mind to show them what gold and blue look like when they're mixed with red," another Valderran growled, near to her.

"Better you stay your hand." The warning tone in the first woman's voice came through clearly. "The First Sword'll rampage if we gut the fish."

A string of Old Valderran curses followed, along with several remarks about Jale's sapphires and golden raiment, one suggesting a parallel between the negligible thickness of the prince's banquet outfit in Axium and his ability as a leader. A second remark, about Jale spreading banners for his enemies, seemed obscure to Lysande, at first, but once she mentally removed the word *banners*, she began to understand. The speaker received a warm response, and Lysande did not like that at all.

Her shoulders prickled as she moved through the camp; every robe could have been a hooded cloak, until she looked again. Cassia's tent towered, festooned with ribbons of purple and white cloth, easily twice the size of Dante's. A Pyrrhan guard looked Lysande over at the entrance, her bronze armor gleaming in the torchlight.

In the center of the floor, a low table lay draped in a cloth with bronze-colored tassels, surrounded by cushions. The Irriqi sat at the head, resplendent in a deep plum tunic. The jagged white pieces on her choker, she informed Lysande, were leopard's teeth from before the Conquest, though Lysande doubted the verity of that.

She could not miss the way that the candlelight threw a sheen over Luca's dark hair, turning it into streams of black silk. He twisted with ease to speak to the lord beside him, as if he did not know how the facets of the ruby at his neck set off his eyes, nor how the smooth movement of his body made others stare in his direction. A Lyrian noblewoman was studying him, and Lysande thought she saw the Pyrrhan advisor, a small man with a glabrous chin, sneak a glance at Luca over the top of his cup. Again, she observed that there was something effortlessly graceful about Luca, something that only showed itself in motion, always agile like the strokes of a rapier.

"Good evening, Councillor," Jale said, from her right.

"Good evening, Your Highness. Though I find it uncommonly warm in this clime."

"Warm for you Axiumites, maybe. In Lyria, we call this winter." Jale grinned. "When summer arrives in the south, it takes a layer of skin off your heel."

His back looked rod-straight and his hands were clasped in his lap, a little too tightly to be natural. His smile never faltered, Lysande noticed. This is what it means to lead, she thought. To be aware of the threat that permeates every inch of space, every pocket of air; and to keep smiling, regardless.

She beckoned Litany and Derset to join her on the cushions. They took their places beside the noblewoman at Jale's left, who had the same fine cheekbones and blue eyes as Jale but none of his natural cheer; after a brief glance at Lysande, she returned to the task of examining her nails. Further along, a Valderran noble ran her hand over a brocaded cushion.

"Put that down," Dante's voice boomed. "It's not for taking, you bear-witted clout."

Lysande wanted to laugh, yet her levity did not last. She could not shake the thought of the last time they had all sat down to eat, and the spinning of a small piece of metal on a table.

On the other side of the low table, Luca straightened the basket nestled in front of him, engrossed in conversation with two Rhimese, a blond woman and a dark-haired lord. While his attention was else-where, she studied, deliberately this time, the line of his jaw and the soft expanse of throat. She pictured herself putting her hands, gently but firmly, against that throat. Again, she could not say why she de-sired it, only that there was something about the thought of touching him—not to harm, but to exert a pressure—that beckoned her to his person.

It was like wishing to hold an ice-bear cub, those northern crea-tures she had seen drawn in the natural history manual, so soft and beautiful and vulnerable in your hands. And yet she was certain that Luca's soft looks would not stop him from lashing out with a bite if she came too near.

A clatter of brass brought the table to attention as Pyrrhan atten-dants carried in plates. Lysande glanced quickly at Litany. There were times when you wished for a shared language of breath, a grammar of the eyes, a vocabulary of touches, so that nothing needed to be risked through sound.

She leaned over to Litany. "Sarelin told me that when she was trav-eling in Rhimese territory, she had her food checked for —"

"Venom of the blue adder, nightroot, and lover's poison."

Lysande met the girl's stare. "Quite right," she said, slowly.

Litany's expression did not weaken. "If I pretend to be hungry, it'll be less noticeable. In case you don't want to offend."

She had looked at Litany so many times, but this was the first time she had really seen what was there.

"We have not discussed payment for this," Lysande said.

"Not yet," Litany said.

Their gazes remained locked. Litany did not move a muscle.

"I suppose you are trained in this field," Lysande said, at last.

Litany nodded, smiled demurely, and reached for the nearest plate. The girl tried each of the rice balls and little parcels of leaf-wrapped cheese before passing them over quietly. Her manner of eating con-veyed the right amount of famishment, each morsel snatched up. Ly-sande felt a stab of guilt as she watched, but did not speak.

"You may drink from any bottle," Cassia announced. "Tonight, we make merry."

Something growled outside—a faint rumble that sounded near, and that Lysande hoped was only the wind. She tried to reassure herself that Chidney was at the ready.

Talk began, winding through topics as a stream winds through a wood, never pausing long enough to pool; trying not to focus too obviously on Litany testing the food, nor on the thought of the bear that was supposedly pursuing them, Lysande listened to the discussion.

"Six months left until the wedding, and everything paid for. A shower of doves every week with new details. Honestly," the noblewoman beside Jale said. "All the fortune falls to my brother."

"The fortune of being shackled to a ram for life, Élérie?" Jale returned.

"You are betrothed, then, Your Highness?" Lysande asked.

"To the heir of Bastillón, Princess Ferago. You can thank your Iron Queen for that," Jale replied gloomily. "She bargained me off as soon as I took the throne. Everyone wants Lyria—we've got the delta, troves of the most famous art, and the bank. Not that my uncle Vigarot put up much protest . . . I'm sure it was just a coincidence he got a fat gift of gold and two hundred mules into the bargain."

Dante frowned. He was watching Jale closely, and in his regard Lysande observed something of the intensity that Jale had displayed when he looked at Dante in the Great Hall—like a thirst that could not easily be quenched. Looking away at last, Dante picked up a bottle and held it above the table.

"Wet Crowns," he said.

All the city-rulers raised their goblets.

The game, Lysande learned, involved drinking a goblet of wine for each year you had been on the throne, along with one for each elemental you had caught. Lysande did not like that idea, but she had no chance to stop it. Soon they were crying "Down! Down! Down!" as the Councillors threw back the goblets. Cassia plied Lysande with enough Pyrrhan red that despite her lack of experience, she matched the others' pace; the vintage was sweet on her tongue, but the richness of the grapes weighed her head down, and she soon regretted her participation.

Dante was not following the latest round, she saw, and was looking down at his goblet. Something in his eyes gave her the impression that his attention had traveled beyond the game.

She had her own concerns, aside from the wine. She had searched her mind for an answer as to why Litany might possess a comprehensive knowledge of poisons, and could find none that set her at ease.

The final course arrived—slices of date bread accompanied by dollops of cream that Cassia's cook had somehow transported on the ride—and wine was replaced with song. When the last chorus had been howled, Dante suggested that they turn to the ordering of the armies. "We need to consider our borders if the White Queen . . ."

The clink of spoons against plates echoed for a few seconds. No one seemed willing to make eye contact, nor attempt to thaw the chill that three words had caused.

"Let's have one night without maps and stratagems," Cassia said.

"A toast to the Council of Elira!" Jale proposed, waving his goblet.

"Elira!" they all cried, and drank.

Another growl sounded outside—this time louder and less easy to brush away. Lysande muttered her concern to Cassia and the Irriqi nodded. It was not that her senses were heightened from scale, she told herself; Sarelin would have checked her surrounds, here, too.

"The puzzle realm," Luca said, when they had put down their goblets. "Where jungle and desert and ice are to be found within the same borders. The puzzle of many pieces—the tapestry of many colors—where five cities keep their customs, but share a common crown."

"Well put. I had no idea you had a knack for poetry," Jale said, flashing a smile.

"Prince Fontaine is quoting," Lysande said, taking another piece of date bread. "From the second volume of the Silver Songs: Cicera's speech about the Unification of Elira."

Yet another growl sounded in the distance. Lysande glanced at the tent wall. She noticed Cassia whispering a few words to her advisor, who rose and hurried out. Catching Cassia's eye, Lysande mouthed the word *check*, and Cassia nodded.

"Very good, Councillor Prior. And do you know why the speech is so famous?"

"Because it is the first written work to define what Elira stands for," she said, meeting Luca's stare. "In Royam, the newer race holds power over the ancient one, and in Bastillón, those with silver hair oppress those with gold; but in Elira, all are equal, the poet Cicera argues. That is why the founders chose the motto *diversity is our strength*."

"There's eloquence in those old poems," Cassia said, nodding.

"Sarelin Brey thought so." Luca was still looking over his chalice at Lysande, not relaxing his grip on the cup. "She loved referring to the Silver Songs when it suited her, to make herself sound like Queen Illora. What an idol. No wonder she got you to translate the Silver Songs, Councillor Prior. A copy in every household, so that everyone could understand the allusions to the Conquest's brave leader."

"I should hardly credit Queen Illora with the Silver Songs. Organizing the great Surge, to take advantage of the elementals' truce? Undoubtedly. But poetry?" Lysande said. "No one really knows who authored the Silver Songs."

"Our late queen was very good at spreading those poems about, though." Luca's smile was as cutting as his stare. "So long as they colored history in her particular palette."

"And you think it was unwise to circulate our finest art to the populace without a fee, for the betterment of their education?" Lysande heard her own voice growing louder.

"I think it was very wise. Control people with a sword, and they resent you. Control them with a song, and they plead for more."

"It sounds as if you find the Silver Songs distasteful, Prince Fontaine." Cassia raised her goblet. "Perhaps the 'Tale of the Drunken Soldier' is more in your style."

The others laughed, but Luca did not join them. He was not smirking now. "I merely point out that if we are the puzzle realm, we leave out one piece of the puzzle whenever we write poems of glory."

"You think we should glorify the elementals?" Dante said. "And shall we let them walk freely in the streets, burning houses and flooding whole towns, too? See their cairns piled on every slope, threatening murder? It's enough that Councillor Prior has stopped killing them in Axium. I suppose you'd like to loose them on the villagers, Prince Fontaine."

Lysande's shoulders tensed. Charice's face swam in her mind, her friend clutching the chimera drawing to her chest, on the day Lysande had first seen it. Then she pictured the treatise on the concealment of magical powers that she had found nestled among Charice's books. Anyone who knew the history between them would say that she had failed Charice.

She heard Sarelin speaking of elementals, the steel whipping in her voice. And she remembered the way that Sarelin had described the rebels' flames sweeping through lines of guards, leaving charred bodies behind, the day she had made her last stand. Yet it was not as simple as choosing to honor Sarelin or to help Charice.

If you wanted to arrive at your own view, you had to stand above others and look beyond their heads, to take in the horizon from a new height. You had to choose that precise level for yourself and decide what you wished to see.

I made the right choice about the executions, she told herself. No woman was born a rebel: she had to stand on her own platform and choose to become one.

Cassia's advisor slipped back through the tent flaps. The woman wore a relaxed expression as she shook her head. The Irriqi shot a look at Lysande and leaned over. "No dangers. None that Pyrrhan guards can spot, anyway. We check *every* tree."

Lysande tried to let herself accept a modicum of good news, but the fact that she alone had seen the rider nagged at her. Should she walk out, now, find Chidney, and scour the whole camp? She wanted to check for herself; and yet she knew that it was imperative to remain in the tent, for whatever drinking games and arguments might yet come, if she truly wanted to be considered one of the Council.

"Thank you," she whispered to Cassia. The Irriqi did not speak, but her nod was slow enough that it might have been a smile.

Across the table, Luca's eyes flashed. "If you're asking whether I think every magical woman is a White Queen in the making and every elemental man is some budding tyrant, determined to destroy us— then no, Dalgëreth, I do not. The captains had to die, and the White Queen had to be brought down. But what of the other elementals? The ones hiding across the realm, the ordinary people? You can hardly blame them for resenting us, when we chop their heads off or lock

them up for the crime of existing. The way I see it, they have been ex-
traordinarily lenient. Do you not think they could raze our cities if
they wanted to? That they could not burn our palaces to the ground in
minutes, and make a new empire of their own?"

"The way *you* see it," Dante said, scowling at Luca. "Rhime has a
weakness for unnatural things."

"Come, now," Jale said, laying a hand on his arm, "let's all cool our
heads with a Triumphal-era red."

Dante was muttering something about Rhime and illegal books on
elementals, but at Jale's touch he fell silent. After a moment, he patted
Jale on the shoulder, uncorked a bottle of the wine, and poured himself
a goblet. The conversation began to flow more freely—like the Trium-
phal red—and when she had judged that Dante was more engrossed in
Jale's company than in quarreling with others, Lysande moved to sit
beside Luca. He did not shift away.

Reaching to his collar, he loosened the button and removed the
jewel, pushing the fabric down a few inches. The act exposed more of
his neck.

Had it been a coincidence? He was looking at her, and again there
was the sense of an invitation, delicate and barely manifest. She struggled to determine if it was a deliberate gesture, or her imagination,
daring herself to glance at the bare skin.

"Jails are being built as we speak," she said, quietly. "Comfortable
jails, while I consider new ideas. But none so radical as yours."

He did not reply. Lysande looked down, then quickly met his gaze
again. "Sarelin said that if elementals were allowed freedom, they
would use it to rule over the rest of us." The argument rang hollow
even as she voiced it.

"Then Sarelin Brey knew as little of elementals as she did of tact."
Luca looked closely at her. "Oh, I don't deny our late queen had her
talents. She could swing a sword and fling a good dagger, everyone
knows, but she missed the opportunity to reach out to elementals after
the White War. Easier to keep lopping off heads. Never mind distinguishing between those who supported the White Queen and those
who didn't. No, Prior, prejudice and fear have dictated the law. And
where prejudice rules, the crown weakens."

Somewhere in her mind, Lysande knew that there was some truth in his point, but she was so angry at the way he had spoken of Sarelin that she could feel heat running through her neck to her cheeks. This should have been the time to talk of the plight of magical people and to discuss the state of the poor, and perhaps even, in some roundabout way, to bring up Charice.

"You should pay more attention to the gift I sent you, Fontaine," she snapped. "The flower of manners."

"Very clever, yes. But I believe you have exhausted that metaphor."

"The gift will only be exhausted when you take a lesson from it."

He dipped his head, a shift from argumentative to something else, visible to only her. "And are you to be my instructor?"

She was prevented from responding when Élérie Chamboise leaned forward and vomited into the middle of the table. It caused such a commotion that by the time the mess had been cleared, everyone had quite forgotten about the near-argument. The sky looked black by the time they returned to their tents, Luca departing alone and Dante escorting Jale away. Lysande insisted that Litany go to her own bed—the questions brimming within her about her attendant's knowledge of poisons would have to wait until she was more alert, and Chidney was hovering, waiting for the right moment to take Litany off her hands, claiming in a rather too-concerned tone that there was an issue with her tent and she would need Litany's advice. Yet Lysande had no sooner turned away than she found Derset holding a dove for her. The advisors' further claims of a Bastillonian attack at sea did not calm her mind. She sent Derset away, too. Pacing by the light of the candle inside her tent, she felt the hilts of her daggers in her belt.

She prepared some scale, taking out one and a half spoonfuls again and heating it over a candle. It was not a risk to drink more than the usual amount. Surely not. It was a necessary measure, even if her stomach crackled and fizzed; even if her whole gut seemed to writhe and her heartbeat knocked so furiously that she had to sit down for a moment. The night-quartz could stay wrapped inside the chest, as it was supposed to be.

The scent of dew, faint and fragrant, reached her in waves. Breathing it in, she located the specific moment that she had smelled it: on her first ride in Axium Forest, with Sarelin, when the queen had sent her riding-party back to tail them from a distance, so that they could be alone together, their horses keeping neck-and-neck amongst the ferns. The dew had enfolded them with its sweetness. The whole forest had seemed to welcome them, that day.

Of course, this was a memory, an echo of that day drifting up from a vial. You could not stretch time and bend it back to you, no matter what mixture you poured down your throat.

She downed the remainder of the contents in a single swallow.

At last, the distress melted from her, yet she knew that the golden feeling would not last forever, and that itself brought another kind of disquiet, one which must lie for now beneath the glow of the room. Guilt over the squandering of her wage, and over the abuse of her body, which Sarelin had taken care to protect—that would waste the precious effects of the scale. Avoidance was better. Always.

It was useful, as it had always been, to draw out the barbs that stuck in her; to forget the way the staff all looked at her in the dining hall, the rapidity with which the silverbloods declined to see her as soon as Sarelin had left a room, and the silence that spread through a corridor when she entered it, pervading every inch of chambers and stairwells. In the face of everyday life, a certain blue mixture could be relied upon, no matter what after-effects transpired. She held the jar up and watched the flakes of chimera scale for a moment, tipping them from side to side so that they slipped between the shadow and the light.

Once her head grew heavier, she undressed and put on the first night-shirt and thin trousers she could find. She stared at her dagger-belt for a few moments, then took two blades out and tucked them under each side of her pillow, positioning them so that they would not pierce through the feathers. Copying Sarelin's precaution seemed both a tribute and a necessity.

She was beginning to doubt that the cloaked figure would turn up, but it was precisely when you were doubting that you needed daggers. That was what she had written in *An Ideal Queen*. Queen Jebel had been repaid for her trust in safe passage by waking to find her lover and entourage slaughtered—and Lysande had never forgotten that story, with its descriptions of severed torsos and congealed blood.

She climbed into bed and opened a book. The candle flickered but never guttered out, and she found herself yawning and stretching as she plowed through the newly circulated *Astratto Formulas*, the tome propped on her thighs. Somewhere after the eighteenth equation, she slipped into a dream of an ancient peak . . . she was climbing onto the chimera Oblitara's back, soaring up into the air. The eastern country-side flew past below, farms and manor houses, mounds of olives on platters in the shops at Ferizia, squares of vineyards at Spelato, and the deep green lumps of the Emeralds. The colors danced before her again, a palette of heat and light. There was a figure moving among them, following her, always out of reach.

She woke to a pressure on her mouth.

"I haven't come to hurt you," a man growled, "but if you squirm, Councillor, I might change my mind."

The hand clamped over her lips was tight enough to muffle her shout. Above her, a man stood, clad in the same hooded cloak as the rider who had darted between the trees. It was obvious at once why he had hidden his face—scars criss-crossed his countenance, and his cheek was calcified in patches and smooth in others, so that the skin wore its history.

Lysande's right leg twitched. She fought the impulse to kick.

"Good." The man gave her a mirthless smile. "They told me you were a bright one. Now get dressed, Councillor."

He removed his hand from her mouth and stepped back. They looked at each other. The man lifted his sword-hilt a few inches above the sheath.

She weighed whether she could notify her guards before he stabbed her, and examining the odds, decided that they did not fall in her favor. Moving as fast as her trembling fingers would allow, she pulled on a shirt, trousers, and jacket while the roar of an animal sounded in the distance, and she wondered how far away the creature was. Her captor walked to the tent flaps and stood in the entrance, silhouetted against the candlelight. If he was concerned by the sight of her fastening her daggers into her belt, he gave no sign.

"You have no right," she whispered.

"Someone wants to speak to you."

"If I come quietly, do I have your word that I won't be killed?"

He shrugged off his hood, exposing the whole map of upraised skin, slowly, very slowly, as if he knew what effect it would have. "For whatever you think it's worth," he said.

Lysande laced up her boots. A sound rang out across the camp—a guttural roar, like an animal about to devour its prey, much closer now. She had not imagined it this time. Her hand flew to her belt.

The man drew his sword. They stared at each other again, and Lysande knew as she took in his face that attempting a dagger-throw at this juncture would do no good.

The night air tickled their necks as they emerged from a gap the man made, at discomfiting speed, by untethering the cloth at the back of the tent. Lysande's guards were still standing by the entrance, out of range, and her heart sank as she saw that the smaller tent opposite was bare too. She thought she could make out an animal running on all fours at the other end of the camp—a crowd of guards from all five parties chasing it with swords outstretched, running swiftly—before her captor twisted her arm and pulled her away. The scent of musk permeated the clearing.

Then they were moving through the back of the tents and into a line of trees, and there was no one to hear her footsteps, no one to see her running as they passed further and further from the torches of the camp.

Seven

The farmhouse stood in the middle of a group of fields, half-shrouded by the darkness. They came to a stop, panting, while a woman stepped out from the doorway. Lysande took in the hooded cloak and the thick hide of the boots.

"How'd the bear go?" the woman said, looking at Lysande's abductor. "Did it kill anyone?"

"Hate to disappoint you."

"I suppose it's for the best. Bit of a waste, though." The woman smirked. "Don't tarry. He's been waiting."

Lysande's captor pushed her through the door and into a small chamber, then through a kitchen, a bedchamber, and a study—all empty, and lit by candles—and she observed as much as she could without slowing down. The room in which they stopped was at least three times the size of the others. It was occupied by a table covered in papers and envelopes, with a candelabra mounted in the middle of the wood, and at the far end of the table she could see a figure in a chair; the sitter's distance from the light made it impossible to discern the face. She could only make out a glint of white hair.

"Welcome, Signore Prior. Do come in and take a seat."

The voice carried across the table, a mellifluous tone honeying the words. She distinguished the shape of a brimmed hat in the gloom.

"I do apologize for the nature of our lodgings—they are somewhat frugal out of necessity—and I must extend my apologies for sending Signore Welles to fetch you. He is skillful at handling a bear, but he grew up north of Valderos, and I am afraid his idea of courtesy is cutting your throat with one stroke instead of two."

The scarred man chuckled and stepped back against the wall. Lysande walked to the end of the table, one hand reaching for the gold dagger at her hip. Her fingers trembled against the hilt. Be imperative, she told herself.

"If I cannot see my captor's face, I demand to know his name."

"I would take my hand off that blade if I were you, my dear." The speaker leaned forward. "Queen Sarelin may have trained you, but my weapon does not need to be drawn."

Wind engulfed her as the figure in the chair lifted his hand. Lysande scrabbled to grasp the corner of the table and several sheets of paper scattered onto the floor. She steadied herself until her host lowered his hand. The wind ceased as quickly as it had begun, leaving in its wake a probing disquiet, as if someone had been blowing a gale inside of her, disturbing the private chambers of her mind and body.

"Sit, Signore Prior," the man said. "I mean for us to be friends, and there are no formalities between friends, are there?"

Lysande sat. The chair at the end of the table creaked as she moved it, but she barely heard the noise—her mind was already racing through everything she knew about elementals. Of course Welles had not been concerned by her daggers. Of course the big man had been able to subdue and transport a bear without losing a limb—he could probably move fire, or water, or air, too—she should have worked that out already. But if these were the White Queen's people, why was she not dead? She quelled the trembling of her fingers. "Forgive me, signore, but I do not believe I know you."

"My name is not important—to those who matter, I am simply called Three." The man in the brimmed hat leaned back in his chair.

"How long have you been following me?"

"Signore Welles here has been following you. I prefer to rest on the margins of the page. But as for you, *Councillor* Prior . . . it was curious for Sarelin Brey, the Iron Queen of seven battles, to pick a scholar for her companion, was it not?"

"You seem to know a lot about me." Lysande kept her face impassive. "But when it comes to you, I confess I am in the dark."

Three rose and walked to the window. "Perhaps it will help if I permit some light."

He pulled the wooden boards open and streams of moonlight washed over him. The man she saw was tall, though his frame lacked the breadth acquired by soldiers through years of hefting a longsword; his angular face might have been classically beautiful, before it had acquired its sharper, wiser aspect. Despite the brimmed hat and the embroidered doublet, Lysande saw nothing to identify him, no crest or motto anywhere; only a triangular pendant of silver dangling in the middle of his chest. The hair that hung down his back was a pure white, yet he could not have been much older than thirty-five. She did not look away.

"You need not fear that I will detain you long. Prince Fontaine, the Irriqi, the First Sword, and that charming boy-prince would miss you if I kept you here. Fontaine in particular." Three gave a smile as he said this, sitting down beside her.

They eyed each other. Lysande sat straight as a blackfoot tree, working to keep her feelings off her face. She searched for words from Sarelin that would help. *Iron bows to no hand.* Was it enough to rely on Sarelin's wisdom, though?

"When you look at me, Signore Prior, what do you see?" Three said.

Lysande's eyes passed over his person, coming to rest on the pendant.

"In ancient times, the triangle was a symbol of magic. Three sides: for fire, water, and air. You're an elemental, and you're bold enough to carry a symbol identifying you as such."

"Very good."

Her heart was fluttering in her throat. "You had a man lead a bear to our camp to get me away. You bring me to a farmhouse in the middle of the night, with the help of people who all wear the same cloaks . . . so you deal in secrecy, and you're highly organized."

Three regarded her without speaking.

"The last clue is your name. Since you already wear a triangle pendant, I'd say that Three does not refer to the elements. And since you have people working for you, I'd say you're third in charge of some magical group."

"Excellent." He looked pleased. "But you have omitted the name of our organization." His smile turned sly. "I should have thought it was obvious to a discerning mind."

Her pulse should not have been racing. Sarelin would have faced these people like a slab of thick marble, without even the tiniest crack; if she tried hard enough, perhaps she could manage something of that façade. Yet emulation was not the limit of her strength. She delved inside herself, seeking the determination that had carried her through the long night after Sarelin's death, through the silent screams in her bedchamber when her ribcage threatened to rend and her jaw ached.

"Even a scholar cannot deduce a fact from thin air, signore," she said.

"You have heard our name before." Three tilted his head, and moonlight struck the brim of his hat. "You simply need to remember."

As she stared at him, she caught a smell wafting from one of the pages on the table, and it only took her seconds to identify the scent of rose-oil—faint and fragrant, but unmistakable. She remembered bending over the fireplace and picking up a corner of paper in the royal suite. The explanation that had been hiding among the fears and anxieties of the last twenty-four hours blazed forth, and though she knew she was guessing, this guess fit.

"You're a member of the Shadows," she said.

He nodded and, walking around to the side of the table, lowered himself into the chair beside her. Up close, she could see the experience written on his face—and the urge to reach for her dagger died as she looked into his eyes, taking in their quiet power.

A note from her compilation came back to her, leaping out: *According to Kephir's study of etymology, to be elemental is simply to be made up of smaller parts, some of which are hard to see, to perceive, to understand.* She gazed at Three.

"You will be wondering who we are and why we have so rudely transported you here." He leaned back in his chair. "I expect you have a multitude of questions, Signore Prior."

Lysande had spoken with enough courtiers lately to know when she was being invited to contribute. She also knew when it was better to stay silent. Three clicked his fingers at Welles and the scarred man disappeared into the house, returning a moment later with the woman who had greeted them.

"Six, my dear," Three said, "would you be so good as to show Signore Prior your face?"

The woman dropped her hood. In the moonlight, the burn that disfigured her right cheek was painfully clear: a twisted expanse stretched from the hairline to the jaw, suffused with the angry red that could only have come from a magical flame. Lysande could not help gasping.

"Tell me, how do you think the White Queen persuaded fifty elementals to fight in her army? Powerful people, many of whom thought her a tyrant and a threat to their own land?"

Questions like that had come to her when she had first begun compiling the notes for her treatise. Seeing the aftermath of the White Queen's impatience was quite different. "Not by asking politely," she said.

"Swords, knives, hot irons, and flames . . . she took her time with those who refused her. You need only look at Welles here."

The scars on the big man's face took on a different aspect as she looked at them again; it was not fear she felt, this time, but something she could only have described as a kind of understanding . . . the kind that came when you dug through some of your own prejudices, clearing away the dust. She marshaled all her effort to put up the façade again.

"And what about you, signore?"

"Some scars lie below the surface." Three adjusted his hat, and for a while he let a silence linger between them. "In addition to being able to move the air, I have what is called a power of the mind," he said, at last. "The White Army had to try different methods on those like me. Even a boy was worth keeping alive for months, if there was hope that he might be broken. Any brutality was justified to win the prize of a power of the mind for the White Queen."

Sarelin had read her a sermon, once, which claimed that some elementals used darker powers, forces that drew upon the depths of their "depravity." It was impossible to forget the fire in those words, and

Sarelin's voice rising to declare that Fortituda and Vindictus would "smite the damned lot of them"—impossible not to shiver, still.

But with time, understanding could flourish. She had come to realize that if Charice was a person like any other, so must other elementals be individuals; that reverence for Sarelin did not have to cloak the truth.

"You must have escaped her, to be sitting here today," she said.

"Some would call it an escape. Others who fled her clutches know better."

Lysande was silent, reflecting on the causes of hair turning white before old age.

"I had been living in a sewer in Axium for eight months when I came across others like me: elementals who had escaped. Some more scarred than others. We formed a group to share food and a roof, and when we had lived together long enough to trust, my new friends introduced me to an organization." As he spoke Lysande glanced again at the pendant on his chest. "A group of elementals who felt that they should use their talents to hold back the White Queen. They saw the way forward for our people as peace, not tyranny, and they were neither of Sarelin Brey's army nor the White Army."

"The Shadows." She felt the weight of the word on her tongue. All those moments. All those times in the midst of her grief when she had railed at herself for not knowing what Sarelin had meant; they melted away now that she truly understood.

He nodded. "Our goal then—as it is now—was to know things. To find out where the White Queen's soldiers were going and what her plans were. To have hands among her papers. Ears on her walls."

If Sarelin had known about a magical intelligence service, why had she never mentioned it until she was dying? And why had she asked Lysande to find this group of elementals? Did the city-rulers know about the Shadows? And what about Charice—what knowledge had she been privy to? Too many questions, like fibers fraying at the end of a sleeve, threatened to unravel her thoughts. She searched for simpler words. "If you were loyal to the realm, I thank you."

"We serve only our own people."

"Yet if you have a structure, you must have a leader."

"I beg your pardon?"

"Above a Three, there is a Two and a One," Lysande said.

"We have a system, in the way that a paper castle has a system behind its intricate construction, invisible to all but the creator. Each of us knows only the people we need to know. Secrecy is our religion, Signore Prior. In fact, I can assure you that the name of One is not known to any but herself."

"Then how can you be sure that it is not 'himself'?"

He regarded her closely, over the top of his folded hands. She was not sure if she had imagined the twinkle in his eyes.

"I see my colleague Two was not wrong about you," he said.

A clink interrupted them: Six and Welles had slipped out some time ago and now they returned with plates of cheese and baskets of bread, setting them down in front of Lysande. The bread was roughly cut, and it gave off a tempting smell. "Please, help yourself to some bread and cheese." Three waved a hand. "And perhaps Six will bring us a little water . . . I expect you do not want wine, after all that drinking."

"You are singularly well-informed of my doings, signore."

He passed her the nearest basket. There were no cured vegetables or honeyed cakes here, but there was enough to stave off the hunger that had woken in her since her run through the fields. Lysande made to reach for the platter of cheese, and paused with one hand upon it.

"You need not fear poison here," Three said. "But I admire your suspicion."

He pulled the platter nonchalantly over and, closing his eyes, chewed a wedge of cheese slowly. "Pescarran, I think. Of all the Rhimese towns, Pescarra is the one to stop in for goat's cheeses—make a note of it, my dear. You never know when you will need good cheese."

The cheese was indeed good, but the bread was better, crusty on the outside and soft on the inside. Lysande's body felt too taut for her to really enjoy it, yet she forced herself to eat, aware that food in her stomach would help her to stay alert. She considered all the dangers that might come next. Three left the room with Six, the pair whispering to each other. They did not return until she had devoured nearly half a loaf.

Lysande's eyes slid to the burns on Six's cheeks. She had heard of the crown's enemies ever since childhood, in every lesson about the hidden people, biding their time, waiting for the moment to strike and seize control once again. No one had spoken of the hidden people attacking each other. That would surely have disrupted the accepted story.

Three placed something on the table, something bright, and it took her a few seconds to realize that the rainbow of plants on the square of black cloth he had laid down was familiar; that the sprigs of crimson, yellow, and white were wild heather, the lime-green stalk crowned with purple was a queensflower, and the dark green leaf, shining almost black, was a piece of eastern ivy.

"Strange, isn't it, how the meanings of things are determined not by their essence, but by what they symbolize. Take this little symbol." Three nudged the queensflower with his finger.

She picked the purple flower up. "Surely, you can't deny that this is a cut queen."

"It is a tribute to a queen. Not a literal queen, necessarily, but any person who embodies the qualities of a queen: strength, wisdom, majesty. Sharp edges."

Another pause. Lysande watched him for a sign of deceit. He rose and walked about the room, and Lysande turned over the queensflower in her hand, before placing it in front of her.

Staring at the flower, she thought of the night Charice had spoken of the creative spirit of nature, her friend pressed thigh to thigh with her on the sweat-flecked sheets, Lysande kissing the nape of her neck and relishing the shiver that came in response; Charice's voice swelling, growing sonorous as she argued that magic was derived from the life-giving rhythms of the seasons, the elements, the land itself.

Something in her stomach had kicked while she was listening to Sarelin raging about elementals, months later. Words were not supposed to mean so much, but they did, and words like *pernicious* and *unnatural* evinced a determination to stay around for a long time after you first heard them.

"The Old Signs appear threatening, like peaks viewed from the other side of a cloud bank. But when swirls of gray mist roll back and reveal the emerald summits, you see that they are not jagged at all."

Three let the words linger for a moment. "The Shadows wish to make you an offer, Signore Prior," he said, as he sat down again. "Work with us. You have the connections to help. Take our information and our advice, and use it to defeat the White Queen."

In the silence between them, responses curled and uncurled. Lysande pushed a lock of hair back from her face. She understood, now, where all this had been leading. "The White Queen may be dead," she said, stolidly.

"I think we both know that that is as likely as snow in Lyria." His voice was still kindly, but there was something of a merchant leaning across a stall-top in it. "There are many things I have confirmed about Mea Tacitus. And some of them concern Sarelin Brey, too. You would be surprised to hear what we know."

Three kept his hands folded in his lap. Nothing in his face suggested he was going to answer anything she might ask. Lysande was reminded of Luca's words at the Arena: his provocation, by suggesting that Sarelin had known Mea Tacitus as a girl. Three could be bargaining on the strength of rumor, of course. There was no way of being sure.

"Even if you're certain that she'll attack again, I fail to see what I can do to help."

"We need someone at the highest level of rule to work with us. If we are to defeat her in any permanent capacity, it must be with the support of the crown, as I tried to convince our late Queen Sarelin."

Lysande smelled the rose-oil, again, floating up from one of the pages on the table.

"Your letter was the last thing she read," she said.

"It was the last letter of several. I tried to warn her that an attack was being planned for a hunting trip—I wrote with increasing urgency, stressing that she should avoid riding out at all costs."

How easily she could picture Sarelin reading that letter, giving a snort of contempt, and tossing the missive over her shoulder into the fireplace.

"So you do serve the crown," she said.

"I serve magic, Signore Prior." Three touched his pendant again, stroking a carving of a smaller triangle within the triangle. "Sometimes, that means choosing one leader over another; but always, it means acting for our people."

As she considered his proposition, feeling the weight of what she had been offered, she remembered Sarelin hacking and coughing, jerking on the grass, urging her to find the Shadows, and then going still: cold and still in her arms. Sarelin had always charged into the things she thought necessary. She might have done so now. Lysande was well aware of the differences between herself and her queen, as well as the similarities.

"You must understand . . . I prefer to be certain," she said.

"Of your safety?"

"Of your information."

Three's hands unclasped and he regarded her for a protracted moment before nodding to Six. While the woman rummaged among the papers on the table, Lysande maintained eye contact with Three. They did not speak. Six selected a number of pages from the mess and dropped them down in front of Three; he unfolded them one by one, revealing messages written in Bastillonian, modern Eliran, Royamese dialects, and snatches of the ancient wayfarer tongues of the Periclean States. Even Luca would have marveled at such a range. Cartography was not the only discipline to draw the lines between the Three Lands—the study of language, too, had made its mark.

"Letters from our correspondents. Remarks our people have overheard while we track her spies. I see you have noticed what we have," Three said, as Lysande reached for a page. "She moves around in our neighboring lands, where even the most determined of our agents struggle to trace her. Most of the time, we fear, she has been further north." Three's mouth pursed. "Across the North Sea, the Exalted are not so scrupulous about driving out tyrants when the tyrants can pay. Some of our recent information is tenuous, but still . . . we suspect she is selling heirlooms she stole in the White War."

A description of the map Lysande had made of the White Queen's known and suspected thefts during the war sprang to her tongue, but she held it there. Something, deep in the part of her that she suspected was not very sensible at all, still believed that the map was for Sarelin's eyes only.

The next page appeared to be a transcription. Was she holding the words of the greatest enemy of the crown? No . . . the greeting was addressing a "true queen." As she smoothed the paper out, she saw that the first line had been written in Bastillonian, followed by a few words in Eliran and Royamese.

"We leave Axium Palace in the morning," she read aloud, decoding the author's neat letters. "We will take the Scarlet Road and most likely camp near Ardua." She dropped the page as the words sank in. "This was written yesterday!"

She had known that a viper was slithering around her. It was something different to see the fact of it inked out on paper, the intercepted message inches from her. The letters were shaped elegantly on the page; a little too elegantly, perhaps, as the author had achieved a style devoid of all vigor and personality, a style that could not be entirely natural.

"I'd like to say we catch doves mid-flight all the time. But I was raised not to lie." Three smiled ruefully. "Six snagged this one as we neared your camp, carrying the letter. Only someone with an intimate knowledge of this Council's movements could have sent such a message." He tapped a finger against the page. "Possibly one of the city-rulers. The White Queen's servant, as you can see, is a woman or man of talent, with several languages at their command. Someone resourceful enough to send a dove unnoticed amid a crowd of guards."

"Someone who has no scruple to throw our trust to the wind!" If she spoke hotly, she did not care. The nerve of it. The sheer disrespect for the Council, already, when it had scarcely been formed. She knew someone who had prowess with several languages, of course, and although she knew, rationally, that he was unlikely to parade the basis of his deception about, she indulged herself by directing all her frustration toward Luca.

"The White Queen addresses them as the Umbra. That is all we have—they cover their tracks so efficiently that I suspect some magical method may be involved."

He seemed to be plunged in thought for a moment. Lysande had driven past apprehension to reach impatience, however. "That is all?"

"Almost all. We know that the Umbra has no great love for Sarelin Brey. In one letter they refer to her as a 'cur'; in another as a 'brute.'"

Like my dear Lady Pelory. But Pelory could not have sent the dove, being dozens of miles behind them in Axium. It was hard to think when her mind was encumbered by wine, fatigue, and emotion.

"Could this Umbra have been the one who killed Sarelin?"

He did not pause; the response flowed from him as if it had been composed some time ago. "The White Queen is careful not to say so directly. But what we hear hints at it. I am personally sure that her Umbra performed the crime; the White Queen's tactics are written all over it." With a meaningful look, he added, "I take it you know of Orbonne."

No, she considered saying, I have been living down a country well. Even the northernmost farmer knew what had happened in that Lyrian town, and Lysande had translated the soldiers' accounts of that infamous encounter in the first year of the White War, detailing how the White Queen had attacked a legion of Lyrian guards outside the large town of Orbonne, using a group of archers dressed in Lyrian armor. While the guards were blaming each other and brawling, confused by the assault from what seemed to be their own people, the White Queen's soldiers slipped into the center of the town. They destroyed most of Orbonne with elemental flames within minutes, and where one family had lived, the only object to remain was a thumbnail, blackened and thinned, like bread that had been left in an oven. Sarelin had said that Elira learned at Orbonne that it was not fighting a short campaign.

Lysande had heard some guards retell that story with relish, but she had never found it gratifying.

"Two strikes. One to distract, the next to destroy," she said.

Panther and poison. Silent sword and wolf. The problem, Lysande thought, was not identifying the White Queen's tactic, but trying to guess how she would use it next.

She tapped a finger on the table. Logic. You had to use logic at times like this. Many things were opaque, still, and she found herself trying to think like the White Queen, trying to stretch to her reasoning. The first step had been to murder Sarelin, she guessed. After that, the city-rulers would squabble for the crown. Presumably, the Umbra would maneuver their way to take the throne, then leave the way open for the

White Queen to sweep in on a tide of blood. Yes. That would make sense. Reduce the work by setting up a puppet to control the realm; transfer power, *then* attack. The White Queen would not need to squander so many resources.

Yet the opposite had happened. Lysande had thrown her plan into disarray by forming the Council. Now Mea Tacitus had several Councillors to outmaneuver, instead of a single monarch. And all of the Councillors were surrounded by the best guards from every city . . . she had not realized, until now, just how lucky her decision had been. From now on, strategy should come first in her priorities. She should lay out all the possible outcomes as beads on her abacus, sliding one forward, retracting another, letting them click.

"Why not attack us from the Periclean States, now that assassination is hard?" she said.

"Her funds will probably stretch to a legion or two of mercenary soldiers, but crawling through the frozen northlands to attack Valderos, the only impregnable city in the realm—is that a brilliant plan?" Three ran a hand along his angular jaw. "We believe she has adopted a tactic from the Conquest Era. The employment of diplomatic deceit comes more naturally to some than others. The hints from her spies suggest she aims to poison our relations with our neighbors. Turn them against Elira so that she can penetrate their thinking, and penetrate their inner councils." Nothing lightened in his expression.

"Oh, Bastillón and Royam will be ramparts in our defense," Lysande said bitterly. "One border riddled with arrows, another decorated with a wall."

The fact hit her that the effort was already underway. The news of a Bastillonian attack on an Eliran ship had reached her right after Sarelin's death. It could have been subtly done, a false report about a ship here, a description of a captain there . . . could it not?

The prize jewel in the Three Lands' trading crown had always been Elira. Anyone who had ever read a history knew that; their neighbors would not like to lose their flow of goods, yet if Elira launched a counter-move to the sea attack, might not Bastillón avail itself of the opportunity to seize those goods, under the guise of responding?

She knew the frustration of the wealthy, who had been raised to embody the spirit of profit, even though she had never had the luxury to nourish it in herself.

It wouldn't take much, she thought. Just a spark to light the tinder.

"Tell me, then, if you're abreast of it, who can I trust?"

Three turned one palm up. The invitation was not subtle, but the way it had been reached was almost an art: *work with us*, first, and then *work with us or the realm burns.* There was a bite in that. But she had been getting to know people with sharp teeth.

"Any woman who agrees to help elementals without asking what they want from her is dancing on a precipice." She tried to sound firm and calm. She was not sure that she managed it.

"We ask only that you be on the alert in these next weeks. Intervene, where you think a lie has been planted. Find evidence of treachery, and hold it up where all can see. Rumors will not suffice. You will need proof, Signore Prior—hard proof—and once you have it, you must stop the Council from doing anything hasty. Need I remind you that this is about more than such players as you and I—that on this stage, the realm's longevity is at stake?"

"I can't imagine telling Dante to put down his sword." She heard the note of bitterness in her voice. "I may be a Councillor, but I am still a member of the populace in the eyes of the world."

"You have read histories and poems. You should know that sometimes the lowest-born can climb like a mountain rose. A palace scholar thinks deeply and knows the shadowed places, the quiet corners that silverbloods would not deign to step into."

What was it he had said before? *I prefer to rest on the margins of the page.* She watched the candles flicker, casting light and then throwing gray shapes over his face.

"You are the only Councillor without years of ties and obligations to a court." Three pushed a strand of white hair out of his eyes. "Of course, you have no family name, but equally, you have no family ties."

"So I am the most convenient choice."

He said nothing, only fingered his pendant again, tracing the edges of the triangle.

She thought of the girl with the braided hair who had shouted "Prior" at her in Elsington, running toward her. Something had swelled beneath her, in that moment, lifting her with a force that did not lift the others; and for all that it flattered her, she was astute enough to know that it came from the people. *Prior.*

From horseback that day, she had glimpsed a place where the sphere of politics was different; where the velvet and jewels slid away. She had seen it roll toward her. A system where a palace scholar could step off the top rung of the ladder and ascend, and where ink counted as much as silver blood . . . it had lasted for less than the length of a breath, but she had seen it, and her imagination held it.

"And what do you offer me in return?" she said.

They stared at each other for a moment. Lysande was determined not to drop her gaze first. After a while, Three bowed his head. "I cannot shower you with riches," he said, "for we do not pay our informers in cadres, mettles, or rackets, lest they begin to behave like mercenaries. But I can offer you revenge for Queen Sarelin. And for your parents."

"I never knew my parents, signore."

"That is precisely my point."

He folded his hands. The words resonated in Lysande's head. The White War was just a series of events from before her time, to be plotted on a map, distant as a story in a book; she had never thought about it in terms of blame. Yet she had spent eight years in an orphanage thanks to the same war. She had lost her queen, the only real parent she had ever known, at the hands of the woman who had led the rebellion. The glimpse she had caught of a picture of Mea Tacitus in Sarelin's vault came back to her: curiously bright, the woman painted on a crag, with her ink-black hair writhing in the wind and her cape the color of bones sweeping the rocky ground—every part of her vibrating with light, as if bathed in an aureole that had been starved of all color, while the landscape seemed to grow duller, to fade in her presence. Lysande had walked toward the painting, compelled to see it up close, until Sarelin had blocked her path.

"There is one more thing." Three's rich voice interrupted her thoughts. "If you are loyal to us, the Shadows will commit all our resources to answer one question of your choosing."

She considered this slowly, studying his hair. It was not queer, like hers; not full of an angry glitter, nor hued in a silver that was either too bright or not bright enough; yet there was more than one way to be marked by the nearness of death, and she saw the reminder of that in Three's long, white locks. She had heard it in his voice, too, when he made the offer.

What are the long-term dangers of drinking chimera scale? Is Charice safe, or lying in a ditch somewhere—and why did she leave Axium? What do you know about Sarelin and Mea Tacitus? Who left the queensflower in the Great Hall? How much chimera blood is left in the Three Lands? Why "Fontaine, in particular"? There were too many questions to choose from. But there were certain things that a group of people who could create fires, floods, and storms might discover. "I will think hard on it," she said. "As to your proposal . . . I accept."

"Excellent."

Lysande barely heard the remark. Her mind was already sizing up the task ahead, assessing where the spy might have opportunity to cause a rift with their neighbors. It was not until she was deep into her appraisal that she realized she was breathing fast—that the thought of working against the White Queen had not deterred her but set her whole body humming. All the more reason, then, to pull herself back; to impose restraints upon her speech, lest she reach too far toward these people.

Restrain, constrain, subdue. The words had worked into her consciousness, like the grain in a piece of hewn oak.

"When you have something to report, send a dove at night." Three clicked his fingers, and Six brought over a speckled dove. "My bird, Cursora, always knows where to find me."

"I should have thought you used chimeras."

He smiled. "Our powers stop short of resurrection, Signore Prior."

Three rose, and Lysande rose with him. She cradled the dove in her hands, and they walked back through the farmhouse. The light was still dim, but Three's white hair shone brighter than the candles, guiding their way. His gait was even as he led them out.

"Good luck, my dear, and remember that you go with our protection."

She had been moving in another realm ever since she walked through the farmhouse door. She ran a hand over the dove's back, quelling its cooing. "Three."

"Yes?"

"The question I can ask you . . . it can be anything? Even if it seems impossible that you could answer it?"

His smile had more than a hint of amusement, and he regarded her for a long moment before he opened the door. "Naturally," he said. "I detest boasting. But in thirty-six years, I am yet to be confronted by an impossible problem."

The township of Castelaggio bordered the river, a cascade of brown stone houses, almost twice as long as Spelato and Ferizia. Amber wine from Castelaggio flowed freely in most of the towns around Rhime, and its inhabitants had built their villas off their trade, shaping themselves into a silver-studded community: well-to-do merchants promenaded down the widest main street, while the square bustled with women and men laughing and chatting, some wheeling themselves about in the contraptions the Rhimese were known to construct for people with illnesses and injuries of the body. Walking and wheeling citizens merged in the fast-talking milieu. Lysande scarcely saw the township as she trotted through; she could hear the lively song of the eastern vowels, but her thoughts were back in the farmhouse.

In the light of day, the letters on the table and the sight of a brimmed hat in a shadowed room seemed anything but real; only the speckled dove that was now nestling in the bird-cage assured her that she had really met elemental spies. The bird, positioned carefully out of sight in the wagon, reproached her with a chirrup every few minutes.

By accepting Three's offer, she had put herself in the palm of a man who might close it and crush her with ease. The rush of the wind knocking into her and those papers leaping into the air were all too vivid.

I may not have an elemental power, she thought, yet I have my wits about me.

Her head was assaulted by the same pain she had been fighting for days, now coming in spurts and bursts. Every so often, it seemed to move to her throat; the same crushing force squeezed her windpipe, until she almost could not swallow. Lysande forced the ache to retreat. She could already picture herself with a spoon and a goblet and blue flakes, in a chamber that night, although she wanted to believe that she was not compelled to heat the mixture; that she might push the scale away, calming her mind with gentler pursuits. Although she tried to focus on the route ahead, her gaze roved over Luca's figure several times, and she told herself that it was at least a distraction from the pain.

"You seem troubled, my lady," Derset said, when they had passed out of the town's southern arch.

There was nothing sharply elegant in Derset's manner—it was like soft cotton, where Luca's was dark silk. That was not to say that it lacked appeal.

"A panther, poison, a silent sword, a wolf, and now a bear. It would be strange if I were not troubled, my lord."

"That bear looked monstrously fierce. I am only glad you were taking the air when the animal came upon us—though you must not wander off like that again." He glanced at her. "There are queer and dangerous folk afoot after dark."

More dangerous than you know, and more queer than you imagine. "How did the guards trap the bear, in the end?"

"They chased it into the trees, but they couldn't get a clear shot. The animal moved deeper and deeper. I saw Prince Fontaine lay out all the fruit in his supplies in a trail and leave a starfruit at the end. The bear took so long trying to open the prickled skin of the fruit that the archers managed to sneak up behind it and get a clear shot. It was busy clawing."

Lysande shook her head. "He is a clever man, Prince Fontaine."

"Cleverness, my sister once said, is a good quality in a banker, a merchant, or a captain. Not a rival." Derset smiled.

Are Fontaine and I rivals? It was a curious thought. To be a rival, one had to be a contender for something. Her eye fell on Luca's tightly laced doublet and took in the sleek fit of his riding trousers, which scarcely creased as he rose, surveying the land from his horse.

The fields had opened up to broad expanses of grass and meadows of pink-and-purple flowers, which the Rhimese used to make perfume, and Lysande caught sight of a group of red deer standing on a hillock amongst the blooms. She recognized the rare breed of Rhimese hinds that Haxley had written of. At night, she sketched a picture of them, making notes on hoof shape and coat splotching, distracting herself from the thought of a certain city-ruler's profile.

Another day at good pace; another night with plenty of wine and song, and thankfully, no bears. By the time they began to slow on the third day, the rolling fields of the Rhimese countryside had given way to a group of gentle ridges. The riders stopped on the last one.

Straddling the banks of a river—the same thread of blue that had run through Castelaggio—a city of white stone sprawled before them, all the way to a pair of hills. White buildings jostled with more white buildings: so many dwellings sat side by side that they seemed to be looking at a carpet of ivory. Rhime offered none of the capital's broad roads forming intersections with ruler-sharp lanes; its streets wound and wove across each other, disappearing suddenly into cul-de-sacs or forking out into paths that divided again and again. Lysande felt the presence of concealed things, a city within a city, as she looked out.

"A domain with a black flag, built of white stone," She halted her mare on the edge of the grass, examining the straggling buildings. "I suppose that's the castle?"

"Where?"

"The hump on the skyline—the round building by the river?"

Derset followed her finger. "No, my lady. That is the Academy. The best minds of Rhime work under that domed roof." He pointed. "Go higher still."

Tilting her head, she saw it, then: a cluster of white towers perched on the very top of the left peak, surrounded by a moat and grounds. The fortress rose in solid stone, its buildings jutting, a garden of white teeth above the city. Even from many miles away, she could see that someone had sculpted two cobras onto the front wall, so that the snakes loomed over the doors, their ruby eyes staring down. The enormity of the statues and the vivid hue of the jewels made Lysande feel that they were alive.

"What do you think, my lady?"

"The castle is . . . unique." She shook her head. "Any attacker would have to climb the slope into the arms of waiting guards. The cobras, though, are surely a little imposing . . ."

Shouts rang behind them, cutting through the morning air. Lysande turned to find the group parting and a woman in black armor pushing through, hurrying toward Luca.

"Riders, Your Highness," she called. "Three of them."

"Our people?" Luca said.

"I think so. It looks like Captain Targia with two of her guards."

Luca rode after her, the sun throwing gold-dust into his black hair, illuminating his profile, and Lysande followed him through the group of riders. Three figures in the distance were galloping over the ridges. They wore the Rhimese doublet with the red cobra on black, and she made out a burly woman flanked by two smaller soldiers, all carrying bows.

Luca stared for a long moment. "That is not Targia," he said, slowly.

"Your Highness?"

But his expression was changing quickly from curiosity to alarm. "Get down! Everybody, get down! Guards—nock your arrows! Now!"

The arrows came so swiftly that Lysande heard them before she saw them—the whizz of shafts in the air, so close that they almost grazed her ears, and the rhythm of arrow-tips landing. Horses reared and shrieked around her. Two of the Rhimese women to her right toppled from their mounts, their bodies trampled at once by panicked hooves; the riders came at them steadily, firing so fast that their bows seemed an extension of their arms.

A youth in fur fell from his horse with shafts lodged in his stomach and his head. Further along, a man slumped forward, the feathered end of an arrow protruding from his neck. A red flower sprouted from his wound, thickening by the second.

Lysande's limbs seemed to have lost the ability to move. She forced herself to push her horse through to the Axiumites, yelling at them to take out their daggers. She saw Luca draw an arrow from his quiver and line it up in one smooth movement, his black hair splayed.

"Now!" he cried, as he let the arrow fly. "Shoot for their necks!"

The riders were keeping up a steady volley as they rode, but Luca's arrow caught the man on the left straight in his heart. He fell, half-entangled in the saddle, his corpse dragged along the ground until his horse was stopped by a Valderran guard. Lysande threw a dagger at the nearest rider. She noticed, as if through a haze, that Litany had whipped out a dagger of her own and was throwing it, but she scarcely understood it.

"Fire, you snakes!" a Rhimese woman shouted. "They're getting close!"

A steady rain of Rhimese arrows struck the remaining two riders, finding the arms and chests and eventually the necks—but not before the attackers had killed several guards, a Pyrrhan attendant, and a Lyrian noblewoman. Lysande felt her hands trembling. The southern woman lay on her back in the dirt, her gold cloak daubed with blood. Everywhere, people were shouting, and someone began to sob behind Lysande, a hoarse, terrible sound. She swung down from her horse and pushed her way to where the city-rulers were standing.

"Bring me the bodies," Luca said, wiping a patch of mangled flesh on his shoulder without so much as wincing. "Freste, Malsante—I want those dead riders over here now."

The dark-haired lord and the blonde noblewoman lifted up the corpses of the attackers. Other guards brought their fallen to their leaders; Lysande hurried through the group, checking left and right. She was relieved to find all the Axium Guards unscathed. The friends of the Lyrian woman wept as they clustered around her body, some of them dropping to their knees, unaware of the dirt streaking their gold trousers, their cries directed to ears that no longer heard. For the first time, she saw, the northerners and southerners were not bickering— though several of them seemed to notice the hug that Dante gave Jale, an embrace infused with relief, and they exchanged dark looks.

Luca dismounted and scrutinized the faces of the dead attackers.

"Hired killers," he said. "These dogs have seen many fights."

All three faces were marred by old wounds, and the man who had been dragged by his horse was missing a chunk of flesh under the eyebrow. Even beneath the fresh blood, the bruises on his jaw stood out.

Lysande watched closely as Luca unfastened the black cloaks and checked them for hidden flaps. Thrusting his hands into the

trouser-pockets, he rummaged in the first two soldiers' without suc-
cess. On reaching into the big woman's left pocket, he smiled.

The purse that he pulled out was no cheap trinket. Even before the
cadres were emptied from it, Lysande could tell that much. The stitching gleamed a rich bronze, and the leather looked soft in his hand; as
he turned it over in his long fingers, she caught sight of an animal's
head with whorl-like horns, embroidered beneath a pair of blades.

"A ram under two crossed swords." Luca's face had settled back
into a cold, unreadable façade. "Usually, Bastillonian travelers want to
drink my wine, not my blood."

The looks on the others' faces were grave. Even Jale did not venture
a remark; the death of the Lyrian woman seemed to have put a stop to
his usual banter.

"See that all the wounds are bandaged, and take the group through
to Rhime," Luca told Malsante. "Ravelli," he said to a slender lord,
"with me. Bring ten of our best guards."

"You're riding ahead?" Jale said.

"I'm afraid so."

You must stop the Council from doing anything hasty. Three's words
sounded in Lysande's mind. She moved quickly to Luca's side, not caring about blocking the others from hearing her, not caring about the
stares she attracted. Her fingers took hold of his, interlacing with them.
"Listen, Fontaine, you won't do anything without the Council, will
you?"

He had frozen. It took a moment to recognize this and ink it down
in her mind to be analyzed later, before she let go of his hand. Luca
climbed onto his horse and looked down at her, holding her gaze.

"I only mean to invite the Bastillonian ambassador to dinner this
evening," he said, with the little half-smile that made his mouth so
dangerous. "We owe her a proper welcome at Castle Sapere."

He rode on without waiting for a reply, a party of guards falling
into place behind him, their doublets turning to specks of black as they
flew down the slope and toward the city, moving faster and faster, until the horses entered the gates. Lysande watched them disappear into
the tangle of streets, her boots mottled with red, her frown engraved.

Eight

The corridors of Castle Sapere snaked around like the emblem of their prince and disappeared into sealed wings. Arches and domed rooves curved everywhere, staircases boasted banisters shaped like cobras, and courtyards burbled with water. White ceilings glittered with onyx patterns featuring designs of a coiled adder, a bull, a double-headed wasp, and an eagle perched on a battlement, with a family name etched below each emblem.

The artistry drew Lysande's eye as she was led through the castle, passing clusters of Rhimese nobles, yet she also spied devices among the decorations. She noted the appearance of a timepiece with eight hands, three pendulums, and a set of pipes that puffed out wisps of white smoke. In one tower she observed a water mill generating light, and in a glass case, she glimpsed an enormous bow whose placard proclaimed that it could fire arrows over a mile. The western courtyard boasted a tubular object pointed at the sky, which she deduced was for observing the stars' paths; yet even this could not compete with the fountain that flowed without an apparent source, cascading jewel-bright water over tiers of marble.

She kneeled beside it, on the pretense of adjusting her boot. Taking a long time to examine the circulation of the water, she reflected: one had to consider the possibility, the very real possibility, of a self-enclosed system. Certainly, the lack of proximity to a spring suggested great technical skill. Yet something beyond the design of the fountain heated her imagination: a certain luster where the glare of the sun met the pearlescent sheen of the foamless water, refracting and entering her mind, setting off thoughts of ancient beasts and their scales. She had the sense that she could spend all day in this spot.

These were Luca Fontaine's inventions, an attendant declared. She wanted to linger and write an appraisal of them, to see if she could understand the man whose eyes cut through her, and whose remarks stung in a manner that was ruthlessly precise, but on the afternoon of their arrival, the shadow of the attack hung over the Council and the castle. Whispers came to her ears from the groups of people in black and red velvet, couched in alcoves. Some were leaning against statues or sitting with their feet propped on antique chests, others leaning over their wheeled chairs, all conversing with an ease that the Axium nobility typically reserved for the most intimate of friends. The word *Bastillonians* drifted to her more than once.

The Council delivered their wounded to a physician, and Lysande was escorted through the castle by the blonde woman from Luca's entourage, Carletta Freste, who possessed as much warmth as one of the denser northern glaciers. Lysande attempted to dally by a cabinet full of first-century scrolls and found herself ushered into the glass dome of the Observatory.

"We can spare more Pyrrhans for the western border," she heard Cassia say. The city-rulers stood around a table of rich night-oak, poring over a map. The Irriqi pointed her finger at a line. "And the Rhimese will send more guards to the eastern border." Had Cassia swelled inside her armor, or was it something intangible that she gave off whenever she issued an order: the impression of an enlarged capacity, a natural skill in command? As Cassia's finger jumped to the north, Lysande edged around to join her. "The rest of you secure the east. Each takes one segment of the border. If that's all right with you, Councillor."

Lysande nodded. Reinforcing the borders, she felt, would be on everyone's mind, given what they had just endured. Yet Three's warning still rang in her ears: they might inflame tensions with their neighbors even while protecting themselves. If any group was likely to forfeit their trade benefits out of sheer, petty anger, it was the Bastillonians; histories had furnished her with enough examples.

"Each to their own territory," Dante said. "I like the sound of it."

"Our enemies will like the sound of it even more." Luca stood at the

end of the table, his hands resting on the surface. He had not clenched
his jaw, but everywhere a tightness manifested, from the set of his
shoulders to the fault line of his smile; yet his wound, now bandaged
and hidden beneath a fresh doublet, did not appear to trouble him. "The
Bastillonians don't divide their legions by weapon. Ferago's women
and men will have longswords, smallswords, bows, hook-swords and
daggers, all in one force. If we don't want to be diced like a Pyrrhan
fruitcake, we'll need the same."

Lysande let the words wash over her. The city-rulers had all grown
up commanding captains and training armies, while she had spent her
days reading and writing in the royal library. Of course, she had combed
through military accounts and letters to prepare for her treatise, but
when it came to actually taking charge of defense . . . she could not proj-
ect the confidence that Sarelin had always thrown out with a single
booming word. But she could pretend. If you wanted to dance with rulers, you had to move like your legs could not falter, surely. She had practiced her tone and posture, nights ago, with the gold quill in her hand.

"Your Highnesses," she said, butting in when Dante drew breath,
"I think we should weigh the cultural difficulties of joining our forces,
as well as the military advantages."

All of them turned to her with surprised expressions. When the
moment had passed, Cassia nodded, a fierce smile spreading on her
face. "Of course, my friend."

This was the Irriqi of Pyrrha, Lysande reminded herself: the woman
who tamed leopards; the woman who took precise steps in the Arena
and then flung her sword into an opponent's thigh. There was no reason
to be pleased that Cassia approved of her contribution, when a friendship with Cassia would be a risky gamble. No rational basis for it. So
why did her whole body straighten when Cassia addressed her that way?

As the others debated the benefits of combining armies and the dangers of Lyrians and Valderrans working together, she studied their faces.
Luca argued his case with perfect clarity, yet every so often she saw him
glance away, out of the glass walls. She observed a furtive manner to his
behavior as he drew something out of his pocket. A small stone, black
and smooth, caught the light. He rotated it slowly, rubbing the surface.

She watched his fingers turning it over: fingers of such length and dexterity that they could play a harp or load a crossbow, their skin lacking the scars from brawls.

"Fine!" Cassia declared, throwing her hands up. "If you all refuse to give in, a combined army it is! So long as my friend does not object."

Again, that word: the thrusting of endearment into the open, so different from a soft-voiced mark of praise; and again, she wondered what purpose Cassia had in applying it to her. Her thoughts ran to strokes of a quill, to letters composed for the White Queen.

After a moment, Lysande realized that all eyes had fixed on her. "I have no objection to combining my guards with yours. But I stipulate that Captain Hartleigh retains control of my guards." There. Imperative. She could do it when she tried.

"Let's deal with the ram scum first. Pay Bastillón back threefold," Dante said.

"Come now, Dalgëreth, where's your sense of hospitality? I have invited the Bastillonian ambassador to dine, and I intend to serve her well," Luca said.

"I don't mean to be abrupt, but—"

"—a Valderran childhood naturally curtails eloquence. Say no more, Dalgëreth. I'm sure that you'll join me this evening at six o'clock in the Room of Accord."

Dante looked across at Jale, but the prince made no motion. Dante sighed.

"Excellent." Luca smiled as he walked from the room. The stone had disappeared from his hand. The guards at the door marched out after him. Lysande noted the cheer of the whole procession, which sat in contrast to the cold fury she had glimpsed on Luca's face in the pass.

"Well," Jale said, "He seems in a good mood, for once."

Yes, Lysande thought, watching the last of the guards turn the corner at the end of the corridor. That was the worrying part.

The Councillors were kept so busy throughout the afternoon that Lysande found herself bustled from one entertainment to another without even a chance to see her suite. A quartet of Rhimese musicians serenaded them with the "Serpent's Triumph" in the gardens; the guards put on a show of archery, shooting to split arrows in targets (which were no longer comprised of "a selection of conspirators," Freste remarked, a little wistfully), and they were taken to a luncheon of cold delicacies served with fig wine, at which Luca did not make an appearance. Lysande felt another twinge of guilt as Litany tasted each of the dishes. There was a conversation she still needed to have, about rare poisons and how Litany had come to understand them; about sharp daggers and how Litany had come to wield one; and about an increase in Litany's wage, with everything it symbolized. It was easy to tell yourself that you were postponing a confrontation, far easier than admitting that you were afraid of it.

As she ate, she was beset by thoughts of the Shadows, but she gave up trying to strategize when the crushing pains in her head and throat returned.

It was not as if she had just taken scale. Did she not have a right to expect that the dosage would stop affecting her over time—or was she to bear this load of pain always, like a wincing pack mule? Surely, you could become truly liberated from the consequences of a very modest, a very occasional indulgence?

If you persisted through the discomfort, it stood to reason that the power of the sensation would gradually diminish. So she had been telling herself as she continued to dose her body and mind. The justification had begun to take on a familiar ring, like a written fact.

Searching for fresh air, she left the hall and set off for the maze garden at the back of the grounds. A circle of brambles shielded the maze from passersby. Within it a latticework of hedges spread out, green walls twisting in all directions, curving into nooks; some of the enclaves offered seats shaped like figure eights, while others held high-backed chairs or stone benches. This was somewhere she could imagine herself coming alone, with a quill and paper. The prince of Rhime probably felt similarly, and she tried not to dwell on an image of Luca walking here on a summer night, his doublet unlaced, his skin soft as tracing paper, streaked with silver light.

Wonderful, she told herself. We're almost at war, and I'm thinking about Luca Fontaine unclothed. A spurt of pain at her temple stopped the thought, threatening to crush her mind.

She took one of the torches from beside the gate and wandered in. Somewhere a bird was singing, its melody deeper than the thrushes she had heard in Axium Forest. Although she passed several lighted spots, she continued into the heart of the maze until she could see nothing but the hedge around her.

Sarelin had traveled to Rhime and had grumbled to her about being surrounded by scheming easterners for three days. Had Sarelin come to this garden, too? Sturdy boots might have compacted the ground where she walked. Why was it that the memory of Sarelin's gait and her open smile hurt more than that of her body on the bier? A number of quotations came flying from the shelves of her mind—Cicera on the "exquisite pain" of loss, the scholar Mavotto on tricks of memory, the physician Maqbani on the observed effects of grief on the body. None of them seemed to help.

She walked on, trying to dispel the head pains, which refused to dull, and she had nearly reached the center of the maze-garden when a voice penetrated the wall on her left.

"You must know that you are beyond compare in the Three Lands."

Squinting through a gap in the hedge, she spied Dante in the nook on the other side, pacing and holding a sword which sparkled under the light of his torch. "The sun may shine brilliantly above us all, but in my heart you shine brighter. And so I ask you to do me the honor of accepting my hand and making Valderos richer for your warmth and light. No . . ." Dante ran a finger over the sword's edge, "greater for your warmth and light . . . more powerful for your warmth and light . . ."

He seemed to be addressing the air, and he was frowning as he rehearsed his speech. The urge to laugh overcame Lysande. She suppressed it with effort. The softness to his words pleased her as much as it surprised her; she had never imagined Dante capable of proposing anything except a duel. There was something about hearing courtly speech emanating from such a solemn man that seemed inherently wonderful, reminding her of the day she had seen Sarelin hold a small butterfly in her hand.

The sword drew her gaze. Lettering stood out on its blade, words in the Old Valderran alphabet carved into the steel and painted a gleaming silver. The engraving was too small for Lysande to make out, however. Above the blade, small jewels of many colors covered the guard and grip, a giant diamond taking pride of place in the pommel; this, combined with the sword's strange size, being between a long-sword and smallsword in length, led her to guess that it might be more of a decorative item than a weapon.

One of Dante's fingers tapped a large engraving near the tip of the sword, an image which looked like an ice-bear. The animal's distinctive horns leaped out against the steel, small and curved.

"For you see," Dante began, "I have searched the depths of my sentiments, combed through the silt-bed of my life, and I find no love like the one I hold for you—a devotion of such fury, I do not know myself— you burn . . . no, that is not what I mean to say . . . you make *me* burn . . ."

She did not think that Dante would take kindly to being observed, and after a pause to muse on the proposal, she hurried on, striding through the maze until she reached one of the little nooks. She managed to cast Dante's quest for a metaphor from her thoughts.

Hard proof. She sank down onto a bench. Proof was what Three had advised her to find—but without looking at the coin-purse, how could she tell whether the riders had really been in the pay of Bastillón? If she could only get hold of the purse, she could analyze it. Her word would be nothing without evidence. That would mean asking Luca to help her, and she did not feel pleased about that.

The way he had looked at her as he bowed in the Arena . . . there had been a dark beauty in the way he moved, the sun tinting his black hair. She pictured him shifting and coiling. He wore his beauty with perfect scorn. That smooth skin cloaked an edge which she felt sure was capable of inflicting damage before an enemy even knew they had been struck.

Perhaps there was another way. She sat there, considering tricks to slip past the Rhimese guards, stemming a tide of anxieties until the air grew cold. When she returned to the castle, she found Carletta Freste by the doors with arms folded. The onyx patterns glittered in the glow of the torches. As Freste opened the door to her suite, the light glanced off a snake's-head key.

"Prince Fontaine has honored you with his finest chambers, Councillor," the noblewoman said, nudging the door open with her foot.

"The monarchs of Elira have always stayed in the Painter's Suite. Queen Brettelin Brey declared it a divine harmony of colors, though she chose to eschew our banquet."

The enormous room that greeted her boasted four dark oak cabinets. Silk curtains billowed and swelled, the blood-red material dancing in and out of the torchlight. A fountain flowed by the bay windows, the water trickling slowly over three small bowls. One of Luca's inventions, she guessed, as no pipes adjoined the fountain on either side.

"Thank you," she said to Freste, who was still hovering in the doorway as if she expected Lysande to bow. "You may convey my thanks to Prince Fontaine, too."

She stood by the black stone fountain for a moment, dipping her fingers. Three's warning still nagged at her. Yet she could not help but appreciate the colors and materials of her lodgings as she inspected the writing desk and the cabinets, running her fingers over the rubies inlaid in the wood.

On a small table she found a vial of pale, orange liquid, resting on a note:

> *This is a Rhimese concoction. For special maladies.*
> *It even works on Axiumites.*
> *Take one sip when you feel a headache coming on.*
>
> *L.F.*

She frowned. For all that he could act out of cold anger, Luca seemed far too astute when it came to her own needs. Of course, she could always ask Litany to taste the medicine later . . .

She thought of Luca leaning over to whisper in her ear, his voice soft against the roar of the Arena.

Why give the best rooms to me? As she stepped into the bathroom, notes of Rhimese flowers overwhelmed her—it was as if someone had picked a bloom from every field south of Castelaggio and compounded them. More extraordinary than the perfumed air, however, was a set of three luminous frescoes on the bathroom wall.

A ray of sun pierced the window and threw the colors of the

paintings into relief: pastel pinks and blues mingled against a background of midnight black, and each frame showed a youthful figure, a
man on either side and a woman in the middle, all staring ahead.

Did Fontaine want to show this off to me?

All three wore gotas, the long robes from before the Conquest
which tied over one shoulder. Lysande bent down to read the plaque
beneath the frames.

"*The Maturation*, by Vitelongelo."

She observed that the man on the left wore a golden triangle on his
forehead, while the woman's triangle sat at her throat, and the last
man's decorated the middle of his chest. She could see no indication as
to why. Three's triangle pendant leaped out in her memory; could it be
that these portraits had some link to the ancient symbology of magic?
Or was she looking at an artistic use of geometry?

At least it was clear why the suite had earned its fame. Rhimese
artists were rarely a match for the southern virtuosos, Sarelin had said,
but Lysande thought that Vitelongelo could stand beside the best of
the Lyrians for style. She stared at the painting on the right, absorbing
the silkiness of the man's skin, the soft throat that reminded her all too
clearly of—

"Is there anything I can do?"

Litany was standing in the doorway, clutching a pile of towels.

They stared at each other for some time, before Lysande said, "You
do much more than I expected." Litany flushed. "But I will take a bath,
if it's no trouble," Lysande added.

She wrote a letter to Three while the water was being poured, and
Cursora had only just flapped away from the window when Litany
returned. Her attendant padded over the floor, taking Lysande's arm
and leading her to the bathroom with a grip that was becoming familiar. The silence between them felt new.

"Where did you learn to identify nightroot, venom of the blue adder, and lover's poison?" Lysande said at last.

"In Axium Palace."

That opened up more questions than it answered. "I remember the
first time you dressed me, you ran one of your nails under my sleeve.
It was a test. I didn't realize it at the time. But I think you also learned

to use balm of red death in Axium Palace—did you not?" She had pieced that together on the ride. It had taken some time to work out. The method of identifying poison residue through the application of a reactive toxin was not a subject she usually considered, while guiding her horse past fields and copses.

"The balm enables—"

"I know quite well what it does," Lysande said. "If I'd been found guilty, you'd have already carried out the sentence."

They faced each other. Litany, she thought, knew when to speak.

"If you were blameless," Litany said, "there would be nothing for the balm to respond to. With no catalyst, no transformation: so the physicians say."

"I believe that maxim refers to healing."

"Councillor Prior, if I have given offense in the process of tending to the realm—"

"So tell me, then. What makes you feel you have the right to tend to anything, without my permission?" Lysande heard her words clatter and felt the reverberation of their edges throughout the room. The girl avoided her gaze for a moment.

"There's a shaded garden," Litany said. "At the back of the pear orchard in the palace grounds. When I was a child, I used to play there with another stable-hand's daughter, using sticks to fight. My mother wasn't aware that Queen Sarelin went walking in the pear orchard. I think the queen must have been watching me for some time before she approached, because she called me the silent girl. She said I never grunted or made a noise when I struck."

Lysande could picture the back of the pear orchard, and the wooden poles that the servants used to fence. Often, at dusk, she had heard the clack of blows there.

"My mother had kept secrets for Queen Sarelin. I saw her tending to the horses just before the Bastillonian ambassador was thrown from her mount—an inconvenient accident, the easterners said. The ambassador was detained in Axium while she healed, long enough for Queen Sarelin to thrash out a new trade deal on silver with her. And another time, quite by chance, you know, my mother had been feeding the horses just before the Rhimese envoy was due to leave. It was said that the Rhimese mare took ill on the journey—simply would not budge. The envoy had to walk quite some way to find a farm with a horse to sell. All her doves had escaped from her luggage, too: an unfastened cage. The news of Queen Sarelin's new tax reached Rhime the morning after it reached the other cities. My mother had had a feeling it would."

"Your mother must have been a very prescient woman."

"Prediction comes naturally to some people." Litany glanced down, but as she looked up again, her surreptitious grin did not escape Lysande. "But it was her close-lipped nature Queen Sarelin cared for."

Of course: the skills of the populace were worth recognizing, when they proved useful for Sarelin's purposes. Lysande wondered what deprivations a stable-hand would have endured if she were not recruited by the royal household. Then there was the matter of elevation to private service, of a personal retainer in mettles . . . and an allowance of fine leather boots and warm coats. "You said that Sarelin approached you in the garden."

Litany drew a breath. "The queen asked me if I'd like to keep secrets too. Once I could taste and identify poisons, she had me practice other things. Fetching objects. Throwing daggers. Fighting, not only with a sword but with my hands. The kind of things they don't teach silverbloods."

"Your grip . . ." Lysande recalled the grasp of that slender hand, unyielding, in the moment when they had both reached for the bottle. "Never mind. I suppose Sarelin was very confident in your mother's loyalty."

"I used to think it was about loyalty." Litany's voice had dropped. "Then I saw how other poor children did not prosper like myself. My mother taught me that's what it means to be an Axiumite: *everything in its place*. Even the humblest of us have a duty, a purpose."

"But?" Lysande said.

Litany frowned. "I beg your pardon, Signore—Lysande?"

"I can hear a *but* circling in the air."

The frown dispersed, and Litany met her gaze at last. "Queen Sarelin gave me a duty, right enough. But for all that we talk of duty and higher purpose, I think that it is in doing that we find meaning. Unlike others, I had the chance to find out what I could do. For me, that isn't sewing clothes or shoeing horses." She folded her arms. "I know how to steal and never be caught. I can follow someone without the person ever knowing I am there. Striking down an attacker in the darkness: that is purpose, to me. There's something tangible in using your hands for taking things, and for stopping . . ."

Neither of them finished the sentence.

"Going through my chests, before the ride . . . you weren't just trying to sneak in jewelry, were you?" Lysande said.

"I needed to see if you were Queen Sarelin's murderer."

Lysande could not blame the girl. After all, had she not asked herself the same question—who profits by the queen's death?

"I might still be a traitor," she said, watching Litany's reaction.

"When you invited me into the box, at the tournament . . . there was no food to taste. You included me, and not so I could serve you." Litany held her head high. "One who kills to rule does not wish to draw others closer to them, least of all a commoner, from whom they can gain nothing. Besides, I saw you crying. After you visited Queen Sarelin's tomb."

The soft voice and the timid air. That's part of it. Isn't it? You are the veiled blade; the defender that nobody suspects. Lysande motioned to Litany to begin unlacing her doublet. She watched her clothes fall onto the tiles. "So many secrets, swirling around. I am beginning to learn why Sarelin used to curse so often."

"I can leave, if you wish." Litany mixed a teaspoon of salts into the bath water.

"No. I would have you tell me what you want from me."

"Want?"

"Do you expect me to believe you are a paragon of selfless striving, Litany?"

Litany looked at Lysande and something hovered over them, something bright and mutable: something that no silverblood would ever need. She felt it, even though she could not see it. When you had refashioned your identity, you were drawn to others who had done the same, however diverse their circumstances.

"I suppose," Litany said, carefully, "I want to continue my employment, using my particular skills, with the stimulus of interesting work—of missions that require discretion."

"Good. Very good."

"And half my wage again, on top of the usual amount, each month."

"A quarter again," Lysande said.

"A third."

"Deft bargaining. I accept. In these times, I may have use of deftness." Lysande climbed into the bath. "There is a coin-purse with a ram's head under two crossed swords stitched on it in bronze thread. It will probably be in Prince Fontaine's chambers." She looked into Litany's eyes. "You have until dinner."

Litany gave a nod and retreated from the suite. Lysande marked how quietly her personal attendant moved.

How old was Litany? Eighteen? Nineteen? Perhaps a higher figure? More of a young woman than a girl, in truth, but she had always thought of her as a girl because she was small and quiet. A needle was always small. A pinch of nightroot, sprinkled into a dish, could be quiet.

Lysande was left to soak in silence, gazing at the *Maturation*. There was a weariness in her bones that might have been soothed by a handsome poet, or perhaps by a musician with elegant hands. She well remembered the flute player that Sarelin had teased her about, two months ago, when she had lingered in the palace kitchen after midnight, she and the woman talking of the carving of instruments and the positioning of lips on the flute for optimal performance, until they made their way back through the corridors, Lysande steering the woman by the arm. The two of them had tangled themselves in Lysande's bed, eventually finding other uses for lips.

And there had been the jeweler from Bastillón, whose smile had flashed at her during an envoy's visit to present an ornamental sword: the man had danced with Lysande after dinner until she whispered words less polished than his creations, which he did not dislike. That night, the jeweler had wandered into her rooms and submitted to her touch, letting Lysande wrestle him onto the bed. His pupils had widened as she pinned his arms down and waited, counted to two, three, four goddesses in her head, until he smiled.

Now, for the most fleeting of moments after she dressed, Lysande hesitated, thinking of Luca again—what it would be like to take control of those long fingers, or to walk him back against the wall. A sliver of instinct told her that he would like it if she approached—a sliver that had nestled in her head since they first met—and yet she wondered if he would allow himself to show his sentiments. It would be exciting to see him struggle to hide his reaction. But was she deluding herself, conjuring pieces of enthusiasm to please her imagination?

She reached toward the blanket-covered chest.

If you don't know its properties, she heard Charice saying, *you should exercise caution. Or invest in a good physician's service.* She pushed Charice's countenance away.

One and a half spoonfuls.

It was not much, if you were practiced in ignoring some of the effects.

When the glow had filled the room and faded away, her heartbeat had slowed, and her forehead had cooled at last, a determination spread through her. Her mind seized on a link between the purse and the way the riders had charged. There were loose threads, she thought, but she needed time to knit them together. The thing that had shifted inside her told her that she could do this; hesitation would not be necessary.

The old chant of the Axium orphanage still reverberated, but she was beginning to learn how to push it away with fewer qualms: it was becoming less and less desirable to *restrain, constrain, subdue* as she worked to knot and retie alliances.

The corridors began to fill with attendants as the hour drew closer to six, and the preparations were accompanied by covert looks and shielded giggles among the staff. Tapestries were being cleaned in the Room of Accord, producing a swell of excitement. Derset offered to divert Lysande's anxieties about the dinner with a walk through the greenhouse. Strolling through a panoply of rare plants, she searched the archives of her mind and passed swordlace vines with barely a glance.

Returning to the Painter's Suite, she examined the doublet laid out on the bed, taking in the embroidered sleeves and the intricately laced neck. Even looking at the garment felt uncomfortable. She pulled on a pair of trousers, buttoned up a plain doublet, and added an emerald necklace, and was about to begin plaiting and pinning her hair when the doors burst open.

"I hope I'm just in time, Signore—Lysande. The Rhimese attendants were swarming."

Lysande took in the flush in Litany's cheeks. Without hesitation, the girl drew a soft brown object from the pocket of her doublet.

"It's this one, isn't it? Prince Fontaine'd put it underneath his pillow."

Lysande closed the door and took the object from Litany.

"I had to wait for the guard to change. I borrowed a uniform from the staff closet."

"Sun and stars." Lysande held the purse up. The ram under crossed swords gleamed on the side. "'Just in time' is about right. Litany—you treasure—this is brilliant!"

"My service is yours now. That is—if we understand each other." The girl colored a deep vermillion.

"I believe we do. And as for the increase in wage . . . we will draw up terms tonight."

Lysande studied the leather for a moment, going through everything she had read about foreign materials. There had to be a clue, somewhere. If the White Queen had set this up, there must be a way to show it; every object told a story. Her body was humming, and she was aware of her excitement, again, at the opportunity to solve a puzzle.

"Let's examine this together," she said. "I wonder if the leather—"

But a knock at the door cut her off. They looked at each other.

"Councillor Prior," Carletta Freste shouted, "The ambassador has arrived. Prince Fontaine requests your presence in two minutes."

Lysande nodded to her attendant, slipping the purse into her pocket. The girl bobbed her head in return. No meekness, now; only a practiced calm and a readiness to move.

The Room of Accord could only be reached by a long and narrow hall adorned with an even longer and narrower black carpet, along whose sides Rhimese guards raised their ceremonial rapiers, the blades meeting in the middle to form a steel roof. Lysande, Litany, and Freste passed below the weapons. A dark-haired man, whom Lysande recognized from the ride as Lord Malsante, stepped forward to meet them. "What kept you, Freste?" he hissed.

"Councillor Prior required more time to prepare." Freste cast an acid glance at Lysande. "How's the sea inside?"

"Choppy at best."

Lysande was still trying to analyze the purse, turning the object over in her pocket. They passed into a room where Cassia, Dante, and Jale stood in front of a table, flanked by various advisors and guards, while Luca leaned on a chair, wearing the black crown of Rhime. Its three ovular rubies sent out beams of light as he looked up, cutting across the floor. His gaze passed over Lysande, traveling upward from the toes of her boots and coming to rest on her unpinned hair, and Lysande knew that he must be noticing the tress of deathstruck silver: the bunch of glittering strands that she had not had time to cover. She fought the urge to flush.

Litany broke off from her with a whisper of "Call on me, if you need it," uttered low.

"Is anything amiss, my lady?" Derset whispered, as Lysande joined him.

"Nothing I can be certain of." She fingered the purse.

Derset laid a hand on her arm. The touch felt gentle, almost like that flute player's. His hand stayed there for the best part of a minute while Lysande gathered her composure.

As if Derset could read her agitation, he remained silent until she gave a soft squeeze with her fingers. He nodded toward a plum sitting atop a bowl of fruit on a stand. "Do you know Chasseur's *Ode on a Summer Night*, my lady?"

"The poem about eating a plum?"

"The same."

Lysande looked at Derset. He was aware, she was sure, of the mood in the room, and yet he had chosen to steal a moment with her amidst the tension, nonetheless. "Devour it slowly—that wine-colored bliss of queens—when the moon stripes your chamber with silver spells," she recited.

"My schoolmaster seemed to think the poem immodest." Derset smiled.

"Well, Chasseur was a Lyrian. She'd tasted a few plums."

They shared a quick glance. She saw something more than amusement in Derset's eyes. "Like all good Axiumites, I was raised to hold back from ripened fruit," he replied.

"Still, there is something to be said for a ripe plum on a summer night."

She pretended that she did not notice his stare at her remark; the interest blossoming in his eyes. What she felt about the difference between Derset and Luca had not changed. But Luca was a prince of Rhime, and Derset . . . well, right now, Derset's hand was exceedingly warm. She moved her arm out of his reach, yet kept the gap between them narrow.

Derset said nothing about her deathstruck hair. If he had noticed the exposed lock, he had enough manners not to inquire about it.

Taking a look around the room, Lysande saw that the table's silverware had been polished, its candles set in clusters of four in respect of the goddesses, and that the other Councillors were dressed lavishly. Across the room, Chidney nodded to her. Lysande's eyes traveled down her captain's armor until she realized what was missing. "Has everyone forgotten their weapons?"

"Prince Fontaine's orders," Derset said. "No swords are to be brought in."

Lysande was about to ask why anyone had agreed to such a demand, but she saw something shine in the candlelight. Scenes of rapier attacks pursued images of beheadings through her mind, all the more vivid because she remembered stories of Rhimese ambushes where blood flowed like thick wine; but it was only thread, she realized. Pairs of tapestries had been hung on each wall, their silver cloth showing scenes of conciliation embroidered in fine thread: Princess Isadonna Salla led her supporters through the capital, ending her war with Axium; Prince Cesaro Ursini knelt to lay an unlit torch at the feet of a Bastillonian king, on the banks of the Cordonna; and unlike in the paintings in Axium, she saw no symbols of power over elementals inserted, no chimeras with wings folded and horns broken beneath leaders' boots.

There was something about that shining thread that triggered an idea, though.

Before she could develop it, a blast of trumpets rang out and a herald strode in. "Her Excellency Gabrella Merez, most honored representative of King Ramon Ferago of Bastillón, greets the Council of Elira with the full embrace of the east."

The guards tensed. Lysande could not help thinking that if Raden were here, he would have made some remark about easterners' embraces and the scars they left. She had to focus on the purse. The truth behind the attack was so close, she could almost taste it . . .

She felt the room stiffen as the herald peeled off. A party of women and men in pale blue robes filed in, flowing into two groups and leaving a corridor, their silver hair attracting a murmur of interest. The Bastillonian attendants who followed wore their golden hair tied back, and each walked with eyes cast down, behind a silver-haired dignitary.

The Elirans began to whisper to one another, and Lysande heard the word *servants* passed around the room. Her stomach knotted. Gold and silver had only been paired as metals, until now.

The Bastillonian ambassador marched in, assessing her surroundings. She stopped in front of Luca and regarded him down the length of her nose, like a woman inspecting a polished dish—and judging by her expression, she had found a few specks of rust. Gabrella Merez was not a formidable woman in size or build, but she sported an aquiline nose, tufted brows that sat low, and a chin that seemed to have been shaped with a chisel for the sole purpose of appearing in profile. She gave the rest of the Council a proud but not unamiable glance.

"King Ferago sends his warm regards to the Council of Elira," she said, in a voice that lacked any warmth. "And his heir Princess Mariana, his wife Persephora, and his sons Dion and Anton also wish you well in your new arrangement. May the Three Lands flourish."

Lysande was aware of her guards watching from all sides.

"May the Three Lands flourish," Luca said, inclining his head. "Elira always rejoices to welcome the citizens of Bastillón—silver-haired or gold."

Merez ran a hand over the chain on her chest, stroking a ram's-head pendant. "Strength without swords. To enforce your city's motto upon guests and friends alike seems irregular," she said.

"You will forgive our eccentricities in Rhime. No swords are permitted in the Room of Accord. The only blades here are drawn metaphorically."

Merez nodded curtly. Staff hurried in with miniature fountains that flowed with water, red wine, and Castelaggian amber, and set down platters of wheat knots in a rich tomato paste, sliced olive-bread, and wheels of the colorful baked dish that had been served at the Axium banquet. Lysande observed the Bastillonians whispering among themselves. As soon as the plates had been set down, the guests and Elirans were ushered to their seats, Merez taking precedence at the head of the table. Lysande tried to picture the purse, turning it over again in her mind, searching for the answer that felt so tantalizingly close.

The conversation flowed steadily. Once the ambassador's tongue loosened, she complimented Luca on the wine, and the Rhimese attendants began to serve. It became clear to Lysande that Merez was studying her hosts.

"We have never met, I think, Princess Ahl-Hafir," the ambassador said, as one of the attendants cut her a slice of olive bread.

"We take the term Irriqi, in Pyrrha," Cassia said.

"Oh yes, you jungle people have your own ways," Merez said, with a chuckle. "My king read of your defeat of the Qamaras with some interest. An innovative siege, I hear. Word is you lost your husband in it."

One of Merez's hands reached toward her robe, Lysande noticed. She would have taken it for a commonplace movement, except that the ambassador did not adjust the garment, only let her fingers hover near it. Merez was like a bee; if you took your eye off her, you might look down to find a sting lodged in your thumb.

"I've lost three husbands in total," Cassia said. "Some call it careless." She picked up an unraveled wheat knot, twirling it around her fork.

The stares of the Pyrrhan guards seemed to convince the ambassador that the topic had been exhausted, for Merez turned away and looked straight into Dante's face. Her hand seemed to hover toward her robe for half a heartbeat.

"His Majesty's first son, Anton Ferago, thinks much of your exploits in the Ice-Rose Campaign a few years ago, First Sword," Merez said. "Strange that a man with your military glory should not have been able to find himself a partner in marriage."

Dante's stare in reply would have made a lesser woman quail. When Merez turned her gaze to Jale and produced her first true smile, the whole table relaxed.

"Now, here is someone we have all heard much about in Belága," Merez said. "We look forward to welcoming you into the bosom of our capital, Prince Chamboise."

"Oh, topping," Jale replied, through a mouthful of olive bread. "I daresay Princess Ferago is full of vigor and spirit, as everyone tells me."

"And Councillor Prior. I shall not ask *you* about marriage. It is said in Bastillón that a scholar's only wedding is to her books."

Lysande had been following the conversation and watching Merez's hands with such interest that she had almost forgotten she was a member of the Council. Suddenly, she was aware again. "Books are rewarding companions, Your Excellency," she said. "A good poem can speak to your soul in ways that people rarely do, and every relationship with a book is a mutual one. Stories are never forced to accept your affection."

Merez gave a shrug, but opposite her, Lysande saw Jale glance up, and thought that her words had stuck their target.

"I appreciate your enthusiasm, Councillor. Yet I know little of your family name," Merez said. The ambassador's smile was a little too innocent. Derset's mouth opened slightly, and Lysande was aware that several of her guards were stepping closer to the table, fists clenched.

"I was found during the White War as a child, Your Excellency. I suppose that makes me lucky: to be found, not burned. Not lucky enough to have rescuers who thought up an original name, though." She produced another smile. "In Elira, children abandoned in the War were named by those who saved them, and my rescuers must have been Valderran, for they named me after an Old Valderran word. *Prior.* It means fire. The blaze that destroyed the carpenter's shop where I was found left my skin untouched, you see, but it turned this lock a rare kind of silver. Queen Sarelin called it deathstruck." She paused, while the Bastillonian dignitaries peered down the table, gazing at her tress of silver hair as if it were an artifact from the Periclean States. "As for my first name . . . its meaning eludes even a palace scholar."

The whole table was listening—Councillors, Bastillonians, and their advisors were staring at her. She noticed Cassia's interest as the Irriqi peered at her hair, the wrinkle in Dante's forehead as he surveyed the deathstruck lock, and Jale's pleased yet curious look, as if he did not quite know what to make of it. Only Luca did not share in the reaction.

They had all seen her hair when she walked into the room, of course. Her difference had not been named, then. Now that it had been spoken aloud, people on every side looked at her without restraint, and she had the sudden feeling that it would have been better to stay silent.

"When you say that you were found . . . surely it is rare for noble children to be lost?"

"Councillor Prior is not from a noble family, Your Excellency," Luca said, putting down his goblet. "She is an orphan. Perhaps you are not aware that at my table, it is considered ill manners to inquire into the breeding of my guests."

"I assure you, I meant no—"

Luca's body, as he rose, reminded Lysande of a tightly coiled spring.

"But since I like to be a generous host, I shall do you the favor of finishing. Councillor Prior is an orphan, as I say, and I am a bastard son: my father was Prince Marcio Sovrano, and my mother was a Lyrian attendant who scrubbed his floors. I took her name because she was worth more than the fool who parted her from her child." He smiled coldly. "So now that you have the blood of every member of the Council noted, you can give your king a full report. Would you like a goblet of water, Your Excellency?"

Merez had opened her mouth to speak, but she paused. "Yes," she managed, "I will take a goblet."

Luca's gaze cracked like a whip across the ambassador's face. The conversation turned to safer subjects, with the help of Derset and Hussir, Cassia's advisor: the heavy snows north of Valderos, the last Sapphire Ball in Lyria, where two hundred dancers had twirled, and a tournament at which Sarelin had fought, unhorsing ten nobles. Lysande's eyes sought out Luca every so often, but he did not look her way, sipping his wine and talking to the guests.

Gabrella Merez spoke rarely after the first exchange. Lysande saw her stare at Luca from time to time. She did not like the look Merez exchanged with one of her dignitaries; it was sharper than Sarelin's battle sword, and far dirtier. A silence eventually descended on the table. One of the Bastillonian noblemen, goblet in hand, broke it.

"King Ferago was gratified to receive your *Astratto Formulas*, Your

Highness. He delights in receiving documents signed by the author—he displays them prominently in the royal library."

Luca nodded briefly. Lysande had the sensation of having missed a stair while going down a flight, and flailing for a moment. How had she not known that Luca was the creator of the same formulas she had wrangled with late at night in the camp? Those thorny strings of numbers . . .

"Yes," Merez put in, "though some might consider scribbling away at equations an odd occupation for a prince."

Luca waved a hand at the wall on his right. Lysande glanced at him, and even as she righted her reeling mind, she appreciated the dangerous politeness of his expression and the tightly enunciated words that followed. "There are eight tapestries in this room, Your Excellency. What is eight multiplied by four?"

"Thirty-two."

"Precisely. And that is an equation that no one here can fail to appreciate. Thirty-two bows are very effective in a small space."

Luca clapped his hands twice. The tapestries on the walls fell to the floor. It took only one pull to bring each one tumbling down, Lysande saw, thanks to the guards standing behind them, holding silver bows. The Rhimese soldiers packed into the hollowed-out cavities in the walls nocked their arrows, four behind each tapestry, all pointing their weapons at the table.

"Sun and stars," she breathed.

She saw Dante shake his head, his mouth half-open. Several of the silver-haired Bastillonians rose and exclaimed in their own tongue. Lysande signaled to her own guards to wait—Chidney had already taken two paces forward. Her own body seemed to be moving automatically, running on some unknown fuel. Be a leader, she implored herself. Think of something. Now.

Two of the Valderrans rushed to Dante's side, shielding him. Litany stared at Lysande, silently entreating her for direction.

"The women and men aiming at you right now are Rhimese archers, trained from childhood," Luca said. "They can hit a target so small that it can fit on the end of my thumb. You might take down one or two of them if you had a crossbow, but unarmed . . . well, even your pure-bred heart would be pierced in seconds if you did anything to displease me."

Merez reached into her robe, drew out a vial, and sloshed the black liquid inside as she held it up. Little prisms in the fluid shone from several feet away. Lysande smelled burned cinnamon rising through the air and felt the precise terror of recognition.

"My reply," Merez said with a sneer, "might seem small, but what it lacks in quantity, it makes up for in efficacy."

Matching the combination of the shade, the prisms, and the smell to a paragraph in Montefizzi's manual, Lysande felt her stomach turn to water, and wondered how anyone could hold Bastillonian python venom with such equanimity.

Two Rhimese archers stepped toward Merez. Lysande's shoulders tightened.

If the contents of that vial were anything like she'd read . . . who could forget that the worst assassination of the Steelsong Era had taken place in Belága with a bottle of python venom? The description of the hapless Eliran envoy, daubed with poison by an eastern agent, screaming in pain for so long that the Bastillonian queen shot him out of mercy, had kept Lysande awake the night after she read it.

Several of the Bastillonian dignitaries pulled out their own vials, including one very close to her left elbow. Lysande tried not to look. She saw Dante shift his position, moving between Jale and the nearest Bastillonian, his forehead riven with lines of concern. Both Chidney and Litany slipped over to Lysande, shooting swift glances at each other as they took their positions side by side.

"Now that we're equally armed, perhaps you will tell me the meaning of this," Merez said. Luca rose slowly. He regarded the ambassador, a dark fire burning behind his eyes. He did not acknowledge the Bastillonian who was brandishing a vial next to his cheek, and Lysande had to admire his sheer gall, even as she felt her hands clench.

"You know perfectly well why you are here," Luca said. "But for the sake of clarity, let me remind you. Three riders attacked our Council yesterday on the Scarlet Road. Their bulging purse bore the Bastillonian crest. Did you hope to eliminate the leaders of the five cities in one swoop, or would killing half of us have been good enough? You must understand, I am devoted to detail." Luca gave a flick of one finger, like a trainer signaling to wolfhounds, and the archers tightened their bowstrings. "Confess—admit your king's plan. Tell me why he tried to assassinate our Council. Or all thirty-two of these arrows will come down upon you, and believe me, they hunger for places to rest."

As she listened, Lysande tried to concentrate on the image of the purse in her memory.

"There was no such attack," Merez said, looking from one Councillor to another.

"Some of my people died," Dante put in. "Are you telling me I imagined the arrows in their necks?"

"Perhaps there was an attack—I could not say—but if there was, it was not ordered by us." Merez bristled. "You, on the other hand, have been scheming against the greatest monarch in the Three Lands, like your ancestors have for centuries, holding back steel and tempero, keeping us in need. Do you think we missed your foray at sea, too? We see your base tricks." She sloshed the venom again. Three of the Rhimese guards who had been moving tentatively toward her arm took steps backward. Lysande's mind spun and spun, turning over the object in her pocket.

"You claim *we* attacked *you*?" Jale said, not bothering to stifle his laugh.

"Poorly, too. That ship you sank failed to harm us. And as for the incident two days ago, in court . . . we did away with your assassin before she could throw her filthy darts."

None of it made sense. There had to be a pattern somewhere, though . . . if she could just piece it together and find the reason . . . she wanted to wrangle with this problem, and she was sure, somehow, that she could do it.

"Every word out of your mouth is a lie," Cassia said. "The warriors of Pyrrha make flutes out of liars' bones. Do you want to become our new instruments?"

"I could say the same to you, Irriqi. Where is this purse you speak of?"

Luca looked across at Freste, who was standing by the door. The noblewoman shook her head. "You were told to bring it," Luca hissed.

"Your Highness, I looked everywhere."

Lysande rose to her feet and cleared her throat. She had the feeling that this was her only chance, before the situation turned ugly, but she had not expected such a heavy silence to fall.

"I have the purse," she said, pulling it from her pocket.

At any other time, the look on Luca's face would have warned her to keep silent. It reminded her of an adder about to descend on an unguarded nest. But as the light from the candelabra fell on the stitching, a wave of realization washed through Lysande. The clouding of her mind, the frustration of the last day: it all disappeared.

"I believe we have all been tricked, Your Highnesses," she said.

"If you're concocting some scheme, Councillor—" Luca said.

"Observe the sheen of this stitching—the iridescent gleam." She was struggling to keep her voice cool, like a noble's; the words tumbled out, chasing her thoughts. "You cannot see it in shadow, but in full light, it shines silver."

Luca stared at it for a moment. "Diamond thread."

"Exactly." She lifted the purse high so that the whole room could see. "Named as such because it is as rare as diamonds, and as strong, once sewn. You only find it in the west and the Periclean States. A blend of fibers used in Royamese ornamental tailoring, almost impossible to obtain in Elira or Bastillón for over a century, thanks to the restrictions on western trade." Her hand was trembling. "What are the chances of Bastillonian assassins carrying purses stitched with a foreign thread?"

"What are you suggesting, Councillor Prior?" Merez said.

"The attack—it was set up carefully, the riders paid handsomely. But there were three of them, pitted against a large, armed party." She looked at Luca, then across to Dante, Jale, and Cassia. All of them had seen the cadres tumbling from that purse. She hoped, desperately, that they would not see her interjection as the raving of an upstart; that they would absorb her words. "Someone needed them to attack five city-rulers in a situation against great odds, where they would surely be killed. That purse was meant to be found."

She saw Dante and Jale share a look, and Cassia raised a hand to her chin, stroking it. She could feel her own pulse drumming in her chest.

"The stitching," Merez said, lowering her vial slightly. "On the assassin's cloak, back home. The crest of Elira. The reports mentioned that it was unusually bright in the torchlight. But I didn't think . . ."

"The Royamese have stayed out of our affairs for centuries," Luca said. "Why would their Sovereign want to make us cut each other up?"

Lysande forced herself to listen to her breathing. In. Out. She could do this, surely, if she could face a group of elementals in the middle of the night.

"It's not Royam I'd look to," she said, enunciating her words. "If the Royamese wanted to take our land, they would have done so in the war, when our forces were spread thin. They didn't risk upsetting the trade lines and suffering a huge dip in their own supplies. No, someone else wants to start a war." She drew a breath. "And that someone wants Elira to believe that Bastillón is trying to attack us. If Mea Tacitus can sow enmity between the Three Lands, she can persuade Bastillón to let her travel to our border. We all know she is coming for our throne." She lowered the purse. "This sprinkling of lies across land and sea, it is part of her strategy. Ask yourself—when Bastillón cuts all ties with Elira, who profits? Do we? Do the Royamese, if the scales of trade slide left and right, up and down, unpredictably weighted? Or is it the White Queen who profits from our discord?"

There was a pause as they all looked at each other, and Merez's expression wavered between realization and indignation. Lysande guessed that she was struggling to keep the veneer up as she exchanged glances with her advisors. Her own veneer was barely in place. It did not help that she locked eyes with Luca and caught the interest flashing in his eyes, flaring for the merest of moments, before he veiled it.

"This farce of a dinner is an insult," Merez said, corking the python venom. "His Majesty will demand an apology for your insolence, Fontaine."

Luca fingered the rim of his goblet lazily. "Let him."

"Do you scoff at the king of the east, signore?" Merez drew herself up, bristling, and rose from her chair. "By Fortituda, bastard, you go too far—I will await your apology at the ambassadorial manor, for these insults and for your foul thefts at sea. And if I do not have it within a week, I will see that His Majesty knows about this little charade. Come!"

This last was addressed to the Bastillonian dignitaries, who rose and followed her out. The golden-haired servants trailed behind them in silence, and Lysande felt a surge of hot rage at this separation, this delineation between people of different appearances, so well-ordered that it spoke of long practice. Luca waved to his archers, and the women and men around the walls lowered their bows.

Lysande's knees trembled, and she realized that she had been holding the tension in her body. She gripped the table, breathing in.

"Wonderful," Luca said, wheeling on her. "You really smoothed things out."

"Councillor Prior was trying to save us from a war," Cassia said. "Cool your ears."

If Luca had resembled a snake, she could now see the points of his fangs.

"Negotiation only works from a position of strength. You must have an advantage before you begin, or you need not bother at all." He stepped toward her. Those long fingers almost brushed hers. "Thanks to Councillor Prior's help, we have just ceded the only advantage we had."

Luca turned and walked from the room, and the archers followed him. Freste whispered something to Malsante and they stared at Lysande, then hurried after their prince.

"Don't mind Fontaine, my friend." Cassia reached over to pat her on the back. "You just saved two realms from starting something that would end with a levy of blood."

Lysande's smile did not convince Derset or Litany, she was sure, but it seemed to suffice for Cassia, Dante, and Jale. They did not know Axiumite manners well enough to tell when she was shaken. She bowed and walked out.

Her hand was trembling again. Luca Fontaine was arrogant—she certainly had no reason to care for *his* opinion, when he lacked all courtesy. It was not at all rational.

She shut the door when she reached her suite, took a torch, and walked to the fireplace, trying to keep her fingers steady. She was used to holding them over fire, thanks to Sarelin's makeshift meals on hunts in the forest, and she lit a blaze. The sight of the flames crackling away soothed her nerves, though not enough that she resisted thinking of Luca's taut neck and his half-smile.

There was no question of holding back the urge this time. The jar called to her. Two spoonfuls of flakes fell easily into the vial, her sugar and water mixing in and dissolving, sending up a smell that was part pipe-smoke, part worn book covers, part spiced wine. Lysande ignored the reverberation of Charice's warning in her head. It was hard to say how long she sat there, watching the flames and drinking, enduring the hammer-on-anvil blows of her heartbeat and feeling the glow of the scale. The golden calm spread through the room, melting away some of her frustration, while her insides felt the wrath of the dose, crackling like the fire, and she felt her own weakness in yielding to numbness. She did not care. All her problems rolled away.

At last, a knock came at her door and Litany called out her name.

"You did well," she said, letting her attendant through.

"I was awaiting your command, all that time, in the room." Litany almost hid her disappointment.

"And I gave none. So you did well."

The girl bowed, though she still looked a little crestfallen. "I will have those terms ready for you by dawn," Lysande added. Another knock sounded, and Lysande heard the distinctive cough of an Axiumite trying to be discreet.

"Your advisor, Councillor." Lysande recognized Chidney's deep voice.

She dismissed Litany, and as the girl slipped out, she saw her brush against Chidney's arm in the doorway. The captain stared at Litany as if she were a finely decorated cake. Lysande had never seen Chidney betray her emotions so openly before, not even when the captain had received a silver brooch from Sarelin during the last jubilee.

It seemed to take a moment for Chidney to remember where she was. When Lysande cleared her throat loudly, the captain bowed and exited at last, with only a tiny glance at Litany.

Derset entered with an apology.

"You did the right thing, you know," he said, when the door had closed. The fire crackled, throwing a few sparks into the air.

Neither of them needed to speak. She rose, and they warmed their hands on the rail of the fireplace together. A long time passed before Lysande looked at him.

"Nobody likes to feel the sting of a rebuke, but it will not help to blame yourself, when Prince Fontaine seized a chance to humiliate Bastillón," Derset said. "That, and I suspect he does not often experience the feeling of being outsmarted."

"Perhaps he was right to slice me open in front of everyone."

"You have been a Councillor for all of a month. Yet I see in you a rare skill, a rare wisdom, and that which is rarer still—a hunger. For something bigger than yourself."

Another pause; the flames burned brighter. The future beckoned her, quarrels to come, blades drawn, an army marching on Elira. No matter who the Umbra was, their silent campaign could only end in blood, and Luca Fontaine would not mind if her blood was part of the price. In a second, as if a shard of spectral light had split open a chamber inside her, she knew that she had been right to accept Three's request.

It was not a change of heart stealing through her. This was simply the revelation of something that had been dormant in her since that day in the rose garden.

Derset was right. She was hungry for this. The stones in her body had not sunk her, but strengthened her core. She wanted something beyond the Councillor's staff, something like sliding tactos pieces into the middle of a board, but it had not seemed possible until she had halted the executions with clear words.

Oh, you could tell yourself that you were doing it for the people and you could turn the pages of tracts in your mind, making all the connections to justify it, but it was still a ladder, stretching up into mist, the top obscured. *For the people*—the other side of that coin was *the people for oneself.*

Glancing across at Derset, she saw that he was leaning toward her, as if he would like to reach out. She remembered how he had placed a hand on her shoulder in the Arena.

"It's queer, but no matter how long I sit here, I feel cold," she said.

It was the first excuse that popped into her head. But he did not laugh: only took her hand between his and rubbed it, until his touch slowed and he looked up to catch her gaze.

For a long moment they looked at each other. The fire had turned his cheeks golden. Everything about him seemed to shine. They had crossed some kind of porous border, and Lysande knew it, but she did not wish to stop. She took his wrist within her grasp, feeling his pulse, the flutter of it like moth's wings under her thumb.

She exerted a slight pressure. Derset's eyes approved, and she reached for one of the buttons of his robe. Why was it that buttons were always coming undone until you sought to undo them, and then they resisted you with the effort of a legion repulsing invaders? He helped her finish and removed the tunic underneath; below that, a collar of black cloth wrapped around his neck; the design was simple, but it was still easy for Lysande to recognize the skinbrace of old Axium custom, the symbol of obedience to the goddesses and to tradition. Only someone like Derset could wear that without an air of excessive piety. She enjoyed the look of it, and traced the band of fabric with her finger, following the line around his neck.

"Just once," she said.

Derset brought his face close to hers. "I could offer to carry your sword. But somehow, I don't think it's what you want."

A spark leaped high in the fire, burning scarlet in the air, then falling again.

"I thought you only had devotion for Sarelin," Lysande said.

"But then I saw you stand up in front of that room of dignitaries and explain diamond thread to them. That's when I realized: there's more than one kind of queen."

She knew that he was not going to take the lead. She kissed him, pressing her upper body firmly against his, and forgot about her irritation while they embraced. In truth, she had guessed that he would not move forcefully—anyone who had loved Sarelin could not desire command in a liaison—but she was surprised by how gently he followed her movements. It was as if he was still feeling his way into her affection.

In the center of Rhimese territory it was good to hold an Axiumite, to let skin brush skin in a way that was not too forthright nor presumptuous. She did not know if this moment was real or an illusion of the night. Perhaps it did not matter. Derset was older, and yet Lysande's mind had flourished beyond her years; Sarelin had once quipped that she was born at the age of twenty, and the gap between herself and Derset felt more like a hairline crevice than a breach, their fingers moving to a slow rhythm, as if they were two quills tracing the same lines.

There were different types of physical attraction, the notorious and widely-restricted royal manual, the *Mirror for a Monarch,* explained. A leader should choose according to her needs and temperament each day. One type of attraction was passion, of the highest ardor, that nearly consumed the lovers. A second type was infatuation, more a whim than a life-changing desire, an excitement of the flesh but not the soul. But a third type could be described as comfort, where a woman or man did not so much set one's heart racing as ease its pains, like the crackle of a fire in winter.

Lysande did not flatter herself to be a queen. Sarelin had given her a copy of the manual on her eighteenth gift-day, though, with the stipulation that she study it, and she did not have any trouble recognizing the reaction that Derset's touch provoked. She held his hand against her thigh, and he stroked the spot where she placed it.

Lying with him was not unlike eating a slice of warm dragoncherry cake in the evening; it was a balm to the prickling in her sentiments that Luca's rebuke had caused; and it was, she felt, what Sarelin would have advised. Comfort had always seemed the most elusive of the three types, until now.

A face hovered at the edge of her vision, and she looked up at a pointed countenance, into shadowed eyes that fixed her with disapproval. Charice shook her head. As Charice's mist-wreathed shape dissolved, Lysande almost called her name, but was there a point to it? Even in imaginary form, Charice would not commit to her. She lowered her gaze.

Derset lay beneath her, almost entirely revealed, and the skinbrace added a certain flavor, she thought, running a fingertip over it again. After she had undressed, she mapped his body with her hands, touching the skin and feeling where it was soft, where there were firm regions. She took his hand under hers and guided it over her waist. They fell into a rhythm as easily as a timepiece marks the seconds.

"Lysande," Derset whispered, when she pushed her fingers through his hair. She twined her fingers around a lock and tugged it, just slightly.

"Yes?"

A smashing noise, like the breaking of a glass bottle, rang out in the courtyard below, followed by the distinctive sound of drunken giggling, and voices bounced off the walls of the corridor, along with footsteps. Lysande clamped her hand over Derset's mouth. She moved out of instinct, conscious of the guards passing close to the suite, and when the tramping of boots in the castle faded eventually, she realized that Derset was looking at her with a changed expression. It felt good to take control of his body with a single movement. Was it supposed to feel good? She was fairly certain that she should let go and apologize, yet the look in his eyes suggested that he wished for no such thing.

He watched her for a moment more. With deliberate restraint, she leaned against his chest and loosened her grip on his mouth.

"You were going to tell me something," she whispered.

"Nothing important." He did not move a muscle.

"One moment it is a cacophony out there; the next, complete silence."

"I think you like silence from a lover."

They looked at each other for longer again.

"And if I do?" Lysande said.

Derset pushed himself up slowly, very slowly, until their noses almost touched. "I like what you like."

He did not attempt to touch her but studied her face, as if perusing a book. She could have resisted the urge to kiss him—perhaps she should have resisted it—but what would be the point? His mouth was so warm and soft and close, so ready to be consumed.

Once their breathing rose and fell for the last time, they lay facing the canopy of the bed in a stillness that seemed to wrap them up. Lysande thought that it was the most pleasant and gentle rest she had ever shared on a bedsheet. Derset was the first to rise. He pulled on his tunic and rebuttoned his robe, lifted up the long, double-woven riding-cloak that Litany had draped over a chair, and stepped around beside her.

"You must let me warm you, my lady."

The formal term had slipped out quickly, but it was changed now, even though the words were the same: something had shifted in the meaning of *my lady.*

She stood while he wrapped the garment around her, tying it under her neck. When it was secure, his hands moved up to her shoulders and lingered there, a soft pressure, just enough for her to feel the touch.

"You need not endure a chill," he said. "Queen Sarelin's fire lives on in you. You are her Councillor, appointed on her authority, as a seal presses into wax and marks it out. And if I may make so bold as to say it . . . you are my leader, marked or not." He dropped his gaze, and she knew that they had slipped back into their roles and ranks, but again she noticed that something had altered slightly, a stitch unpicked in the middle of a seam. *I like what you like.*

They stood there in silence, watching the fire burn. When she reached at last to remove his hands from her shoulders, he moved to her side, then pulled a small pouch from his pocket and held it out.

"For some time, I have been waiting for this moment. Well—that is not to say—I did not expect—but I hoped to find a time when we were alone."

The string came undone on her first attempt. Inside she found a silver chain, so thin and light that it could have been liquid, shining in a way that no overly polished merchant's jewelry shone. She held it up, watching it shimmer in the light.

"It's beautifully crafted."

"It was given to me when I took up my post as an advisor. Queen Sarelin wanted to wish me luck on my first journey to Bastillón." He looked at the chain, and his gaze rested on it sadly as well as fondly. "I like to think it has continued to be a light for me after her own light went out."

A lump rose in Lysande's throat and lodged there. "You should not pass on such a precious gift to me."

"On the contrary, my lady. It is because it is precious that I give it to you."

He lowered his head slowly and touched his lips to the back of her palm, keeping his eyes locked on hers, as if to make sure that the gesture was allowed. She returned the kiss on the back of his own hand, then flipped it over to kiss the soft middle of his palm. Once she drew away, he moved back too, bowing and walking out, with the presence of mind to close the door. She lingered by the fire, watching the blaze in silence.

After the embers had died, she drew the chain around her neck, looking at the thin silver in the glass.

Sarelin's necklace was still fastened against her skin when she slept; the landscape of her mind rolled out in a pure black, unadulterated by dreams of triangles, until a twinge of pain cut through it. The agony had moved to her throat.

Once she was truly awake, she thought about speaking to Sarelin, her words falling softly into the half-dark, telling the queen what had just transpired that day, focusing away from the pain. But the thought of Sarelin was painful, too. Her stiff figure among the rose petals; the way she had treated elementals; everything Lysande had come to confront; it was a whole lot of twisted-up things together, and Lysande did not know which of the queen's two bodies she would be addressing, the woman or the state.

She picked up her quill and unrolled her notes for *An Ideal Queen*. The material on the five cities and the foreign lands was growing. Paragraphs and lists welcomed her.

After some minutes had passed, a tapping sound broke her reverie. She padded to the window and took in the bruise-purple dawn that had engulfed the clouds, then opened the sill, gazing out toward the eastern border, to where Elira became Bastillón by the stroke of a paintbrush. In the quiet of the morning, she mused on the mutability of lines, on borders and their dissolution, before scooping up the speckled dove that was waiting with an envelope in its beak.

Nine

Carriages and carts emerged from nowhere. One moment, the stream of traffic contained riders and people; the next, a vehicle was pushing through, leaving everyone to disperse and congregate again. Women and men stepped out from arches, talking at a pace that might have served in an auction house. The buildings Lysande passed seemed to have been jumbled together; apartments rubbed shoulders with bakeries, and apothecaries flourished beside jewelers. As she led the Axiumites through the streets, she caught the stares from doorways. The Rhimese regarded her with neither resentment nor disapproval.

I am a spectacle, she realized, when a father carrying a basket of eggs pointed her out to his son, nearly dropping his cargo. And not just any spectacle, either, but one with a dozen Axium Guards trailing.

At least her hair was plaited and pinned tightly again, with the deathstruck tress covered by her red strands, the hard glitter of the silver now entirely concealed.

"Shall we keep going, my lady?" Derset said, in a tone that rang with a little too much formality.

A ring of spectators surrounded a pair of duelers in the next square, while hawkers wove through and offered quince pies and bags of spiced almonds. It would have been easy for Lysande to forget her purpose if there had not been a bag of mettles tucked in her pocket. The softness of the leather under her fingers took her back to the steward counting out her travel allowance, while she sat, transfixed by the fine exterior of the three bags, unaware that once the coins had stopped clinking, she had not performed the expected way: that she had gawped instead of snatching up the money with disdain.

"I have a load here, my lord. It needs to be lightened." Two-thirds of the silver she awarded to the guards, with the remaining money split between Derset and Litany. Derset tried to refuse, but she insisted that he buy himself a new chain: it was not at all improper for a leader to bestow a present upon her advisor, she told herself, meeting his eyes and finding a subtle glow there.

Litany was less reticent, accepting the coins and slipping alongside Lysande. They did not need to speak of the agreement on wages they had made before leaving the castle, nor to confirm again that Litany's income was officially guaranteed. Some threads only needed to be woven once.

Lysande took Chidney, as well as her attendant, and set off from the center of Rhime, moving south. The map she had received at dawn led her through a tangle of alleyways to a narrow lane, the only sign of a prayer-house being a series of little steps leading up to a pair of doors. She mounted the first stair.

Inside, she found a small but ornate hall, lit by candles. Sculptures of princesses and princes of Rhime dotted the prayer-house on stands, yet it was the scene on the domed ceiling that made her breath hitch.

Someone had decorated every inch of the plaster to create a vista of the goddess Cognita emerging from the sea before a crowd of admiring humans. The faces stared down at Lysande, in such detail that she could discern the scars and blemishes on their cheeks. Earrings and buttons and laces shone; tiny figures in the corners of the ceiling had been edged with gold, and seemed to stand out from the roof. Cognita clutched her staff, her emerald robe billowing as her chariot broke through the waves. Another goddess, Lysande thought, would have forced the people to bow or commanded their respect, but Cognita, without demanding, drew them to her.

Her gaze passed down and she gave a slight gasp. A chimera presided over a clutch of eggs in the bottom right of the scene, its tail arcing up above its wings, the pointed tip almost touching one of its horns; to see it painted alongside one of the goddesses was . . . heresy,

if you liked the language of priests, or treason, if you preferred monarchs' speech. Whatever the case, she felt that the painter was being
unfairly Rhimese.

She thought she heard a footfall. No . . . it had been Chidney's
cough. "Guard the doors, if you please. Take Litany with you," she
said.

If Chidney looked surprised at being paired so closely with the attendant, she also looked like a child whose gift-day wish had been
granted, her grin new-minted. Lysande had a feeling that the barrier
between the two women might eventually dissolve, and filed it away as
a matter for future thought.

She made her way slowly past the scattering of worshippers and
stopped at the purging-booth. Slipping into the visitor's half of the
box, she slid the door shut.

"Welcome, child," a woman's voice said.

"Thank you, Your Beatitude." A grate separated her from the priest.
How long had it been since her last trip to Discuss? Long enough that
Sarelin would have shaken her head and tutted.

"Those who enter must admit their sins. Have you murdered or
stolen, child? Have you eaten of animal flesh or acted out of cruelty or
greed? Harmed your friends or kinsfolk? Or neglected to defend the
realm in a time of need?"

"No, Your Beatitude."

"Then I fail to discern what brings you here today." The woman
spoke slowly. "The Discussion is a serious matter, my child; the goddesses speak through their ministers."

"Then I must confess . . . that I have come to speak with he who is
more than two and less than four."

There was a click from the grate. The partition opened and Lysande
gazed into the face of the woman who had greeted her at the farmhouse. Six's hooded robe concealed most of the twisted flesh that disfigured her cheek. "Good timing, Councillor."

They exited through the back of the purging-booth, moving to the
very end of the prayer-house, where a triptych of scenes lined a nook
in the wall. Lysande followed Six to the paintings, which showed the
warrior Titarch's journey through the desert to Lyria, rendered in the

same high style as the ceiling. She had little time to appreciate the brushwork, for a footfall sounded, unmistakable, from somewhere in the balcony level above.

Lysande turned to face a blur, her attendant crossing the floor, leaping over a rope, and landing beside her. Chidney ran, too, hurrying to her side. The three of them stared upward.

"Was that—" Chidney began.

Her next word was swallowed by a shout from Six, and the whistle of something as it plummeted through the air, landing with a smash on the prayer-house floor.

Lysande jumped back, dodging a piece of marble. Shards bounced and flew. Chidney clutched her boot, hopping, still reaching to push Lysande clear of the rubble, and Litany leaped to block her from another falling piece. Although the bust had splintered upon impact, Lysande spotted a piece of a familiar face fashioned from stone, and she recognized, with a dull and disembodied feeling, that seconds ago it had been a bust of Sarelin.

Litany sprinted to the stairs that led up to the balcony. Chidney rushed after her. The captain drew her sword and was halfway up the stairs behind Litany before Six's scream cut through the air, just louder than the shouts of the worshippers as they ran from the prayer-house. Was it the warning shout that prompted Chidney to swerve, smacking into the stair-rail, or was it blind luck? Whatever the reason, the next bust missed the captain by an inch. She gasped her relief.

"Get down, Councillor!" Litany called.

A second replica of Sarelin in black marble struck the floor and rolled, fire licking its sides and lighting up the dim prayer-house. Fire on marble, Lysande thought. But how? The bust rolled further and set a fallen scarf aflame before Litany ran over and stomped the fire out. "Fortituda's fist—excuse me—but take cover!"

Lysande could see no figure on the balcony. Surely, she should be solving this: working a trick with strategy. She looked at Six. The woman shook her head. "Let the two of them handle it," she said. "This is our opportunity."

I think that it is in doing that we find meaning, Litany had said. The girl was moving so fast across the floor that a captain of the Axium

Guards could not keep up. Catching Six's gaze, she felt certain that Six was noticing Litany's talents now.

Chidney made up for her shock, bounding up the stairs, following Litany and drawing level with her, the two of them walking side by side. They advanced along the balcony from which the busts had fallen, weaving around sculptures and tiers of candelabra, the big woman and the smaller one moving to a wordless music of their own.

Lysande called to Litany that she would return, clapping her hand to her chest as her attendant turned. The girl clapped her hand to her chest in return. The salute came as they had agreed, with easy confidence, and Lysande tried to let her doubts be assuaged.

Six turned again to the triptych and pushed the side of the frame on the right. It swung backward. "Quickly, Councillor, if you please," she said, pushing the painting further back.

Lysande had to stoop to get through the gap, and the top of her head bumped the stone, sending tendrils of pain through her skull. She moved into a cavity, where two tables waited. At the far one she made out a familiar white-haired figure, sitting with a candle and dishes of honey-glazed nuts, herb-bread, and stiff-crusted cheese before him. The goblets on either side of his bottle brimmed with wine. "Fine work, my dear."

"Someone just set a bust on fire out there and hurled it at me," Lysande said.

"Congratulations."

"*Congratulations?*" She stared at Three.

"To make someone want to eliminate you that much, you must have taken a firm position on something. Now, I insist that you take a seat."

Lysande sat down slowly and took a sip of wine. Three pushed the dish of herb-bread wedges across the table. "I am confident our friends out there will deal with the problem. And we have little time—so let us examine bigger events. I expected you to make some kind of intervention in the Room of Accord. But even by our standards, you performed admirably."

Performed admirably . . . aside from angering Luca Fontaine. Apart from the sudden violence of the prayer-house, there was only room for the recent incident in Castle Sapere in her thoughts. It should not be this hard to expel Luca's cool stare and swift exit from her mind. Ever since he had sent her a black rose wrapped in summersilk, he had worked his way into her thoughts with discomfiting skill.

The rest of her was calming down, slowly, though she still wondered how Litany and Chidney were doing. When two women were throwing themselves into the paths of marble busts for the sake of her neck, she could not so easily shutter her conscience.

Three studied her. She gazed back at him. She was aware that much had changed since their meeting in the farmhouse, and not only in terms of archers stepping out from behind tapestries. Something in her had altered when she held the purse up and addressed the room; or perhaps, something had grown, a vine that had only needed an opportunity to climb.

That's when I realized: there's more than one kind of queen. The comment echoed in her mind. *Restrain, constrain, subdue* . . . the motto always returned, but its words seemed a little duller now, and Lysande had an inkling that it faded a little more with each day that she made decisions as Councillor.

A plate of pale and shining objects that she recognized as quail's eggs accompanied the bread. At Three's insistence, she peeled the shell and bit one in half, savoring the taste of the warm yolk. She noticed that a sprig of yellow heather had been pinned to Three's hat.

"Two was very pleased," Three added, taking a wedge of bread. "To dissolve the threats without an arrow being fired or venom thrown: it was the resolution we hoped for." He touched his pendant, that same movement that she had observed throughout their first encounter. Lysande watched him and realized that she was no longer on edge; that despite her best attempts to stay aloof, she was enjoying this, as she had enjoyed solving the purse.

"Some would be shaken, after a flying bust," Three said.

"I am."

"So I see. Positively trembling." He was looking at her hands, folded neatly in her lap. In a seamless movement, he rose, walked to the second table, and picked up several papers. Lysande noted the gray paper: ragged sheets, with dark veins running through them. The Periclean books in Sarelin's library had been made with paper like that. She had already guessed that Three had not risked his safety to come into Rhime merely to congratulate her.

"Thoughtful of you, to bring a present for me."

"These messages may not be easy to unwrap." Three dropped the papers onto the table. "They cling to their secrets."

Why did that make her think of Luca again? She should be harboring resentment towards him, after his callous rebuke of her in the Room of Accord, she reminded herself—she was not supposed to be thinking about what she would say to him if they found themselves alone, or how she might try to strip his secrets from him.

Setting to work on the first letter, she translated the sentences from Old Rhimese into modern Eliran, untangling the phrases; several of the lines had been coded in a rudimentary cipher and required even more unpicking, yet falling into the dance of alphabets, she forgot about the shattering bust, about everything but the strokes of ink. She managed to make out the details of an exchange. Gold was flowing across the North Sea, under the guise of shipments of grain.

"The White Queen is trading with merchants in the Periclean States," she said, putting the letter down. "Unless her spies seek to deceive us about her servant."

"There is too much of a pattern in the remarks we have overheard. Our neighbors may have turned her away, but large sums of money are being passed back and forth by her people on the other side of the North Sea. We think the Umbra coordinates it from here . . . I don't like the skill of it."

Lysande wondered if Three ever felt outmaneuvered; if he was ever afraid.

Sometimes I think the White War was a stocking-up exercise, Sarelin had said, once. Lysande could count on one hand the number of times that she had heard doubt creep into Sarelin's voice. But she remembered well the way Sarelin's countenance had darkened, that day. *I wouldn't have put it past her to slaughter all those ladies and lords just to loot their castles*, the queen had said.

"If you had walked through the docks of the Periclean States, you would know that there are many mercenaries in need of coin and food in the north," Three said. "We have heard of Pericleans being offered handsome payment—ex-soldiers, able-bodied, lacking work."

People did not become desperate on a whim. Poverty pressed its teeth to your limbs, wearing away the fat and gnawing until it had made an indentation in the bone, not ceasing until it had collected its due.

Lysande thought that something in Three's voice belied a knowledge of this. But did it matter? She had taken on this task with the intention of sharpening her thoughts, pointing her quill, and wielding words. Her mind would produce ink enough for the job.

She looked through the remaining letters without comment, but with each page, her spirits sank lower. There was no acknowledgment of the strengthening of the border guard. If anything, the Shadows' spies quoted Mea Tacitus' servants speaking in a buoyant tone.

A yearning, a familiar feeling stirred in her, and she tried to quash it. Maybe later. A dose might help . . .

"Your thoughts, Signore Prior?"

Lysande weighed the parts of the situation. "Before, she was recruiting a few mercenaries. This seems like much more." But it was not only the soldiers that worried her. Not compared to the web of fine threads behind them, which had begun to catch the light. "Let me put something to you," she said, "that has been formulating in the back of my mind. The Irriqi nearly choked on a silent sword. That weapon was first devised to be used against elementals at the Conquest."

The pause in which they looked at each other elongated.

"I have asked myself, many times, why the White Queen continues to attack us now that Sarelin is dead." The breath she took traveled down to her core. "I think she means to show us that she will do as non-magical people did to elementals. A great Surge." Take the whole realm, Lysande thought; not just the crown, nor the cities and towns, the forests and rivers and hills, but own the spirit of Elirans; take enough land to dictate the scope of their choices. "Conquest-era tactics, as you yourself pointed out when we first met. But this time, she will use our neighbors to wedge us in politically."

"Must I remind you she is shifting to the Periclean States?"

"Why assume she has given up on Royam or Bastillón?" Lysande had spent enough nights studying her charts of the war. "Returning to our neighbors with an army might place the White Queen very differently in their eyes. Force begets force." Who had said that? Volerus. And not with praise. The thought was not comforting, as quotes from ancient texts were supposed to be. "Bastillón and Royam did nothing during the White War, but it was not so in ancient times, if one reads the histories. If she intimidates them now, well . . ."

Three smiled wanly. "Tell me," he said, "why do you think Mea Tacitus calls herself the White Queen?"

"Some banned sources suggest—I mean, if I had access to them, I might know that Mea Tacitus wore a white cape into battle. When soldiers saw the spotless white cloth, they knew that no one could come close enough to stain it with blood or dirt. Everyone who saw it understood how powerful the White Queen was."

"I have always liked banned books the most." Three's smile remained faint. "Yes, the *white* part of her name has been much discussed. But why do you think she chose her particular title? Not the White Warrior, or the White Rebel . . . but the White Queen?"

She remained silent.

"It is a game of image. A White Rebel exists only in opposition to a regime, but a White Queen . . . she could take the throne and rule. When elementals hear her name, they do not picture themselves fighting and struggling. They picture themselves winning. And while a White Warrior sounds violent, bloody, perhaps even chaotic, when people hear the word *Queen* . . . they think of order, control, and calm."

"No one who remembers the White War could believe that." Sarelin had spoken of whole villages full of hacked-up corpses; the histories overflowed with blood, and she had seen the drawings that accompanied them. Never mind the legacy of children left parentless, like herself. Again, she felt the desire for scale rising in her.

"Twenty-two years have passed since the White War, my dear. Years in which elementals have not been treated kindly, by anyone's measure. They are broken and scattered. All Mea Tacitus needs to do is offer them hope."

The memory of the women and men hunched on the executioner's cart, peering up at the palace, from faces more bone than flesh, resurfaced in Lysande's head. The image had not grown softer around the edges; if anything, it had sharpened in her mind. Sarelin shouldn't have let this happen, she thought. She shouldn't have allowed the executions.

The idea had popped up from the bottom of her mind again. She had to remind herself that she was not leading only for Sarelin—that she had chosen to lead for people who were sent to bait wolves, for people who hid while their shop-fronts were smashed. People like Charice. People who liked to read histories, dream about ancient creatures, mix medicines, and keep heather sprigs. People, in short, who had all the desires and hopes and weaknesses of any others, but not the voice.

And it was not only elementals she thought of now. Members of the populace had broad shoulders on which fellow members could be lifted, and Lysande could imagine where she might be borne. She saw herself bobbing atop that tide.

Of course, though, this was about doing the right thing. There was no merit in thinking about where she, herself, might rise. Was there? Three's hand pressed something into her own, and she uncrumpled the piece of paper.

The last missive reported a single comment: *We will do this in the sunlight.*

"I suspect there may be a metaphor lurking in that sentence." Three tapped the page.

"If she kills the whole Council in public, she serves two purposes in one stroke. Terrify the realm, and show elementals that she can restore them to power."

"It is pleasing to meet someone who shares my pessimism."

Lysande took another egg and sliced it open, looking at the daub of orange against the white. The glob marked the place where life might once have been. Three let her chew in silence until she had finished, sipping his wine and watching her. It seemed, as she ran through maps and old conversations in her head, that she knew more of their attacker than most of Elira, and still not enough.

"Our border defenses are strong," she said, when she had reflected for a while. "The troops have been reordered; the last legions should be at their posts within a week. Even if the White Queen acts fast, Cassia says she wouldn't get her army past the eastern border."

"Perhaps you are right. There is something else, however."

He reached inside his cloak and, from a pocket that had been sewn into the lining, produced a coin of a dark color. The metal was bumpy under Lysande's fingers, and turning it over, she saw a crown carved in the middle, but not one that she recognized: she noted the rounded points. The band around the bottom bore a name.

"Chamsak." She remembered Sarelin repeating that word before the twenty-year jubilee of her victory, when she had bought chariots, finely wrought cages, and several exotic animals from a merchant's helper in a western cloak. Sarelin had ranted to Lysande that it took some kind of jumped-up Royamese merchant to send an envoy in her stead; Lysande felt the weight of the memory.

"I do not wonder that Signore Chamsak uses a crown as her symbol, since she rules the world of trade. This," Three took the coin from her palm and held it in his thumb and forefinger, "signifies a purchase of great importance." Lysande waited. "While I do not mean to alarm you . . . Signore Chamsak's specialty is weaponry."

She felt a chill that had nothing to do with the cool air.

"Nine took it off a man who was trading for the White Queen in the Periclean States—the man had an accident, poor thing, and got swept off his horse by a gust of wind." The casual manner with which Three said this reminded Lysande what kind of people she was dealing with. She shifted in her seat. "In his saddle bag we found this token, along with a receipt of purchase from Signore Chamsak."

From the same pocket he brought out a slip of paper. Lysande read the figure on it once. She read it again. Her lips moved silently, trying to come to terms with the amount of money written on the paper. "That has to be most—if not all—of what she owns."

Three nodded.

"If something's worth that much to the White Queen, I don't like to think what it is."

She knew that they were both thinking the same thing. A weapon of great power could turn a fight. Coupled with the unknown, possibilities bred . . . even a simple weapon could destroy chunks of an army in seconds, if that army had no idea what it was facing.

"This must be why the White Queen is confident," Three said, after a moment.

Put it all together, and you had an army, a weapon, and enough experience to assemble any number of dangerous tricks. You only needed the will to act. Fear surged, and she worked to push it down.

"It is also why Elira must not give her the chance to stage an attack. I would have you avoid a public event. Perhaps you are right about her strategy. But if she works on our neighbors in the hope of building a bigger force, she may still be aiming to deal a swift and public blow to you as soon as she can. While you attempt to smooth things over with Bastillón, keep your eyes and ears on alert for a ball or a festival—hold your Councillors back from crowds."

"Oh, I'm sure they'll jump at my order," Lysande said.

"No need to fear, Signore Prior. I have confidence in you. A good leader makes themself water, not rock."

Who was he, to throw out aphorisms? But she thought of Derset's words last night: *there's more than one kind of queen.*

Three took a long sip from his goblet. "Let us hope your jail is finished sooner rather than later. Other elementals are stirring. A little respite does not sate an appetite for liberty, but increases it."

Lysande knew better than to ignore those words, after the flaming bust. She nodded. Questions were planting themselves in her head, ugly bulbs that sprouted quickly, their stalks piercing the soil of her mind. Why did Three not support the rebels? Did the Shadows not feel the same desire as their sisters and brothers? If you had a reason to attack, then you needed a better reason to exercise restraint. She would wonder, later, about that.

Now, there was little more to say. By the time they had drunk the last of their wine and he had thanked her for her help, Six was waiting with one hand on the back of the painting, and the frame swung forward soundlessly at her touch. Lysande gave Three one last look before she climbed through.

"If I were to ask you a question, but not *the* question . . ."

"One may always ask."

"Three." She drew a breath. "I have this lock of hair—this queer, silver lock." She loosened her hair and pulled the strands on one side free of their pins. "You see it there? It was changed by the fire I survived as a child, during the war. I wish to know why I am the only one with this mark, so far as anyone knows."

"On that matter, I am afraid, your guess is as good as mine."

"There is no magic that might explain it? It could not have been created by a spell?"

"Spells do not exist. We only use our powers. And I do not know of any power that, when cast, simply gives the target's hair a different color and consistency."

Lysande thought she saw him smile faintly from under his hat. She nodded, and passed through the gap created by the picture frame. It was difficult to resist the urge to turn back again and ask him if he was being honest with her.

In the prayer-house she found the shattered pieces of the bust removed and her captain and attendant guarding the door. She stared up at the elegance of the chimera bathed in shining paint, and waited for her mind to stop whirling; looking up at the ceiling and fingering the chain around her neck, she wondered if there was any hope of avoiding a war. She pulled her gaze away from the adulation on one painted admirer's face as Chidney and Litany came to her side. Despite the pair's curious looks, they asked no questions.

Everything in its place, Lysande thought, thanking Axium upbringing. "Is the prayer-house secure, captain?"

Chidney nodded. "Your attendant did more than I could, Councillor."

"It was like chasing an element." Lysande could hear the forlorn note in Litany's voice. "I can vouch that the flames that blocked us from them burned twice as long as they should have. In fact, I could swear that they were . . ."

She placed a hand on Litany's shoulder and patted her gently. "Let us walk into the sunshine together before we say too much. One is bound to speak hastily, after a shock."

Halfway through the doorway, she turned to look back at the trip-tych. The frame was back in its place, as if it had never moved.

The serpent of the Flavantine ran through a world where the bustle and sound of trade disappeared entirely, bordered on each side by a bounteous green bank. Lysande strolled northward with Chidney and Litany, watching rowers skim over the water in long boats and dip their oars, still thinking on her meeting with Three. She spotted play-ers bent over tactos-boards in a pavilion by the water, staring intently as they slid the pieces back and forth. For a moment, she yearned to do the same; everything became much clearer when she was playing tac-tos, as if she was looking at a world of glass. She was about to turn away when she picked out a face among the spectators.

She moved toward the crowd, ignoring Chidney's "Councillor?" and breaking into a run. By the time she arrived, the figure was gone.

"See something?" Litany said, softly, coming to hover beside her.

"Only a ghost."

"If it's a Rhimese ghost, it might charge you for the haunting." Chidney grinned as she sidled up to Litany.

Lysande stared for a few seconds more, waiting for another glimpse, but only the Rhimese remained, talking among themselves. "Yes," she said, "perhaps we had better avoid the fee."

She had probably imagined the face. It would not be the first time she had hoped.

Chidney drew her sword while they walked up the steps toward the vast dome of the Academy at the northern end, but at Lysande's prompting, she sheathed her blade again. The armed guards flanking the steps would not attack, she assured her captain, hoping that she had not overestimated Luca's welcome.

So many Rhimese peopled the foyer of the research library that she paused for a moment, yet when Chidney explained to a smiling atten-dant that Councillor Prior wished to visit, the man scuttled off at once and disappeared into the bowels of the building, reemerging with the head librarian, Signore Marchettina, whose grip could make a wrestler wince.

Reading rooms with desks on which glasses of wine nestled beside books; halls dotted with people arguing over plans and bustling through with quills; laboratories where women juggled vials, bottles, and long-handled spoons . . . the Academy offered chambers upon chambers. An attendant in black livery emblazoned with the red cobra admitted them to the library, where waves of books stretched back to the walls. The section in the far-right corner, cordoned and guarded, drew Lysande's eye. She caught a glimpse of a triangle embossed on one spine and slipped away toward the cordon rope. The guard barred the rope as she approached, and she was taken by the elbow while Signore Marchettina steered her firmly on.

The shelf of material on the White Queen turned up little of use. She had looked for something that might hint at a weakness, yet she found only jubilee verses condemning the "demon" who had ravaged the realm, and a copy of the law banning portraits of Mea Tacitus, cobbled onto the end of Queen Illora's Precept by Sarelin. She resorted to borrowing the one book that predated them, a volume of military accounts from the White War, preserved with its spattering of blood, and tried to feel hopeful about it.

The Council was not to meet again until the evening, so she had the whole afternoon to read. The thought of returning to her chambers did not appeal, however. With the open mouths of Rhimese streets and the salons flowing with conversation and music before her, the practicality of finding a quiet place to peruse the book was dubious, anyway. She wound her way through the streets to the southern half of the city, keeping Litany and Chidney close—though the pair seemed to stick together naturally, now. Entering a courtyard fringed by tall villas, whose gardens overflowed onto the cobbles, she bumped hard into someone, and her apology caught in her mouth when she saw who it was.

"Signore Fox!"

"My dearest owl."

"I thought you'd have run to the far-north mountains by now!"

"You're the one running." Charice's eyes were following Litany and Chidney. "You know me. Never been one for crowds. Can we speak alone?"

Lysande waved the attendant and guard back until they were standing further away. Trying not to gawp, she faced Charice, book in hand, and examined her friend.

The merchant's robe was gone and the supple gray leather boots had been replaced with a pair that were worn on the toes, and Charice's demeanor was more harrowed than usual. But she was alive and in one piece: that was more than Lysande had dared hope for. You did not know the shatterings you had imagined until you saw the jewel intact.

"I'm going west," Charice said. "Only a few more days in Rhime, then I'm out."

"Why are you here at all?"

"Mostly because there's not a mob at my heels in Rhime, and I value my life."

Some pauses came like a thump, like a beat, like a word that was felt even though it was unspoken. The vibration of this pause carried through Lysande's flesh. She should not be feeling guilty—it was not her fault that they had parted on shifting ground, the peat-layer of safety crumbling beneath Charice's feet. Or was it?

"I deeply regret what happened in Axium. I deeply regret what happened to your premises."

"Regrets are a bronze racket apiece. You can fill your pockets with them, but they do not add up. Apologies, though . . . I'd say an apology is worth a bag of gold cadres, at least," Charice said.

"I'm sorry that fate has treated you harshly." The words came stiffly from her lips.

"Fate? I've never met fate. Fate never touched the skin of my neck. I know the culprit who has been running a knife-edge along my jaw, though—she's indifference: sheer, human indifference. That's the criminal."

Lysande wished that she could rewrite the story of the last few weeks or find some thread of comfort to offer Charice. She was very aware of her own fault in the matter. Yet she was already being pricked by a different thought. A question waited on her tongue, one that she had long wanted to ask, and yet she could not bring herself to cast it into the world; how did you inquire politely whether your former lover had assisted in the queen's murder?

"Regarding Sarelin . . ."

"Oh. I see." Charice let out a short laugh. "My dear scholar has more pressing concerns."

"Charice, I only wanted to know—"

"You always did wish to garner every detail, every fact. But I confess, I cannot see why you should doubt me at all."

They understood each other too easily, Lysande thought. Guilt pierced her again.

"I recall the time you blasted back a sunsnake with a jet of air," she said, facing Charice over the uneven cobblestones of the Rhimese courtyard. "You opened your palm and the air shot out, striking it right in the middle of the body. The magic. The fall. The thump. It was beautiful, and it was terrible."

"And now you wonder if I have had a hand in other terrible things."

Behind them, a chirrup issued from a branch. The sleek body of a starling flapped upward, taking flight over the garden of a villa, shaking another trill from its throat.

"If I were her murderer, would I have waited until the capital was in an uproar, raging citizens destroying shops, the mob hoping to snap me like a quill too? Would I have chosen the most dangerous moment to flee?" Charice said.

"You make a strong case," Lysande admitted.

Charice folded her arms, as if no reply was needed.

"The capital's calmed down," Lysande said, not without a little guilt. "You could have your shop back."

"And if I'm arrested and put in jail? Or worse—if I spend my days as an actor, playing out scenes for all to approve? I won't live a lie, Lysande."

Lysande realized that in all the moments she had worried about Charice since the uproar in the capital, she had not spent enough time considering how Charice would feel; she had focused too much on whether or not Charice would survive. The two were separate issues. She wondered if remorse showed on her face. "Perhaps memory of your power has guided me unfairly," she said. "I can offer you my protection."

"Have you forgotten what I told you? There are other people one can seek out. But leave that aside." Charice had never sounded so breathy. "I'm the one who must give you charity—though I confess, I wonder why I do."

"You'll have to speak to the point."

"There's something I have to tell you. It concerns the queen you liked so much—I think you should know it before—well, just in case."

"Then lay it bare."

"Not here." She could tell, from Charice's face, that this was not open to negotiation. "I have something to show you, too. Meet me by the Flavantine, near the pavilion where the tactos players sit. A week from now, at midday."

A noise came from the street behind them: a group shouting about something, some of the voices indignant, bickering. Charice stared at the crowd. "I must go." She clasped Lysande's hands, arms crossed, and bowed. And then Charice was striding away, her boots slapping the cobbles.

Lysande watched her leave. She recalled their last meeting: the vase empty of heather, the glass tinkling in the street outside.

Had she been wrong to raise a memory? Was it not natural, to think of the potency of the magic she had once seen? It might have been un-just, to cast doubt on the woman she had missed so often, and yet Charice had left her so quickly—had always been good at leaving her.

Walking under the stone cobras and into Castle Sapere's eastern courtyard, she heard a shout and a clang. She nearly strode into a group of Cassia's guards chasing each other with serrated swords. Her thoughts left Charice out of necessity.

"I doubt you've seen real western discipline before." The Irriqi emerged from the shadows, taking Lysande by the arm. "Those who lose a finger while training are not fit to be part of the Pyrrhan Guards. You should stay and watch the wrestling."

"I'm afraid, for all my years with the queen, I have no taste for combat."

"Then you should develop one." Cassia's pat on her shoulder was light-spirited, but there was perspicacity in her glance. "I have a feeling this Council will face a war soon."

There was nothing she would have liked more than to speak openly with the one city-ruler who called her a *friend*: a word she did not yet trust but which reverberated within her mind, leaving echoes in parts of her consciousness. Perhaps she should ask Cassia exactly how far a friend would go to protect elementals, if pressed.

Instead, she asked if Cassia had been to the Academy. It was easier to keep the concerns about Charice at bay if she could listen, rather than talk. The Irriqi launched into an appraisal of the archive on magical beasts. "They have the oldest descriptions of the striped fire shrike there, you know, the very first type of chimera to be observed. I found notes on the hazel-furred flier, too. And then there is that drawing of the Royamese white—still disputed—I could not find another opinion to verify it." Cassia's voice took on a hopeful note. "As a scholar, I suppose you have read that scroll about the thirteen reported varieties of the ancient creatures and how they differ."

"Not recently." Lysande had never guessed that Cassia studied chimeras with such passion. "You seem able to name every fact about them that has been transmitted to paper." Was it that the encounter with Charice had left her prickling? She could not stop a question flying onto her tongue. "Strange, is it not, that a woman may know so much of ancient beasts and yet never recognize a Conquest-era weapon, even when it nearly lodges in her throat? I wonder at the curiosities of interest."

Cassia made as if to speak, then stopped midway, staring at Lysande. "Ah."

Lysande had expected her stomach to sink like this. She forced herself to keep her posture upright.

"I knew this day would come. I simply did not think it would be you, my friend. You know, I entertain all kinds of thoughts, myself: I wonder about the queen, too. People think I had no love for Queen Sarelin, because we disagreed at times, but I offered her my opinion in the palm of my hand, where all could see it. There were plenty who *appeared* to be close to her, in that palace full of statues and gleaming slabs, where even the bedposts are polished. One polishes to keep the guests focused on surfaces, rather than on the true nature of something." A pause, just long enough to give her a chance to interrupt. "I wonder about her scholar, sometimes. But do you know what,

Lysande? I prefer not to distrust. Because I see you and I think, here is a woman who could prove to be a friendly face. One lacks a friendly face when wolves are circling."

"It is an honor you do me." Lysande chose her words as if searching among plums on a tree, looking for the fruit that was not hard, nor overripe. "I hope you can forgive that I harbor some suspicions when I think on what befell the woman who was dearest to me."

"And I say you must be aware that I feel the same."

"The same?"

Cassia smiled tightly. "Perhaps I chose my words hastily. I mean that I feel something for Queen Sarelin. You might call it respect."

"She lies yet unavenged, Cassia."

The word had jumped out of her throat, unbidden. She had intended to use the proper title, but somehow, in the heat of argument, the Ir-riqi's given name had slipped out; any moment now, Cassia was going to take her to task for it—to point out that it was a noblewoman's right to address others how she pleased, but not Lysande's right.

Yet Cassia was looking at her with a smile that spread, slowly, upward.

"Now, revenge. That is something a Pyrrhan always understands."

A poem sprang to mind, an ode on the subject of recompense by an unknown author. Lysande was aware that she did not have the leisure to explore this avenue further, nor exonerate herself, nor even assess how friendship might balance with suspicion to reach a workable state. Physical exigencies pressed upon her.

When a burst of pain tore through her throat, she winced and ex-cused herself, pretending not to notice Cassia's look of surprise. She retreated through the grounds. Having enough respite to forget the pain was worse than having a short relief, for the ache seemed doubly vicious upon returning. She was not desperate enough to try Luca's orange medicine, and discussing the pain with Derset would mean confronting what had passed between them last night; on top of this encounter with Cassia, she did not think she could countenance it. Thanks to the aid of scale, she had long been accustomed to avoiding emotions that became complicated.

She headed to the castle stables and saddled her mare. At the back of the gardens lay a ramble that Luca had designed for his personal pleasure: the wild patch of land covered in bracken and conical trees stretched out to the very edge of the peak behind the maze garden. The pain could not be wished away. Perhaps she could ride it out. Since the expanse of green and yellow and blood-red bushes offered no clear path, she set off down the middle, and after half an hour she felt the agony began to melt away in the sun.

She began to picture Luca riding here, his body crouching atop his horse then descending again, the lines of his physique pressing against the leather of a tight jerkin. Her mare's cantering sent larks and finches flying from the branches, and she raced past several little hedges. She could not resist approaching one, preparing for a jump.

"Come on," she said, patting the mare's neck. "If Fontaine's horse can do this, so can you." The horse whinnied and pawed at the ground, its piebald coat accruing mud. "I'm not above bribing you with sugar," she muttered, nudging it toward the hedge.

Further into the ramble, blissfully removed from all eyes, she veered west until she found a little lane of trees and halted under their interlaced branches; when she emerged from the shade, she caught a glimpse of blue and cantered into a clearing. An expanse of sky welcomed her, and beyond the grass, a sheer drop stretched to the foot of the hill.

"Sun and stars!" she cried, struggling to rein the mare in. "Stop! Stop, there!"

"Dramatic, isn't it?" said a voice behind her. "Of course, it wouldn't be half so beautiful if it was cordoned off. The thrill arises from the danger."

She whirled around. Luca was sitting on his black horse, regarding her from the edge of the trees. Her eyes ran over the trousers tucked into black leather boots and the black cloak that rippled behind him, held together by the single ruby at his neck. A pair of black gloves finished his outfit. She was struck again by how the shade seemed to suit him, not only for his dark hair and fine complexion, but for some other reason she could not identify.

Not a tight jerkin, then, she thought, trying to steal another look at his waist. "What are you doing here?"

"It may have slipped your mind, Prior, but these are my grounds. I do ride through them from time to time." He dismounted and tied up his horse. "A picturesque view, wouldn't you say? That is the best part of Rhime—from across the Flavantine, there, you can see to Pescarra. Princess Abella Targia once executed her whole court at the top of that dale, wrapping wires around their unsuspecting necks. These days, the Pescarrans do all their cutting with flavor. Cheese-makers." He waved a hand across to the western half of the countryside. "You ride well, by the way, but you should be bolder when you jump. A horse will never do as you bid if you ask it politely."

She took in the little smirk around his mouth. Climbing down off her mare, she tied the animal up beside his.

"Boldness can lead to errors in judgment—even diplomatic mistakes," she said.

The edge to his smile told her that he had understood her meaning very well, but he made no reply. They walked to the brink and stood side by side, looking down on the sprawl of buildings. A cart was meandering down one of the lanes, stopping at every house to drop off its goods; as she watched it, she was conscious of the proximity between them.

"I suppose you thought that diamond thread was clever," Luca said.

"It wasn't bad."

"Didn't anyone ever tell you that modesty is one of the Axium virtues, Prior?"

"I have heard that tact is one of the Rhimese talents, too. You didn't exactly exude it in the Room of Accord."

"First impressions can be misleading," Luca said, turning back to the city. "So often, one welcomes those who sow discord, and conversely, one suspects the wrong person."

"Yet suspicions can be removed."

"They can." He kicked a stone and watched it bounce down the cliffside. "Without your interruption—clumsy though it was—the White Queen's stratagem would have succeeded. I have often thought two exceptional minds are better than one, though I have had no way to test the theory, growing up around my father and brother."

"You and I? Working together, Fontaine?"

"The orphan and the bastard . . . it has a ring to it, don't you think?"

She looked at the ruby under his chin; the absolute stillness of his jaw. "We'd trip each other up before we'd run a race together. How is an Axiumite to trust a Rhimese?"

He was quiet for a long while.

"You know, the first time I came to Axium, I saw a sea of Fortitudas. Statues, amulets, paintings, even the chamber pot in my suite had an image of Fortituda thrusting her dagger up, on the side." His mouth curled up on one side. "Defender of the privy realm."

"The priests do a good trade in her likeness."

"Our Rhimese priests don't sell much of the goddess of valor, did you know? Too heroic, for us. And while we approve of smiting, Vindictus' methods are a bit like an iron bar, striking in the sun. We prefer a shadowed rapier, you see."

"Cognita, I suppose."

"She gets the most orders in smiths' workshops. Although it's not uncommon to have one statue of Cognita and another of Crudelis on the same shelf. The incarnations of wisdom and passion: a constant dialogue."

"Passion? Or should that be love? A subtle difference, wouldn't you say?" Lysande could not resist responding. "The same concept, for the same goddess, but different words . . . one for Axium and another for Rhime. I wonder how the Rhimese define their term."

He did not reply for a long time again, only watched her.

"When I think back to the first time you ever spoke to me, through an inkflower and a note, I see that you dangled that puzzle in front of me as bait," Lysande said. "Goading me to dance for clues and prove myself to you. At the same time, you sought a tactical advantage, trying to gain my interest." She paused. "If we are to be allies, Fontaine, you must have my position clear. I have nothing to prove to you. I have nothing to give you, either, unless it is earned."

"I believe you have already administered a check to my manners." His half-smile tugged at one corner of his mouth. "Twice."

"And yet I do not believe you have learned."

"Will I mount some effort to gain your trust, you mean? Shall I kneel and kiss your boots?"

It was her turn to remain silent.

"We are colleagues, Prior. Trust is not a useful currency. We pay each other with more practical coins: deals, votes, information." He sent another stone skipping over the edge and Lysande was reminded of the black stone he had toyed with. "I'm going to smooth things over with Merez as recompense for what I said."

"And then we will walk off together, laughing and planning our reign?"

"We will see how we proceed from there." She looked to see if he was joking, but there was no sign of levity on his face; indeed, he was looking at her with an expression that was impossible to read.

"Your hair, Prior."

Her hand flew to her head. Of course. After she had loosened the deathstruck strands for Three to see, she had forgotten to re-pin them; but then, Luca had already gazed at her silver lock when she entered the Room of Accord. Why was he staring again?

"Don't worry," she said, lightly. "I will cover that bit and pin it, as soon as I reach the castle. There will be no risk of it standing out again."

"You must be the judge of your own style. Not I. Yet I think you assume my opinion to be other than it is, so I must correct you." He came slightly closer to her, without touching. "I like the way you stand out."

They stared at each other, while the breeze stirred a few pebbles at their feet.

She placed a hand upon his shoulder. The touch was soft, a promise of collusion, and she thought of Three's new evidence, of the risk of an attack, and of the flaming bust hurled at her guards. But it was not only an alliance she was thinking of now. Her eyes found his neck. Why was it that, again, she felt the urge to grip it? Would his flesh give way to her hands, like a foal to its trainer? It was not a coincidence that she felt this way, she knew, but a product of his stillness, that deliberate passivity which had an effect on her.

She became aware that he was still watching her. "If you fix things with Merez, we may talk further. I have a feeling you'd like to hear what I've learned," she said.

"Curious. I was about to say the same to you."

Lysande was prevented from speaking by a rustling and a flash of gold in the bushes; a second later, a woman emerged. The attendant ran up to them, straining to catch her breath, the sleeves of her doublet flapping.

"Excuse me, Councillors," she said, bowing. "It's Prince Chamboise."

"Don't tell me the Lyrian beauty has come to some harm," Luca said. "Has he collapsed under the weight of that ring at last?"

"No, Your Highness."

"Or fallen onto Dante's sword?"

Lysande guessed that he had chosen that phrase deliberately.

"No, Your Highness." The woman heaved another breath. "The prince has gone missing."

Jale had not arrived in his suite for a prayer ceremony that morning, nor had he turned up to bathe in the afternoon. The main floors of Castle Sapere had been scoured within the hour, but there was no sign of the youngest prince in any of the chambers; even the kitchens and cleaning cupboards were searched, their brooms pulled out and shoved back in. Lysande's guards joined the Lyrians in combing the grounds.

The Valderrans gathered at the back steps of the castle to watch the search party. Lysande did not have a good feeling about the way they were standing in a knot, talking. "Maybe he's plotting with the hidden people," one of the Valderran guards said. A big woman, who Lysande recognized from the group that had cursed Jale in the camp, spat on the ground. The talk stopped abruptly when their leader rounded the corner; Dante cast a look at his guards and uttered a few sharp words, and they dispersed.

Lysande hastened her journey to the Painter's Suite. If she took Litany with her to search for Jale, she might have a far more effective hunt, she reasoned. The snake's-head key rattled in the lock. Entering the bedchamber, she was halfway through calling out a greeting when she stopped.

Litany stood by the window, holding a jar of a familiar blue substance. A chest sat at her feet, now divested of its blanket, its lid hanging open. The girl met her gaze.

"Litany." She closed the space between them.

"I didn't mean to pry, this time. I thought it was the chest with your doublets."

"I won't ask you to excuse—"

"My mother was stable-hand to an apothecary before she joined the palace. She unloaded and unpacked the goods for the back room. Sometimes, there would be a special delivery. I know shredded chimera scale when I see it." Litany cupped the jar in her hands. "And I might've had no right to unlock the chest, but I must say something, Signore—Lysande."

Lysande waited. She felt as she might have done if the air had been sucked from the room. Litany stood on tiptoe, seeming to swell as she spoke.

"If you mean to poison whoever killed Queen Sarelin, I'll help you."

A laugh came out of Lysande, involuntarily. She clutched her stomach but could not stop another laugh, and another. By the time she stopped, the girl was blushing. "Oh, Litany."

"I mean it; I'll find the right substance for you. Better than slow-working scale. This, I enjoy doing."

Hardly necessary to remind her, after the prayer-house. "I believe you. But this isn't for poisoning." She gestured to the jar. "Well, at least, not in the way you think. There are some scholars, Litany, who know the properties of chimera scale well enough to prepare it as a sort of . . . medicinal treatment."

Litany's eyes added the question: *for what?*

This time, the silence was hers to break, and she held out a hand and took the jar. She pressed her other hand to Litany's own. "It dispels the cares of this world. Some people know how to unburden themselves of the particular effects of living in a place where you feel like a jeweler's rag, always in contact with diamonds and emeralds, but only to show up their quality. Others require assistance in unburdening." And without Sarelin, without her laugh to fill the corridors . . . without her smile to distract from the way they all stared at her . . . "There are some more pious citizens who might disapprove of the way I've been assisting myself."

Litany stared at the jar for so long, she might have been studying to paint it. "No one can be very pious," she said, at last, "if they judge a soul for enduring. Fortituda understands that there are different types of valor."

The words caught Lysande in the chest. It was not the goddess that mattered, but the fact that Litany had invoked her. Scratch an Axiumite, and you found reverence for Fortituda; Luca might joke, but it was no small thing for a woman of the capital to call upon the divine embodiment of valor.

After a moment's hesitation, Lysande wrapped her arms around Litany and held the girl close. The fountain burbled beside them. It flowed on and on, after they had finished embracing, and Lysande could feel gratitude still flowing through her. "Your work goes unappreciated by almost everyone," she said, gently. "It won't always be so. One day, I think, you will serve me in the light."

Litany bowed her head. She did not look as pleased as Lysande had hoped.

"One more thing. Queen Sarelin died of her wound. That is what the realm believes, and what it must continue to believe," Lysande said. "There are some truths we carry in our hearts. Others, we bear in our mouths. You are an intelligent woman; I know that you will understand this."

Her attendant bowed again and stepped back.

"For now, let us return to our task. If Prince Chamboise cannot be found, we may all need to think creatively. Somehow, I think you will manage that."

Litany smiled, and they parted, each silent.

Castle Sapere swarmed with staff in black and red livery. Lysande took the stairs to the second floor and searched the rooms one by one, Chidney and a group of Axium Guards trailing her. It occurred to her, as she walked, that there was one place the staff had not looked. She remembered from her studies that Lyrians sought out the sun in times of distress: Princess Gaincourt had retreated to a rooftop after a bad omen about her army. The uppermost floor had been pronounced empty, but Lysande had overheard two Lyrian attendants discussing how no one but Jale was supposed to enter "the sanctum of the sun."

She shielded her eyes as she entered the Observatory, deflecting the sun streaming through the glass walls. At the far end of the room, a blond figure sat, gazing out at the grounds.

"Jale."

He turned his face away from the glass, and she saw streaks shining on his face. "Oh dear . . . is the whole Council looking for me? I should've run to the cells."

"There's no shame in being low. It only means you'll take a while to rise." Lysande knew how it felt to hide several floors up above the rest of your peers, hugging your feelings to yourself. She signaled to her guards to wait in the doorway, and approached him.

"Dante wouldn't cry, would he?" He wiped his cheek. "Luca wouldn't shed a tear. I don't expect Cassia even *has* tears. She's probably forgotten what they look like."

On the floor beside him, a prayer bowl was half-full of water, a few petals submerged beneath the surface. She knelt down and took care not to knock the bowl over, aware of the preeminence of water and sun in Lyrian rituals, so far removed from the clipped and ordered objects of worship she had seen laid out in Axium prayer-houses, always perfectly still, always lacking the ripple and glow of nature. This water shimmered, its surface quivering from the vibration of her body. She had learned from dealing with Sarelin that it was often better to wait than to speak, and she sat for a few moments, watching Jale.

"A dove arrived." Jale drew a deep breath. "It's Merez, you see . . . she's been speaking with my uncle Vigarot."

"The Bastillonian ambassador?" That made little sense after the scenes in the Room of Accord. She was glad that Merez had not sent python venom with her note.

"Apparently, King Ferago's made a deal with Vigarot. Bastillón and Elira are to be friends again; the whole thing's been carried out behind our backs. Very neat. A few quick doves to Lyria and the deal was struck, without the Council having a say." He gave a bitter laugh. "My uncle seems pleased with himself; more pleased than usual, that is."

Her other concerns melted, ceding to the urgency of the news. It was not what she had expected, certainly, but with a neat bit of manipulation, Vigarot Chamboise had saved the Council from groveling to the east. That was something the Council would be grateful for, but it also made her neck prickle. She tried to recall what Sarelin had said of this man, who could control the south with a stroke of his quill.

"He says he's letting King Ferago open a trade route to the delta," Jale went on, "so the Bastillonians can buy spices and metals from Lyria. Everyone knows Ferago needs tempero and steel more than he needs gold. Oh, I'm sure it'll shore up our countries' ties for an age. The old ram's dipping his snout in our pond—I don't think dear uncle Vigarot realizes he might drink it dry."

"I don't see why a trade route should bother you."

"It's not just trade. Don't you see, Lysande? The Bastillonians want proof: hard proof we won't break our commitment." He gazed out through the glass wall. "Might as well put my hands in golden cuffs and lock them in. As of today, my marriage to Princess Mariana will be brought forward and conducted within the month. They've signed it over in ink—there's going to be a Sapphire Ball in honor of the occasion. I can't get out of it, now."

"Ah." Lysande looked keenly at him.

"Princess Mariana—pride of the east—lady of wit and valor. There's nothing wrong with *her* at all." He turned his face away. "No, she's every blessing."

Whenever she had walked in on Sarelin in a bad mood, Lysande had opted to listen until the dust had settled from the queen's tirade; yet as Jale continued to stare through the glass, she considered that he might prefer a change of subject. Her thoughts were drawn to Dante and Jale leaning over the banquet table in Axium Palace, joy rippling across Jale's face like early morning sun across a clear lake; to Dante and Jale embracing in the Arena, Dante's hand lingering on Jale's shoulder for longer than necessary; and she thought about raising these memories in an attempt to cheer Jale up. It was possible, however, that Dante's affection was very much linked to Jale's current mood.

She set to distracting Jale with questions about the ball, instead, trying her hardest to draw him into discussing it. Officially, she had read in *A History of Modern Elira*, a Sapphire Ball was a celebration for the wedding of royalty in Lyria, dating back to the Classical Era; its role was enshrined as the final ceremony before a coronation. After listening to Sarelin talk of the most extravagant party in the realm, she had suspected that the Sapphire Ball was as much an expression of Lyrian identity. Quaffing of wine by the jug, dancing in elaborate costumes which unraveled in pace with the festivities, and carrying out of a wide range of liaisons in candlelight or in shadow: these all featured in Sarelin's stories of the ball, which had been passed to her by her grandmother. Lysande had the impression that Queen Brettelin had not approved of Lyrian dancing, with its infamous pressing of body to body.

"Tell me more about your favorite parts of the . . . more colorful preparations," she said.

"The courses must be symbolic, you see: milder dishes to start, before the dancing, and spiced food for when passions rise. And then, you know, we have some desserts in Lyria that are made with such a sweet blend of liquors and fruit, they are almost intoxicating."

"That would certainly excite the guests from the capital."

"All the better, I say. If one cannot read something salacious into the food, then what good is a banquet?"

"Indeed. Your stewards will be run off their feet, arranging things, no doubt."

"Oh, I like to get involved myself when we welcome guests." Jale's expression turned a little bashful. "Uncle Vigarot says it is vulgar for a prince to be friends with the cooks and the Overseer of Wardrobe, but I do not give a leopard's ar—that is to say, I have different views on the matter."

As the minutes passed, he spoke more calmly. Lysande tried to remember what it was that silverbloods did at their marriage ceremonies: she had covered food, music, and vows. "You must tell me about the dancing, of course."

Jale smiled. "You're a good listener, Lysande. Has anyone ever told you that?"

"Sarelin was too busy talking to notice, most of the time."

"Well, I need not blather on to you any longer."

"Blathering to a friend is an excellent cure for melancholy. Several texts concur."

He shared another smile with her, this one unfurling gently, a southern water-rose. "You will see it all for yourself, soon. The Council must be in attendance at the Sapphire Ball, of course, to show the crowd that Elira and Bastillón stand together, and you will dance as well as any of us, I am sure."

The word *crowd* hit her in the gut. She remembered what Sarelin had said of the last Sapphire Ball. All the most important people in the realm would be there, the queen had told her: poets and nobles and merchants of importance, artists and captains. *They wouldn't miss a Sapphire Ball if their fortunes depended on it*, Sarelin had declared.

She stared at Jale for a moment. A public event . . . an attack in front of a crowd . . . her conversation with Three had not been so long ago that she had forgotten the White Queen's new strategy. Visions of soldiers pouring into a palace were coming fast.

She excused herself and strode from the room. The others were still searching the rooms on the second floor. She was sketching out her response as she descended the stairs and walked into Derset. They dipped their heads to each other, and Lysande recognized that the veneer of politeness they had maintained since last night had fallen; she flushed and saw redness answer her in Derset's cheeks. There was something in his gaze that was not just the awkwardness of their circumstances, something soft, and subtly welcoming, and she could not persuade herself that she disliked it.

She imparted Jale's news without any personal remarks, and Derset took her lead, speaking only of the wedding's implications, his eyes flicking between her and the floor. Quickly, they agreed to split up and call off the pursuit, and she hurried downstairs.

It should have taken some time to gather the Council, as the southerners were milling about, muttering darkly about the Valderrans' lack of help, but Litany wove her way through the throng of guards, bowing left and right, her back straight and yet not overly stiff. "If you please," Lysande heard her say to one guard, and "if I could trouble you," to another, and "I believe something most pressing is about to happen" to yet another—couching her phrases in Axiumite formality, then slipping in a request to move. The guards complied without seeming to notice they were being manipulated. Lysande whispered a "thank you" in Litany's ear as she passed by.

Jale locked the door of the tea-hall and faced the city-rulers.

"I do apologize for my sudden absence," he said, "and for my sudden reappearance. I suppose I must cap the whole thing off with a sudden announcement. Unless anyone would prefer me to draw it out?" Catching the looks of his listeners, he heaved a breath. "Word from Vigarot. I'm to be married this month, in return for a new route between my delta and the capital of Bastillón. Traded for trade, you might say." He drew another breath. "There's to be a Sapphire Ball, too."

"What?" Cassia shouted, just as Luca cried "Already?" Lysande suspected that she was the only one who heard Dante's quiet "No."

As a mêlée of voices broke out, Lysande stepped forward, stumbling through a response. "The forging of a bond between realms, in front of royalty, with the most notable people from each country watching? That would be a gift to the White Queen. By any measure, the opportunity would be too tempting for her not to take advantage. Think like a woman who is desperate to rule, Councillors. Think like a tyrant in the making." She glanced at Cassia as she spoke, quickly enough that she might get away with searching for a sign of suppleness, looking for anything that had begun to soften since their last conversation. "We must cancel the ball. When we seek to show strength, she sees a chance to prove our weakness."

"I can tell you that strength begets victory. I scared off a battalion just with the sight of my army in the last Pyrrhan war." Cassia folded her arms. "I say let us join these Bastillonians, and we will meet the White Queen's army with a gory embrace."

"And if I had intelligence that the White Queen will attack the ball?" Lysande said.

"Intelligence from who?" Dante said.

"By all means, produce it, my friend." Cassia returned her gaze.

Lysande glanced from one to the other. She was on the verge of sending for Litany to fetch the map-book and discussing the White Queen's tactics, but as she took in their expressions, she knew that it would not be enough.

"Axium spies," she said. "I would not ask for your support unless the circumstance was as dire as it is now. My sources believe she has both weapons and troops."

Dante's laugh told her how convincing her delivery was.

"Axium spies," Cassia said. "Where did they get this evidence about the ball, when we've only just heard it's to be held?"

"Perhaps we should consider the odds of a heightened risk," she heard Luca saying, but Cassia argued on, and Dante and Jale, to her disappointment, sided with the Irriqi, even though Dante looked like a man wounded by a savage bull. She suspected that as far as Valderran opinion went, he had no choice. By all logic that could be openly declared, the city-rulers were in the right, she knew. Vigarot Chamboise had played his cards skillfully, with his hand concealed.

Yet he could not know that the White Queen had bought a weapon that cost several fortunes in gold.

She bit her lip. Gathering her determination, she shaped her fears into lists, marched them into formation. "Councillors, we cannot afford not to consider the risks of the wedding. I leave you to reevaluate your positions. Jale, it is your wedding, and your vote must carry the greatest weight. But I ask my friend from Pyrrha to consider my words and to take my concern as a gift—if she still bears me any good will." No one cut her off; they were all gazing at Cassia, who looked like a woman who had been readying herself to shoot at skylarks, only to find that the songbirds had been packed away and the sport abruptly called off.

Cassia watched her. She watched Cassia back. The silence stretched like skin, threatening to break but never quite giving way.

"I will not reconsider without evidence," Cassia said.

Lysande pulled her gaze away and turned as she did, hiding her face so that the hurt written there could not be glimpsed. She left the other Councillors talking among themselves, signaling to Derset to remain with them. Litany was in the Painter's Suite when she arrived, tidying her desk. The attendant looked up from brushing an ink-pot.

"Bring me the map, if you please," Lysande said.

The parchment had been commissioned for Sarelin. It gave off a cloud of dust as she unfurled it, spreading it out to cover a good part of the floor. Naturally, Sarelin had never done anything on a small scale; the realm rolled out in detail, offering up the glaciers, the mountains, the great lakes around Valderos, the jungle that surrounded Pyrrha, the stretch of Axium Forest above the capital . . . everything was inked in, right down to the names of towns.

Lysande edged around the map. A thick line bisected the swathe of the Lyrian desert, branching out into the three prongs of the delta after it reached the city. She grimaced. The Grandfleuve seemed to her the quickest route, but it would also be full of ships and checkpoints, and for secrecy, it would help little.

There might be a way, provided there was a head start and orders were followed. She could not rely on others. It had become her own task to parry the White Queen.

"Stay there, Litany. I would have you take a letter." She walked to the window, composing her thoughts. "Make it out to Captain Hartleigh in Axium Palace." She willed her breathing to slow. "Dear Raden. Kindly bring two hundred of the best Axium Guards together for me; equip them for a long journey, disguise them, and assemble them in secret."

A bird trilled outside while Litany's quill scratched over the paper.

"You must make no mention of this to anyone. When this is done, you are to make preparations for the group to travel through the desert. I want them to leave as soon as they have their boots fastened."

"The desert?" Litany looked up sharply as soon as the words had passed her lips. "I beg your pardon, Councillor—I didn't mean to ask."

"You might well ask. And when you hear the answer, you might well ask again. We will soon be going to Lyria, for a wedding that requires a Sapphire Ball. Put that in your letter." She walked over to the girl. If Litany could tell that her whole person was tingling with the excitement of making the decision, she did not mind. "Tell Captain

Hartleigh he is to spare no expense. My secret guard may have what-ever weapons it can carry on muleback."

Litany nodded, her hand flying, and Lysande waited a minute or so while the attendant caught up. She could feel her pulse galloping. She had a feeling that Three would approve of her plan. This was the most logical way. Luca might be less pleased, but he had said that trust was not a useful currency, so he could not blame her for failing to trust him with this. The way he had watched her from atop his horse . . . and the way he had stood so near to her on the cliff-edge, so deliberately close . . . and the way he had looked at her as he remarked: *I like the way you stand out.* She impelled herself, with difficulty, to push those thoughts aside.

In her mind, she called up other maps: drawings of the desert that she had copied into her booklets.

"When you've written that, ask Raden to come to me at once," she added, glancing at Litany.

She waited while the girl fetched a dove. As the bird winged off from the window, she watched it arc up into the sky, a white shape against clouds pregnant with a storm. When the pale spot had disap-peared, she turned back, arranging her countenance.

"Take my daggers, Litany, and have a guard sharpen them." Ly-sande unfastened the sheaths from her belt and handed them over. "And retrieve your daggers. I know you have them here, probably wrapped in lace and packed in a chest of my softest tunics. You're go-ing to train with me."

"It would be an honor to be your throwing partner."

"I hope, in time, we may call each other friends. In the meantime, we work." She pretended not to see Litany's barely restrained smile. "There's going to be an attack, unless I'm much mistaken. And I don't mean for us to perish in it." She folded Litany's fingers over the dag-gers. "We are an 'us,' now, Litany. You, I, and Lord Derset. We face this with solidarity. And with adequately sharpened blades."

The girl bowed, then saluted with one hand to her chest and hurried out, looking back once more from the doorway. As her footsteps died away, Lysande opened the window and stood facing the clouds. A gust of wind whipped through the frame. She dug her hands into her pockets, feeling something in one of them and pulling the object out. It was the golden quill, the one Sarelin had given her the day before she died.

She had forgotten that she had slipped it in there. She clutched the stem, feeling the jab of the tip into her palm.

The girl with the quill. It was impossible to count all the times Sarelin had called her that. A girl with a quill might yet have a place in the business of war. Could she really counter the enemy's moves, trusting to her own deductions, though? What of military experience? Of battle planning?

She had known, in the Pavilion, that she wanted this. As she thought back to that moment, sitting at the table and raising her goblet to join the Council, it occurred to her that there was a different kind of knowledge, one which could only be acquired with experience. She had not known, in the Pavilion, what it meant to challenge a ruler. Now she knew the rush of zeal that accompanied the fear of failure; the way that fervor and determination entwined.

Experience was more than that, though. It was also the sound of your name shouted by a girl in Elsington, a girl who had tied her hair in a braid because she could not afford a pin.

Prior.

Her fingers touched something hard. The feather's tip. She felt her chest rise and fall.

She was standing by the window and holding the quill, facing the clouds, when the northerly came in and painted her cheeks with rain.

Ten

The strings of the harp and viol sang out across the stones, accompanied by the warm thrum of the lute, the click-click of castanets, and the unwavering rhythms of the pipe and tabor. Laughter and chatter permeated the music. Above the courtyard, Lysande pulled her curtains open and peered down at the crowd of people in black doublets trimmed with scarlet.

"Did they give a reason for this refusal?" she said, turning back to the room. "Or are we simply to bow to their whims?"

"There was a reason, Councillor." Lady Pelory stood by the writing desk, holding a thick, leather-bound book. Her fingers were encased in soft emerald gloves. "Lady Bowbray insisted that while they have restored Prexley Castle to your wishes, the advisors cannot make it into a jail. Quite impossible, she said. A former symbol of great nobility, fitted out, only to be given over to elementals—there might be a petition to remove you. The court would prefer that you use the existing jails, even though they are cold and cramped."

Lysande moved away from the window. The laughter from outside reached her like a boot rubbing on a doorstep, muddying the newly swept stone of her mind. "And the accounts?" she said, walking over to the desk.

Pelory opened the book and flipped through the pages, before stopping at one. "It would seem that your suspicion was right, Councillor. I took the liberty of perusing Lady Bowbray's private books and found several entries that indicate funds are being siphoned off. From the charities, you see." She pointed to a string of numbers. "The Treasurer is restoring smaller castles with the money: decorating four properties."

"Whose castles?"

"That is the question, Councillor Prior." Pelory smiled mirthlessly. "They belong, it seems, to the families of Bowbray, Addischild, Chackery, and Tuchester."

The castanets began to click at a swifter pace and boots drummed on cobbles. Lysande had seen the Rhimese nobles dancing in pairs around the band, parting and rejoining, snaking back and forth. She blocked out their sound, thinking far beyond the castle, to the faces in the Oval in Axium Palace. She could picture Bowbray's mouth pinched into a hard line. Time taught you some things later than you would have liked; only now, after conversations with city-rulers about borders and negotiations with elementals, did she see that Bowbray's stiff smile had not been a stroke to end a phrase, but the beginning of a reply.

Was it treachery, to restore a castle for each of the advisors in Axium? Or should the author of *An Ideal Queen* call it clever politics?

"A lively tune, isn't it?" Pelory gestured to the window. "I walked past that nest of snakes on my way here and asked Lady Freste if this was a celebration. Certainly, she said. When I asked what they were celebrating, she said that Prince Fontaine orders a concert every time he hangs conspirators." Pelory paused. "How does a man reputed to be as cold as a Valderran floor manage to know everything going on his city? Does he have some special talent we might extract?"

"I assure you, Prince Fontaine is not entirely aloof."

"Well, you may be right. I suppose it depends on who is standing next to him."

Lysande said nothing but bent over the book, ignoring Pelory's probing gaze.

"I assume you want me to stop the advisors from restoring the castles," Pelory added.

"On the contrary. We must allow Lady Bowbray and her colleagues to fit out their spare dwellings with every luxury. Do nothing to stop them. But see that every cadre, mettle, and racket comes from our restoration fund—that is my only condition. Perhaps Lady Bowbray was right to object," Lysande said, straightening up. "I find it not compassionate to crowd all the prisoners into one jail, with no privacy. Four jails, on the other hand . . . that should ensure that elementals have all the space they need." Not to mention a sanctuary from a mob ready to pounce at the slightest provocation. "They will be handsomely accommodated, don't you think?"

She was pleased to see that Pelory could not hide her surprise. She had seen nobles shocked into silence before, when Sarelin threw out an order while smiling.

"And another thing."

There were times when you connected your ideas slowly to an action, and there were times when your body made the link for you, shepherding you through the motions. The order had come neatly from her quill, that morning, just as it had appeared in her mind.

All persons in Axium found to be acting as vigilantes, against elementals, the poor, or any others they persecute without evidence, shall be jailed forthwith.

It would have been sweeter if Charice were the one unfolding the piece of paper now; if Charice were the one raising her eyebrows as she read the order and took in the signature at the bottom; if they could embrace, drain their cups, and lay out the cards for a new game.

"I ask you a favor. Alas, I have no noble blood, Lady Pelory. There are no family ties between us." She waited for Pelory to lower the signed paper. "So I will offer you an exchange. I will give you something else to impress your husband, since you've already taken him to the perfumery."

"You followed me?"

"Only with my nose. Your robe has a distinct scent of lavender oil. I detect dragoncherry oil, too: an expensive fragrance." Lysande looked closely at her. "It might be hard to improve on a Rhimese perfumery, but if you do as I ask, I will give you something that you could not buy, even if you had all the gold in the realm."

"And what is that?"

"An invitation to the Sapphire Ball in Lyria." Lysande took care to enunciate each word. "And there will be another prize waiting for you if you seize the four castles once restoration is complete. Lord Derset tells me your villa lacks a title—that the Pelory family desires a castle with a hereditary line and a generous estate. One may be procured. Provided, of course, that the crown taxes the property, and all such income flows into a new fund which I am establishing for the living expenses of the poor. As of today, it will be known only to the two of us. We will call it the Leveling Fund."

Pelory's hesitation was just enough to constitute a pause. That's right, Lysande thought, examine your circumstances; think on the perfume bottles and the chestnut pony that you have bought for your husband on this trip alone, think on the way his pretty face lit up when he received your latest gift, according to the perfume merchant, who was all too happy to talk after I parted with a few cadres; then consider your own style of living, for rainbow heartstone does not come cheap, and you are not a woman to parade about in motley.

Lysande extended a palm. Pelory unclasped her emerald gloves and smiled mirthlessly.

"To the future," Lysande said.

Pelory gripped her hand and shook it. "To foundations."

The eastern breeze blew more kindly than the Axium wind was wont to do when Lysande returned to the pavilion by the Flavantine. She was aware of every sound, every snatch of conversation as she combed the bank. Among the dallying Rhimese she spotted no familiar Axiumite. She sat down, plucked a weed from a clump of queensflowers and tossed it into the river. For a while, she watched the ripples on the water, yet there was a rippling within her, too, and she reached for the memory that was shifting in the corner of her mind.

That day in the forest . . . before she discovered scale, before Charice discovered black-market trade . . . it belonged to another time. Yet she had thought of it so often, it was as she had inked it onto paper. She could pick out every part of it. The warm breath of summer had hung upon Axium as they marched into the silver birches, chattering. When Lysande and Charice had broken away from the other students, Lysande had felt a rush of heat in her neck: the two most studious pupils caught up in a whispered pact, at last; an expedition for their own curiosity. They had found themselves in the heart of Axium Forest within an hour. She remembered entering a grove where the sound of birds retreated and looking at a ring of tree stumps streaked with white.

How well she recalled it, even now. The white substance that sent translucent beams over the soil, purer than starlight. She had smiled until her lips could curve no more.

"Chimera markings," Charice had declared.

They must have debated the markings for an hour. Why did the white streaks feel so ancient? What could anyone really know about chimeras and other magical creatures and artifacts from before the Conquest? Lysande had not been used to talking so freely, but Charice had spurred her to new questions about the markings, their ideas running to the potential messages the beasts might have left. A deep breath; a deep pause. She remembered that moment of realization. It should have been easy to find the group again, she had told herself; surely, the singers and chatterers among their classmates would guide them back.

The silence ripened around her. The forest seemed to get denser and denser as she and Charice walked. Then a leaf crunched, and something dragged through the undergrowth.

Lysande saw it, again, like a picture repainted in sharper colors. She had drawn her tiny knife from her pocket, unsheathing the blade. A rainbow of scales flashed as the sunsnake slid forward; she stepped toward it, brandishing the knife; all she knew was that she had to fight to save both of them, to dart the point of her blade between those little eyes. Before she could attack, Charice thrust out her arm.

Wind blasted from her friend's palm, and Lysande felt a hollowing inside herself—a strange and terrible rawness.

The sunsnake soared into the air, spun over and over, plummeted, and fell with a thud onto the soil. Snake and attacker stared at each other, waiting.

Lysande's legs had frozen on the forest floor. A queasiness came over her: it was as if the wind had passed through her body, through flesh and bone and blood, and stirred up her emotions, leaving them tangled in her stomach. She saw the sunsnake give a hiss and then disappear into the undergrowth, and Charice drop her arm to her side. In the quiet that followed, a few leaves had crackled.

"I'll confess," Charice had said, quietly. "I expect you'll want to tell the headmistress once we're back. But there'll be no need to. I'll be blunt and quick. I've heard the queen looks you in the eye when they do it—right before the axe falls."

The last hour of conversation had run through Lysande's head, a haze of animated discussion, peppered with anecdotes from histories, stories and poems the two of them had read. She had grabbed Charice by the forearm. "No," she had blurted. "Tell me you don't feel the same, like we could talk for days?" Like Obera and Rousse, she thought: the moon-crossed friends, meeting in the secret library in the Silver Songs.

Charice had nodded slowly. "But," she began, "the snake . . ."

"Didn't harm anyone. I don't think it should be punished."

They looked at each other. A butterfly landed on one of the tree stumps and fluttered off again, its wings like garnets, gleaming in the dim grove.

They clasped hands and shook. Lysande refused to let go until Charice did.

They had lost the party for good. But they talked long into the night, and by the time they slept, the stars poked holes in the canopy of the sky. Lysande lay next to Charice, the mossy slope cushioning her head, and watched the gold points needling their constellations into black silk. The future seemed to expand above her, rolling out across the firmament. There was something warming which was not only the night air, and she fell asleep to the sound of an owl hooting, somewhere far away in the birches.

Now, she let the memory ripple across her mind, leaving traces.

She could have publicly declared that anyone targeting elementals would be punished. She could have protected the woman who guarded her own secret, the woman whose body had spoken of her care for Lysande as she had knelt on the floor and bent herself to a task with more concentration than a scholar, looking up every minute or so and meeting Lysande's eyes. How warm Charice's tongue had felt against her own skin. *You're always cold to the touch*, Charice had told her once, and she had thought that her body only heated under the influence of scale, during those blissful moments when the world receded. Charice had proven her wrong. She had taken time in the disproving, too, drawing patterns of heat with her mouth, until Lysande's skin transmuted under her touch.

They had journeyed a long way, from classmates to friends, friends to lovers, to . . . whatever this state of disequilibrium was, now.

Softly, she spoke Charice's name into the wind, and thought she heard the ghost of a reply.

As she turned, her hand struck the toe of a worn boot. The breath rushed out of her. Charice managed a faint grin, and Lysande leaped to her feet and made the old gesture, wrists crossed. Litany had edged forward and Chidney drew her sword, and Lysande ordered them back, until both halves of her escort hovered by the water.

"You're safe—you're still—"

"Wish I had longer." Charice pressed her lips to Lysande's, then withdrew, watching her. It was as much a question as a kiss. Lysande leaned in, driven by the part of her mind that worked on instinct, and claimed Charice's mouth for a moment, wrapping both hands around her waist and tightening her hold.

"I'd forgotten you liked to do that," Charice said.

"Grip hard?"

"Mm." A pause. Lysande let go. "As I said, I wish I had longer." Charice pulled a tiny, gauzy bag from her pocket. "Perhaps we'll see each other soon, though, one way or another."

A silence rippled between them, sudden as a breeze flecked with snow.

"Which side of a sword will I see you on?" Lysande said.

"Hasn't anyone told you that it's impolite to refuse a gift?" Charice pushed the bag toward her before she could respond.

Lysande opened her hand and took the delicate gauze. There wasn't much to examine; the silver locket tumbled out of the bag easily, and she found a finely detailed engraving of a bear inside it. The bear's mouth hung open in a roar.

"If this belonged to who I think it did, then . . . words alone won't do."

"I thought you'd assume as much." Charice wore an odd smile. "Sarelin Brey never owned this locket, though. With the Brey family emblem swimming around her on goblets and hangings, I don't think she needed a keepsake. No, this belonged to a member of the Brey family who is rarely remembered as a Brey."

A moment's hesitation, timed exactly where the rhythm of the sentence tapered to an elegant close: the kind of timing that did not occur by chance. Lysande knew that Charice did not usually rehearse her remarks. She wondered why her friend was determined to do her this favor—if it was some ethical imperative or pangs of guilt that drove her. A voice in her head that she did not like raised the question of whether it could be something more insidious.

"Second cousins to the queen aren't exactly celebrated. The royal family thought so little of this girl that they made her clean up after Queen Sarelin, darn her clothes, look after her daggers, practice foreign tongues, and go through books with her, all while both girls were scarce half-grown. The scholarly tasks hurt her the most, I think. Those were the times she could tell how close she was to the queen's ability . . . so near the heir, and so far, like the rag that wipes a diamond clean."

"That is the exact metaphor I should have chosen."

"I know," Charice said.

Another silence.

"I thought any rumors about Sarelin's youth were never . . . substantiated."

"We know each other, the hidden people in Axium. We've a community. And I found out that a woman who visited my shop every week had been a personal attendant in the household of Sarelin Brey, when she was a girl—before she was caught stealing a silver plate." Charice smiled sadly. "When you've been cut loose from your work, you don't have much to pay with, but truth be told, I felt sorry for her . . . enough to accept a locket thieved from her former family of employment as currency."

"And you went from shop talk to discussing Sarelin's slighted cousin?" Lysande said.

"She was a handsome woman. Of course we lingered a little, into the night."

"Of course you did." Lysande paced, glancing at the murky water of the Flavantine. "You must think this important, to risk finding me."

"I wanted you to hear it from me first."

Who else would she hear it from? The question was practically forming itself. But from all the hours she had passed with Charice, she could judge when more was coming.

Charice folded her arms. "You should have seen the way Perch came flying at me the next day, telling me that he'd found my visitor's body in the gutter, her chest pierced through. Apparently, there'd been a half-dozen Axium Guards outside the night before. It turns out the queen didn't like anyone hearing about her second cousin and the way she'd been treated."

"Her second cousin," Lysande said, "the White Queen."

She had guessed, the moment Charice mentioned Axium Guards. Lysande had spent many years around Sarelin, enough to know what made the queen react.

She ran a fingernail over the tiny bear engraved on the locket. It shone so brightly, for nobles, the family crest; so brightly that even to tarnish it once was to reduce its light forever. In Axium, a cousin with magic would have been a stain indeed. She could guess why the Breys had made Mea Tacitus a servant to the heir. She saw the dual purpose, teaching Mea to grovel and enabling the family elders to keep an eye on her; it would have seemed a wise solution, enabling them to control the elemental girl. Researching for *An Ideal Queen*, she had seen the same thing, only in smaller manors instead of palaces. Silverblood families thought along remarkably similar lines.

But as so often happened, in a city whose nobles thrived on hierarchy, the Breys had overlooked that most crucial of factors: personality.

"I think a woman as ambitious as Mea Tacitus could not accept being a link near the bottom of a chain," Lysande said. "I suppose she was just Mea Brey, then."

Charice looked down. "*Tacitus* means silence in the old tongue. Perhaps that's what I should have done. Kept silent." The waver in her voice did not go unnoticed by Lysande.

Charice folded Lysande's fingers over the locket.

"Grant me this," she said. "When you see me next, do not be too angry."

"Angry? Why should I be angry?"

Charice pressed her lips to the back of Lysande's hand, and this time, it was not a fleeting kiss but a touch like a seal pushing into wax, as if to preserve a farewell: *with this crest, I remain.*

"Be proud," Charice said.

Like the breeze, which passed in a fragrant whisper, she was bowing and then gone. Lysande knew her friend too well to attempt to chase after her. Everything that had been said would take time to sink in, anyway, and it was more sensible to focus on that, surely: on the knowledge, and not on the tightness in her chest that increased with every second that she thought on Charice's harrowed face and tattered cloak.

Making sure that Chidney and Litany were still a fair distance behind her, she plucked a queensflower from the ground and began to roll it between her fingers.

Her fingers pulverized the flower, sharp leaves and thin petals both, and she stared ahead at the water, not seeing it. The wheels in her mind were spinning freely now. This revelation brought her a dance-step away from the White Queen, and she knew it; and yet she could not make that last step. She longed for a few more pieces of information—just a few shreds more.

Something tickled the back of her neck. The old instinct to call Sarelin's name was there, but only the breeze came to her side, and she trudged back to her waiting mare.

That night, she brooded on Charice's words. The goblet of scale she poured fizzed and hissed, with two spoonfuls mixed into the water. It was only a temporary increase, she told herself, in a time of stress. The tremor in her conscience refused to entirely disappear, but she did not reach for the night-quartz. Spreading the map-book and her compilations of notes before her, she drank while she read, feeling the writhing in her stomach, the burn of her forehead, and the angry pace of her heartbeat—physical stimulus and mental calm, a paradox she knew well. She concentrated on the gold sweeping through the room; the torrent of rich light.

Two vessels anchored by the side of the Grandfleuve; a ramp of wooden boards ran down to water that gushed and roared, carving a swathe through the land. The nearest ship boasted twenty-four sails, half with the image of the Pyrrhan flag and half with the Valderrans', so that purple leopards billowed from the front and pale gray ice-bears fluttered at the back. A prow jutted out in the shape of a spearfish spike, dawn tinting the wood a faint ochre.

Gasps and cries escaped the crowd as they took in the cages that were positioned on either side of the main viewing deck. Lysande tried to accept that she was seeing a live leopard and a gray ice-bear, the latter sporting a pair of horns that were short but undeniably sharp, poking out from the roof of its cage. The animals growled and snapped.

There was no way any attackers downriver would fail to notice a craft decorated with bright colors, an ice-bear, and a leopard, yet Cassia looked so pleased that Lysande managed to conjure a smile. It served you well to smile when you did not know if there was still a crack between you and a colleague, to scatter sand over whatever fissures might remain and pretend that suspicion had been buried beneath the grains; yet Lysande did not have to search hard to find an expression to suit the circumstance. As she took in the grin brightening Cassia's face, her own heart juddered in her chest. While the Irriqi and Dante boarded their boat, she walked over to Raden.

"My horse is still sleeping off the gallop. It's been quite a ride, since your letter. Feels as if I spent most of it jolting around on a stubborn child with hooves. At least I won't be wrangling a mule for the next leg of the journey, unlike some . . . Fortituda take pity on them." He looked more tired than he sounded.

"I still wonder if two hundred guards will be enough," she said, low enough for only him to hear. "Telling Jale might be wise, too."

"Prince Chamboise's uncle doesn't have a reputation for welcoming Axium Guards." Raden looked darkly at a pair of Lyrians. "He tried to turn one of my officers away from Lyrian territory with her whole legion, last year. Better not to risk more, if you're asking me."

Derset came to her side and nodded cordially to Raden. Lysande watched Raden's face, but if there was a knowing look or the slightest hint of disapproval, she did not detect it; of course, it seemed to her that the mark of certain private activities with her advisor must be stamped across her face. Yet she had kept her façade up, had she not?

And the way Raden had snuck a glance at her entourage told her that he was more concerned with what he had raised with her when they last spoke—she had not forgotten that remark about power sitting on her easily, like a mantle.

Derset leaned forward to converse with Raden about his journey, making inquiry after inquiry: Was Captain Hartleigh enjoying the mild eastern air? Had he found adequate time to leave instructions for the officers who were maintaining order in Axium? Only when Raden was in full flow of discourse about the effects of the wind on their impending voyage did Derset's glance stray toward Lysande. The style of it was almost formal, if you missed the affection couched within.

She decided not to tell Raden or Derset what she had learned from Charice; time was needed to work through the implications, no matter how tempted she was to share.

The Axiumites filed along the bank to the second vessel. The topsails of the craft, fashioned from gold cloth, blazed in the morning sun; the mainsail billowed sapphire blue, with a spearfish embroidered on it, and she saw that each prow bore swirls of pearl. Beside a sail with a Rhimese cobra, another sail had been embroidered with the Axium crown and letters in silver thread:

COUNCILLOR PRIOR
ORPHAN PRINCESS OF AXIUM

Lysande stared, and turned. "Jale!"

The Lyrian prince looked up from where he was chatting with two women in feather-light outfits and waved to her.

"Was this your idea?" Lysande called.

"Thought you'd like it!"

"I'm not a—" But she saw how he was smiling and sighed. "Never mind."

"I think there's not enough silver on the design, though. We should have added a border of crowns, and a new crest of your own—and a dash of diamond thread, of course."

"Diamond thread would suit you better, Your Highness. It shines brightly, no matter how it is used."

Jale's smile gave way to open beaming. He nearly knocked into one of the noblewomen as he turned back.

Lysande happened to catch Dante's eye, on the next ship, and received the full blast of his approving stare, which she had only recently learned to distinguish from his disapproving stare. She suspected that a compliment to Jale had bought her some good will.

If it had not been for the archers forming a solid border around the deck and perching themselves by the prow, she might have felt nervous as they pulled away. They made quick progress, to the whistles and cries of the sailors in the rigging; the northern half of the Grandfleuve carved through largely uninhabited scrub, and the weather, though warm, did not build to a southern pitch. The Council had the river mostly to themselves, the archers keeping guard, and Lysande spied no suspicious figures on the banks. She slipped down to her room, ducking her head beneath the low doorway, and drew out her daggers, ordering Derset to fend off anyone asking after her.

Since she and Litany had practiced with weapons last night in the ruined Montinetti Castle in Rhime—an arrow shot across the floor here, a rapier swung over the marble curls of a bust there, their banter cobbled together from advice, comparisons, and jokes—she felt invigorated. Now, she threw a dagger at the board Raden had set up on the wall, concentrating on landing the blade in the middle. The hardest thing about throwing daggers was not hitting the target—it was doing so quickly, flicking her wrist and sending the blade flying out of instinct rather than calculation. She tried to call on Sarelin's training. Litany, as she had expected, had proven to be an excellent shot, and Lysande worked on copying Litany's firm stance from their practice last night.

The crew amused themselves by gambling with the Axium and Lyrian guards, and even a few of the nobles rolled dice on the deck. The Rhimese set up their tactos-boards at the rear end of the boat, staring each other down. Their leader did not take part in their silent war, and Lysande searched the ship for him in vain. It should have been relief that she felt, surely, rather than disappointment; she was only seeking to debate the *Astratto Formulas'* workings with Luca, she tried to tell herself. Not looking to study the soft underside of his jaw.

She joined Jale, who was looking out at the water without seeming to see it, his gaze sweeping across every so often to the other ship. Over a few cups of cinnamon-spiced tea, she insisted that he tell her about the arts of the delta.

"I go in for the choir, myself—but when you see the palace dancers perform the Song of Sun, well, you know you're alive."

"Do they really climb over each other's shoulders and form steps?"

"Oh yes. You needn't sound so astonished, you know; we are quite limber in the south. My mother used to dance every year in her own jubilee, with dark wings fixed to her back, surrounded by white-winged dancers of every age and shape, recreating the tale of the first messenger doves. She had a famous partner from the dancing school— a young man who leaped and twirled around her more gracefully than any other performer."

"She sounds a Lyrian ruler indeed," Lysande said.

"When I asked her why dancing was so important, she would quote the poet Verlaude: that if a princess can leap and slide on stage, she can sidestep in a courtroom, and if a prince can dance before a crowd, he can win his opponents' hearts. Of course," Jale gave her a sideways look, "my mother was more concerned with winning bodies, for the most part."

"I take it you have not been tempted to traverse the same path?"

"There is but one deer for me. That's how you Axiumites put it, isn't it? Love and the chase are the same to your poets. Sometimes, I wonder if I am the pursuer or the quarry . . ."

He glanced out across the water. It took a moment for him to notice that Lysande was attending his words, but he showed no inclination to finish the sentence.

They shared stories about their cities, and as the time grew, so did their ease with each other; when Lysande told a joke about Axiumites trying to make a river flow on time, Jale laughed heartily at the punchline. Although his melancholy seemed to have mostly dispersed, at one point she noticed him gazing at Dante on the next ship. The First Sword did not look his way. Jale's demeanor seemed to droop slightly, and Lysande noted it.

With some reluctance, she looked down to see a bird landing on her arm. The speckled head of Three's messenger nudged her, and she took the envelope from Cursora's beak. The dove soared back into the clouds.

Lysande made her way down into the hammocks, pushing past guards clutching their stomachs and cooks chopping vegetables, until at last she found the door to her box-like chamber. The dimensions seemed to have been intended for someone much shorter than her.

> *My dear,*
> *Congratulations on your new plan.*

A surge of relief passed through her. Three was not furious, after all.

> *But I am afraid we have reason to be concerned about*
> *your safety. Elementals whose voices never sound in the*
> *halls of power . . . these in anger outrank the most*
> *envious of nobles.*
> *Nothing is certain; only hints. We will investigate. Keep*
> *your eyes and ears open. With warm regards from a*
> *warming clime,*

> 3

She folded the paper up, unfolded it, and read it again. Gratitude filtered through her mind, tempered by frustration. Would it have hurt him to explain how and why her safety was at risk? *Be clear, damn you.* A poisoner? A party of archers? A great rock on the river-bed?

Though she knew what she really wanted to write: *Tell me everything you know of Sarelin and Mea Tacitus together. Bad or good.* The locket bulged inside the inner lining of her doublet. It seemed to grow heavier as she dwelled on the thought of the White Queen.

She locked the letter in a chest and strode out. In the room at the end of the corridor she found Derset and Litany hunched over a table, and together they shared a half-bottle of pepperwine—the Lyrian wine, with glittering peppercorns mixed through it, left an aftertaste that was half-sweet, half-spicy, and entirely memorable—while Derset recounted a few tales from the delta. She could not help smiling at a fable about a drunken captain who mistook a crocodile for her horse. One lingering glance reminded her of how Derset's skin had felt warm against hers as they lay on the blood-red bedsheets in the Painter's Suite, but she had to put that comfort behind her. It was easy to fall into a pattern, and she did not need another dependency.

As Derset was beginning to describe Princess Ariane Chamboise's duel against Captain Rodrillaud of Bijon—"the handsomest duel that ever was fought, with swords that gleamed blue with sapphires"—a roar of voices cut him off.

"What in the Three Lands was that?" Lysande said.

They all raised their eyes to the roof.

"Your reception, my lady."

The dice had stopped, and feet were moving about on deck. Lysande emerged to find everyone pressed to the starboard rail. Derset kept a careful distance from her as they made their way through to the front. A platform balanced on stilts, further down the riverbank, and she took in several hundred women, men, and children, all of them yelling and waving. No city colors daubed the throng, only rags in drab hues.

She turned at the sound of her name. Luca was beckoning her from the rear, Tiberus coiled on his shoulder like a dark epaulet. Finally, he stood above-deck.

"Word travels fast," Lysande said, stopping by his side.

"When you've little to talk about but your next meal, word travels like a flaming dove in search of water. I expect that since the Council was formed, that lot've been hoping for a glimpse of us."

"They are not from the cities, by the look of them."

"Villagers from the central scrub," Jale said, coming alongside them. "Bone people, my mother used to call them. They have so few possessions that they sell the bones of their dead to traders. Insufferably hard existence, between Lyria and Rhime. My mother said it was a funny thing that in a country with so many leaders scrapping over land, there could be a place that no city-ruler was allowed to claim."

"I fail to deduce the humor." Luca gazed out at the crowd.

Staring in the same direction, Lysande could well believe Jale's remarks. The same plague that had whittled the flesh of the elementals on the back of the executioner's cart in Axium was present here, too: starvation exacted the same price from magical and non-magical alike. Bile rose inside her, the beginning of a nausea that was bred of guilt. She made to return to her party at the rail, but Luca's fingers curled around her arm.

"Aren't you eager to greet your reception party, Prior? We can't deny the people their orphan princess."

Although they were too far away to make out the deck in front, cries of "Irriqi!" told them that Cassia must be waving, and Lysande could feel a flutter in her chest at the thought of the attention. She straightened. She pictured Sarelin standing on the palace steps, a year ago, before the jubilee crowd, her shoulders squared to the people. Were these spectators not part of the populace she had claimed to rule for?

By the time they walked to the front of the boat, the faces in the crowd were close: couples barely old enough to be carrying children jostled for space behind the rail, old men and toothless women pressed together at the front, and a smattering of youths waved. Paper, Lysande thought, looking at their skin. They were made of paper. Easy to crumple.

Jale stepped forward to the prow. The cheers swelled to a roar as he began to wave back, beaming and calling out, greeting the crowd with a smile. The bone people shouted so hard that their throats must have ached, lavishing rounds of applause on the prince. When Jale returned to her side, Luca walked forward.

You never knew what a prince looked like until you saw him reflected in the faces of a crowd. The spectators shouted and hailed him, clapping, even holding their children aloft to see; Luca did not beam but greeted them in his own fashion, raising a single hand. Tiberus had coiled around his arm, and man and snake seemed to wave together. Lysande concentrated on the lines of his body, repressing her own anxiety.

"Surprised?" Jale said, at her side.

"He doesn't seem an obvious choice for the people's hero."

"Oh, I don't know; he's got a dashing side to him, the mysterious prince of Rhime."

"The mysterious prince who murdered his brother, you mean," Lysande said, thinking of Dante's remarks.

"It's because he murdered Raolo Sovrano that they're cheering." Jale's voice dropped to a murmur. "My mother told me about Luca's brother."

Lysande could not remember hearing any tales of Raolo. Sarelin's comments about Rhime had usually encompassed the court and city, her dislike firing like a storm of arrows rather than a single shaft.

"Apparently, he was a Quester. I used to think that fanatics who believed in renewing the Conquest were all talk—Mother said they were zealots clutching their books—but Raolo was more of a doer. He rode through the poorest villages from time to time and shot anyone he accused of being elemental. He was 'cleansing' the realm."

Lysande stared. "That's madness."

"Oh, I suspect he was all too much in command of his wits. Questers close in on their prey. Sometimes Raolo would pick on those who'd been rumored to have harbored elementals, or told fortunes, or even kept a chip of glass they called a magical stone."

Lysande could not find a reply. She could see the girls and boys, lined up to be shot. It was one thing to believe the ludicrous notion that anyone who associated with magic was committing a crime against the state, but to actually carry out a punishment . . .

Sarelin could not have known about this. Raolo Sovrano must have hidden it from the crown. *But Sarelin killed elementals*, a voice in her head chanted. If Sarelin could conceal the fact that Mea Tacitus had spent her childhood working for her, relegated to the place of a servant in all practical ways, what else might she have tucked away from Lysande?

She stared out at the paper creatures before her.

Could she lead for these people—the people who could not afford to bribe her at a banquet? They were all over the realm, people like this. If not so dire in circumstance as the bone people, then they were at least old friends to poverty, and she had done . . . what? Stopped the executions of elementals. What of housing? Of safety? Of food and water and crops?

The crowd on the platform were still cheering, and she realized with a jolt that they were waiting for her. "It'll only take a minute," Jale said gently. "You just have to wave."

"Come on," Luca said, sliding his palm beneath hers. "The scholar needs a hand."

He made to escort her forward. The touch was molten, every bit of her aware of his skin. Instead of unclasping, she gripped his hand with every bit of force she could exert; his chin jerked toward her and she read the expression written on his face, before it disappeared, and as she understood the sharp excitement there, she squeezed harder. They were almost level with the platform now. The ship had slowed, and as Lysande turned to face the crowd, the sound washed over her: stomping, applause, and a single word.

"Council! Council! Council!"

"They like us," Luca said. "Curious, but there you go. Give them a wave."

All those faces stared at her; all those people, chanting, waiting for her response.

"I'm a commoner in royal clothes," she said, quietly. "An impostor."

"That is precisely the point, Prior. Everyone in that crowd looks at you and sees themself in a better doublet."

The face of a boy at the front struck her as she gazed out. His cheeks had sunk so deeply that they seemed holes, the skin stretched tightly from jaw to ear like a skull wrapped in plaster, yet this skeleton was smiling. His eyes lit up as he saw her, and he bowed, exposing the vertebrae in his neck. *Like the elementals, driven into hiding.*

She did not pause to consider propriety. She bowed as low as she could in return, her hair falling down around her face and dangling, and she held the pose even when it began to hurt. The noise of the crowd dropped away, but when she straightened up, the storm of cheering swelled beyond anything that had come before.

"Prior! Prior! Prior!"

She looked back at Luca. His gaze was fixed on her, though whether it was with irritation or admiration, she could not be sure.

The front row of the platform bent down into a bow; behind them, the next row followed, and the next; an old man at the back stooped last, his withered frame just managing to bend. Lysande looked at them all, taking in the tops of their heads. She bowed again. The second time, she was conscious of the effect of her bow, and Perfault's words swam in her head. *Confidence before the nobility. Humility before the people.*

The word *Prior* filled her ears, and she was not sure if it was the sharp movement or the sound of her name that caused the dizziness when she straightened up.

Of all people, she could act. There had to be more that she could offer; more than bows and smiles and waves. A wave had never bought a loaf. Bowing did not pay for grain or offer an uncracked pot. It did not protect you against Questers riding through the desert.

The chanting, the cheering, and the churning of the river: it all merged into one rhythm, following her as they sailed on. Yet it was the boy's face that stayed in her mind: the hollow cheeks, the neck like a notched rope, and the eyes, shining so brightly in that skull. Those eyes never left her, even after the ship had rounded the bend.

The snarls of grass and the parched soil that had surrounded them all morning ceded, and the brown of the riverbank gave way to gold—a vista of undulating sand, stretching for miles. Lyria's territory, Lysande noticed, contained only a few trees that pushed up from the desert like forks, their branches bristling with spines, and tiny pools in the sand crawling with mosquitoes. Insects slipped beneath their collars and sleeves on deck. A flying beetle stung Litany on the nose, and Lysande tried to slap mosquitoes away, but by the second day, a trail of little dark blots decorated her ankles, wrists, and the crooks of her elbows. She did not envy the archers standing at the rail.

Below the deck, the atmosphere felt little better, thanks to a current that surged and roared; guards and nobles alike retched into pails, and Lysande decided to spend most of the journey above. They were lurching through one of the coils of the Grandfleuve when the prow of their vessel bumped Cassia and Dante's craft, and a crowd of Valderrans turned.

"Ahoy there!" Jale shouted, waving.

Dante was among the group staring back at them. He waved, but only for a moment. The Valderrans were shirtless in the heat, and a few of the noblewomen around Lysande giggled and pointed, yet Dante locked eyes with Jale, unheeding. His face creased deeply.

"Have Prince Chamboise and the First Sword fallen out?" Lysande said, turning to Derset. Nothing could stop the surge of warm curiosity through her.

"I do not like to give tongue to rumors, my lady."

"Yet I would know them, if they exist."

"Well, it is only speculation." Derset ran a hand through his hair. "But since Prince Chamboise agreed to marry Mariana Ferago, there have been whispers that Dante Dalgëreth objected to the match—that he spoke passionately against it behind doors. It is only gossip, as I say. Whispers that should be taken with a spoonful of salt."

As Dante left the prow, Lysande realized where she had seen him glare like that: at the dinner table in the Room of Accord, when Gabrella Merez had questioned him about his lack of spousal prospects.

"Do you think that Dante might be in love with Princess Ferago, my lord?"

"I could not say."

"You cannot venture an opinion on love?"

Derset smiled wryly. "I know plenty of devotion. In that area, I might venture, if a goddess should approve of my ministrations."

Lysande was not blushing. She was just a little heated by the Lyrian sun, she told herself, turning her face away from Derset. She refocused her attention on Dante and Jale.

There was a more likely explanation, of course. But Sarelin would have called it a poison brew—an idea so stupid that it was akin to drinking your own poison by accident. A First Sword of the north might marry a woman or a man, a suitor with gray hair or honey-brown curls, a noble or a new sword-champion . . . but the one person they might not marry was a southerner. Dante would know that as well as anyone. Lysande guessed that if he did not, the scowls of his guards would remind him.

She watched the land. A plume of smoke rose from a fire, on which a few bone people were roasting something. She checked the sand for any sign of movement, wondering all the while about the look between Dante and Jale, and the way Dante had leaned across to his friend and begun speaking at the banquet in Axium, as if there were no one else in the Great Hall. Had Jale's face not lit up, too, upon seeing the First Sword? They had drawn close to each other naturally, as if they did not need permission to inhabit each other's space.

Her mind had run ahead to several possibilities, since she had watched Dante holding the bejeweled sword in the maze-garden, rehearsing his speech. If she really had borne witness to the makings of a proposal, then perhaps some prelude had taken place . . . a declaration of amorous sentiments, or perhaps even a dialogue. There was a language of touching and caressing, of advancing and seizing. Something in the way Dante looked at Jale told her that he could speak that particular language very well.

They would not take such a risk, surely, surrounded by soldiers who sang "The Land of Gold and Blue." They must guess, as she did, that the queensflower had been left on the Valderran table in Axium for a purpose, and that there was no way better to rekindle an old north-and-south enmity than by blending it with magic.

The ship cut smoothly through the clear water. By the third day, Derset had removed his jacket and boots, and Litany had stripped down to her drawers, but as their leader, it seemed inappropriate for Lysande to remove her doublet. For the first time, she gazed at the flimsy skirts and gauzy overlays of the Lyrian nobles with envy. She joined Derset, who was reading a book of poems at the rail, frowning as he perused one particular ode, and though Lysande could not see the whole text without making her curiosity obvious, she managed to glimpse the first line: *If ever I should choose to hunt.*

She had an odd feeling that she had read the full poem, but she could not recall it, and the gap in her library of memorized pages bothered her.

On her other side, Chidney and Litany discussed the speed of sail and the methods of navigation, Chidney guiding Litany's hand in the direction of the topsails and somehow forgetting to let go of her fingers. Lysande could not help smiling as she watched them; it was like watching a bear paw gently at a kitten. While the pair debated the chance of wind, her thoughts drifted to Mea Tacitus as a young girl, cleaning Sarelin's chambers and darning her clothes.

A pain stung her throat, and she clutched the rail.

"If you are seasick, my lady, I can fetch you a pail."

"Thank you, my lord. But it is only a slight—"

The agony that ripped through her struck lower this time: a stabbing in her chest, entering her lungs. She steadied herself with one hand.

"My lady, you are unwell." Derset placed his hand gently on her arm.

"So it appears." The deck began to wobble. "But I think I would rather do my retching in private. You stay here, my lord. Litany, with me."

In her room, she unlocked the chest where she had stowed the remedy Luca had left outside her door, and drew out the little glass tube. The contents swirled about in the vial, glistening the color of ripe tangerines. She toyed with the stopper.

I will be fine, she told herself. In an hour's time, the effects of all that scale will probably disappear.

Yet she uncorked the vial and handed it to Litany. The attendant drank a little of the potion and waited a half-minute to gauge the taste before nodding and handing it back. Taking a sip, Lysande closed her eyes.

As the first drop of liquid slid down her throat, the pain dissolved, melting away and leaving a viscous coating in its wake. One mouthful cleared her chest entirely.

"Sun and stars," she breathed.

There was enough in the vial for one more swallow. The glass clinked against the wood as she locked it back in the chest. She inhaled, feeling the air rush in.

The heat had become oppressive in the windowless room, and in her haste to return to the deck, she almost ran into Lord Malsante. "Prince Fontaine requests your company, Councillor," he said.

She found Luca by the prow, his hands folded behind his back, gazing out at the Grandfleuve. A table and chairs were set up next to him and a tactos-board laid out.

"I don't know about you, Prior, but I find this heat brings on boredom."

"This is your request?" She eyed the board. "A game of tactos?"

"You might indulge me for a quick bout. I've beaten envoys, priests, and nobles, but I am yet to defeat a scholar."

He turned, the sun catching his dark hair from behind, and the look in his eyes made her silence a sharp response. Something eddied in those eyes, a dark ripple of intent. Tiberus reclined on the chair closest to her, so she took the other, and Luca scooped up his cobra and sat down. After they had both studied the board, he slid one of his guards forward two squares.

Lysande made an advance of her own. They watched each other over the board. Move by move, they began the dance of Elira's oldest game, sliding the pieces or moving them in jumps . . . guard, noble, city-ruler, queen, king, or chimera: each attacked in a different way. Lysande had always been able to anticipate how her opponent would play, from calculation, and from years of practice in the staff kitchen.

Luca's moves proved challenging. Bluffing, then striking, and sometimes capturing three pieces in one go, he played without letting his emotions show, working his guards and city-rulers and only moving his queen and king when he needed to take an important piece. His fingers moved silently across the squares. She yielded several of her guards early in the game, taking the opportunity to note his responses. When her first princess toppled over, he folded his arms. "It won't work on me, you know," he said.

"I beg your pardon?"

"I'm not Sarelin Brey, Prior. I know when someone is letting me win."

Lysande stroked a fallen guard on its head, considering the formations on the board. "No need for my submission, then."

"You mean to survey my strategy and use it against me. I am quite aware."

It was as if he knew that she had a series of diagrams of tactos moves in her compilation of political notes; as if, somehow, it was discernible in her face.

"Perhaps I will win, and you will submit," she said.

His little half-smile curled the corners of his mouth.

She shrugged and picked up her queen. Her hand skipped over the board, taking five of his pieces, mercilessly exposing the flaws in his formation and knocking down his monarchs. She rested her own queen in the back corner, surrounded by her guards. Luca's silence lasted for longer than she had anticipated; he gazed down at the ruins of his army with one hand propped against his chin. Lysande let her eyes wander over his fingers.

"You're contemplating whether to yield now or to finish the game and be officially decimated," she said.

"Aren't you forgetting something, Prior?" He picked up his chimera. "A whole army of guards . . . a queen and a king . . . they are nothing to the most powerful piece on the board."

After a fleeting pause, he moved quickly, sliding the chimera out in a diagonal line: not to attack her own as was customary, but to place it equidistant from her queen and king. The act threatened both monarchs at once. It was so audacious that it stole her breath, and for the first time, she realized, someone had made a move in tactos that she had not foreseen.

"You were pretending all along," she said.

He gestured at the board, where only six pieces remained: three black and three white. "Shall we begin the game, now?"

She noted that his collar had slipped as he leaned over. Without the ruby or the cloak, more of his throat was exposed than before. She could not say how or why she did it, but her hand reached toward him and wrapped around one side of his neck.

The flesh felt tender, as if she could reach through it and touch the very pulse.

The deck around them had gone unusually quiet, and a glance showed her a ring of guards and attendants watching, all of whom found things to do immediately upon catching her eye. Excellent, Lysande thought. We are the main entertainment for the voyage. Derset was watching her too; he caught her eye and looked away at once. She turned back to meet Luca's gaze. He was sitting still. He had not removed her hand from his neck, but his eyes flickered over her face. Slowly, Lysande slid her fingers across the soft skin of his throat.

Some games you played by moving stone pieces. You calculated the moves, strategizing carefully. Other games, you played without knowing why, steered by a force beyond your control.

Pressing the skin was an art: a sculptor's touch was needed, careful but firm. It might have been her imagination, but she thought his pupils had widened. He looked away quickly, and she took her time before pulling her hand back, removing her fingers one by one. A whole variety of parts of her body had awakened. She was not about to let it show.

She examined the board. There were only a set number of strategies that could be used at this point, and it all depended on which one Luca chose. She pretended to consider her queen's position and stole a glance at him. His eyes were definitely brighter now.

Reaching out, she seized his wrist and held it for a few seconds, this time making certain of the flare of interest across his face before she let go.

"You have a crushing grip, Prior."

"I do apologize. It was a moment's whim."

"I never said I disliked it."

Lysande could feel a current eddying inside her.

"I've never had a colleague," Luca remarked, sliding his chimera to the left. "I suppose you've heard this from Dalgëreth—he always tries to attack my image with the subtlety of a man wielding a blunt axe— but I prefer to work alone. It's not that I shun company. It's just that I like to work among equals."

"That excludes everyone else, I presume."

"Almost everyone."

"Your modesty is intensely charming."

"You should be pleased, Prior." He blocked her king and captured her last guard in a single move. "There aren't many people I place in the category of similar wit."

Had he been on the verge of saying something more? Lysande was determined not to speak of touching his throat a few moments ago; it felt like a challenge not to mention it again. He had veiled that bright look, and she managed to match his insouciance. As she was contemplating her next move, a man in black armor approached, drawing near Luca. "Your Highness, Lady Fabbriani thought she saw fire."

"Where?"

"Over to the east, Your Highness."

Luca followed the man's finger to look, and surprise spread across his face. "Fire."

Lysande turned to see a ball of flame speeding through the air toward her.

Everything seemed to happen at once—the deck became a blur—guards running at her; several Rhimese soldiers shielding Luca; Litany speeding at her, hands outstretched, so fast, impossibly fast; but Derset arriving first, from her left: Derset knocking her to the ground. His knee wedged between her thighs, pinning her against the deck. Flames rained down around them. A few smaller fireballs struck the deck, and guards rushed to stamp the blazes out, leaving black and twisted wood. Women and men shouted furiously to each other, waving away smoke. Lysande felt Derset's hands gripping her shoulders and tightened her grip on the solid warmth of his torso, pulling them closer together, feeling the thumping of his heartbeat.

Warm. The world was warm, and soft, and quiet. There was only the gentle heat of Derset's body, and only that sound. Thump. Thump. She could feel it through his skin, a fragile, flightless thing: a prayer.

Then the incantation of his heartbeat dissolved. She saw Raden rushing through to the side of the ship, pushing Lyrians out of his way. "Elementals!" he cried. "Over there!"

As the archers opened fire into the desert, she glimpsed several people sprinting behind a dune. The deck was still smoking. She and Derset leaped to their feet and looked away from each other quickly. He glanced back just as she did. She moved a slight distance away from him, and then they were checking each other over for wounds before rushing to the rail, Lysande feeling a fogginess in her mind. The balls of fire had stopped coming, but Cassia and Dante's ship was aflame, an embroidered leopard smoldering on one sail. Something quivered behind her, a movement of rope, a shifting of shadows: Litany dropped from the rigging to land on the deck.

"Look, Your Highness!" Freste cried, pointing to the desert.

The sand sped in a ridge along the top of one dune. To Lysande, it looked as if the desert itself was moving—chasing their attackers—but as she watched, she spotted four people running behind the bandits, their ragged cloaks flying in the wind. She picked out a sheaf of white hair streaming in the sun.

The sand whirled and reshaped itself into the form of horses. Four golden beasts chased the attackers. "Downstream, and spread some sail before they strike again!" a sailor in the rigging called.

Three held his hand up, angling his wind. Several of the bandits stumbled in the force of his gust. A ball of water arced over the top of the speeding sand-horses, sent by a woman who looked like Six, and struck one of the bandits on the neck. Lysande leaned on the rail, staring. She watched the stricken woman fall to her knees, screaming a cry that was whipped away by the wind. It happened so fast that she almost felt sympathy—especially since the woman wore clothes that were ripped and patched, and her face was haggard, like the bone people.

A little respite does not sate an appetite for liberty, but increases it. For the first time, she understood what Three was sacrificing, to work against the White Queen; it was all too easy to imagine the Shadows siding with these rebels, otherwise, and she wondered to what degree commitment could be measured: weighed and sifted, like flour.

The woman's companions sprinted, looking back every few seconds. As Three sent another blast through the desert, the horses galloped on and grains swirled, settling in a wall and blocking the fight from view. Cries of frustration sounded across the ship. The thought stuck in Lysande's mind that there was no one else to take charge of her people.

She looked around the deck, surveying the people on board. A few guards nursed burned arms or fingers; Lord Malsante held a boot that had been seared through the sole, and Chidney had taken a spike of wood to the arm, but no one looked to be dead. She drew a breath and issued a stream of orders to the Axiumites nearest her: find the physician, take the injured below, clean up the blood, check their position with the helmswoman.

She seemed to be running on something raw. Her mind called out for blue flakes.

"Praise Fortituda. You're not hurt," Derset said, beside her.

"I owe you my thanks, my lord. If you hadn't grabbed me, I might not be here."

"I hardly deserve thanks for doing what any servant of the crown should do." The warmth tinging his words exceeded the bounds of the statement. They faced each other. Lysande moved a fraction closer to him, laying a hand on his arm, and he glanced quickly around. "I must warn you . . . but no . . . may we speak in your quarters at Lyria, instead?"

She nodded and stepped back, a little too slow to create a distance between them.

Raden and Chidney came to report on the state of the ship, but after seeing Litany's concerned look, Lysande allowed her attendant a moment alone with Chidney. When the pair had finished their awkward half-embrace, she drew Litany aside. "I supposed you learned how to scale masts in Axium Palace, too?"

"Who do you think cleans the walls of the staff tower? They get grimy." Litany leaned in to whisper. "I recognized her among them. The sharp-faced woman."

"I'm sorry?"

"I only caught a glimpse before she took her fight behind a dune, but there was no mistaking; it was the woman you were speaking to by the Flavantine; all cheekbones."

Charice would have been amused to be called "all cheekbones," Lysande thought, suppressing a laugh of disbelief. *When you see me next, do not be too angry,* Charice had said. No wonder she had not explained who she was meeting.

"Could you be certain as to which side of the fight she was on?" Lysande said.

"Not at first. I climbed into the rigging so I could be sure. She was helping those who defended us, the white-haired man and his group. They attacked in formation, together."

Of course, Lysande should feel pleased. Knowing that did not stop frustration from creeping through her. If this was not being dangled in Severelle's middle space, between visibility and nothingness, then what was it? The worst part was that she could not say that she had had no warning, for Charice never truly let you all the way in—you came right up to the latched doors of her heart, and you waited on the threshold, listening to the occasional sounds from within, hoping.

"I suppose they were the White Queen's people," Jale said, stopping beside her.

"I'm not sure, Your Highness," Raden said. "Looked like two

groups, to me. Forgive me for stretching Queen Illora's Precept, but the first group of elementals threw fire at us, and the second lot . . ."

"Defended us." Luca joined them. "Don't let Axiumite manners hold you back, captain. You may as well say what we're all thinking. That little incident would seem to shatter the notion that all elementals are scheming to destroy the crown." He turned to Lysande, who was holding back her thoughts on the attack with great effort. "You've sprung a leak, Prior. Shall we find you a bandage, or would you like to keep painting the deck?"

Lysande looked down and saw that her wrist was bleeding. A piece of wood had cut her, somehow, without her realizing. She was about to signal to Litany, but Luca clicked his fingers at one of his guards. "Let me."

The bandage arrived, and he drew out the tiny slivers of wood that had lodged in her skin. Winding the cloth around her wrist until it quenched the bleeding, covering even the smallest parts of the wound, he worked, his gaze focused entirely on her wrist. When he looked up again at last, pleasure melded with something indecipherable in his countenance.

Most of the boat was crammed up by the rail, staring at the wall of sand, yet Lysande knew that they would not find what they were searching for. If Three had blocked off the fight, there would be no more glimpses; she felt certain of that. In her mind, she still saw the sand-horses champing.

After the last wounded guard's hand had been shaken, Lysande rejoined her Axiumites. Her gaze sweeping the vista, she searched for a glimpse of white hair or a cloak, yet there was nothing except miles and miles of golden grains, tapering into the distance until the mirage met the sky.

The first port in Lyrian territory swarmed with traders, thanks to its position as a gateway to three towns—Bref, Villechaud, and Cléche-fort. While Cassia and Dante haggled with the merchants, Jale suggested a trip through the desert to the tiny township of Bref.

Lysande took Litany, Chidney, and a few guards and joined the party. Despite the obedience of the desert mule she was given, she found herself missing the whinnying and stubbornness of her piebald mare. The road meandered on, and Bref arose from the sand in ten rings of shining stone, the sun glancing off the walls of the town. Lysande and Jale led their party through the fort-like buildings, until the attention of a trail of agog citizens forced them to speed up and duck into the largest building.

"This is the thing to see in Bref," Jale said, waving around the front room. "Those gold-fingered Coûteuse sisters set up the Raffiné Gallery from their personal fund."

Paintings hung on every side, some as large as those in the prayer-house she had visited in Rhime. Jale whirled her through the hall and pointed out pictures of bejeweled rulers and scenes of Lyrian warriors piercing opponents who wore brown capes, a distinctly Valderran garment. The picture in the far-right corner caught Lysande's eye.

A scene from the White War, it showed the Mud Field covered with soldiers and a familiar figure in armor, brandishing a dagger, and Lysande had to smile—for Sarelin would never have removed her helmet in battle, making herself a target. The queen's black hair streamed around her face, and her lips were parted, as if giving a battle cry. It was not hard to spot the homage to the last charge, dots resembling crimson embers dancing around Sarelin's face, a detail from a day that should have dried and set by now but was always being repainted on the canvas of her imagination. Somehow, this defiant Sarelin seemed more real to her than any of the posed portraits in Axium Palace.

Despite everything I've questioned about you, I feed on the times we laughed, she thought. *The nights we swapped stories of nimble deer and even more nimble men. Your smile, spreading, the first morning I managed to hit a target. The black flames leaping into your eyes when you mounted your horse and wheeled it round . . . when you boomed out a command to the hunters. Your arm linked in mine as we walked across to a dead stag.*

Jale demonstrated a sudden interest in a portrait on the left wall and left her in as much privacy as she could enjoy with more than twenty guards milling about, and she quietly told the painted Sarelin everything that had happened since her death, leaving out only her abuse of chimera scale.

"You'd say I must step into your boots. But you were a masterpiece; not a mold. I think that means I must lead my own way. It's like one of those paradoxes of the early philosophers, isn't it?" She breathed in, regarding Sarelin. "Emulating you, by not emulating you. There's more I can do." *And where there is need, there is opportunity*: Perfault had written that. "Elementals . . . the poor . . . they're just people, Sarelin. That's what I find written in my mind, when the ink dries. They can turn on you, but they can shout your name, too. Loud and clear with a single voice." Lines cracked her brow. "Not just a damned plugged-ear idealist, now, am I?"

When they left the gallery, Jale helped her back up onto her mule and they set off again, the animals plodding, swatting clouds of flies with their tails. It occurred to Lysande, as they moved through the desert, that Jale might have invited her to this gallery to see the portrait of Sarelin; when she caught him darting a glance at her, she was sure of it. She searched for a topic to break the silence. "Do you take a personal interest in art, Your Highness? Or do commissions and selections become a chore?"

"Anything but a chore. You don't know how jealous I was when you got the Painter's Suite in Castle Sapere." Jale sighed. "Vitelongelo's a true master. That balance of color he manages. What I'd give to look at the *Maturation* as I was sitting in the bath . . ."

He was soon rhapsodizing about the *Maturation*, praising the frescoes and comparing them with the Lyrian works, and Lysande's thoughts had skipped to images in shining paint when one remark brought them back.

"But of course, the real subject is magic."

"Magic?" She gripped her reins tightly. "If I'd known the *Maturation* was about elementals, I'd have . . ."

"Studied it, probably." Jale flashed white teeth. "It's a secret, of course, unless you've had the facts passed on to you. My mother drummed it into me once a year. 'Elementals aren't born with their powers, Jale. Pay attention, Jale, and stop plucking that damned harp.

First the brain, then the blood and the tissue: their bodies change and they go through a painful transformation, which is called a maturation.'" He looked at her and, seeing that she looked more puzzled than amused, repeated, "A maturation."

"I've never heard such a thing." It certainly hadn't been in any book in Sarelin's library. But then, had she not copied out Queen Illora's Precept herself, stating that all discussion of magic—from the White Queen's survival to the kinds of elemental forces—was banned? Should *she* not know, better than anyone, how much knowledge had been hidden?

"Some of them are young when they mature," Jale said. "But some of them are almost twenty-five. Wish I could remember all of what Mother used to bang on about."

Charice was scarcely ten years old. But then, Charice had always hinted that the incident with the sunsnake was a surprise—that her power had erupted early.

She wondered if Sarelin had known about maturation. If there had been another secret the queen had kept from her scholar, for so many years.

Again, her thoughts touched upon Mea Tacitus working in Sarelin's chambers.

"Mother liked to lecture me about it, in case I ever had to deal with elementals. When they've matured, they can move one of the elements or use their powers of the mind, she said. Of course, talking about this is banned by law, you know. But we're not discussing magic, are we? We're just appreciating art."

"The most captivating of subjects." Lysande smiled. "I wonder where the references to the transformation are, though. My knowledge of art is grounded in the Axiumite school. You must be an expert, I imagine, growing up in a palace."

"It's all in the triangles, you see." Jale made the shape of a triangle with his fingers, and Lysande remembered the golden symbols on the women and men's bodies, shining in the creamy paint. "They represent the different stages of magical maturation. One on the forehead, to show the head pains; the second shows pains in the throat; and lastly, one over the chest, for the pains in the lungs." Jale waved a hand airily.

"Mother seemed to think it was useful to know this stuff. Used to pour goblets of cherry-brew while she lectured me—it's a wonder I remember any of it. They're supposed to be cowering in caves and sneaking around in the mountains, she'd say, but they're not all hiding—you never know when you might run into an elemental."

Lysande feigned illness from the heat and dropped to the back of the mule-train. As thoughts chased each other through her head, she felt muscles tightening in her jaw. It was impossible to avoid checking off the symptoms in her mind: head, throat, lungs. A ruthlessly clear list.

When they arrived at the ship, she thanked Jale and made her way below. "Did you pack my books in the mahogany chest?" she asked Litany, once they were in her chamber.

"Of course." Litany's gaze skipped across her face.

"I need the book on the White War—the one I was reading last night." She hoped that the desperation did not show in her voice.

"The one from the Academy? That old collection of military accounts?"

"The same."

When the spattered tome was in her hands, she flicked through chapter after chapter, thumbing the pages rapidly until she found the passage: a description of a capture from the White War. She read through it twice.

> To check that the prisoner was indeed magical, the most honorable Prince Marcio Sovrano performed a test devised by the researchers in his Academy. He bade Captain Feronna of the second legion cut the prisoner's arm. A sample of blood was taken, and the captain poured it onto a silver plate.
>
> When, after a minute's passing, the silver turned black, there was much rejoicing in the camp: for it was declared that the prisoner must be an elemental captain, as proven by the Academy's esteemed science. The guards sang the "Serpent's Triumph" and toasted to His Highness, and Captain Feronna gave her soldiers a ration of wine.

Lysande snapped the book shut. "Would you stand outside the door, Litany?"

Her fingers slid a dagger from her belt as the door closed. She hunted through the jewelry box on the floor, pulling out a silver bracelet and placing it flat on the table. Trembling, she held out her left hand.

It was hard to keep still, but she knew that she would need more than a nick on the finger. She sank the tip of the dagger into her flesh. The steel bit into her palm, and she made sure the blade was wet before conveying it to the bracelet.

The minute she waited seemed more like ten. The hand on her time-piece inched around. When at last it had completed its rotation, she gazed at the bracelet, watching.

Nothing. The blood was red—the same color as when it spurted from her finger. Had she really been so mad as to think that those pains could be something so dramatic, and to transpose Jale's words onto a mere human sickness? Had she fallen victim to delusions in the aftermath of a violent attack, like the paranoia Montefizzi described in her manual? Had she succumbed to utter mental disintegration as the result of an excess of scale?

She was about to turn away when she saw the dark tinge spreading across the silver.

She was not conscious of dropping the dagger. It clattered on the floor, and she felt pain slice through her chest, but could not bring herself to move.

Black. The silver had turned black.

She breathed out, and a hundred daggers sprouted in her lungs.

Eleven

The fragrance in the palanquin cloistered her in notes of starberry and anise, yet not with such a power that she could stop peering out, studying the people along the ceremonial lane and taking in the parasols that stretched five feet above their heads. Groups of Lyrians pointed at the procession, smiling and talking, their gauzy trousers falling to their ankles. Beyond the curtains, the sun beat down, and the crowds and the sugar-palm trees seemed to shimmer brighter than any painting she had seen; it could have been a scene from the Silver Songs, if not for the pain in her chest.

The stabbing had been coming and going, coming and going. Now, it was definitely coming. A bubble of panic was rising inside her, swelling with each jolt of the palanquin. Jale had said that the maturation was a painful process, but there was a gap left by the failure to define *painful*—a gap of sensory knowledge that her body was beginning to fill. She felt another jab in her chest and pictured her legs giving way, in front of all these people. It was too easy to imagine the change of blood and tissue contorting her body on the way to the desert palace— the guards running their swords through an elemental—the rending of gristle and the shattering of crisp bone.

"Are you well enough for this, my lady?" Derset must have seen her clutch the corner of a cushion.

"It is only the heat, my lord. This torpor is foreign to me."

A smell of spice and incense wafted from the street, and a dryness weighed down the air, pressing upon her shoulders. How could Jale be so sprightly and full of cheer, she wondered, being raised in a place like this? Most of the Lyrians seemed happier to see their prince than their guests, running up to Jale's palanquin and throwing handfuls of rose petals, which perfumed the air with a nectarous scent. Coins showered into the lane, thrown by a group of elders dressed in golden robes. Lysande glimpsed one of the many sandstone façades behind them, a building whose gilt letters proclaimed B.O.L.

The Bank of Lyria. The biggest monetary institution in the Three Lands. Lysande recalled reading about the bribery they had carried out during Ariane Chamboise's reign. *Established in the forty-first year of the calendar—the only place in the south to store your money safely, provided you can afford a rate that changes every seventh moon.* She tried to think about the bank; tried to focus her mind on something other than her pain and fear.

Just as the cymbals and brass stopped around them, their palanquin lurched to a halt, and an attendant held the curtains open. They climbed out onto a flight of steps.

They had passed through the wall that encircled Rayonnant Palace, and they seemed to be facing a sea of gold—gold columns, holding up a gold-plated roof, and the gilded arches of a reception hall waited before them, in front of which another band was playing "Flowers of Old Lyria," the tassels on their caps gleaming with gold thread. While Lysande tried to adjust to the glare, a man with a pearl-and-gold chain dangling over his doublet walked out to the top of the steps. She could spot the resemblance at once—the fine bones, limpid blue eyes, and elegant bearing—but while this man shared Jale's looks, his smile offered none of the same warmth.

"Uncle!" Jale said, bounding up to embrace him. "You've been busy, eh?"

"I have found time to look into a few profitable endeavors." Vigarot Chamboise detached himself from his nephew. "Your marriage among them. We should celebrate your last days of unwed bliss, Jale. But you must introduce me to your friends—I fear they do not have the stomach for our sun."

Lysande worked hard to exude what she hoped was a serene aura. Hands were shaken, introductions given, and each of the Council made their courtesies and compliments. Vigarot Chamboise gave a curt bow to Cassia, Luca, and Lysande, yet he did not bow to Dante, who merely raised a hand. The Valderrans kept their fingers on their swords as Jale led them through the columns.

Lysande made every effort to repress the pain in her chest. She could feel the bubble expanding and expanding inside her, threatening to burst, but it would not do to collapse on ten thousand cadres' worth of rubies. Her footsteps echoed across the foyer of Rayonnant Palace. She passed over a tile encrusted with so many gems that it might have been a rainbow: mosaics of bulls fighting and lovers riding a swan, and a smooth stone set with a school of fish swirling in an arc of sapphires; strange, she thought, how even if you saw the underbelly of the system that built such wealth, you could still be arrested by the sight of the glories it produced.

Yet she was hurried through without much time to be awed. A herald in blue-and-gold livery bowed to Jale and flung open the far doors.

"His Acting Majesty Vigarot is pleased to announce the return of the jewel of the south and the true son of the desert: the radiant Prince of all Lyria, Jale Chamboise!"

Instead of a vaulted ceiling, Lysande found herself walking under a dome with a hole at the top, through which rays of light streamed. Gold wreathed the dozens of people in thin raiment who rose from their benches. A shower of sun fell on headpieces and heraldic pins, illuminating every member of the court, and on the far side, the beams glanced off five throne-like chairs, each embellished with the letter of a city: L, V, A, P, R.

Lysande decided to concentrate on those letters. If she did, she could almost ignore the agony in her lungs and her thoughts about what the eyes traversing her body might see.

"And with him comes the Council of Elira," the herald cried, "soon to celebrate the union of our great land with Bastillón! Your Councillors, Lyria!"

Thunderous applause; Jale beamed and nodded, and the rows of nobles bowed to him as he led them through. Derset pointed out the noble families of Lyria in a low voice as Lysande walked: the Chateliers and the Gaincourts, sporting so many bracelets and necklaces that they seemed to be competing with sapphires; the De Clair sisters, holding their ceremonial swords, and the Prichet family, who had recently survived the spotting-plague.

Lysande surveyed her hosts, noticing, even through the haze of anxiety, the fine edgework on their necklaces and bracelets. No commoners here, then. Logic told her that none of these people in their elegant clothes could have guessed what she was feeling, but something else made her fear that they would know the silver had turned black: that she was being stabbed from the inside.

At least my jail will be comfortable. She heard trumpets blare.

Vigarot Chamboise ushered the Council to the gold chairs at the end and asked Dante to remove his outer fur, and although the First Sword did so without any ill grace, the Valderrans muttered and cast dark looks at Vigarot. Lysande felt a spurt of relief when Jale stood up and silenced the room.

"Ladies and lords of Lyria, I've assured our guests that they will be treated with more splendor than you can shake a sword at. Let's show them what we do with southern gold!"

More applause; louder cheering. One of the Chateliers jingled a wrist enthusiastically. Lysande saw women and men gazing at Jale with chins tilted toward him, some with eyes brightened and cheeks flushed, not bothering to hide their admiration.

"They say a ball in the north is an event you remember all your life," Jale went on, raising a hand, "but in Lyria, we don't call it a celebration if you can remember your name in the morning! So let's make this a Sapphire Ball . . . not to remember, but to forget!" The court whistled and laughed. "Before we get to the preparations, however, my uncle has a proposal."

Vigarot Chamboise stepped out in front of the chairs. From the look of polite inquiry on Jale's features, Lysande guessed that the prince had not been privy to the idea.

"On the Council's journey here, there was a heinous attack on our ships," Vigarot announced. "It would seem that elemental scum are on the move again, and if they strike on the Grandfleuve, who is to say they will not strike at us here, downriver? To protect our Council and citizens, I move that the Lyrian guard be doubled at the Sapphire Ball. A special guard for the ballroom, to be selected from our elite ranks."

He looked around slowly. "And new swords for every woman and man in armor."

Muttering and whispering broke out in earnest. Luca leaned forward, Tiberus coiling around his neck. "Convenient timing," he said.

"What do you mean?" Cassia said.

Lysande felt a rush of desire for the calming effect of scale and fought to concentrate. Vigarot turned to face them. "I believe Prince Fontaine wishes to remind you that it is the responsibility of the crown to pay for security at such an event," he said.

"Of course," Dante said, loud enough for Lysande and the others to hear clearly. "You refit your army at our expense."

"Devils who channel primal forces are afoot. You must see the need for the ball to be adequately defended, First Sword." Vigarot kept up a beatific expression. "Assuming, that is, that you *want* it to go ahead . . . I would never doubt your commitment, but others will talk."

Lysande could not see a hint of geniality in Dante's eyes. The First Sword gave the slightest inclination of his head. "Valderos supports the decision of the prince of Lyria."

The court was peering at them. Vigarot Chamboise flashed a particularly bright smile before turning back to face the benches.

"Let it be known," he said, glancing at Dante, "that *Lyria* supports the safety of its Council. And we hope that by forging a chain between my nephew and Princess Ferago, our land will be safe from elementals." He unsheathed his sword and raised it. "The vermin who gnaw at the foundations of our culture may scuttle to their leader again, but Lyria will hunt them down. Glory to Elira, the puzzle realm. And death to all elementals!"

The cheering reverberated around the circular room before any of them could speak. It pounded in Lysande's ears like a drum, and though she saw Luca frown and Jale look displeased, none of them rose to silence the crowd. Family by family, the nobles stood, drawing their smallswords and echoing the cry: "Death to elementals! Death to elementals! Death to elementals!"

Vigarot Chamboise bowed and smiled so politely that his face seemed to strain. Lysande did not really see him, however—she saw the blotch on the bracelet in her mind's eye, the black tinge creeping

across the silver, and as the cheering reached its final crescendo, she felt
the daggers in her lungs begin to thrust again.

Defense diverted her as soon as she left the courtroom. Raden rode
back from a nearby town, wearing a grim smile. The secret party of
Axium Guards possessed weapons made of the finest capital steel, he
assured her, and all of them knew how to use them; sixteen of the
twenty elite dagger-throwers had been spared from their posts, and two
hundred of the most dangerous women and men waited in Flemency,
just five miles from the city.

Lysande found this one piece of good news a tonic for her spirits.
She had a longing to sit down with Litany and Raden and a bottle of
wine, and ease her soul further with a hand of cards—or ease it in other
ways with Derset—but there were more pressing games to play.

If the rules of honest and open engagement were to be respected,
then she should have been collaborating with Luca in this strategy. She
knew it, and yet she brushed it aside. The kind of collaboration she
imagined having with Luca was not the kind that involved military
preparation.

She gave orders for the guards to be dressed as pilgrims and brought
to inns across Lyria, trying not to dwell too long on what Luca might
say if he found out. A careful dispersion seemed necessary, since two
hundred Axiumites in robes would not escape notice, and Vigarot
Chamboise had given strict orders about the number of guards each
city could install. She made plans and drew up lists in her head. The
Axiumites would need crown buckles, robes, and prayer-books to
avoid questioning. She felt a twinge of guilt about the bone people,
who could surely have done with new clothes, but she had to keep that
line of thought in the back of her mind; an invasion could burn through
any reforms like a flame through paper.

"You're all right, aren't you?" Raden said.

She froze, one hand gripping her chair. "Why in the Three Lands
shouldn't I be?"

"Don't know . . . I thought nearly being killed by a ball of fire falling out of the sky might've shaken you a little."

"Oh, yes. Positively shaken."

Calm yourself, she thought. It's not him you have to worry about.

He gave her a mock salute as he strode away, and she managed to return it. Even in a palace decorated with Lyrian gold, Raden still swaggered.

No books on magical powers could be found in the palace library, though she had not really expected to find any; the only references to magic in Axium's collection she had discovered, aside from interpretations of the Old Signs, were records of battles fought and chimeras slain—as if elementals were stock figures to be moved around the stage of history. She could not quite believe that she was one of these people. That was how history worked, though. If you could not write yourself into the long story, the story that wove through decades and centuries, then others would write you out of it. Before you knew it, you found yourself clutching the few pieces of your life that had endured, the words spoken on the doorstep of an orphanage, passed down to you in scraps.

Of all the people she had met since her appointment as Councillor, only Three would understand. Perhaps he would even be able to tell her when she could expect the maturation process to begin. But he was not here. *Damn him.* Instead, she was surrounded by the group of people most likely to notice her symptoms. She ought to be checking over her shoulders. Jale knew about elementals. Luca's gaze could slice through layers of her person, even if he went still at her touch, and he might have deduced her true nature just by observing her. Dante, the hungriest for the persecution of magical people, might know the signs best of all. A week ago, she would have counted Cassia as her friend, but now she had burned that rose garden away. Cassia had as much reason as any to examine her with suspicion.

And then there was Derset. It would be easy to forget about all of this and pull him under her, sliding into a state of solace. She yearned to be feeling nothing but the warmth of one body against another. Breathe deeply, she told herself, and do something useful.

She worked her muscles by practicing in the indoor target range, and she was almost satisfied with her progress when a stab of pain in her lungs sent her tottering. Her dagger spun off course and landed in a potted plant.

"No more strain in this heat." Litany wrapped an arm around her. "Time for rest."

It was a gift that a girl with such sharp skills could care for her. She let herself be bustled back to her suite, which contained everything that might be expected from a palace presided over by Jale: a painting of the coronation feast of Princess Charine Orvergne adorned almost an entire wall, and her bed had been decorated with mirrored glass, covered in blue silk, and draped with a mosquito net flecked with sapphires. A design of a chimera carrying the sun on its back on one of the bathroom tiles did not surprise her as much as it might have; she thought of Severelle's description of the southern practice of sun-worship, a sacred connection embodied in the act of sitting, whether on painted tiles or cracked stone. *In the path of the morning sun, the Lyrians claim, the magic of light reawakens the spirit.*

Had not Charice argued that nature and the elements were as lovers, a fusion from which the chimera had also emerged? Too easy to imagine the spots of color in Charice's cheeks, the spots she had cherished because they were so rarely displayed. She could not help but think that if not for the crown's rules, Lyria might have tolerated people like Charice and Three . . . and herself.

A balcony hung out over the palace gardens, complete with a pool, so that if she chose to swim, she could look down at swirls of pebbles and bowls of heart-flowers. Twin summerharps rested on the stands that flanked the desk. An attendant offered to play them; another offered to change the water in the bathroom, and another offered to bring food every couple of hours; yet the visitor waiting on her window sill pleased her most.

Three's speckled dove cooed softly into her hand. Lysande took out paper and her gold quill, but after several attempts to compose, she merely wrote *Thank you for moving quickly. Come to me as soon as you can*, sealed the envelope, and passed it to Cursora.

Litany garbed her in a thin cotton suit for bathing and escorted her to the pool, where the water was cool and sweet-smelling, and full of some southern crystal that made it sparkle, soothing her skin and senses. The pain receded until it was almost possible to forget the black stain on the bracelet and the sound of the court shouting "Death to elementals!" In the water, it all seemed very far away.

"Come and join me, Litany," she said. "I won't have you scuttling through the halls alone, before you get a moment's rest."

When the stars came out above them, her lungs cleared again and she could breathe in without pain. She did not mind at all that Litany had settled beside her on the ledge and rested her head upon her shoulder: it was nice to stroke the girl's hair and to feel her closeness.

If she knew what I am, she reminded herself, she might not sit so near. The thought of losing Litany pierced her, in a manner that surprised her. She could not bear to think that the attendant who had chewed her food and assessed it, filched a purse from Luca, and climbed into the rigging amidst the attack at sea might turn on her one day, after all that had changed and developed between them.

No pains of a maturation woke her in the night, even though she had feared they would. Mosquitoes butted their heads against the net and circled her; but the city rose before she did, and the buzz of commoners going about their business had well and truly started by the time she sat up. Lysande finished a breakfast of fiery balls of rice and pickled vegetables, sharing it with her attendant after Litany pronounced it safe. While Litany was smoothing down a doublet, Lysande took out her goblet, spoon, vial, and jar of blue flakes and gazed at them for a while. Her hand seized the jar just as a knock sounded at the door.

It shocked her, the speed at which Litany swept the jar from the table, along with the goblet, snatching the spoon and vial in one hand and slipping all four items into their chest.

"Pardon the interruption, my lady," Derset said, leading in a slim youth in gold livery, "but this gentleman insisted on seeing you."

The boy strode in and bowed. "I have the honor to be your guide, Councillor. His Highness wishes to delight the Council with the three wonders of Lyria: the Monument of Silver, the famous Pavilion of Songs, and of course, the Hill of Oblitara—"

"*The* Hill of Oblitara?" Lysande cried.

The guide paused. "Yes," he said, "there is only one."

"I had no notion that we could walk upon a site dating back to the Conquest."

How Sarelin would have smiled to see her visiting somewhere from the Songs she had translated. And yet it felt different to consider the Conquest, now, when she knew which side her ancestors had been on. You could not smile at stories from a distance when you had been written into them.

"We can really ascend to the place where the chimera Oblitara was slain?"

"If we leave before the sun is at is zenith, yes, Councillor."

Derset smiled, and she gave him a look that said she could take a hint. "You may thank Prince Chamboise," she told the guide. "We will only be a minute."

The boy bowed and retreated. "His Highness says you can only climb two hundred steps, however," he added, as he walked out.

She began to gather her belt and boots, and nodded to Litany to leave. Once the door was closed, she gestured to Derset to draw near. It was easier to stand in proximity to him since he had dived to cover her from fire. "We began a conversation on the ship." She fixed her daggers in their sheaths. "I would finish it now."

Derset bowed. "After the attack, it occurred to me—and as I say, I have since realized that it may have been no more than a fancy—that when the first fireball struck the deck of the ship, it seemed to land where you had been sitting. Right on your chair. Prince Fontaine had invited you to play tactos near the prow just before the elementals attacked."

There was a knock at the door—most likely the guide—but they both ignored it. Lysande felt her hands clench. "Go on, my lord."

"The thought crossed my mind that his new alliance with you might be no more than an act, designed to lull you into sitting where he asked . . . that he might have arranged for an attack on you. But I have since reflected that I was wrong to think so. The magical fire was thrown from a long way off."

Lysande could not unclench her fists, no matter how she tried. They seemed to be stuck in a balled position. She reflected on the notes she had made for her treatise. "All the pieces of accounts I've read suggest that the White Queen threw fire with accuracy over the best part of a mile."

"Well, perhaps it was luck that you were sitting closer to the rail. Prince Fontaine was sitting by that tactos-board, too, when the elementals struck." Derset spread his hands. "He might as easily have chosen your chair."

She remembered a shimmer of black scales, and her body recoiling.

"Tiberus," she said.

"My lady?"

Tiberus was on the left seat. The guide's knocking on the door had grown impatient, and she finished tying a bootlace, gathering her composure, and trying to stop her mind from running with the thought.

"We will speak no more of this, for now. But I thank you, my lord, for your honesty. And I would have you help me in my chamber this evening, if you have time to spare and the will for such a . . . chore."

Derset caught her eye and held her gaze. Pleasure chased surprise from his face. "I have plenty of time, my lady. And nothing you ask of me could be a chore."

"Careful, my lord. You do not yet know what I mean to ask."

"I will let my imagination be schooled."

He bowed, with the hint of a smile on his face, and waited for her to lead him out. She wondered what Derset would say if he knew what she was—if he would change his mind about Sarelin having chosen the right Councillor. Would he decline to be associated with her, or do far worse? She had few enough people she could speak to and listen to, without losing the ones she cared for, and Derset, she admitted to herself, was among those few. She chanced a look at him, taking in his steady gait, and catching his glance, she tried to return the smile.

Dante and Jale had left together an hour ago, she was informed by an attendant in the reception hall, for their own tour of the three wonders; whether they intended to fight or to reconcile, the attendant reported that they had hurried into Dante's palanquin and closed the curtains. Lysande's idea of that relationship was firming quickly. Luca had departed alone, but Cassia was waiting downstairs, and she strode over to Lysande, pulling something from her pocket and thrusting it under Lysande's nose.

"I had not thought to see this for many weeks."

Lysande took the proffered branch, a slim curve of honey-colored wood whose leaves sheltered nubs of silver fruit. She looked up slowly.

"Your attendant brought it in waxen paper. The traditional way," Cassia added.

Lysande assembled her best hopeful look. She reminded herself to thank Litany, again, for not forgetting the details she had requested.

"I should ask how you knew that we give the livea branch as a symbol of reconciled hearts in Pyrrha, but I know better than to question a scholar. So, tell me one thing: is this truly an apology?"

"With all my heart," Lysande said.

"I should not welcome *all* your heart. That would leave none for you to give elsewhere, and I think a certain snake of a prince would be first in line for a piece." Cassia smirked. "But I accept what is given insofar as I give the same to you."

"Let us be reconciled, then, my friend."

The Irriqi threw back her head and laughed, the kind of laugh that captains gave when they were utterly delighted with a cleared battlefield. "Yes, friend, indeed. Or is that friend in deed? I have not forgotten that silent sword."

She embraced Lysande, and the pair clapped each other on the back. "Now," Cassia said, "we can tour that glittering chaos they call Lyria."

As she rejoined her attendant, Lysande whispered "good work" in Litany's ear.

There was a brief hold-up at the gates, when Cassia's party of fourteen was asked to trim itself down to six—in Pyrrha, they might be one family, the attendant remarked, but in Lyria, they had to whittle themselves down to close relations—and after much wrangling and several threats from the Irriqi, both palanquins passed through.

The ceremonial lane through the city had disappeared, replaced by a mishmash of traders, and a throng engulfed them as they reached the west side of the city. Lyrians flowed around them, carrying baskets of chilies or rice; bankers glided past on open palanquins, athletic-looking staff in scant clothing keeping them company. While attendants hurried between mules and street-traders with parcels and small sacks, nobles stopped to talk and laugh without any regard for the crowds. To be human was common, Lysande thought, but to be *seen* as human was a luxury that only certain could afford, and it seemed no cheaper here. It was almost impossible for their party to navigate without hitting some merchant or messenger: if Rhime had been madcap, this was pure, unadulterated chaos, without any pretense of direction.

They were forced to push and swerve their way to the Monument of Silver, and Lysande could see that Derset was trying to speak to her when they got out, but the guide drew near to hand her a stick, which, unfolded, produced a handsome parasol.

"Constructed by Princess Charine Orvergne in the year one hundred and eighty-four," the boy declared, pointing to an obelisk behind a ring of rope, "the Monument of Silver remains one of Lyria's three wonders."

They all stared up at the enormous silver column. It dominated the street corner. "Sarelin told me it was built by slavery," Lysande recalled.

Cassia and the guide both turned to look at her.

"Well . . ." She faltered. Best not to think of the black stain on her knife. "She said Princess Orvergne ordered her elemental prisoners in tempero to construct it. They worked all day in the sun with little water or food, and if they asked for a break before nightfall, they were taken to the city square and executed."

"I wouldn't blame her if she put rebels to the sword. If you don't keep them down, they set you alight." Cassia shrugged. "Look what happened on the Grandfleuve."

Lysande turned pale, despite the heat, and Cassia stared at her. Calm down, she told herself, but it did not stop her from thinking of the fate that would confront her if her nature was exposed. Secrecy would have to be her religion, as it was for Three.

The full reality of the law hit her for the first time—and it was not some other, unfortunate soul, some faceless elemental she considered, but herself. She could be locked in her own jail. Her own doing. Not open sky, but iron bars. She could be tied up and forced onto her knees in a city square if some angry citizens gathered in a mob and came after her. No one would blame them for doing so. They would be champions, and she the monster that deserved to die. Perhaps she did deserve to die, if the law of the realm ordered it so.

"Are you all right, my friend?" Cassia said.

"Yes," Lysande said, "thank you; I find myself tiring easily in this climate."

The guide said little as they climbed into the palanquins again. When they reached the city market some half-hour later, he devoted his attention to showing the Pyrrhans around, and Lysande took the chance to separate from the group, instructing Chidney and Litany to rejoin her later. Litany nodded, solemnly, and yet when the she turned to Chidney, a smile blossomed on her face. The captain offered her hand. Litany hesitated, then slipped her palm into Chidney's, and the two of them walked toward a stall laden with spiced figs, bumping into each other's sides slightly as they did so, Chidney leaning over to say something. Lysande watched them for a moment. The pair made the dance of courtship seem easy, even when it was a very awkward dance between a woman who embodied a broadsword and another who appeared deceptively like a sewing needle. It was *too* easy for them. Grudgingly, she turned in the opposite direction.

The rabbit warren of stalls before them spread out under a tin roof, and all sorts of things were dangling from hooks, swimming in jars, and spilling out of bags. She passed herbs for smoking that she suspected were illegal, chilies that had been soaked in honey and flattened, and a bowl of rice that appeared to be moving but, on closer inspection, turned out to be a mound of live ants. The stall-keeper insisted the insects were being sold for "medicinal and decorative purposes" and definitely not for eating.

Somehow, she had found her way into a section of the floor packed with people shouting the prices of grain, and she was surrounded by bargainers pointing to sacks of impressive size. Derset came up on her left. He paused, and Lysande felt that since lying together in Rhime, something had unfurled between them . . . something that had begun to expand even further since she suggested that he join her in the evening.

"My lady, I want to make sure that you will not place too much importance on what I said before."

"Your scruples do you credit, my lord."

He bowed. "I only hope that you will take your time to consider the matter . . . I would not want to hamper your friendship with Prince Fontaine over something so tenuous."

She patted him on the arm, then, newly aware of the warmth of skin on skin, let go.

"Goddess of love," Derset said.

Lysande followed his finger. He was pointing to a stall on their left. Among bowls and plates, a few small statues of a female hunter were elevated on bronze stands, the tiny spear in each figure's hand jabbing up.

"You studied etymology as scholar, did you not, my lady?" Derset said. "Would you answer me something? I have heard the origin of the word *Crudelis* is *cruelty*."

"Yes," Lysande said, absentmindedly, "from the Old Rhimese, you know."

"I saw many statues of Crudelis in Rhime. They love the passion and the pain of that goddess; we Axiumites are wiser."

She nodded, barely hearing.

"At least, we are meant to be."

"Quite." Seeing him had jolted her back to the fact that she was in Lyria, undergoing a tour that most people in the realm could only dream of. The bone people would not be pitying themselves if they were being whirled around the jewel of the delta. Sadness and determination fused in her. You could remind yourself that you were leading for your own safety and still be impatient to make change; that same coin was still there, spinning—*for the people* etched on one side, *the people for oneself* on another.

She left Derset examining a stack of bowls painted to resemble queensflowers and ambled through the lanes. Having dressed without care, she realized that she was unrecognizable as a Councillor, and several stall-keepers cast contemptuous looks at her tattered doublet. One Lyrian was so offended by her sleeves that he pretended not to hear when she inquired about his spitting cats, yet for every merchant who turned up their nose at her doublet, two more waited to sell her goods. She bought as many gifts as she could stuff into her pockets: a peacock quill for Derset; a jar of salted plums for Litany, who had expounded their merits several times on the voyage; a pair of sheaths with suns on them for Chidney; a hunting knife for Raden. At the far end of the market, she found a woman who professed to sell exotic goods from Royam. Among the weapons and shields, something violet sparkled.

She breathed slowly. It was important to breathe slowly if your heart was racing. When she had glanced over both shoulders and ascertained that no one was watching her, she leaned closer to peer at the jar. The shape of the flakes, their ragged edges, the slight luminosity to their surface: yes, there was no doubt about it, except for the color. Had there been purple chimeras in Royam before the Conquest? She could not recall reading if there had even been chimeras in Royam at all. The merchant was watching her now; Lysande reached for a vial of something black beside the scale and became very interested in the contents.

"Powdered chimera talon. Anyone would be delighted with such a curiosity," the woman assured her, eyeing the stain on her sleeve. "A unique product, oh yes; but you'll need eighty-five cadres and twenty mettles for that, and not a piece less."

There was one person she knew who would love that vial. And it was not the formal recognition of her rank but the warmth in the Irriqi's voice that Lysande thought of, now; a warmth that had been renewed when her little present of a livea branch had been received.

When she pulled out her purse and counted out five twenty-cadre coins, a deliberate rounding-up beyond the usual tip, she was thanked and shaken by the hand, begged to visit again, and promised that she would be provided with a bargain on gryphon's tears, or blood of the leaping wolf if she liked. It took all her effort not to look back at the jar of violet scale.

As they arrived at the beginning of the delta, she gazed out. The Grandfleuve diverged into three paths that gushed to the sea, and on the left tributary a pavilion floated—or at least seemed to float, supported by stilts, framed by four pillars shaped like spearfish. She wondered if members of the populace had ever been allowed to visit such a place.

"The Pavilion of Songs," the guide announced, as he led them to a galley. "The very place where the Lyrian royal choir performs every year. His Highness Prince Chamboise sings the 'Hymn of Pleasure' here."

"Of course he does," Cassia muttered. "He's never known anything *but* pleasure."

Lysande smiled, despite herself.

Pieces of glass on the pavilion's roof rained droplets of light over the surface of the river. The only melody that reached their ears as they glided across the Grandfleuve was the scooping of the oars in the water, but it made no matter, for the sunlight felt more ethereal than any song. Once on the pavilion, Lysande really did feel as if she were floating in the middle of the shimmering water. The guide unwrapped parcels of starfruit and snap-flower strips, dipped in a blend of chili and salt, producing an unexpected harmony of flavor.

Lysande produced the vial from her pocket. She had anticipated this moment for the better part of the journey, and Cassia's expression did not disappoint.

"Is it . . . surely not . . . powdered talon? You? I've never heard you once mention you like collecting chimeran artifacts!"

If she bit her lip, she might just stop some ironical, self-loathing witticism about scale from coming out. "Not precisely. But I have a friend who, I hear, spent years reading about chimeras and their powers. Perhaps she would take it off my hands."

Cassia pulled Lysande into a hug that nearly crushed her ribs. It was a feigned alliance, Lysande told herself, a cover to throw over the chasm of suspicion; and yet when those arms surrounded her with their bruising grip, she felt the embrace, almost as if it were Sarelin's. Did it matter if laughter and conversation came easy to them? Was it not wise to keep Cassia on her side? If so, why was it that a burr had lodged itself in her conscience, telling her that she could not be friend and strategist at once?

After they had rowed back to the shore, the two of them chatted in the same palanquin, comparing impressions of Lyria while the palanquin-bearers wove through the traffic. Lysande studied Cassia in the moments when she was silent. For all that she searched Cassia's features, she was relieved to find no hint of scheming; no calculation.

As they approached the Hill of Oblitara, it was hard to say who. carried the most expectation. The Irriqi rattled away to her guards about the distinctive horns of Oblitara and the villages she had destroyed; discoursed about the other great chimeras, Excoria, Ignis, and Eradicus, who had been ridden by elementals into battle, according to an esoteric and probably illegal manuscript that Cassia had sought out; while Lysande, though quiet on the outside, had allowed her thoughts to run to the Conquest and the histories she had read as a child. The formation of armies, the truce, and the great Surge, when women and men rose up against their elemental rulers, slaying the leaders and every one of the chimeras, all played out in her mind. They now touched something personal in her, something that was stirring.

I put it to you that deception is the ink in which all invasions are signed, one scholar had written of the negotiation after the Conquest. Lysande had quoted that book to Sarelin during a night of philosophical jousting, when they had not needed wine to make them loud.

The book had been banned, of course. So too had the works of the elemental scholar Roussant. Lysande had found one of them in the restricted part of the royal library, and she suspected that Sarelin had always known what she had purloined.

In banning our books, our knowledge, and our customs, and in wiping us from the histories, non-magical people waged war on our spirit. It is a war that continues today. For even being subjugated is not so dangerous as forgetting that your people were ever rulers.

So Roussant had written.

No one imagined elementals as rulers anymore. Perhaps memory was malleable—perhaps the collective memory of Elira had melted and reformed, over centuries.

The Hill of Oblitara rose out of a bare plain, and she saw at once why Jale had not wanted her to climb it: the peak that rose above them looked naked of any vegetation, with not even the meanest date tree flourishing on its sides, and only at the top did a few daubs of green shade the earth. The steps stretched up like a ladder under the glare of the sun. She hoped that the palanquin-bearers received a handsome wage, for they began the jerky ascent at a pace that must have strained their shoulders, never pausing to put down their load.

"Imagine burning your enemies with a chimera," Cassia said, when they were halfway up. "Now that'd crush any rebellion, or any jumped-up family who thinks your throne is theirs. If I had an Oblitara to roast every one of the Qamaras . . ."

"Even if they hadn't been dead for four hundred years, you couldn't possibly control one."

"All right." Cassia folded her arms. "There's no need to go throwing facts into a fantasy."

Lysande experimented with a nudge to Cassia's elbow and received a nudge back.

The jolting ceased after an eternity, and they emerged onto a landing that stuck out on the side of the hill. Lysande felt her stomach give a lurch. Looking down was not a good idea; it was much easier to turn her eyes upward.

Two hundred steps, she thought, gazing at the trees on the peak. Better than a thousand. Jale knew what he was about.

She set one foot on the first step and began to climb. Derset walked swiftly to her side, and the others divided into pairs. The last two hundred steps did not seem like a great distance, but the pain sliced into her after just a few minutes—it was different this time—an ache spread through all of her, from her fingertips to her toes. The daggers multiplied. Keep moving, she told herself. Just keep moving, and it'll pass.

She was nearly there, at the spot where soldiers from the first armies had shot down the chimera, and she was going to see it, even if it took all the strength in her body not to wince. The pain tripled, and she fought to put one foot in front of the other. It would be wise to ask the group to pause until the pain dispersed, but she had not come this far to stop, even for a few minutes, and she kept hobbling up the stairs in the sun.

"Are you all right, my lady?" Derset said, as her foot struck the edge of one step.

"This sun is enough to make anyone falter." Lysande wobbled, but managed to right herself. "Only a few more stairs to the spot. I am determined to stand where Oblitara did."

"So long as you don't die on a hilltop like Oblitara did." The trench in his forehead deepened. "Heatstroke is a serious thing."

Eight steps left. Then seven . . . six . . . five. The fourth was nearly another stumble, but she gritted her teeth hard enough to keep her body upright. Three steps to go . . . then two . . .

She had mounted the last stair when she felt the pain cut through her. The knives sliced into her flesh, her lungs, her throat, and her head: it was as if they had entered every part of her, ribboning her veins.

She reached for Derset's arm and nearly grabbed hold of him, but her legs gave way. Her body toppled backward.

Somebody caught her, but not in time for her head to avoid the ground. She could hear Litany's shriek, and Derset's cry of "my lady," and Cassia shouting at someone to get water.

The last thing she saw was the pure, vibrating blue of the Lyrian sky, before everything faded.

Blackness. Blackness for hours, or was it days? She tried to open her eyes, but the pain felt so excruciating that even moving an eyelid was agony. The only choice was sleep. In the blackness she still felt the daggers in her veins, but when she dreamed, their points receded and she could breathe again.

She found herself walking in Axium Forest, on the first morning Sarelin had taken her there. The queen had sent the guards away, and they were talking alone, the shadows of blackfoot branches striping their faces, the smell of animal scat rising, the two of them moving along the trails of pawprints until their voices sank into subsoil. At last, Sarelin put a finger to her lips and pointed. Lysande saw a brown shape move between two trunks; the bear walked toward the queen on its hind legs, its jaws wet.

Sarelin stepped forward to meet it. The animal slowed to watch her, bear opposite human: ten feet of muscle and dark, lustrous fur, facing down a figure in silver armor.

The two gazed at each other, and Sarelin drew a dagger from her sheath. The queen steadied her aim and threw. A hit. Then three more. The bear opened its mouth—bellowed—and crashed onto wet soil, leaving the forest reeling so that Lysande could feel the earth shaking, could see the sweat on Sarelin's brow as she sheathed her dagger.

"Powerful bastard." The queen shook her head and walked over to the huge body, now still. "I saw him on the last hunt, too, but I let him get away. Suppose I sort of got attached to him."

"Why kill him, then?"

Sarelin's smile, as she turned to Lysande, betrayed a hint of sadness. "Any soldier can kill something she hates. You don't feel pain when you destroy an enemy. It's the natural thing to do. It's only when you kill something you've come to love that you learn how to lead." She walked back to Lysande and clapped her on the shoulder. "One day, you'll understand that, Lys."

The agony in her veins returned, and the blackness shrouded her again. She drifted down a river where there was no light, only waves of pain, lapping at a shore she could never reach.

The next time she accompanied Sarelin, it was not through sight, but through touch. A pair of familiar hands lifted her up and placed her into a carriage. She could feel the warm presence of a body on the seat beside her and hear a ringing voice. "There she is, the girl with the quill." Laughter—the scent of thick perfume, of the kind that royals and nobles wore—and Sarelin's arm wrapped around her shoulders.

There were other hands, too. Cool hands that pressed against her forehead and went away again. Hands that pushed her lips apart and gave her water. They held her when the pain finally stopped and when she swam back into the real world, pushing up through the blackness to break the surface.

"Here you are at last," a mellifluous voice said beside her. "Try to lie still. You've had a frightful ordeal; the physicians think it was heat-stroke, the poor souls."

She opened her eyes. A drowsiness hung upon her, but no pains threatened to pierce her; she was lying on dozens of silk cushions in the suite in Lyria, with the mosquito net rolled up above her and the sun gushing in.

Relief swamped her. It took a moment to see who had spoken.

"I thought you'd forgotten about me."

Three's smile was enigmatic as always. He pressed a hand to her

forehead again and held it there for a few seconds. He looked somewhat out of place on the gilt chair beside her bed, attired in his plain
brown cloak and triangular pendant.

"I'm sorry it took me so long to arrive," he said. "I had to clear up a
little altercation in the desert, as you know. Still, I made it here in time
to keep you from prying eyes."

She was not in prison. Nor were her hands shackled in tempero
cuffs. Relief gushed through her again. "Naturally, you stole into a
guarded palace."

"Not I. Well, not first. Why have underlings if you can't ask them
to use their talents? My dear colleague Seven has Lyrian features, a
physician's robe, and most useful of all, the power of inducing extreme
good will. The guards on the door were pleased to see her. Seven even
managed to persuade your attendant that she was being kept informed
of your progress, with regular reports." He smiled.

Lysande imagined Litany returning and returning to the suite
doors, and swallowed.

"By the way, your friend, the merchant Charice, sends her wishes.
It was hard to tell if our offer of safety would be enough for her—she
keeps her cards very close—but then again, she has played many rounds
with a scholar." Three's smile deepened. "Coincidentally, she has
loaned us some potions that are quite hard to come by."

Charice. Of course. The way he spoke, it was as if Lysande had
never needed to worry about her. It was one thing to see Charice fighting alongside the Shadows; it was quite another to hear the word *safe*
pronounced, like a dotted *i* or a crossed *f*, as if the matter were resolved.
Yet in that pronouncement she sensed a little too much surety, and she
wondered if Three knew that Charice lived her life in unfinished
clauses.

Leaving the questions for now, she tried to sit up, but her head
weighed her down, a ball of lead fixed to a twig, and she was forced to
settle back on the pillows.

"You will feel weak for a few hours." Three patted her forehead
again. "The symptoms of this condition include heightened senses, so
acute that they will occasionally drive you to distraction, and the ability to kill with a flick of your hands. Of course, you'll have to hide

these symptoms for the rest of your life, so the scales even out—in a manner of speaking."

"You knew I was an elemental."

"I guessed." He pulled his chair closer to the bed. "But I did not expect my suspicion to be confirmed before the Sapphire Ball. Least of all two days before. Lie back, my dear, and allow me to offer you some of this honeyed gateau; I could not procure snap-flower strips, nor the starfruit that you like so much."

After she had swallowed the piece of cake, she flexed her arms, tested her toes and fingers, and measured her exhalations. Nothing seemed unusual. It might be obvious on the outside, though—the extent of the change she had been through might be sketched onto her features through dark circles under her eyes, a pallor in her cheeks, the red of sleepless nights splashed across her eyeballs—what if everyone sensed the underlying cause and closed in upon her? As she was considering this possibility, Three's words sank in at last.

Two days until the ball, she thought. *That means I've been asleep . . .*

"You have been sprawled on that bed for over a week." He seemed to have read her mind. Or was he simply reading her expression? "It takes time for one's body to transform into a weapon of mortifying force. Lord Derset has been asking after you, most solicitously. And the Irriqi nearly broke down the door. There is also this," he produced a small bag of black velvet, "from Prince Fontaine."

She ignored the look he was giving her, and taking the bag, she traced the curves of an object inside it, pretending not to guess at its nature. "I don't feel like a weapon of mortifying force. My arms feel like limp lettuce."

Even if there was a weapon hidden inside her, it could hardly be strong enough to protect her against everyone in the realm who would detest her.

"It would be unnaturally convenient if there were no gap between maturation and the emergence of your powers. This is what we call the transition," Three said. "Two days before the ball, and you are at the height of volatility: a jet of water or a ball of fire might burst out of you at any moment. You must not drink any more scale for at least a week. I do not imply that you may use night-quartz and expel the contents of your stomach, either—we are talking about a program of outright abstinence."

"Scale," Lysande repeated, thickly.

"Oh, yes, my dear, we are quite aware of your little habit."

"But I—" She felt a panic stronger than that she had experienced during her maturation. Shame suffused her body.

"Forgive me, but we have no time to go into it. No more scale until your powers develop. You are dangerous, not only to others, but to yourself. A state of heightened physical stimulus would only exacerbate the problem." He paused, looking at her, but did not elaborate. "We have infiltrated Rayonnant Palace, and my colleagues can take you through the methods to control your powers, but it is a practical lesson. It cannot be taught until you have your element."

Had Three really spotted clues that she was elemental? How did he know about the scale? Was it really true that a jet of water might just *burst out of her*? It was always when you had no time to think that questions came. As they arrived one by one, she noticed that he was fumbling under the brim of his hat and pulling out a piece of paper.

"You are different now—and yet you are the same—but we must leave that till after the ball. There is something we must deal with first." He held out the page.

"Three." She had only just remembered. "I know what Charice knows, about the White Queen. And I suppose you have the right to know that we met twice in Rhime."

From his unsurprised expression, she knew that she had guessed right about the extent of his knowledge—the information he had hinted at, about Sarelin and the White Queen, when she first met him—and she knew, too, that Charice would have bargained for her safety with other offerings.

"If Mea Tacitus was a Brey—Sarelin's cousin—we have a chip of diamond that may be worth an enormity," she said.

"In my opinion, whether it is a diamond or not remains unclear."

It would have been so easy to argue. She knew that Three had experience in this, and experience granted the upper hand, and yet . . . if only she had time to do as she pleased, to analyze what Mea Tacitus' childhood serving Sarelin meant and how they could use it. Biting down on her words, she took the page.

The gray veins in the paper told her that this note had been inked from the Periclean States. Runic symbols formed lines of even length, dominating the page in black ink. Unlike the other letters she had read, it was not translated, and she felt a small relief at having something tangible to work with, something aside from shame and anxiety to focus on. That Three knew about the scale . . . she had a horrible feeling that he knew about the night Derset had visited her chamber, too, and worst of all, that he could read her thoughts about Luca.

Why was it that some interactions imprinted themselves in your mind like a seal pressing into wax? She could not recall what she had said to Derset on the ship, yet she perfectly recalled the flare of interest across Luca's countenance when she had grabbed his wrist, and his remarks: *You have a crushing grip, Prior . . . I never said that I disliked it.*

"Seven worked very hard to catch that messenger dove and duplicate the note. She took care to send the bird flying off again, as if nothing had ever been intercepted. Yet for such a coup, our efforts to translate have proved fruitless." Three almost managed to suppress the hopeful note in his voice. "Perhaps your not-inconsiderable abilities can be of some use."

It was time to direct her thoughts onto the task. This proved less simple than she had expected. She forced herself to concentrate. The runes that covered the paper were not any alphabet identified by the crown: the shapes were curving yet jagged at the ends, a hybrid of two kinds of ancient glyphs, so rare that she had only come across them in one poetry book in Sarelin's library. She had stored away the meaning of each in her mind, yet she did not feel content to proceed without checking them against a reliable source, and she worked to translate the message with a quill and the *Compendium of Ancient Languages*, fetched from the desk. It felt like butting a mountain with her shoulder, but the translation stimulated her in a way that she needed.

The result, when she had checked the runes three times over, appeared to be strings of figures. "It's a cipher," she said, looking across at Three. "Look here: punctuation marks among the numbers. I would bet that there are sentences buried beneath the code. But don't get hopeful. I have no notion of how to crack it."

"Ah." He reached for the page. "Then I shall pass it on."

Lysande sat up straight. "Leave it."

She was already bringing the paper closer to her face, holding it tightly. She had forgotten about the pair of symbols in the bottom-right corner of the page. *1, 12*. Two numbers in modern Eliran script, but only there. Why the anomaly? Perhaps this pair of figures denoted a chapter and passage in the Silver Songs, or a hymn from one of the city prayer-books that would decode the message. It might be a book known only to the White Queen's supporters, but that would require making several copies, and Lysande felt that that was something of a tiresome task for a woman on the run; for convenience's sake, she would have chosen a book that circulated everywhere. She could not help noticing that it was becoming easier to think like the White Queen with every day that passed.

Running through the Songs one by one, she pushed herself to think while her body was sore, with no scale to relieve the pain, and nothing came up from the verses that could be relevant. She loved the thorniness of the problem, though: the challenge of untangling the threads.

The thought occurred to her that Luca might have knotted them, and a bolt of something warm and bright shot through her. It was frustration, she told herself. She would not permit it to be excitement.

There was "open the way for the Conquest," on paragraph twelve of the first book, but she couldn't see how that helped her to make sense of these numbers, unless the code could be shot at with arrows or stabbed. She bit her lip. "And so she took one in every group of three": the twelfth paragraph of the seventh book sounded more promising, but after putting together every third number, she was still looking at a string of meaningless figures.

The Axium prayer-book that Sarelin had kept by her bed, with its thick hide cover, came to mind. She chastised herself for not memorizing the hymns. There could be something in the *History of the Chimeran War*, though; in her head, she ran through the quotes she had noted down in her string-bound compilation on politics. This would make a useful lesson for *An Ideal Queen*, if she managed to succeed: *The ideal ruler is not thwarted by a coded page.*

"No hope of cracking it, I suppose?" Three's voice still had a distinct note of hope.

"I shall need a few minutes more."

Or a few hours more. She glared at the *1* next to the *12*, blaming the skinny numeral for her inadequacy. As she took note of the number's appearance, she saw that there was a tiny stroke kicking up from the bottom-right of the stem, a mark almost too faint to be seen.

Had she imagined it? She held the page closer again. No; it was still there.

"It's not 'One, Twelve,'" she said. "It's 'L, Twelve.' The number one's got a line veering up at the bottom. I've seen 'L, Two' on one of Sarelin's law-drafts, in reference to a place in the official text; I'd say this comes from the *Legilium.*" She leaned forward before remembering how much it hurt to move; her back protested shrilly. Even that could not stem her satisfaction. Threads of code separated in her fingers. "The numbers will correspond to letters starting from the beginning of the twelfth chapter."

Three clapped his hands. He looked as if he had found a lump of gold in a battered cooking pot. "The book of laws! Excellent work, Signore Prior. A good choice for a key, no doubt. Most city-rulers and nobles keep it nearby, in case they are suddenly required to evade their taxes. They are scrupulous when it comes to acting without scruple."

Who did that sound like, if not Luca? But she was not supposed to be focusing on him.

"I don't suppose you happen to have the *Legilium* at hand?" Three said.

Vindication pricked at Lysande as she directed him to the chest of books that she had convinced Litany to pack. Three rummaged through the manuals and histories and poetry volumes to find the dog-eared *Legilium.* Lysande opened the law-book to the twelfth page: a chapter on the crime of using a magical power, she noted with an ironic smile. Skimming through the passage, she had just enough strength to hold the book beside the creased piece of paper, and once she could balance it, matching the key to the message was no problem; she counted the letters in her head and jotted down the right ones.

Holding the paper up, she looked over what she had written.

"Make sure you have won Prior over by the ball," she read. "All will be ready."

Three said nothing in reply. He stood up and walked to the window, and Lysande grappled with the message, telling herself to breathe. "Win me? Why in the Three Lands would the White Queen want her servant to win *me* over?" she said.

Three was gazing at the lotus pond below. She had the impression that his thoughts were far away from the flowers.

"Perhaps she has guessed that the 'heatstroke' that laid you up in bed was not quite what it seemed. Or perhaps she has discovered that you are working with the Shadows." He walked back to the chair and sat down. "Perhaps she thinks that because you are new and inexperienced, you can be killed in some manner that will shock Elira. Only one thing can be assumed. Whatever she has in mind for the Sapphire Ball, it will revolve around you."

A wave of disbelieving laughter rose in Lysande's chest and subsided again. She had just discovered that she was elemental, and the Council would be within their rights to have her killed as an enemy— and now their real enemy, the White Queen, wanted to kill her too. It was a play without an end.

"Well, I may not be Dante Dalgëreth, but I can defend myself. And I will have two hundred elite guards waiting for my word." She could feel her jaw tightening. She would not give in to Mea Tacitus, not yield to a woman who refused to take form, to a hand that moved others into the line of attack. Whatever Mea had endured as a servant to her cousin, it did not weigh against murder. Not in the reckoning of Perfault and other ethicists . . . and not in her own, for she had devised her own standards since Sarelin died. "Even if the Umbra leaks the positions of the Lyrian guards to the White Queen, they cannot know about my troops."

As she spoke, it occurred to her that there was no means of absolving Three from suspicion of being the Umbra, or absolving the rest of the Shadows. She held the thought, for a moment, before shelving it in her mind.

"I expect you are right. Hand me those papers, Signore Prior."

Lysande passed him the letter and the translation, and he folded them up and tucked them back under the brim of his hat. He pushed a lock out of his face, and as the Lyrian sun streamed in and fell on the strand, she saw the pure white shade of it against his cheek: the tress starved of color. It took her a second longer to notice his frown. "You're not telling me something. Do you think two hundred of the best Axium soldiers will not be enough?"

"What is defense, after all, but putting up walls? You use an army to erect a wall between yourself and another army, or a shield as a barrier against a sword. Mail, weapons, personal guards: they all provide walls with which we hope to keep out death. But can you put up a wall around your own mind, Signore Prior?"

She was silent. Charice risked death, she thought. The bone people faced death each morning.

"Consider that if she seeks to win you over, she may work to gain your trust; few of us have a fortification against our emotions and our anxieties, and the Umbra may have been working on yours already. We have analyzed her deceit against Bastillón and Royam. We have scoped out the building of her armies. Perhaps we should have looked at a different kind of campaign, though. I know that no chain mail or armor plating can protect you against what she will do to you if she breaks into your head."

"Do I have your assistance?"

He looked at her for a long moment, his hands folded, his eyes crinkling at the edges and lending him a manner that was both kindly and sad. "The Shadows will do what they can from the margins. Your Axiumite friend is lending us some very unusual medicines, which I hope we will not need. I make no promises, but if things look grim, Six and I may even step into the light. In the end, however, we rely on you."

"Then I must not disappoint you. I must set about putting up the best wall I can." Dante, Luca, Jale, even Cassia: none of them could be trusted until the ball was over. Why did she feel so heavy inside? "I will be impermeable."

"Impermeable." Three straightened his hat. "I thought I was impermeable, too, until she shattered me. Very well. Sleep, my dear, and you should be recovered enough to go over the defenses tomorrow. Send word if you feel a stirring."

He bowed and rose. As he stood up, Cursora came flying back through the window, landing on his wrist as naturally as if she were a part of him: her feathers shone the same unnatural white as his hair. He placed the dove on the desk and left her to peck among the papers. Lysande watched him walk across the room.

She thought she caught a hint of consternation as he regarded her, like a man weighing up his odds and finding them longer than he had hoped, before he turned the handle and walked out. The pendant disappeared beneath his cloak.

Only when the door had clicked shut did she realize that, in the shock of the maturation, she had quite forgotten to tell him that she had stood on a hilltop in Rhime, gazed down at the sheer drop below her, and agreed to form an alliance with Luca Fontaine.

Twelve

It took nearly a half-hour for the palanquins to navigate through the pleasure district of Lyria. Lysande stared out at theaters, salons, and academies of dance, all decorated with gold statues that resembled spearfish and seemed to protrude onto the street. In the western quarter, a less-refined range of establishments promised "prize fights" and "exceptionally skilled dancers," and the signs disappeared altogether once they passed into the southern quarter.

Lyrians beckoned to her from doorways, dressed in clothes that revealed more than they covered. A little further along, a man sauntered into the street, clad in what seemed to be a scrap of silver cloth suspended by a multitude of strings, eyeing the palanquins over the top of his goblet. Lysande could not help blushing. The Axiumite in her was too strong to stare, but she allowed herself an occasional glance. It was hard to tell whether there was any point in observing propriety in Lyria, when minutes ago, a doorwoman had invited them to "better connect the flesh with the divine power of the sun."

A jolt of the palanquin made her wince. She put a hand to her chest, rubbing the flesh where a tenderness remained, and thought of writing, of her quill, of anything but the caress of blue liquid on the back of her throat.

In the quarter marked PLEASURE DISTRICT SOUTH, the buildings gave way to a wide, open area where groups of Lyrians chatted. Sweet-rice carts trundled between groups of card-players, and smaller carts distributed pepperwine and iced dragoncherry juice. The palanquins jerked to a stop, and her gaze swept the plaza, finding its object on the edge of a fountain.

Luca sat, reading, clad in an unadorned shirt and trousers. If the shimmering coil of Tiberus had not rested on his knee, he might have not have attracted so many glances from the crowd. He shut his book as she walked up to him, and its spine shone like a ribbon in the sun.

"At last," he said. "I was beginning to think you'd never find time to converse."

"That was no excuse to pelt me with doves. Why here, of all places?"

"Why else but to delight in the Fountain of Southern Cheer?" He gestured to the bubbling water behind him. "Of course, that's not its real name . . . like so many historical terms, it was mistranslated. In the ancient Lyrian, it was *fontaine de vivre*. The water of life."

"Throw a coin into it, and it brings you glory. Dip a hand in the water, and it heals the illnesses that plague you." Lysande had not forgotten the cramp in her palm from the hours she had spent translating the section on Lyrian myths in the Silver Songs, so many years ago, when Sarelin had presented Ariane Chamboise with a copy for each of her mistresses.

"Perhaps you should dip a hand in it, Prior. A heatstroke that lasts for ten days—that must have been a very tenacious ailment."

She ignored the remark and led her guards past; he followed her, lifting Tiberus up onto his arm. At the rail around the circular area, they stopped. She waited a few seconds, inspecting his face before turning back to the fountain.

"I opened your gift, Fontaine."

"And did you get so far as forming an opinion?"

"I find it repulsive."

"I see. You don't know how to use it."

"I understand perfectly how it works, thank you. I simply do not find it amusing."

In front of them, a group of girls tossed coins into the water. An old man stooped down beside them to tip a bag full of brass shavings in, and shook his offering out bit by bit.

"Speaking of gifts," Luca said, "those coins and trinkets don't stay in the fountain. At night, a member of the royal staff comes out and trawls through the water with a net, to catch coins and smaller pieces that may not look valuable: chips of gold, gems, slivers of copper."

"I sense a metaphor in the air. What is the net, Fontaine? Justice? Power?"

He moved closer to her. "We Rhimese are different from you. Axiumites learn to gather news when their backside touches the throne; in Rhime, we do it to survive. I've been marshaling spies since I was eight, Prior. I caught two of the Ursinis plotting to slit my throat on my sixteenth gift-day. Now, like that net, nothing slips past me." He fixed his stare upon her. "Even when I'm sitting in Lady Pendici's courtyard, I catch every whisper in the inns . . . and if pilgrims are lodged near Lyria by my colleague, well, I catch that, too."

Lysande pretended to study the peaks of water as they rose and dissolved.

"You may be surprised to hear it, but we Rhimese have pilgrims of our own."

"How many?"

"One hundred and fifty. Specialist pilgrims, you might say. They have a very good aim with their . . . blessings."

They looked into each other's eyes. Lysande weighed the desire to avoid disclosing a secret plan against the risk of crossing Luca Fontaine. Something always held her back from walking away whenever he was near, and there it was, again: a certain brightness in his eyes when she moved a little too close. She thought of the touch of her fingers against his neck, on the ship; of the way he had looked at her as she pressed them against his throat, his pupils widening ever so slightly. It was impossible to forget.

"I have a hundred pilgrims," she said.

"Good. Perhaps we could arrange a gathering, to coordinate our hymns."

A man with a pierced ear in the style of one of the Periclean States' fashions wandered past the fountain, and she caught something odd about the man's garb, but her mind was still working out what Luca had discovered. Had he followed her to her meetings with the Shadows, too? Could he tell she was lying about the number of guards? And what of the bigger secret—the transformation that had wracked her body and mind?

Something warm and heavy on her wrist prompted her to look

down. Tiberus had wriggled his way off Luca's arm and was wrapping himself at a leisurely pace around her own. "Fontaine," she said, through gritted teeth. "I am not a pillow for a snake."

"Some would consider his attentions an honor." He reached over and lifted Tiberus up. The cobra gave Lysande a reproachful look, re-settling himself on Luca's forearm.

The Periclean walked past them again, and she realized at once what had niggled at her: the man's outfit draped him, the thick cloth hang-ing all the way down to his boots. It looked like an advisor's robe, ex-cept that this man did not have a learned manner, and she thought that his shoulders exhibited the bulk of a soldier. As she watched, the man shot a glance at them.

"As a matter of fact," Luca said, patting Tiberus' head, "I was wondering—"

Lysande's mouth opened, but before a warning could form on her lips, the Periclean lunged at Luca, smallsword flashing in the sun. The blade went through Luca's shirtsleeve and drew blood. Luca moved, and she saw a blur, a whirl of linen and flesh, the prince pulling his rapier free of the sheath even as he turned. Tiberus hissed and reared.

It was Luca who struck, though not by thrusting. The attacker ad-vanced, pushing his way to Luca, and the prince appeared to receive the blow—it was an art, Lysande thought, to kill by taking an impact instead of giving one, yielding like water. The man had not spotted how Luca had avoided the edge, and where he had positioned his own blade, close to his body.

A red stream leaked from the Periclean's chest. He tottered, a stunned look in his eyes, and clutched Luca's arm. Luca pulled the ra-pier out and let him fall.

"Not a bad effort," he said, looking at the man. "But far too hasty, for an assassin."

He stepped back from the body, ignoring the shrieks around them—people were running, some fleeing back into the street, others hurry-ing over to gawk at the dead man. The fluid that had burst from the man's heart spread and soaked the ground. Lysande felt a crackling in her stomach that had nothing to do with scale.

Luca ripped a strip of cloth from his sleeve. Binding his arm, he stared down. "Let's see if our friend wears his allegiance under that ugly collar."

He ripped the man's robe upward, exposing a mark just below the collarbone. An image discolored the flesh, the skin tainted black as if from some disease, but surely this could only be a brand. The shape was unmistakable. If someone had copied it from an illustration in a history book, the winged beast could not have been clearer.

At Luca's whistle, two Rhimese guards appeared beside them—they must have been hovering nearby all along, Lysande realized—and the soldiers dragged the dead man through the group of spectators, a smear of red following the body along the ground.

With brisk strokes, Luca wiped his hands on his shirt. The Rhimese hefted the body and disappeared into the traffic. Just a second ago, a man had come out of nowhere with a sword; Luca's sleeve had been slashed, his arm bloodied, and yet he did not seem troubled.

"It's a late request, Prior but I have to ask . . ." He wiped his hands on his shirt again, daubing more red onto the white.

Lysande's mouth felt dry. She could see the dark lake on the ground out of the corner of her eye. "Yes?" she said.

"Would you lead me into the dance at the Sapphire Ball?"

Possibilities, probabilities, and likelihoods ran through her mind as the palanquin jerked its way back to Rayonnant Palace. She recognized a familiar yearning, and without the warm, golden glow of scale to still her anxieties, she considered who she could turn to.

The upper dining room was nearly empty, its open windows allowing the sun to pour over the table, illuminating bowls of blush-melon and plates of spiced noodles. The court of Lyria was putting on a comedy in the grounds; Jale had dedicated the performance of *The Merry Sword of the North* to Dante, to sniggers from the Lyrian nobles; but as she had hoped, a familiar figure sat by the left window, a ray of light blessing the poetry book on his knee.

"Better to sit, for what I have to tell you, my lord." She raised a hand as Derset made to rise. "In fact, better to drink, too."

He bobbed his head, with an ease proportionate to that which

Lysande had felt around him ever since they fell together onto the ship's deck. It was not the time they had spent in her bed that had changed things most, desire moving between them like the swell of water at high tide; it was the moment he had rushed to knock her out of the path of a fireball that had eased them into a state of nearness— the kind of nearness that could be felt.

The sight of the poetry book reminded her of the line she had glimpsed Derset reading on the ship. Jolted by the visual, she remembered the rest of the verse:

> *If ever I should choose to hunt*
> *A poor shot would I be—*
> *But I would gladly lay before*
> *The one who hunted me*

A fragment of the fourth sonnet in Inara's *Courtship of the Black-foot Tree*—was it not? One of the poet's lesser-known works, Lysande knew, perhaps because the sequence of sonnets was so long and was known to be more romantic than respectable. She was one of the few who cherished Inara's musings above the moralizing poetry of the Steelsong Era, and she was proud of the eight hard-bound volumes containing her personal translation of the sonnet sequence, stored in her chamber in Axium Palace. To see Derset reading such a poem, however . . . a sonnet about wishing to be pursued and pierced . . . was it inappropriate for the acting leader of Axium to be deeply intrigued?

She took a jug and two goblets from the table and poured the wine. "Before we speak of plots, let me say that I should like to request your company again, this afternoon. In my chamber. Provided you feel that it would be beneficial to you, of course . . ."

Derset looked down, smiling, and when he met her gaze again, it was with the kind of agreement that could not be mistaken. *If ever I should choose to hunt.* Lysande took a long sip of her drink.

Over the Lyrian white, she recounted her organization of the secret guard, beginning with the day that she had learned of the possibility of an attack at the Sapphire Ball—though leaving out the meeting with the Shadows, attributing her intelligence to Raden's range-riders. She detailed the selection of two hundred special fighters, the disguise and dispersion through inns, and the plan to bring them to the palace. It was strange how secrets layered: once you had one, you had another, and then before you knew it you were buried by them, struggling for a lungful of air. This was her chance to breathe.

Derset listened in silence.

"I could hardly blame you if you were angry," she said.

"Angry? No."

"You do not feel I should have consulted you?"

"Bowbray or Tuchester or Pelory would have felt so, I am sure. They have always made it clear to me that an advisor's role is to direct their ruler. But I am of the opinion that the best leader is one who knows how to direct herself." There was his gentle smile again. "Of course, I am a little taken aback that you worked so industriously in secret."

He reached to brush a piece of dried leaf off her sleeve. Her hand fell onto his and she let it linger, a little longer than usual, pressing down against the firm length of his palm and thinking of the moment they had been pressed to each other on the ship's deck. There had been nothing but warmth in the world: his warmth, and the thumping of his heartbeat.

She had to force herself to return to strategy, relating her meeting with Luca and his request to merge guards, and coming to the Periclean man's attack.

"It may have been that the White Queen's spy was trying to kill Prince Fontaine, just as it appeared. If Prince Fontaine is truly your ally, the timing of the strike on the Grandfleuve may have been a coincidence. He may have been defending himself today. I think it not impossible," Derset said.

"Not impossible. A glowing vote of confidence in Prince Fontaine, then."

"My lady, I would not wish to suggest—"

"Speak plainly, Lord Derset."

Derset put down his goblet of wine, his brows knitting. "Then I think we should also consider the possibility that Prince Fontaine is tricking you into yielding information. If he arranged for a soldier to run at him, he might be seeking to gain your trust by slaughtering the man in your presence—could anyone deny that it would work to his favor? The fox knows the shaded path to its lair far better than its prey ever can." He paused and met her glance. "We cannot ignore that he is a master of stratagems, after the Room of Accord."

She could still see the blood spreading across the ground from the assassin's body. "I knew you would strike the nail on the head."

"By merging with you, he gains the precise details of your plans, for some purpose or other. I do not say that it is an ill purpose—perhaps he merely wishes to make sure of your loyalty." He gave a polite but rather unconvincing smile.

"Perhaps." She rose and paced to the window. The White Queen had used the expression *won Prior over* . . . and was it unreasonable to suppose that a request for a dance was somehow part of a campaign? She pictured Luca's face again, after he had killed the assassin: his eyes closed shutters.

"I think we should attempt to protect ourselves against him," she said. "Give him some of the guards' locations in the inns, to pacify him, for he has gleaned them already; but give him false details as well." Nothing covered a lie so well as a little truth. She had written that at the end of the third chapter of *An Ideal Queen*, after analyzing the bloody string of first-century conspiracies.

"A good plan." Derset considered, taking another sip. "A risky plan, too, but I suppose so long as you act with great care . . ."

She walked back to him. "I told Fontaine I only have a hundred guards."

Derset's goblet clinked against the table. He was looking at her as one might regard a markswoman who had just hit a target. Ever so slightly, his mouth quirked. "A bare-faced lie to a prince. You remind me of someone, my lady."

"And who is that?"

"Her late Majesty, Queen Sarelin."

She laughed. When she was back in her suite without an advisor to face, and without a mask of confidence to assume, she did not laugh any more. She took out the gold quill and held it in her palm, unbuttoned her doublet, stood in front of the mirror, and looked at the chain of fluid silver around her neck. The links caught the sun, dripping radiance onto her skin: a curve of metal singing.

There was no such thing as being left alone when you were a Councillor of Elira. Dante and Jale called on her at separate times that afternoon, but she sent Litany to make her excuses. She suspected that her supposed ailment was forgotten in the excitement that followed. Dante had bloodied the jaw of a Lyrian guard who muttered an insult at him in the corridor, and although competing versions of the guard's remark were circulating, Litany had gathered that it had had something to do with the north being the last refuge of savages who thought with their lower parts, illegitimate brutes seeking to rut, who had no right to pursue southern leaders. She also reported that the Valderrans had cheered Dante on as he laid a blow.

"It's odd, though, isn't it?" Litany said. "The First Sword's reviled by the southerners. Yet last night, it looked like he was heading toward Prince Chamboise's quarters."

"Mmm," Lysande said.

They looked up and their gazes met.

"Do you think they . . ."

"Possibly," Lysande said.

"I have heard the Valderran guards boasting of the First Sword's virility. They say he has bedded some of the most famous noblemen in the north. Yet he does not marry. They say he looks for a better match."

"Maybe it is all rumor." Lysande's tone failed to convince even herself.

"Maybe. But it seems to me that Prince Chamboise would be a great prize. He has royal blood and a fortune beyond any in Elira. And as for the other side of the match, well," Litany blushed, "the First Sword is very handsome."

"You astound me, Litany."

"Have you not noticed that he has the build of an athlete?"

"Of the two, I must admit, Prince Chamboise is more to my taste."

Litany grinned. "'The balm of a pretty man's face.' Callica's phrase?"

"Inara's. But do not get your hopes up, Litany. I doubt either one of them is looking our way." Lysande ran a finger over her sword-hilt, remembering the moment she had watched Dante pacing in the maze-garden. "And besides, I would be very surprised if the First Sword sees Prince Chamboise as a prize. He takes oaths seriously. I think it very likely that he takes love seriously, too."

She resisted the temptation to ask Litany what she thought of love. Some things should not be broached with a person who could split an arrow in the middle of a target.

In the aftermath of the altercation between Dante and the Lyrian guard, Lysande managed an hour of quiet study, poring over her charts of the White Queen's past maneuvers. Cassia's attentions were harder to avoid than Dante and Jale's, for she turned up in the thick of a group of armed soldiers and insisted on being let in. Litany went out not twice, but six times.

Impermeable, Lysande thought, as she looked at the bouquet of fiery red flowers Cassia had left her.

She turned to studying the book of military accounts she had taken from the Academy, but the records of the war served no use except to tell her what she already knew: that the White Queen did not like risking her own neck when she could send another to attack in her place. More hours passed, and the difficulty of holding off from her store of scale increased. She tore strips off her nails several times. The more she tried not to think of blue flakes, the more she found herself dreaming of the room transmuting to gold around her, of the feeling of quiescence washing through her, and the scent of spiced wine lingering in her nostrils, like the ceaseless thrum of Sarelin's voice, pushing her concerns into retreat. The heat searing through her forehead and cheeks, the writhing of her stomach, the knocking of her heartbeat like an angry drunkard against her ribs: those effects of scale, her memory chose to sift out.

Even though she had told Derset to meet her in her suite, she had forgotten about it whilst plunged into the depths of research, carried away by books and charts. A gust of wind caught the door as he entered, banging it shut, and they both jumped.

There was no need to pretend that they wished to talk or check arrangements; the look that passed between them said enough. Lysande grasped his hand and led him to her bed, feeling his body respond as she pressed it down.

Inch by inch, leaning over him, she lowered her mouth to his earlobe, then ran her teeth over the skin without biting; stopping; then shifting her body to kneel over him. For a moment, it was hard to read his expression. Then he smiled, ever so slightly.

"Are you sure you want this?" She could not help the words from slipping out. Was it naïve, to ask? She thought of the woman in the orangery, years ago, backing away from her.

"You're forgetting." Derset's glance deepened. "I like what you like."

"I have seen you reading poetry."

"My lady?"

She quoted the verse in full:

> *If ever I should choose to hunt*
> *A poor shot would I be—*
> *But I would gladly lay before*
> *The one who hunted me.*

The words rang out in the airy chamber. Derset was looking at her with appreciation. "You are observant, my lady."

"I like to observe you."

Was he blushing? Surely not.

"And how do you find Inara's sonnet?" he said, at last.

"I relate to the hunter." Lysande met his eyes and saw approval again.

They took longer than before. Considerably longer. The encounter almost relieved her inner ache, and his movements matched her own, responding to her restlessness with speed. She unbuttoned his robe, like the last time, though soon his hands worked more swiftly than hers. At one point, she pressed so hard against his brace that he flung out a hand to grip the sheet, his fingers tangling in blue silk.

Yet even amidst the press and yield of limbs, there was something pricking away at her mind, a tiny but steady jab that she thought was the effect of going without the familiar concoction of sky-blue flakes, sugar, and water. Just when she was about to swim away from the craving, into deeper waters, the jab came again.

Other preoccupations resurfaced, too. At one point, she realized she was thinking about Luca's pulse beating under her hands, her mind fixed on the moment when she had leaned over the tactos-board and touched Luca's neck.

It rose and subsided, and rose and subsided, the hunger, the need for satiation. Derset did not question her or ask how she felt. He was adapting to her desire, she could tell, and she did not like how easily she had accepted that.

A ruler's work will not bring her pleasure. Her pleasure, therefore, need not bring her work. Convenient, how the *Mirror for a Monarch* could justify your needs.

Derset's final gasp softened into suspiration, a half-voiced prayer.

They lay still on the silk, still enough that they might have been sleeping. After a few minutes, Lysande trailed a finger down Derset's hip. He turned onto his left side, and she ran her palm down his back, feeling the warmth of the skin, and glad that he could not see her face as she thought: *This is mine, this living thing.*

When he had gone, she tried to ignore the guilt that had crept, like a many-legged insect, into her consciousness. Should she not be working to *restrain, constrain, subdue,* pushing down those desires which threatened to flow out of control? She stood at her desk for quite some time, sipping honey-water, trying to force herself back into the flow of her duties, telling herself to make use of her research in the most practical way: by making a counter-move.

She slipped down to ground floor of the palace to meet Raden, making an excuse for her tardiness, and they edged their way past the Lyrian guards to the area where items were being carried to the back door. Tables were lugged past, sometimes in pieces, other times whole. Tanks of something covered in cloth were bustled along, and great quantities of mesh that Lysande presumed was some kind of decoration were brought to the door. All in all, the procession seemed more expensive and a lot noisier that it would have been in Axium.

"Do you see what this means?" Raden said. "They're holding the ball outside. We don't have to station the guards in one or two rooms."

"The back wings, the stables, or the gardens . . ." She peered out of a gold-edged window. "What does a captain's eye make of the layout?"

Focusing on details of fronds and foliage, she kept her mind off the lure of a vial of blue flakes. She considered the spare rooms on the ground floor, which were easy to break into, and the possibility of stowing the guards with the horses; yet the only place that was likely to hide them all, in Raden's opinion, was the palm garden behind Rayonnant Palace. Jale's mother, Ariane, had attempted to gather ten of every kind of palm in Elira—the result, Lysande thought, looked leafy enough to hide a legion of guards.

Separating her other hundred guards from Luca's would be more difficult. But had she committed to her role for what was easy?

As she went over the positions of the scouts with Raden, she wondered what Vigarot would do if he knew that Axium Guards were being smuggled in under his nose. She was risking a breakdown of the Council, she knew. Some people probably found it simple to take risks. They probably didn't feel a churning of anxiety.

If I've managed this far, for those like me, I can damned well keep on working.

It was not only the crowd at the ball she was protecting, she reminded herself, but all the people across the realm, the destitute and hidden and starved people, who would feel the White Queen's wrath too. And no matter how altruistic it might look on the surface, these people were the ones who cheered her name louder than those of the other Councillors. She knew from where she might draw her base.

Yet another thought kept popping up in her head.

"So, we put half the scouts along the Grandfleuve, a quarter in the desert, and a quarter along the coast. They've got hundreds of doves. We'll know as soon as there's any sign of an army. Then—are you listening to me?"

"I was wondering," Lysande said. "Raden, would you still want me as leader of Axium if you knew that my parents were . . ."

"Were what?"

"Well, not Axiumites."

He shrugged. "I suppose I wouldn't mind if they came from another city. So long as it's not Rhime, of course." The force of his hand gripping hers took her by surprise. "The way I see it, you're not your parents. And whoever they were, you've made your own way without them. That's true as a leather sole." He let go.

Lysande felt a little surge of relief and smiled as they pulled apart. She had the urge to clap him on the back, but she knew, from one memory of an encounter in the Axium Palace grounds, that Raden did not take hugs lightly—they were far too intimate for a man raised on salutes. A handshake was already pushing the bounds of propriety. "In a time like this, it means the world to have a friend of many years on whom I can rely."

Raden smiled and gave a quick nod. She recalled the day they had sat beside the lake, while dappled light filtered down to them through the dragon-willow leaves, and how Raden had waited patiently as she tried to calm her breathing, recovering from the sight of four guards carrying Sarelin's body. As he walked away now, she noticed his steady strides.

It was with more energy that she finished running through their plans and left Raden to write to the scouts. The image of scale appeared occasionally among her thoughts, but she managed to push it away. She was almost back at the Axium rooms when she felt the itch.

It began in the middle of her palm and spread. Halting next to a statue of a pair of twined lovers, she scratched at the skin with her fingernails, raking the spot.

This was a time for concentration. She should be thinking about what she had she just witnessed. Every detail of the ball's layout might be crucial in stopping the White Queen. But she was thinking of her palm, instead. She ran a finger over it again. She could not forget that she had five days until the maturation, and when it happened, the ball would be over, and she could retreat to a house in Ratchley or Weicester outside the capital and remove herself from the public eye. *And learn what kind of monster I am.*

The early evening inched by, in a string of cravings that saw her pacing around her suite. The thought of the calm, golden glow that just one small spoon of scale would afford worked through her like viper poison. She resorted to re-reading the map-book and compiling a list of spots where the White Queen might infiltrate Elira. Target practice and a final check of plans with Raden did not go quickly enough.

An hour before the ball, Lysande made her way back to her suite. A cloak had arrived with Jale's compliments—a voluminous emerald thing with silver trim and tiny white jewels in the shape of Axium crowns dotting the lower half, it left scarcely any space on the bed-cover for her doublet and trousers. She stood side by side with Litany, staring at it.

"What do you say to a dressmaker's fee, Litany? I pay uncommonly well."

"I beg your pardon, but the cloak is already—" Litany caught her eye. "Oh."

Lysande picked up the long garment for a moment, letting the soft material flow through her hands. "This is of Lyrian make, you see. Light, for the desert. It will blow open in the slightest breeze, exposing the dagger-belt, but I am rather proud of my daggers. If a woman is likely to be attacked, she does well to have several hilts at hand, even if her enemy sees them." She laid the cloak down and picked up the doublet. "If she is taken, on the other hand, she requires a garment with certain capacities which must not be seen."

Litany turned her face away. When she spoke, her voice was rich with emotion. "I thought you would ask me to fight her."

"Fight Mea Tacitus—alone?"

"I have worked my whole life to defend the crown, Councillor."

Lysande saw that the girl was looking at the floor, her lips pressed together, a narrow seam. You could see the motto *everything in its place* hovering around the ears of most Axiumites, waiting for a moment to slip into the ear canal and travel all the way to the brain, so that all the pages and the cobblers and the stable-hands and the smiths stayed *in their place*, and Lysande knew the look that the dutiful wore: a kind of hopeful daze, as if they might be rewarded at any moment by those above them. Litany had never worn that look. She could think of several reasons why Litany would mention her years of service now, and none of them had to do with blind commitment to hierarchy.

The girl had her own kind of ambition. Lysande understood, better than most.

She laid a hand upon Litany's shoulder. "I brought an army here. I mean to use it. Armies are blunt weapons, even when they win, and you are a very fine instrument—I shall need you by my side, to protect me, if a battle breaks out tonight." She gripped Litany a little tighter. "You can shadow me in a way no one else can. I do not ask purely for my own sake. You told me once that in doing, we find meaning—and I think you have so much more to do, in the years to come. I should bet on it."

"What kind of bet do you see yourself making?"

Lysande eyed her carefully.

"Double your current pay," she said.

The tension slowly melted from Litany's face. It took a few moments, but in time, she looked down, and nodded.

"My advancement is your advancement," Lysande said. "I have a good memory for debts, and I know what I owe. But to pay it, I must defend the Council, and survive."

"I suppose I must let you be right."

"And you must survive to create our strategy of defense, in a truly coordinated way, against threats to come." Lysande smiled. Slowly, Litany nodded again. "Now, you see, this doublet does not look very different from any other doublet," Lysande said. "That is the trick. It is not the outside, but the inside that needs work."

Litany carried off the doublet with a muttering about making "adjustments to the inner fabric." Lysande felt a twinge of gratitude for the ease with which the girl understood her.

Her books had disappeared into their chests, and the desk had been covered with an array of jewelry. A necklace of square-cut emeralds accompanied a set of earrings shaped like the capital crown, and twenty-four hair pins inlaid with tiny chips of emerald glittered, along with other rings and baubles that she could not possibly wear. She wondered if the bone people on the platform would have cheered her so loudly if they could see all this show. Sorrow and shame rose at the memory of the boy smiling at her, the skeleton with the bright eyes.

Later. Always, later. It did not feel good to relegate them to a lesser rank in her mind.

Nor could she entirely push that sphere she had glimpsed, where Lysande Prior might be anyone and anything, into some dusty corner of her thoughts—no more than she could forget the sound of sunlight and steel in her voice as she ordered Raden to halt the executions.

She imagined laws as winged creatures: pictured Pelory giving her new order to the advisors, the guards, and the steward, and each time, the words flapping up, soaring toward the ceilings of Axium Palace and butting their heads against it.

All persons in Axium found to be acting as vigilantes, against elementals, the poor, or any others they persecute without evidence, shall be jailed forthwith.

What was she hoping for? It was only a little change that she had asked for, but still, a little change was a beginning. *Where prejudice rules, the crown weakens.*

Luca had said that to her.

She pictured him getting dressed, now—standing before a mirror, in all his smooth-skinned delicacy, while the men of his chamber pulled his trousers over his calves and thighs, laced up his doublet, and combed his hair. Or did he do that himself? Did he slip on his garments as he slipped on a layer of unwavering defiance each day?

She had scarcely donned her own trousers and the doublet that Litany returned to her, and shrugged on the cloak, when a knock came at the door. "The Overseer of Wardrobe of Rayonnant Palace," Litany announced.

The Overseer flounced in in head-to-toe gold, took one look at Lysande, and shook his head. "Oh, dear me," he said. "You—attendant—outside."

It took ten minutes for Lysande's cloak to be tied perfectly and adorned with a crown pin; another ten for the sleeves to be brushed and the shoulders plumped so that the swirls of silver would show to their full advantage; a half-hour for her hair to be arranged with two plaits pinned back to frame her natural waves. Her deathstruck strands disappeared beneath the left plait, pinned so tightly that there was no chance of them coming free. It was hard to say if she was pleased to see them hidden so well, or if she wanted to see them displayed . . . ever since she had seen the black stain creeping across the silver dagger and felt the terror of knowing how her blood marked her out, she had begun to wonder how it would feel if everything strange about her was no longer concealed.

Soon, Lysande began to understand why Raden said torture was worse than a swift death. By the time a few touches of silver powder had been applied around her eyes, she was wondering why any ruler bothered with balls when they could stay at home and dance around their throne in ordinary clothes—or whatever passed as ordinary when you had grown up swathed in velvet. A vision of herself charging at the White Queen and tripping over her own hem did not help.

The Overseer of Wardrobe sent for two assistants, who brought in a mirror and held it up. Her gasp drew smiles from them. The person looking back at her in the rich green cloak and the emeralds was not the scholar of Axium Palace—she could pass as a silverblood.

But if you were smoothed, your ink flecks removed and your straggling locks pinned back, perhaps you could still be tangled on the inside.

"There we are. You're a proper Axium girl, now," the Overseer said.

Lavish the costume might be, but it did not cling, nor expose her skin. The shoulders puffed up, like new muscle. No, she thought, staring at it. Not a girl. A Councillor.

Litany was allowed to come in at last, and when the door was closed, Lysande turned to her. "Go on, then. Show me the work."

A deft movement, and practiced hands opened the cloak, unbuttoned the doublet beneath and exposed two pockets sewn onto the left side of the lining, just below the breast. Two more adorned the right side of the lining, with a further pocket positioned toward the very front of the doublet. Lysande drew in her breath. It was the work of a minute to slip a few of her daggers into the slim pouches and tuck the gold quill into the outermost pocket, before pulling the doublet shut. She ran a finger over the boiled leather of the exterior and admired Litany's handiwork, noting how well the garment hid its secrets. Even if it had bulged, however, she would have been glad for the advantage of her cargo.

When she leaned to the right, she felt the tapering point of the quill, close to her as blood to bone.

She slipped Sarelin's gold dagger into the last loop on her dagger-belt; some gifts demanded to be used, calling in the voice of their giver.

"It seems dress clothes have a use after all," she said. "They smuggle. Actually, I have a garment for you, too, Litany."

In the closet on the wall hung a silver jacket cut in the Axium style and overlaid with fine Lyrian cloth. A likeness of the Axium crown shone in emerald thread on each sleeve.

"I had your measurements sent from the palace steward by dove . . . I hope you won't think it an impertinence. The first time you dressed me, you fixed crown pins in my hair. They were capital-made. The very same design marks these sleeves." She placed the jacket in the girl's arms. "I should have rather got you a matching cloak, but an attendant can get away with this . . . at least this way, we can represent Axium together."

Laying it out on the bed, Litany turned to face her, and after hesitating for less than a heartbeat's length, threw her arms around Lysande's waist and embraced her fully.

The preparation chamber seemed to be hidden in the farthest point of the eastern wing. Lysande followed her guide out to a staircase and through corridors she had not seen before, decorated ever more sumptuously with gold and jewels. Lyrian guards dotted the walls; the southern soldiers eyed her with interest as she passed, but kept their silence; there were more of them, now, Vigarot Chamboise having got his wish in time for the ball, and the palace had put on a serious air, torchlight gilding the hilts that jutted from leather belts.

They entered a corridor lined with portraits, beginning with Princess Catherique Gaincourt and running through every other Lyrian leader, from Claubert Tancey to Charine Orvergne, depicted next to fountains or the blazing sun, and she felt the weight of history upon her, those royal faces looking down at her from the frames. Tonight, standing in for Axium, she did not feel quite as removed as she ought to have.

Tonight, I could be one of them.

Some thoughts blew through you, a disquieting gale.

The attendant knocked three times on a set of doors at the end and opened them. "The Councillor of Axium arrives!"

The shards of light emanating from a chandelier dazzled her. It took Lysande a moment to see clearly, and when she walked through, she discerned Dante standing beside a high-backed chair. He and Jale stood with scarcely an inch between them.

"I have no patience for his grasping," Jale was saying, as she came in. "And the First Sword of Valderos is beholden to no climbing thorn. Tell him that." The signs of consternation written on his face might have been natural on another man, but on Jale, who was usually so adept at putting on a cheerful mask, they stood out like paint slapped across a clean wall.

Where Dante wore a northern warrior's outfit of a brown cape over armor, Jale sported a blue doublet and trousers, fashioned from a silk that had to cost hundreds of cadres. As the chandelier's light fell on his clothes, they shimmered like waves of the sea. He reached up to straighten the sapphire-studded ring that nestled on his brow. Lysande thought that the Lyrian crown outshone even Axium's jagged silver diadem, yet the look on Jale's face was far from glowing. "You overestimate my courage," Lysande heard Dante whisper to him as she passed. "I've never dared . . ." A shift in Jale's expression, a tightening of his jaw, seemed to set off a shift in Dante, too. "I shall dare it for you," Dante whispered.

The two of them broke off their dialogue to greet Lysande. She kept her pleasantries brief, slipped out of the conversation, and edged around the table, to where the leader of Pyrrha stood upright with arms folded, a sight that comforted her. Anything more polite would have suggested calculation. Lysande could not forget the happiness she had felt when Cassia had hugged her, after she had presented her with the livea branch, nor the sense of companionship she had felt when they had talked of chimeras inside the palanquin: the sense of being joined to her colleague, for better or for worse.

Side-slashed trousers of plum silk, overlaid with a sword-belt that might have even impressed Sarelin, marked Cassia out from the small crowd. She tapped the white spikes in her hair as Lysande approached. "Leopard's teeth."

"You look quite imposing, I assure you."

"Well, let's hope we do more dancing than dicing. I've been longing to speak with you." Cassia's eyes lit up, and Lysande felt another surge of guilt.

Vigarot Chamboise swept through the room with a train of attendants, giving orders left and right. While the staff dispensed sugared nuts of an alarming pink hue, Lysande felt a tap on her elbow.

She turned. As Luca moved into the light, gold beams fell on a black doublet slashed through the sleeves, tied with leather down the middle; with the deep red of the shirt beneath, it gave the impression of flowing blood. The coloring was not the only thing she noticed. Surely, if Luca had been placed in front of a mirror like her, he must know how well his doublet clung to the outlines of his body, and how the cascade of his hair lent a softness to the lines of his jaw, a touch of delicacy against that exquisite sharpness. Was this another move in the campaign?

"This should prove an interesting wedding, don't you think?" Luca remarked, as Vigarot guided the Council into a line. "The reluctant husband." He nodded toward Jale, a smile twisting his mouth. "Have you figured that little puzzle out?"

"I've no notion what you mean." She had no desire to expose Dante and Jale, if she was right about that particular suspicion—not to a man who saw scruples as playthings.

"Indeed. Your attention seems with your handsome advisor, of late."

She was spared any further conversation by the attendants moving them into place. Luca was pulled away from her, and Lysande felt a resurgence of the determination she had felt weeks ago, when she had first confronted the advisors in the Oval.

"Tell me the truth, Lysande," Cassia whispered into her ear, as ushers in gold livery marched past them. "Were you really ill all that time?"

"Of course I was."

"I'm so glad. I thought you might've been avoiding me." Lysande nearly tripped, and Cassia caught her and steadied her. There was no chance to explain, nor to navigate the fine line between logical suspicion and her quite illogical desire to be liked by Cassia.

At a nod from Vigarot, the ushers pushed the doors open, and a wave of hot desert air hit Lysande in the face. She followed Jale and Luca down the palace steps, a roof of gauzy mesh providing the only barrier between them and the sky: the blue a little darker than afternoon but not quite as deep as night. Hundreds of candles flickered in bowls along the ground, lighting the way a few feet ahead at a time, drawing them down a long path until the glow blossomed into full light. Lysande listened for any sudden noise. At the end of the path, they passed onto a low stage, where a wedding pavilion offered her a view of an altar wreathed with sapphire flowers, each bloom fully opened; beyond the stage she spied a long platform with two lines of palms encased in gold running down the middle.

She nearly jumped as something hit her arm, but she realized that it was only water. Flat pools flanked the platform, and as they walked, dozens of little jets of water sprang up on either side, giving rise to applause. The source of the clapping, Lysande guessed to be further ahead, where the platform ended and a path led through a mass of round tables . . . so many tables that she faltered. After Three's warning, her body was on edge, her mind sharpened. It was not easy to fight the soporific power of all this adornment.

Every notable person she had ever seen in Axium Palace seemed be sitting before her. Lady Langlore and Lady Banover, the two Axiumites as famous for their feuding as for their epic verses, shared a table to her right. She recognized a Pyrrhan merchant and several Bastillonian dignitaries—all silver-haired, and all with golden-haired servants standing behind them; a bolt of anger shot through her at the sight and lodged in her. She wondered what Charice would have thought of this unhuman separation; then she wondered if Charice was, perhaps, here somewhere, keeping company with the Shadows, talking to them instead of her.

Lyrian guards ringed the enclosure, she was relieved to see, while the other cities' soldiers prowled. She searched the crowd for any figure out of place, any watcher among the talkers. She caught a movement at the end of the enclosure where six tables stood, five draped with a city crest, one bearing a design of the Bastillonian ram under crossed swords.

"Look," she heard Carletta Freste say, from the table she was passing, "that old stoat Ferago's brought his whole family."

And now she saw the man approaching the Bastillonian table, his sword sparkling in the candlelight. King Ferago walked slowly, a ram's-head crown nestled on his white curls and a great cloak trimmed with ermine trailing along the ground behind him. Both crown and cloak enveloped him, leaving very little of his person to peep out. His wife supplied the height: towering over the heads of the rest of their party, Persephora Ferago looked sharply at the city-rulers, her hand clasping that of a young woman in armor. The princess on her arm reminded Lysande of a warrior in the Silver Songs, who had been tasked with leading a legion through the Tracian Hills in winter, and who had paused every noontime to look for a sign from the goddesses.

What sign Mariana Ferago was hoping for, though, Lysande could only guess. The princess shot a glance across the enclosure. Following her line of sight, Lysande found Dante and Jale—the pair had somehow reunited for a moment, despite Vigarot's best efforts. Dante leaned in to straighten the collar of Jale's shimmering doublet, and Jale laughed, the sound a rush of sunlight. When she looked back, Mariana's face had not lightened.

The two young men behind Mariana glistened as they walked, their confections of chatoyant silk falling over their limbs. One wore significantly more silk across his broad shoulders than the other, more slender son, but each prince carried off the Bastillonian white and blue admirably, Lysande thought. They were staring at the city-rulers, and she saw them lean in to whisper; while she watched, the slender brother pointed at her.

Was she being marked out for distrust? Litany had whispered to her that Gabrella Merez had agreed to appear at the ball, along with the Bastillonian royalty; to Elirans, at least, this was a step toward reconciliation. Yet was it possible that the events of the Room of Accord had lingered on in the collective Bastillonian imagination?

Perhaps she was being unduly anxious. And yet perhaps it was right to remember that the history books were not furnished with examples of the smooth and easy temperament of Bastillonian leaders.

At Vigarot's prompting, they reached the Council's seats. The Axium table brimmed with the people Lysande liked best—Derset, Litany, and Chidney welcomed her. Derset rose as she arrived. Looking at her cloak and then at her face, his gaze moved slowly and lingered on her countenance, and he seemed about to voice some remark when he thought better of it and bowed. "My lady, I am afraid the Axium guests do not like your seating arrangement."

Glancing down the enclosure, she saw several nobles whispering and staring at her. "I believe I was clear on the matter," she said.

"For an attendant, a captain, and even a royal advisor to take the place of nobility . . . it is not protocol, for Axiumites."

That was a word you heard as an excuse, passed down from those at the top of the ladder, Lysande thought. Everyone imbibed it without question. Protocol. A silver word.

"Nobility of spirit is the standard I use," she said. "I am confident that you have all met it."

They locked eyes. Derset did not look away, and she had the distinct impression that something about her had affected him in a new fashion.

Litany's sleeve had scraped something oily and Chidney was cleaning it with a corner of the tablecloth, she saw, trying not to smile. The pair straightened at once when they saw her and greeted her, then fell silent, Chidney opening her mouth and then closing it just as quickly. Lysande poured them each a goblet of wine. "How comforting it is to see you both at my table, and so close together," she said.

"Councillor, I did not mean—"

"I hope you are not about to apologize, captain. I should much rather you explain the dancing to Litany. She has not had time to study it, you see, nor to secure a partner."

Chidney turned to Litany again, looking a little hesitant and yet not displeased. One of her hands, which Lysande had seen frequently gripping a sword or a dagger, came to rest atop Litany's arm. "It is all very straightforward if you know how to fight. Dancing is a lot like fighting, except that nothing gets wounded."

"Except your pride," Litany said, "if you make a misstep."

"Ha!" Chidney leaned against the table as she laughed, sending two glasses clinking into each other. Litany edged closer to her.

Lysande slid into the seat beside Derset's and gestured to him to join her. "Is there any sign of an army yet?" she whispered.

"Your captain says there's been no word from the scouts." Derset squeezed her hand under the table, with barely enough pressure to be felt.

"There must have been a sighting further out, though."

"No doves from the border or any of the towns." Looking at her, Derset leaned closer. "Aren't you pleased, my lady?"

"I wish I could say I was."

Their eyes locked briefly. Lysande watched the rest of the Council take their seats and sank into thought. She heard the clash of an attendant dropping a tray of cutlery, and the curse that followed, but paid no heed. A small army would have pleased her. A large army would have disquieted her; but no army at all meant something different. She put a hand to her temple. Right now, she would have traded all the balls in the world for the golden glow of scale, whatever price it put on her heart and stomach, let alone her mind.

"Perhaps the White Queen hasn't brought an army," Derset said.

She reviewed the string of attacks, from the panther that had clawed Sarelin, to the chimera blood, the silent sword at the banquet, the wolf bounding across the Arena . . . panther, poison, wolf . . . and then the coin-purse that had nearly brought them to war. Each was a move in the same game. She remembered the flash of a sword as the assassin charged at Luca, just yesterday; the bust of Sarelin shattering on the floor; the notes from her readings on the White War that she had gone over last night.

"I don't think she's been deterred," she said, slowly. "If her legions aren't in the desert by now, I believe Mea Tacitus is planning something else."

"We haven't prepared for something else," Derset said.

He almost succeeded in hiding the waver in his voice. Lysande looked across at him. If Derset was afraid, despite all their efforts . . . it was an unpleasant thought.

Before she could respond, Vigarot Chamboise ushered Jale to the front of the seating, and the crowd fell silent. "Ladies and lords," Vigarot said, "Queen Persephora and King Ramon Ferago; Mariana, Anton, Dion; Councillors, distinguished guests, and guards who defend us so bravely: let me welcome you all to the Sapphire Ball!"

She saw Luca Fontaine looking at her across the room as applause broke out. He raised his glass. The red of the shirt under his doublet flashed in the candlelight.

"In Lyria, our motto is art, wine, song, and tonight we plan to give you all three. But first, a taste of our history," Jale announced, spreading his hands. "I give you the illustrious tales of our poets. Here, for you, we present the Song of Sun!"

A troupe of dancers ran in: eight women and men in costume gathered on the stage and bowed, followed by a band of flute-players. At a clap of Jale's hands, a lilting melody began, and the dancers moved back and forth: Lysande recognized the crocodile who had emerged from the river to give birth to Lyria; the bird that laid a golden egg out of which the spirit of art hatched and blessed the city; and of course, the fountain that poured forth southern cheer, created by a pyramid of dancers scattering glitter onto the ground, their blue costumes mimicking water. Each of the desert myths received cheers. When a man leaped from atop the pyramid, Lyrians whooped and hollered.

It was easy to imagine Mea Tacitus seeing splendor like this, in Axium, and standing at the edge of the official crowd, looking in on a realm of glitter and glory yet not being part of it. *Like me.* The thought came swiftly to her. She did not like the way it lodged in her mind.

Lysande glanced around and saw Raden among a group of Axium Guards. Four entrances fed into the enclosure, and he stood in front of the one on the back wall, closest to the palm garden. She watched him raise his hand to her. Slowly, she waved back.

The White Queen's not here, she told herself. She saw Cassia among a group of Pyrrhan nobles, yawning. A lock of long white hair made Lysande sit up, but it was only an elderly woman in a captain's uniform. There had been no glimpse of Three, nor Six, nor even Charice, who might be hiding somewhere. A gust swept through her mind, stirring the anxieties.

The performance had grown more vigorous. A woman dressed as Prince Arle Raquefort began striking another dressed as a chimera with a wooden sword. Across the enclosure, Lysande saw the fine-boned Ferago son looking at her. She stiffened.

The dancers received a warm reception, and they were followed by the even more welcome sight of Lyrian attendants bearing dishes and jugs. The attendants carried food, water, and wine to the Councillors' tables, working their way forward.

"The songs start in a moment, my lady," Derset said, offering her a plate of stuffed chilies. "At a Lyrian wedding, they weave music and food together, to delight both senses."

"Must I dance?"

"You're an Axiumite; so only if the beat is even and well-ordered."

"Sun and stars, Derset . . . was that a joke?"

Weeks ago, she knew, he would not have smiled in response, as he did now. The soil of their intimacy had borne shoots, and he met her eyes again without a blush, a hint of that subtle glow lending a shine to his eyes.

As the band marched onto the stage and struck up the first tune, hands picked up spoons across the enclosure. Lysande watched the slender Ferago son while she nibbled at jasmine-cakes and balls of fried banana. Her gaze jumped every time the light fell on his sword. After the first two courses, the musicians tripled their volume and boots tapped the ground.

"Ah, here comes the dancing," Lysande said, turning her gaze on Litany for a moment. "Did you manage to find a partner, by any chance?"

"I shouldn't wish to ruin anyone's night. I have no talent for leaping and twirling." Litany looked down at the tablecloth.

"That cannot be possible," Chidney said. "I saw you leap into the rigging and down again, on the ship. It was as handsome as a clean shield."

Litany blushed. Lysande noticed Chidney's pleased expression.

Her eyes swept the tables again, finding nothing of note but searching every group of bejeweled figures. Suddenly, she was aware of movement. Heads were turning across the enclosure. Vigarot rose and walked toward the Lyrian table—but Dante had drawn Jale from his seat and was speaking with him. After a few words had been exchanged, Lysande saw the young prince turn on his heel and hurry over the platform, back into the palace. Chairs scraped the ground. The ladies and lords of Lyria knew how long to wait before joining the first dance, she guessed, but none of them seemed to know what to do if the bride and groom did not begin it.

Lysande heard a cough and turned to her side. "Lady Pelory."

Those cold eyes stared down at her. "May I present my husband, Councillor Prior? Lord Clifferd Pelory."

Still conscious of the staring and muttering guests, Lysande nodded her greeting. A young man in a small ruff bowed back, his hands folded, his belt winking with emeralds, his gaze skipping merrily over Lysande's necklace.

Lysande noticed that as he stepped back beside his wife, his hand slipped under hers and nestled there, unmoving, a portrait of spousal tenderness. Pelory smiled—the first genuine smile Lysande had seen her give since they met.

Briskly, Lysande looked around. She weighed the risk of diverting her attention for a few minutes, and decided that she could allow herself one conversation. She recommended the wine to Pelory's husband, and Clifferd Pelory was not slow to take a hint. He bowed, adjusted his ruff, and was halfway to the wine-fountain by the time Lady Pelory had found a chair and dragged it over to Lysande.

"I announced that the four castles would be used as jails for elementals, just before I left," Pelory said as she sat down. "And I introduced your law about vigilantes, at the same meeting. There was an outcry. But my colleagues yielded. Remarkably quickly. It may have been because I brought fifty Axium Guards with me and only waved them through the door once the others had taken their seats. Your letter was most instructive."

It had begun, then: the quiet campaign, which soldiers and captains might never see as an engagement. Yet it was a war; one that had seen its first arrows fired.

"Very good." Lysande smiled. "We understand each other, Lady Pelory. I should like us to keep doing so. I have not forgotten my gift. A small castle, did I not say? A modest dwelling with a hereditary title? But I am afraid I have checked, and there are none to spare."

Pelory opened her mouth, but caught her words.

"That is why I have decided to give you a large castle instead. Prexley Castle should do nicely. It is newly restored, after all . . . I should like it to be a symbol of my reliance on you, and of your support to me."

"Councillor—this is beyond all expectation—I cannot thank you enough—"

"Your *ongoing* support, Lady Pelory. These are such treacherous times. It is good to know that I have eyes and ears in the Oval, or in the manors of Axium; and since Prexley Castle shall contribute a considerable annuity to my Leveling Fund, we shall be closer than ever. Your fortune shall be intertwined with mine."

Pelory leaned back in her seat and nodded slowly. Her face did not reassume its mask, this time; its austerity melted to contemplation. "Just so," she said, at last. "I see a relationship of great profit. I hope you will excuse me for taking a while to warm."

"We speak as Axiumites. A little thawing is entirely necessary."

Lysande almost added the saying that Litany had heard from one of Jale's guards—that in Axium it was cold outside the walls, but warm inside them—yet she suspected that it might have a double meaning which Pelory would deem unfit for polite discussion.

"I have a task for you, in celebration of our new bond." The idea had come to her after seeing the bone people, but it seemed the product of a much longer thread of thought, one that had begun weeks ago. "You see, I wish to survey the state of wealth across the realm. Find out where people are poorest, where they are rich, where they are just getting by. Note down their burdens and their anxieties. Then we will use the Leveling Fund to remedy the state's sickness. Begin small. Take grain with you, from the royal stores, and distribute it to meet need as you go. I think the team of royal advisors should yoke themselves to the task of levying funds from the court, don't you?"

"They will need persuasion to fall under any yoke." Pelory smiled slightly. "But you may depend upon me."

"So I can see. I will look forward to the results, Lady Pelory, and in the meantime, I wish you enjoyment of your new castle and its title."

The Mistress of Laws bowed, and walked away, to where Clifferd Pelory was admiring a statue of Princess Orvergne. The young man bent down to kiss his wife's hand, gazing up at her as he did so, the emerald teardrop of his earring catching the candlelight.

Lysande allowed herself a moment to relish the result. Turning away, she made another quick glance around the enclosure. There was still no sign of an unusual weapon, a figure out of place, or a foreigner in a cloak . . . she looked across the tables and saw the willowy Ferago son staring at her. He began pushing through the guests, excusing himself as he came, making a path toward her table. The motion of his elbows sent several ladies scuttling.

"While I hesitate to discourage anything so joyful as dancing," Derset whispered, leaning toward her, "I suspect your Bastillonian suitor has more than one motive."

Ah. Dion Ferago did not have the flashing grace of the jeweler she had once wrestled onto her bed; nor did he exhibit the sweetness of the Lyrian ambassador's scribe, her first infatuation, a girl for whom she had endured a week of Sarelin's teasing; nor, Lysande suspected, did he possess Charice's penetrating mind and her more physical skills. Who did? He was not ill-looking, yet she considered that his father's reasons might be plain, and she rose from her chair, taking a plate of sun-cakes with her.

She cut a path between two tables. At the great jug on the left side of the enclosure where guests could dip a spoon into honey, she joined the queue, holding the plate of little yellow cakes before her. As she was attempting to survey the enclosure, a woman swept past her to join the queue, arm in arm with a sharp-chinned Bastillonian.

"Prince Fontaine designed the fountains in the pools. You know how he loves to invent." By the paucity of emotion in her voice, Lysande recognized Carletta Freste, the noblewoman who had shown her around Castle Sapere.

"Indeed." Gabrella Merez—for it was she—looked down her nose, regarding Freste. "I have borne witness to his innovation, a little too closely. And the spearfish among the fountains—I suppose they were his idea too?"

"Oh, no. Those are all Lyria's." Freste laughed. "I wish we could claim those vicious little brutes."

They drew closer together, Freste rubbing against Merez's shoulder. Lysande had the uncomfortable premonition that the pair were going to approach and greet her. She looked out at the crowd again. Finding Raden directly opposite, she tried to signal for an update, but he was looking in another direction. She noticed that Dion Ferago had reached her table and was leaning over to Derset, speaking in a persistent flow. She was considering whether to stay in the queue or move away when she felt the sheath of one of her daggers rubbing against her side, through the fabric of one of the pockets.

By the time she had reached beneath her cloak and adjusted the blade within her doublet, the sound of voices had risen. Something metallic caught the light. Lysande turned toward it. Not far from the jug, Vigarot Chamboise held a glittering sword in his hand. It was the same sword she had seen Dante rehearsing with in the maze garden at Castle Sapere, and Vigarot was looking at the jeweled guard and grip and the enormous diamond in the pommel, his face scrunching. Groups of people halted their conversations to stare in the direction of the two men. As Vigarot examined the sword's engraved message, his expression transformed from dislike to open fury.

Lysande hesitated, but after a quick glance around the hall, she stepped out of the queue. No one seemed to notice her, with all gazes fixed on Dante and Vigarot.

"It's merely an ornamental sword," Dante's voice boomed. "I see no slight."

"Don't act smart with me, Dalgëreth. I know the northern customs as well as you do. You mean to wrap your grubby hands around your beloved."

"My hands are clean. Like my honor."

"*I pledge to nourish your spirit and defend your person as long as I live.*" Vigarot flipped the sword over, reading the other half of the inscription. "*I pledge to kiss you from your crown to soles of your feet, and worship where my lips touch.* Is that honor?"

"It is no more than the truth."

"Your hands are clean, you say. But not your mouth, apparently."

"Unlike you, I do not spit the venom of self-aggrandizement."

Vigarot's smile was as sharp as the blade-edge. "You do not lack ambition."

"You conflate ambition with love. A common mistake of smaller men."

There was a pause—in which Vigarot raised the sword—but upon seeing Dante's hand fly to his sword-hilt, he lowered it again. "Slipping this under a platter won't do a thing," he hissed. "Bastillón and Elira are one. The gift's been made. The trade contract's signed."

"Don't think I can't see you looking up the ladder." Dante moved closer to him. "You tried to wheedle your way into Ariane's favor, drumming up fear about my mother. Do you think I don't remember you pouring lies about Raina into her ear? You think your deeds are forgotten, minnow, but remember this. The ice-bear can wait."

"I did what I did for the sake of Lyria." Vigarot drew himself up.

"Bartering your nephew like a trader at a market . . . tell me, Vigarot, can you sell a heart? Even you might find that hard." Dante stepped closer still. "The heart, at least, remains my property."

Whose heart? It had sounded as if Dante had meant Jale's. Only weeks ago, Lysande would have thought a public declaration of love unlikely. For all that she had observed since, she still hoped that she had misunderstood; surely, Dante could not be willing to risk open warfare between the north and south; yet even as she told herself that, she recognized the mark of possession stamped on each word. Whispers broke out across the enclosure.

"This marriage will go ahead," Vigarot snapped. "Valderos will keep its distance."

"Tell me: once Ariane's son realizes he's your puppet, how long do you think it'll take him to cut the strings?"

This time, Dante's words were only loud enough for those nearby to hear. Lysande's muscles tensed. Vigarot looked at Dante, his blue eyes gleaming. His smile had gone. He put a hand to his sword, but hesitated. "Threaten me once more," he said, "and I'll have you taken out to the stable-yard and whipped. I make the rules in this palace."

Dante looked back at him without a hint of fear. "For now."

Lysande did not like the tone of that remark, but before either man could move, a great wave of applause rolled through the enclosure. She turned to stare at the platform.

Mariana was guiding Jale onto it: the prince waved a hand, as if to say that they could all relax now, and the band struck up another tune while Mariana led Jale through the first steps of the lyrianesque. Jale put on a smile that would have been convincing to a stranger. Lysande had studied him long enough to know the difference. Soon, other couples flowed onto the platform to join them, falling into the movements.

Vigarot smiled triumphantly, and turned to find Dante gone.

Lysande passed her plate to an attendant and slipped out from the queue, moving slowly and glancing at the crowd, yet not finding any glimpse of an attacker. She cut through two tables, her eyes focused on a group of Rhimese guards on the far side of the enclosure. As she surveyed the group, she barrelled into the chest of someone coming the other way.

"Councillor Prior!" Dion Ferago cried, his arms encircling her.

"My lord." She extricated herself. "I had not hoped to embrace the east quite so literally. I hope you will forgive me."

It was cunningly risqué, the Bastillonian princely garb: only when you saw it up close did you realize how thin that material was. Someone like Luca could have worn it to devastating effect. On Dion, the upper garment hung slightly loose, as if it were not quite fastened at the collar.

"My father asked—that is, I thought—" He looked down at his feet. "I was wondering if you would do me the honor of a dance."

Lysande glanced at the platform. The couples were performing the sensual Lyrian passedanse, and several of them had drawn so close that there was scarcely any space between them.

She looked back at Dion; took in the waterfall of blue and white silk that poured over his body, and noticed the sword-hilt that poked out at his hip. Searching the tables, her eye fell on the Rhimese crest on a soldier's breastplate.

"I'm terribly sorry," she said, "but the fact is, I've already committed to dance with Prince Fontaine."

"And here I am. Ready and at liberty, Lysande."

Luca had crept up without making a sound, and he was standing at her side. The thought dropped into her head—like a polished stone—that he had used her first name.

He took her by the arm and steered her away, toward the platform, his hand slipping into hers. The pressure was firm, but she squeezed back, making sure she matched the strength of his grip.

"Don't think of running off to your devotee over there," Luca said, jerking his head in the direction of Derset.

"Whatever makes you think I'd try to run from you?" She risked a glance at her table. None of the group were looking her way. Her free hand clenched.

"Good. That should make this a lot easier," Luca said.

And stopping before the last two tables, he waited, and waited, until she led him onto the platform and into the dance.

Thirteen

The band switched from a slow tune to a fast one as they walked down the middle of the platform. Luca placed his hand on Lysande's right shoulder, and she placed her hand on his right hip, in the style of the desert haute-dance. For the first few minutes, she concentrated on going through the motions, and once she had mastered them, she looked up and met his stare.

She had observed him many times before, over a table or across a room, but as they moved together, she realized that they were the same height; he did not look down at her, like Dante, or up at her, like Jale, but straight into her eyes.

"This is the only place we can talk without being overheard," he said. "We don't have much time, so I'll get to the point: I think it's better to do away with pretenses, now." He led her in a circle, clasping her by the arm.

"I don't follow you."

He let go of her as they passed down the line of couples, and they rejoined when they reached the end. She could feel the stares of the crowd upon her. This time, she steered him through one of the dance's swerves, and when she gripped him a little more firmly than was necessary, a half-smile returned to his lips, matching the sudden brightness of his gaze.

"I know exactly what you are. I guessed the day Malsante came into my suite in Castle Sapere and told me Sarelin Brey had chosen someone called Lysande Prior as Councillor. I speak Old Valderran too," he said, following her lead. "Did you know that while ordinary foundlings are named any which way, elemental bastards are named after an element?"

"What?"

"Prior. Fire. Just like you told those gawping fools in the Room of Accord . . . only I expect none of them had heard of magical customs."

Lysande was silent. He's lying, she told herself, her legs moving automatically as her mind swirled. She couldn't have missed something that obvious, all this time; not obvious to most people, of course, but to a scholar who had all manner of esoteric books at her disposal, and who had grown up around a girl who had once blasted a sunsnake into the air . . . well, there was no point in self-chastisement now. She pulled him into the next turn, and the next.

"Whoever found you knew more about you than you gave them credit for," Luca said. "When I saw you wincing, my guess strengthened. There were all those other little flinches that followed. But it was your stay in your suite that confirmed it. Heatstroke for nine days, Prior? I'm not a physician, but that's stretching belief."

It was a good thing that the dance separated them again, because she did not trust herself to speak. Keep your cool, she thought. Be composed, like Three.

"I'm afraid you've let your imagination gallop downhill," she said, when they were close again, their palms pressed together. "I was stricken with red fever as well as heatstroke. That's why I was confined so long. Perhaps you should've given me more of your remedy."

"The concoction I gave you doesn't work on red fever. Did you know that? It relieves the pains of elemental maturation."

"I . . ."

"Don't worry, Prior." He laughed. "If I wanted to expose you, I could've turned you in to the others straight away—the thought of Sarelin Brey picking an elemental to choose her successor *is* rather amusing, since she beheaded plenty of their number. But I want to work with you, not kill you."

"Why do you want an alliance?"

The words burst out of her in a jab. Luca's countenance was all superciliousness. He coiled close to her and stepped back in time with the music. "I'm of the opinion that no one can rule Elira securely while they're wasting the talents of the most dangerous people in the realm by chopping their heads off. Locking them up won't be enough, either. This is a difficult game, Prior. Until we find a way to get elementals on our side, no leader can win against the White Queen—and I mean to win." He leaned forward so that she could lift him into the air and down again. "Why else do you think I put you on the Council?"

It sounded like a potent strategy. She would be the bait, to bring other elementals over. Yet she forced herself to remember the ball of fire rushing at her on the Grandfleuve, and the way he had wiped the blood off his hands after killing the assassin.

Never trust a snake. How many times had Sarelin said that?

And yet dancing with him was so easy . . . like breathing.

The song wound to a close. In front of them, Jale followed Mariana from the platform, smiling brightly. While the dancers rearranged into new couples, Luca guided Lysande from the back of the platform and onto the palace steps. She reached beneath her cloak and grasped at the hilts in her dagger-belt. Luca laid a hand on her arm and said, "A little privacy, perhaps?"

He accompanied her onto the final stair, guiding her by the forearm, and smiled at the Lyrian guard at the top. The other couples were beginning the next dance. She laid out the situation like a puzzle in her head, trying to think logically. If she undid her cloak now, she might draw a dagger, but would he slash at her before she could throw it?

He moved quickly into Rayonnant Palace and pulled her to the left, down the corridor. They entered a closet lined with bookcases, and his fingers slipped over hers. She felt trails of warmth on her skin as he let go. Up close, she saw the length of his eyelashes for the first time—how was it that a man could have such lashes and yet a spikiness to him, like a queensflower?

"Listen to me. This might be our last chance to talk." He closed the space between them and a scent of orange blossoms stilled Lysande. "You're elemental: that means you're a danger to the White Queen. A magical woman in power who isn't her creature . . . who knows what you might achieve? Show a little kindness, and you purloin her followers. Fiddle around with the laws and liberate elementals, and then who will be angry enough to help her?"

"The thought had occurred to me, too." Even as she said it, it became clearer. Nobles did not want to change the system. They wanted to climb to the top and perch there; and that was why it mattered that Mea Tacitus was a Brey, Lysande understood, as she faced Luca. All that time serving her cousin had hurt the young Mea, the way it could only hurt a silverblood who believed a grand destiny was rightfully hers. Threads of reason rose inside her and twined, knotting and unknotting, weaving into patterns that shone. That silent sword had been stamped with a picture of a chimera for a reason, logic dictated to her; that chimera brand on the assassin, too: her mark: a crest, of sorts. *This* was what she could use. *This* was how to really fight the White Queen. Let her focus on dynasties and glory, while there were other, less burnished things that she could put to use.

She was glad, now, that she had sent Pelory off on her mission.

"I can see it in you," Luca said, quietly. "Jails are only the first step. You want more. A mind like yours won't be content with anything but a big change. I'd bet she can see it, too. Call me sentimental, but I wish to warn you, Prior; you're likely to be targeted if there's an attack tonight." He looked into her eyes. "Whatever you do, you mustn't let one of the city-rulers lead you away during the ball."

"One of the other city-rulers, you mean."

"Oh, very good. Interminably witty. I merely point out that I can only protect you if you're in my sight."

"And what makes you think I desire your protection?"

The White Queen told the Umbra to win me over. And here we are, alone, after a dance. If she asked Luca outright where his allegiance lay, perhaps she could catch him off guard. His discretion could not be infinite. Lysande felt a surge of the strength she had been building for weeks, the raw audacity that she had begun to draw upon since Sarelin's death.

"Forgive me for the imposition." He shrugged. "I thought you needed help."

"You're forgetting I was raised by Sarelin Brey. She took me hunting. And she always made me wait until the deer was in my view: never trust the sound, she said, only trust what you can see with your eyes. I find that holds true for you, Fontaine."

"Ah, Sarelin Brey." Luca shook his head; color suffused his cheeks. "She was an exceptional warrior, which is why she was such a middling queen. She had no interest in any of those pesky legal reforms that better the realm. Killing was easier than ruling. And she made no effort to understand those who were different."

She could smell orange blossoms again; their sugared scent was laced with a sharpness, everywhere on his skin, and she leaned instinctively toward him.

"I know the tiers that divide this land," she said. "I know what she stood for. But I also know that Sarelin had more valor in her little finger than you do in your whole body."

"Valor. I have heard it spoken of. Was valor the part where she allowed magical citizens to have their heads chopped off? Or the part where she threw even those elementals who refused the White Queen onto dungeon stone?"

"She stopped a tyrant from taking over Elira." Lysande could feel the heat rising in her body and tried to pull herself back toward logic.

"And let tyranny flourish on her own soil. You ignore her weaknesses and praise her strengths. But I'd expect nothing less of someone who was raised by the Iron Queen." His half-smile had crept back. "She did a good job of glorifying herself—I'll give her that."

It was hard to say whether her mind controlled her hand, or the other way around. All she knew was that she was slapping Luca across the face. He stopped, inches from her, rubbing the spot where she had hit him.

A red mark bloomed on his cheek. She felt a little jab of guilt but not enough to apologize. Surprise flared in his eyes, yet his lips formed a smile, and this time, it did not disappear quickly. The sight arrested her. Lysande was not sure if a prince could be pleased to be slapped, but she had a sudden and unreasonable desire to find out.

"That's not very friendly, Prior. You know, I like you very much, whatever you may think. You have wit, and a good deal of vigor, and a mind that I find very—very interesting. But you need to let go of your loyalty to your precious Iron Queen. It holds you back from the truth."

It was crucial to choose the moment carefully. He closed the space between them with assurance. *This is it,* she thought. She waited until he was upon her before reaching beneath her cloak and drawing a dagger from her belt, holding it still.

When he moved again, Lysande rushed close to him, just as Sarelin had taught her, and thrust it under his jaw. The blade pressed against his skin.

Luca's smile disappeared, yet his eyes stayed trained on hers.

"Go on," he said. "Do it."

"Do you admit to betraying the Council?"

"I admit to having one parent with a burnished name, and one who was cast out with nothing. I admit to reading and writing and building things. And I admit to being a bastard." He placed his hand over her own: the hand that was holding the dagger. "Those are my crimes. If you think them bad enough, use that blade. Later, you can say it was valor."

She held the weapon still for a long moment. Too long, it proved, for he pushed her hand back and snatched at the dagger's hilt.

Lysande darted to the side and grabbed his collar, and with all her strength, whirled him around and slammed him against a bookcase. Volumes rained down over their heads. Some of the books hit the floor and fell open, splayed; others landed shut and made a heavier thunk, like bricks, and the sight of so many poetry collections smacking the floor made her pause, giving Luca the chance to grab at her dagger.

He managed to pry it loose. Lysande kneed him in the stomach, and he staggered to the side. She felt a hot current of anger rushing through her. While she was wrestling the weapon back, he took hold of her wrist. Arms locked, they toppled onto the books and rolled across them, the corners poking into their backs. By the time he was lying beneath her and she could make another pass for her dagger, his rapier was at her throat, and something in her subconscious kicked and twitched.

There was a curious look in his eyes, and as Lysande's fingers pushed the tip of the sword away from her neck, he did not stop her. One of his hands wrapped around her back and rested between her shoulderblades. She pressed a hand under his jaw. This might be the last opportunity she had to prompt a confession, yet her lips would not move, and as she lay on top of him, she dug her left hand into his hair.

His rapier clattered to the floor. Her own dagger fell. She smelled the orange blossoms with their slight bitterness, the scent on his skin a falling sweetness, fading but lingering . . . if she needed to kill him, her dagger was right there, within reach.

Something closed over her hand. It was his palm. His soft fingers moved her hand and pressed it into the side of his neck. She looked down and met the quietness of his gaze.

She became aware of the warmth of his body under her; of the pulse beating under her fingers. She recognized the thing twitching in her consciousness. It had been there on the ship, when she reached out to his neck and wrapped her fingers around him, and it responded to his yielding now, with a quicksilver rhythm that she did not seek to restrain, nor constrain, nor subdue. With her free hand, she ran a nail down his cheek.

He shivered, and Lysande luxuriated in the reaction.

The art of reading a present was also the art of reading a person. Just days ago, he had left a gift with her guards, in a bag of black velvet. She had read a meaning in it, later, turning over her interpretation while wrapped in her soft Lyrian bedsheets, and she had decided, at last, that she had a right to be angry at his presumption: that she would teach him how ill-matched his desires were to her own. Yet even a scholar could misread another's intentions, and he was not flinching away from her. He was leaning into her touch.

You could throttle a man from this position. You could do other things, too. As she grabbed his hair tighter, she felt the pulse increase, and saw his eyes darken with something that was not displeasure.

"Your Highness," a man's voice said, behind them, "King Ferago—"

Lysande had one hand to Luca's throat, and he had one to hers, their noses almost brushing. They looked up.

Lord Malsante was standing in the doorway. He stared from one to the other of them, his mouth slightly open. "Excuse me, Your Highness," he said, "but King Ferago asked me to tell you that they're readying the pavilion. The bride and groom are about to say the vows."

Lysande pulled herself off Luca, leaped up, and hurried out, brushing against Malsante on the way. She made her exit down the corridor and burst through the door, murmurs following her as she ran onto the palace steps, across the stage and past the attendants scattering petals on the pavilion, and over to her table. Panting, she straightened her cloak and slipped into her seat.

"My lady . . ."

"I'm all right." She squeezed Derset's hand.

Luca Fontaine had offered to protect her. He had urged her not to go out of sight with any of the city-rulers. If he had been trying to win her over, why did he bother with a warning—why not simply try to seduce her? She was aware that a few of the guests were staring at her.

Trumpets blared. The Lyrians rose from their chairs. "The Council must ascend to the stage for the vows," Derset whispered. "My lady, are you sure you're all right?"

She nodded. Within seconds, an attendant was waiting beside her, offering an arm. Gathering her composure and trying to look as if she had not just been rolling on the floor, she followed Cassia and Dante up onto the stage, to the left of the pavilion where Vigarot and Élérie Chamboise waited, along with a woman in a hooded robe who could only be a priest. On the right side, the Feragos made a line of silver-haired royalty. Nothing seemed out of place, and inside her, too, nothing had given way; she realized that she had not craved scale during a very difficult moment. The rushing of blood through her body had taken over.

A flash of red drew her attention. Luca was walking down the steps. Whispers ran through the crowd, gaining volume as he slipped onto the end of the line and shot her a glance—in that stare, she saw anger and frustration. Good, she thought. He's failed.

Jale and Mariana made a slow path onto the platform, between the lines of gold-encased palms and up to the stage: slow, because Mariana gave off a glare from her neck to her ankles, her path slightly obscured by the reflection of her gauntlets and greaves. The silver of her armor was clean enough for Lysande to see the first smattering of stars high above the enclosure, reflected in her breastplate: a lacquering of white light. Custom required two Bastillonian servants to trail her, holding a scepter carved with a design of a winged ram, which Lysande suspected was more mythic symbol than ancient beast. None of the

Bastillonians seemed to notice the Elirans' stares at the golden-haired entourage, who bent their heads as they walked, but Lysande was aware of their cringing gait, and she felt as much guilt as disgust.

None of the Council had foreseen this, yet they should have. She herself should have done something to stop it. Could she not have taken Vigarot aside and argued until her mouth was dry?

Jale stopped opposite Mariana on the stage. The priest mounted the pavilion and stood between the silk-decked prince and the princess in armor, creating a stiff tableau.

"It was a good idea of yours to hold the ball out here," Cassia whispered. "Much less stuffy, with netting instead of walls."

Lysande glanced up. "Me? But I had nothing to do with it."

"Vigarot told me—"

"It is my very great privilege," the priest said, "to announce the vows of Mariana Ferago, Princess of Bastillón, and Jale Chamboise, Prince of Lyria."

The group fell silent. Lysande spotted Raden making his way back along the wall at last. He caught her gaze and shook his head, mouthing the word *nothing*.

"If the bride would step forward . . ."

A look around the enclosure showed Lysande that every side was guarded by Lyrians and city troops. She tried to dispel the unease that had nested in her stomach.

Mariana took her place and gazed at the floor. Lysande's attention had scattered too widely for her to listen to the priest's deluge of questions and Mariana's promises to take the prince of Lyria as her husband, to honor her vows, to be true to her heart . . . the list went on and on, Mariana nodding brusquely, uttering "Yes" every time the woman paused. Every so often, Mariana darted a glance at Dante, whose eyes were cast down at the ground.

"And you, Prince Chamboise," the priest said.

"Yes?"

"Do you take this woman as your wife?" Jale made as if to speak, then hesitated. "Prince Chamboise," the priest repeated, "do you take this woman—"

"Er, yes, Your Beatitude," Jale said, "that is—as my wife—yes, I do."

The priest folded her hands. "Do you vow to be true to your heart—"

"Actually, no," Jale said. "Sorry."

Gasps made a chorus in the desert air. Lysande watched intently as Vigarot stepped forward. Jale ran a hand through his locks. "I mean—yes, I want to be true to my heart," he said. "But that's why I can't marry her. I'm sorry, uncle; we'll have to call the wedding off."

Vigarot seized his nephew by the shoulders. "Jale," he hissed, "you are dizzied by the crowd. Pause, concentrate, and recollect your duty."

"I didn't mean for it to happen like this. And I'm frightfully sorry to Mariana, and to all of you who came so far south . . . but the problem is, I'm already in love with someone else." Jale took a deep breath. "There's not a thing I can do about it."

King Ferago was gripping the edges of his ermine coat with a furious intensity, and Queen Persephora's brow had furrowed into copious lines; in the queen's unceasing glare Lysande read more danger than she did in the king's posture. Yet it was Dante's reaction that sent the tables into an ecstasy of pointing. He rose from his seat and stared at the stage. Several of the Valderran guards stepped out from their posts and edged toward him.

"Don't talk nonsense, Jale," Vigarot snapped.

"I'm afraid it's true. You see, I've always known, since the day snow came down on me and hurled itself upon my riding party. My teeth were chattering while it pounded the carriage and covered all the horses, as if a goddess sought to bury us alive. Out of the whiteness I saw a figure, striding—he must have been three feet ahead of all his riders—he kept striding toward me, as if no blizzard in the world could stop him. I thought all the heat had left my body, but when he held me, I felt it come rushing back . . . like a terrible, thawing forgiveness."

Lysande felt her suspicions crystallizing into an explanation she had long considered, and she wondered if she should have told the other Councillors that Dante and Jale's intimacy had begun some time ago. She had guessed, when she first saw Dante smile at Jale over the banquet table in Axium Palace as if there were no Councillors around them, no watching guards, no gawking crowd; and even before

Vigarot had read the inscription from the sword, she had known, somewhere deep inside herself. Dante looked ready to rush the stage now. He was not bothering to conceal it.

At the same time, she heard the sound of boots, well before she saw the guards gathering at the back gate of the enclosure. The slap of soles beat a tattoo that she recognized, instinctively, as a warning. Raden moved to join the commotion. After a hurried conversation, he broke away, running through the tables.

"Your Highnesses, take cover!" he shouted. "Get back into the palace!"

The crowd turned as one, jeweled necks craning. Lysande's whole body stiffened.

"Vigarot," King Ferago said, "restrain that man. He has forgotten his place."

"With pleasure."

"Look up, all of you!" Raden cried, dodging from the Lyrian guards who were edging toward him, and raising his hand to point. "Arrest me, shackle me, lock me up if you like, but Fortituda's fist, look up there!"

A shadow covered the moon. It was moving, and within seconds it dropped from its height to just above the enclosure, where the moonlight bathed it and turned it from a smudge to a winged shape.

The slick, dark surfaces of its scales shone like cobbles on a wet street; they could almost have been mirrors, except that the huge wings resembled skin more than glass or stone. They stretched out and beat the air, sending birds fleeing. Once the body was low enough to be visible, there was no mistaking the horns, the feline head, the black fur that covered the neck and shoulders, and the tail that hung out like a finely honed spear. Where fur met scales, Lysande saw no ridge, only the seamless meld of one texture with another. The pit of her stomach knotted. She grappled with the sight of a fantasy transformed into flesh, and bit her lip; it was fear that gripped her, of course. It could not be fascination.

"That's . . ." King Ferago's mouth had fallen open.

"Everyone, get back!" Cassia cried.

"But that's impossible!" Jale shouted.

There had been no errors. No transmutation of features in ink. Every detail matched the drawings in the history books, Lysande observed with a feverish speed, before the chimera opened its mouth to roar.

Guards rushed toward the platform. Cassia pulled King Ferago and Persephora out of the path of the chimera. Raden made a dash to the Eliran side, and he had almost reached the Council when the creature breathed fire, a great blast that burned through the roof and brought the mesh crashing onto the guests. Lysande leaped clear of a chunk of burning material, with a speed she could only credit Sarelin's training for.

The palms on the platform ignited and a falling frond caught Anton Ferago's silken shirt; the ends of the sleeves went up, the fire moving higher and higher as the material burned. His screams cut across the crackling. Jale tried to put out the fire while Mariana and Dion came running; Mariana fell to her knees and smothered the flames, but by the time she had snuffed them out, Anton lay still. Lysande forced herself to look away and sprinted to the middle of the enclosure, calling her guards to her, Litany running at her side, the two of them heading for Cassia and Dante.

With the rapidity of one practiced in the art, Cassia gave directions, dividing up the guards. Lysande drew a dagger from her belt, even as she realized that they would need arrows.

Of course there was no army, she told herself furiously, as she dodged another piece of flaming mesh, pulling off her cloak, flinging the garment out of her way. Of course the White Queen was moving so much money about in the Periclean States. Of course she could risk attacking the Council. But how, by the four goddesses, did she get hold of a beast that was supposed to be extinct?

Her feet seemed to know where to tread before her mind did. Most of the crowd was attempting to flee into the gardens, jostling at the back entrance of the enclosure, where the cramming of bodies prevented them from breaking free. As they pushed to get out, another sheet of burning mesh fell from the roof and landed on top of them. It enveloped Bastillonian and Eliran dignitaries like a net. Leaping over bodies and pushing through tables, guards of all cities hurried to them, but the chimera sent a fireball down—so quickly that for a moment, Lysande did not know where it had come from—and the smell of burning flesh filled the air. Lysande felt hot bile rise in her throat and pushed it down, barking out orders, dividing her Axium Guards and sending them in two directions. A shape moved at her elbow, and she looked across to see Litany gripping a thick dagger, her body positioned to shield Lysande.

Streams of water flew overhead and scattered the ground liberally with droplets. Lysande muttered a prayer of gratitude to the Shadows, though she could not spot Three, or whoever was commanding the water with such prowess.

She looked up and her thoughts glaciated inside her. A black shape blotted out the sky above her, muscular legs and feet with hooked talons descending. She could not miss the fur, the horns, the scales on the body . . . but it was the great orb of jade with a black pupil in the middle that arrested her, holding her gaze, burning with a deeper intensity than the flames around them.

The eye changed as it examined her, rage ceding to curiosity. The two of them stared at each other. Something stirred inside the heart of that pupil, something that had known prey for a long time, and yet the creature did not pour fire down upon her. Somehow, it felt as if the chimera was inviting her to come nearer, encouraging her to reach out.

Then arrows flew through the air and the thread was broken; the great beast flapped its wings, took off across the sky, and breathed a jet of orange flame onto the tables.

Lysande looked around, willing herself to move. The encounter still held her, the silent conversation working like a kind of inertia. You could not shake off the power of a chimera like an attendant shaking dust from a rug, not when the creature had been within inches of you, looming in awful splendor. Her head swam, and her arms had turned to lead. With great effort, she managed to push herself back into the cacophony of the enclosure.

By now the Rhimese archers were scattered among the other guards, black amid silver and gold and brass. She could not see Luca anywhere. Her hidden Axium Guards were pouring in, some clearing the mesh from the ground, others flinging their daggers. Raden shouted her name, leading a group of them toward her. Instinct urged her to turn, to look for someone who could give orders, but she made a quick decision and waved the guards toward the chimera.

A Bastillonian servant screamed, running down the path between the tables, a piece of mesh melted onto his skin like a molten choker. The pair of Bastillonians near him looked over but did not take a step. The servant flailed and ran at Lysande. Her feet froze, but Cassia stepped forward and drew her sword: it went through the man, and the burning figure heaved a breath that turned into a sigh. Lysande watched him fall. He had the misfortune of golden hair, she thought, another bolt of anger shooting through her, even as she turned to thank Cassia. She felt the staccato rhythm of her pulse.

"Archers!" Cassia cried, scanning the enclosure even as she pushed forward. "Anyone with a bow, aim for the underbelly! Where in Cognita's wisdom is Fontaine?"

A blast of air shot through the enclosure and her next words were whipped away. Tables flipped and chairs scattered; Lysande dropped to the ground as the gust struck the chimera in the side. The animal roared and huffed more flame. Forced back by the blast, it flapped around the side of the palace, shrieking.

Litany jumped on top of Lysande to shield her from a piece of debris, but even as she blocked the way, Lysande thought she caught a glimpse of a tall figure with white hair, behind the group of statues in the back-right corner.

The wind had barely stopped when jets of water arced up over the guards and Councillors and landed on the flaming tables, quenching the fire. Even in the chaos of the smoking enclosure, she could not help but admire the Shadows' skill.

She and Litany picked their way through bodies and mesh, taking in the chaos around them. "Dante!" she heard Jale cry. The First Sword strode toward him at a pace that she would not have thought possible if she had not witnessed it; at one point, he kicked aside a shield as if he barely saw it, his stare fixed on Jale.

The Valderran banner had ceased to burn, giving off a thick smoke, and within seconds, the scene was still. The palms on the platform dropped pieces of smoldering leaf. Between the upturned tables, those who had been struck by the mesh lay wrapped in their golden shrouds. Only the Council and their guards remained, the surviving guests fled, with the bodies of the dead littering the ground. Lysande tried to calm her pulse and dispel the uncanny feeling that had spread through her since the encounter with the chimera, as if a seal had left its imprint upon the wax of her mind.

Dante pulled Jale to him, pressed his lips to the prince's brow and held him tightly, lifting him off the ground a little as he gripped him, before suddenly seeming to become aware that he was surrounded by people, and setting Jale down. The center of Jale's cheeks turned an interesting shade of puce. Looking everywhere but at each other, the two princes formed a knot with the other Councillors in the middle of the enclosure.

Amidst the bustle, Lysande leaned against Litany and whispered her thanks.

"Did you see the streams?" Litany said.

"Streams?"

"Elementals at work. Without a doubt. I saw the water move in arcs—steady as the fountains in Axium Palace." Litany's expression changed. "You're not surprised. Fortituda protect us, you're not even frowning."

Excuses jostled for place in Lysande's head, but before she could settle on one, Cassia was tapping her on the arm. She could not ignore that swift touch, as much as she wanted to reply to Litany and devise something that was only half a lie.

Litany gripped Lysande's forearm. "When that physician met me outside your suite, I thought perhaps—"

But her next words were drowned out by louder voices.

The Feragos had been seen hurrying into the palace after Anton's death, Dante reported—Mariana Ferago was the last to be glimpsed, hefting her brother's body on her shoulders—and no one seemed in a rush to pursue them. They looked to one another, breathing hard. Lysande checked her surrounds for any sign of Three.

"What just happened?" Jale exclaimed.

"A chimera," Vigarot Chamboise said, stumbling out from behind the honey jug. "A chimera happened." He was holding out a small-sword in front of him, as if it might explain the phenomenon.

"How in the name of Vindictus did it get here? They're meant to be dead." Dante's voice would have made a legion cower. "And there were elementals out here, too—her people did magic—water and wind. You saw it. We should hunt them down."

Lysande opened her mouth to interject. The right words refused to come.

"Never mind that. We have to alert the city. Get everyone under cover," Cassia said, looking around grimly. "The first thing you do after an attack is prepare for a second charge—learned that one from the Qamaras."

"For once, you speak sense," Jale said.

"We need armor. Before we go out there." Cassia bent over a dead soldier and removed the woman's plating. The others did the same. For a moment, there was no sound but the clanking of metal.

"Where's Fontaine?" Dante growled, looking around.

A cool, half-amused voice interrupted them. "If you thought I'd run, you're painfully mistaken."

They turned. Luca was crossing the ruined enclosure, somehow managing to find a straight path through the detritus of the carnage. His guards and nobles rushed to him, one of them handing him a bow. "Your voice carries further than rumor. Perhaps you should be thanking those elementals for forcing a chimera back into the sky, Dalgëreth," he said. "To say nothing of putting out the fires. They saved your life, whoever they were."

"Where were you?" Lysande demanded as he stopped opposite Dante. She did not care that there was an edge to her words.

"I was defending us strategically."

"From *outside* where we were being attacked?"

"Never mind that." Dante folded his arms. "This is the White Queen's doing. A massacre. And her helper is somewhere among us, I'd bet." He turned to Lysande and Luca. "What were the two of you doing before, in the palace?"

In the silence that followed, Lysande considered the explanation "trying to kill each other in a book-closet" but abandoned it when she heard Litany call her name.

The girl was pointing upward with an expression of such horror that Lysande followed her gaze. There, high up in the sky but coming closer by the second, was a white shape with a horned head and wings. She could not mistake the creature. It was swooping fast enough for her to make out the golden dots of its eyes, and it was not the spikes on the tail nor the extraordinary power of the chimera—at least twice the size of the first animal that had attacked them—that made her breath come faster. It was the dozens of armed soldiers in the skirt-like armor and spiked helmets of the Periclean States, strapped to its furred shoulders and scale-slick back. Some crouched on the tail, held in place by a complicated rig of ropes.

The city-rulers tilted their heads back. Lysande fought a panic that threatened to consume her. Two strikes, she thought. *Chimera and chimera.*

"Rally to me!" Cassia cried.

A pressure on her arm: Lysande felt the power of Litany's grip and looked into the girl's face. An unspoken question hung between them. Without breaking the stare, Litany jerked her head toward Cassia. Slowly, Lysande nodded.

I trust her.

She hoped the sentiment reached her face in its curtailed form, rather than in full: *I trust her because I want to believe I can.*

So many bodies clung to the backbone that the soldiers scarcely fit on the chimera: the ropes had been fashioned into harnesses, connected to stirrups and tied with knots. Lysande searched for a weak point and found none. The Councillors, guards of five cities, and all others who had been foolish or brave enough to remain closed around the Irriqi. They retreated to the back of the enclosure. Lysande jostled her way through the guards, allowing action to take precedence over fear; somehow, Litany managed to keep close to her side.

They had barely moved to the back wall when the chimera turned into a dive and plummeted, breathing fire as it came.

It landed in front of the platform without a rope breaking. The mercenaries cut themselves free and poured off its back, shouting and brandishing swords. All Lysande saw was spiked helmets and skirt-like armor coming at her, the Periclean breastplates shining like the chimera's scales. At last she understood why Sarelin had prayed before battle; the thought of being protected by the goddesses might have made her feel courageous, even heroic. Instead, she felt like turning and vomiting onto the ground.

"It's a Royamese white," Cassia managed to shout, over the noise. "Got more scales than other chimeras. You can't kill it through the underbelly—have to get it in the neck!"

Lysande saw Luca turn to his captains. "Strength without swords," he said. "Make every arrow count."

Freste and Malsante set off through the throng, toward the rest of the archers. As Lysande watched them pushing anyone who got in their way, it occurred to her that all the descriptions of battles in books had made no mention of all the desperate shoving that was involved. Fighting looked like at least two-thirds shoving, to the tune of ringing shields. She hurried to appraise the formation of the oncoming soldiers and shouted to her guards to gather, trying to keep anything but deter-mination out of her voice.

Dante drew his axe and sword and charged forward at the left flank, shouting "Valderos," and the Valderrans followed him, taking up the cry. Jale moved quickly after them, approaching the right wing of the attackers with his Lyrian guards. The two parties of Elirans met the Pericleans, and for a moment there was nothing but the crashing of swords. A mercenary fell with a blade in her neck. Another attacker tottered with one arm cut off at the elbow, spurting blood. Several Lyrians and Valderrans fell, stabbed or knocked down, and some were trampled under boots.

Lysande appraised the scene even more quickly this time and grabbed Raden by the arm. "We can't have our special guard fighting without its captain!" It was hard to avoid sounding sentimental. "Go to your troops!"

"If you think I'm going to leave you when there's a whole legion of soldiers bearing down on us . . ."

"Now, Raden! Go!"

An agonized look passed over his face. "You know I count you as a true friend."

"And I you. I cherish all our walks, all our conversations. But Raden, you must go!"

He drew a deep breath. "You were a dearer friend still to Sarelin."

A lump rose in Lysande's throat. "This is not the time for speeches!"

"She would have given you this. Take it from our queen, if you won't take it from a friend." He thrust his shield at her and dashed off before she could refuse it, toward where his Axium Guards were engaged. Lysande watched his arm raise a sword aloft and bring it to meet an attacker's blade. She knew she could allow herself no time to bask in his words; the White Queen's people would not slow with her; and yet she felt the glow of the sentiment and guessed what it had cost for him to voice it.

In front of them, soldiers in spiked helmets and skirts broke the lines and advanced. Cassia did not need to call to her guards: they came with her as soon as she stepped forward and massed to form a block behind Jale and Dante. The Pyrrhans took her direction, throwing swords and firing bolts into the mercenaries. Lysande looked quickly around, wondering whether she should make a charge. The Axium Guards who had reached her were waiting for her command, yet it did not make sense to charge headlong into the fray.

She might do more damage to the Pyrrhan defenders than help, when they were working so closely together. What would Sarelin do? But no . . . it was what *she* would do that counted. The change had taken place some time ago, subtly.

"Not going to charge in, Prior?" Luca called. She spotted him behind the mêlée.

"I'd prefer to help us win."

"That's not very chivalrous of you."

"Is there chivalry out there? I must have missed it."

Luca called something to his soldiers. They rallied behind him, and a wave of black flowed around the side of the battle; the Rhimese moved with the same assurance they brought to everything they did, most of them spreading into the seating as they ran. They were not merging with the fight, she realized. Luca climbed onto a table near the front, and Lysande saw the others copy him and begin to shoot at the chimera.

"Draw your blades!" she screamed, turning to the Axiumites.

It was the last shout she managed before the first Pericleans broke through the block.

She was throwing daggers before she could think. Her first blade sank into the gap in a woman's visor and killed her mid-stride. She churned inside, but hastened to pull another dagger from her belt. *Don't look at the blood*, she told herself. *Just look at the target.* She could do this if she immersed herself; blocked out all fear. Ducking under a Periclean's arm with her shield held close, she pulled her dagger from a fallen body, yanking it out quickly and darting back, just as Litany was doing beside her. Litany flung blade after blade into the mass of soldiers; Chidney raced forward to bring the Axiumites beside her, and together they fought to keep the attackers at bay, Chidney hacking and slashing with the full power of her muscles behind her sword, Litany whirling and weaving, flinging her daggers, the two of them pointing out attackers to each other.

The chimeran fire had burned some of the Pyrrhans, and more and more Pericleans were slipping through Cassia's lines. They could scarcely kill one soldier before another arrived in their place, and the lunging of the Periclean soldiers told Lysande that they knew their advantage, swinging their swords without hesitation. She forced herself to ignore the waves of despair breaking within her, focusing on each attack, throwing rhythmically.

She dodged a sword, feinting to the right, and nearly impaled herself on another blade: Litany pulled her out of the way in time. They stared at each other, breathing hard. "Thank you," Lysande whispered, adjusting the shield Raden had given her, and Litany nodded before turning back to the fight.

The tide of soldiers might have proved too much had not a blast of air knocked several of the Pericleans to the ground, the force sending their weapons flying. Lysande felt a tug at her arm, coming from a figure in a rough brown cloak. She knew who would be wearing it even before she glimpsed his face.

She flung a dagger, almost automatically, into the legs of an approaching mercenary. "You mustn't let anyone see you!" she cried.

"My dear, we might all meet the goddesses below. And if the White Queen is here, I mean to help." Three shot a jet of air at another Periclean. "How many chances does one get to test oneself with a chimera, after all?"

"It was you before, then?"

"I cast the air. Six just happened to ignore her orders and came here too." He moved to guard her left. "How in the Three Lands the White Queen got two *chimeras* . . . but never mind. Damn that white beast. Roaming around like a fire-breathing eagle. We can't kill it with fireballs."

She stared around the enclosure, half-expecting to see Luca engulfed in fire. Despite sweeping the crush of bodies with her eyes, she could not pick out his elegant figure. It annoyed her that she felt the need to look for him, even now.

"The archers need to get it in the neck, Cassia says."

Three glanced ahead, in the direction of the platform. "They might, if Six keeps on."

She looked up to the front of the enclosure and saw balls of fire shooting up, causing the chimera to screech and flap its wings. Six was nothing if not determined. Her flames widened in the air and forced the animal higher. Hope began to spread in Lysande's breast. Ahead, several figures were climbing onto the platform; their spiked helms glinted in the light of the elemental woman's fire, and one of them reached into a pouch at his belt.

The object glanced off a Valderran's breastplate and clattered to the ground. Lysande stared at it, but she did not recognize it: a disc of metal with a jagged edge.

"The filthy dogs!" Cassia shouted. "They're throwing coin-knives!"

"What?"

"Tiny pieces of goddess-be-damned death, that's what! Get down!"

The second circular knife whizzed by Lysande and sliced the cheek of one of Jale's soldiers. The woman gave a guttural scream as she tried to pull it out, and staggered, falling into the path of a group of mercenaries. Figures in skirted armor fell upon her.

"Down!" Dante roared. "Everybody, get down!"

The Elirans ducked as more of the sharp pieces rained onto them. Lysande lifted her shield to block the coin-knives, then grabbed Litany and Chidney and drew them close. "Can you cover for me here?" she shouted.

"Yes. But where are you—"

"Take this." She handed Raden's shield to Litany. "Just keep holding them off. You're doing brilliantly."

"Lysande, you mustn't risk—"

She pulled Litany tight to her and squeezed her. It was the only thing she could think of to thank the girl, and as she held her close, she whispered, "Shadow Chidney now. See that she's protected. For your own sake."

Litany nodded, and seemed to struggle with words before running off.

There was one other person who was shadowing Lysande, clutching a shield and watching for arrows, and she turned to him. "Derset, can you bring that shield and run alongside me?"

"Of course, my lady."

He moved to her. Without hesitating, he maneuvered himself to stand between her and the mêlée on her right. His hand clasped hers. The touch came gently, and yet it carried the weight of an embrace, and Lysande was aware of the brevity of the moment, savoring it. She was aware of the other moments that layered beneath this one: those minutes when they had been alone and gasping, but not in pain. Something pulled her away from the thought. A whipping sound came nearer, like wings beating the air.

She looked up just as the beast swooped on her. The power of the gaze hit her in the stomach, the full force of it causing her body to freeze. Golden eyes stared into hers.

Lysande stared back. This time, it was unmistakable—the inquisitiveness, directed at her, overpowering, and her own fascination rising to meet it. The animal might roast her. She could not move, even if she had wanted to, trapped in thrall to the meeting of soft hair and cut-glass scales. When it did not draw a breath and cremate her, she considered what might happen if she reached up, for she felt certain that it was waiting for a signal to approach her.

A thought hit her. Surely, though, if no physician or scholar had ever hinted in any text, after all this time, it could not be that her use of scale . . .

"My lady!"

This was no time to gape at a chimera.

She drew a dagger and forced herself to sprint down the path around the side of the tables, past the statues, the honey-jug, and its pavilion, Derset keeping pace on her left. Armor covered the three Periclean soldiers upon the platform. It would be impossible to get a clear shot through the slits in their helmets, yet there was one place . . . She lined up her eye with her right hand and sent a dagger spinning into the boot of the nearest soldier. The man staggered, cried out an oath, and fell into the pool.

Lysande forced herself to watch. The splash he made was nothing to the flurry of movement around his body: spikes of a grayish hue broke the pool's surface and impaled him from every side. His legs, groin, and chest sprouted with red.

The spearfish leaped onto the body and tore chunks of the flesh, their teeth flashing. They worried the fat from the bones within seconds. Lysande turned her head away, holding down bile. If she could have rewritten the moment, she would have parceled this violence up, exchanged it for something bloodless and clean.

Derset passed her a few more daggers, all battle-stained. She brought down the second Periclean, and the woman's body had already been half-devoured by the time she struck the third soldier—despite everything, she was proud of her aim.

Spearfish turned on each other as they quarreled over these presents, beginning to gore their rivals in the body and fins. Their blood added to the spreading pool of red. Glancing away, she saw Cassia totter; a knife-thrower had landed one of his little pieces in her face, and the Irriqi staggered, clutching her eye. "No!" Lysande shouted.

Pyrrhans thronged around Cassia, shielding her. A rush of blood surged to Lysande's head. She aimed a dagger at the heart of the nearest mercenary and found her mark, and ignoring the rest of the battle for a moment, she threw another and another. Even though she knew she was not meant to care about the city-rulers, her wall was crumbling—it had never been very solidly constructed to begin with, she realized.

"For Queen Sarelin!" somebody cried. "Let's send her some company!"

Lysande turned sharply. She strove to pinpoint the speaker through the crush of bodies.

"And for Councillor Prior!" Raden's voice roared, louder. "Prior! Prior! Prior!"

Her name echoed from the guards' voices: *Prior*. There was a bold music in it that was not the well-measured tune of court dances, nor even the regimented two-step of a march. Lysande noted the wild beat.

Prior. Again and again. She was supposed to be indifferent to such adulation, performing her duties for the Shadows, the populace, the other elementals . . . yet she could not hear that word enough. *The mirror of one's majesty*. The reflection could nearly blind you, she thought, watching the Axium Guards storm through the mêlée.

A crest of silver broke over the sea of swords and shields. The mercenaries shouted words she did not recognize, but she saw the new fear on their faces.

One of the archers had penetrated the chimera's hide below the neck, and the animal came wheeling around in the air, shrieking and sputtering flame. Fires blazed between the tables and encircled the Rhimese as they sprayed arrows into the throng. Lysande directed the Axiumites as loudly as she could over the shouts and screams, letting strategy take over from fear. Did Perfault not claim that the place to debate orders was in court sessions, and the place to issue them was in battle?

"Can you put those fires out?" she called, elbowing her way through to Three.

He looked up, and shook his head. "My dear, I'm afraid my element is air."

"Someone used water to put the flames out, before!"

"So I saw." He cast a jet of air at an oncoming attacker. "But not our someone. Only Six and I are here tonight; I wish my colleagues were as eager."

She was pushed forward before she could ask him more. The Valderrans and Lyrians were leading a surge, driving the Pericleans back toward the chimera, and her elite guards were following Raden after them. Now, surely, it was logical to charge.

Shouting over the clash of steel, she led the rest of the Axiumites forward, bringing them up behind the first wave of soldiers and raising her dagger as she commanded them. The White Queen's people were hemmed in now, but they were giving as good as they got. Close by her, Jale's sister Élérie thrust a smallsword into a mercenary's face before another soldier ran her through from behind; she fell forward slowly, her eyes wide. Lysande heard screams and saw Chidney racing toward the killer. She knew, even as she shouted a warning, that Chidney had not seen the mercenary coming up on her left.

She had a glimpse of Litany tackling Chidney; of the two of them ducking beneath a longsword, scrambling and sprinting, while Raden ran in to cut off the mercenary's blow.

It could not have taken five seconds in total. A swing. A clash of swords. Over the sound of steel, Raden gave a blood-choked cry. Lysande felt that cry echo inside her. The fighters near him moved aside, and she saw the blade that pierced his chest like a jousting lance cutting through wood.

Not Raden, she thought. He could not have fallen: just minutes ago, he had led a charge through a throng of bronze-clad bodies. Before that, her fingers had gripped his shield.

But more to the point, there were all those years between them, all those quieter moments riding after Sarelin, drinking together at night, playing at tactos, throwing darts together with a wobbling aim; and she had not forgotten the small acts of kindness he had shown her, in sharing her company, year after year. She drew a shuddering breath before bracing herself, driving her dagger into the next attacker.

She fought twice as fast, then, raining blows on the woman. By the time she got clear of the next group, Raden lay still on the ground. She found him with eyes open, staring up at the darkening sky.

His eyelids felt soft against her fingers, unexpectedly soft, as she closed them. She pressed her forefinger to each one.

If this was a tragedy, there was no time to mourn. More soldiers were approaching, and she focused on the scene ahead, holding back her emotions about Raden until she could taste them. The Pyrrhans had closed ranks into a knot, Cassia at the front, her left eye a bloody mess and her left cheek streaked with red. The wound transfigured her face into a battle-mask. As she raised a serrated sword, several mercenaries scattered.

"Jale!" Luca shouted.

Lysande rose. She saw a group of Pericleans closing on the Lyrians, some of them splitting off to target a single fighter. She drew another shuddering breath.

There was no way Jale could win against so many opponents. He had nowhere to run to, with the table cutting him off and a fire blazing behind him. She tried to push toward him. With all the power in her lungs, she took up Luca's cry.

Jale did not shrink back: he stabbed one mercenary between his arm-guard and shoulder-guard. The shadow of a big soldier fell across him. Ducking, Jale sliced the woman in the leg and leaped onto her back to slash her throat. Lysande watched him weave around the others like a dancer. The soldiers moved in on him as he vaulted down, and while he evaded two and killed another with a single blow, he did not stop the woman who had crept around beside him. Her sword-point found his shoulder.

Blood painted Jale's arm. Two mercenaries closed in. Another came around on his left in a pincer movement—Lysande screamed a warning—and a brown cape whirled through their midst.

Lysande heard Dante's roar even before seeing him. His axe cracked the helmet of the woman like a knife splitting a walnut. Brains spilled out, and nearby, somebody retched. Dante let the mercenary fall and wheeled around, turning on the others. Hacking, he took an arm clean off one soldier, gouged another in the chest, struck a third below the abdomen, the skill of a butcher and the aim of a swordsman in his strokes. Lysande could not bring herself to look away. Bile was rising in her throat again. A man ran behind Jale and locked his arms around the young prince's neck, nearly choking him.

Dante smiled grimly as he walked toward the mercenary. "There's a punishment for thieves, in Valderos," he said.

"I am no thief." The man's Eliran was perfect, a little too cleanly adapted, but the fear in his voice did not need translation.

"You're holding my jewel." Dante raised his axe. "That makes you a thief."

The soldier let go of Jale, leaping backward, landing against a fallen Lyrian guard and stumbling, and Dante did not pause for even a second; he hacked the mercenary's neck over and over, until Jale placed a hand on his arm, and at last, Dante lowered his weapon. Jale stroked the First Sword's blood-spattered jaw, and Dante leaned down, bringing their lips together as easily as a wave meeting sand.

"Vindictus' gory sword!" Cassia shouted, next to them. "Get it over with!"

Dante did not appear to be interested in following her advice. The northern and southern guards who surrounded the princes were frowning deeply. Lysande barely had time to take that in and to navigate the shoals of her emotions: satisfaction at guessing the truth, relief for Dante and Jale, and her stubborn, accompanying fear for both princes.

She turned, feeling a tug at her arm. Derset had come around on her left and was shielding her. He had found a sword, and his hair was askew.

"Captain Chidney sent me with a message for you, my lady," he said. In the middle of the throng, Lysande saw Chidney fighting an enormous soldier in a spiked helmet, Litany wielding a dagger by her side. "She says we're winning the battle, but she needs you to bring the last group of troops in from the palace."

"We have no more troops!"

"She and Captain Hartleigh stationed fifty guards in the third-floor dining room." Derset pointed toward the palace. Lysande felt a knife-point twist between her ribs at the mention of Raden's name. "They were to be a final weapon. Captain Hartleigh asked to be excused for his temerity, my lady, with his final breath; he thought it was necessary to conceal them."

Lysande just managed to suppress an exasperated retort, though she felt the prick of grief again between her ribs. "I mean to stay and fight," she said. "Send our guards."

"My lady, it seems Captain Hartleigh told the guards to only take orders from you." Derset looked pained. "He felt that if he was busy trying to hold back the White Queen's people here, you should be the one to take command. Please, my lady."

Damn Raden's Axiumite blood. *Everything in its place*, now, of all times?

None of the Pericleans were paying her or Derset any attention. Bronze armor flashed against silver and gold across the enclosure; mercenaries locked in combat with Elirans, cries and screams rising and falling with their blows; the chimera hovered, withholding its flames. Through the crowd she spotted a ring of Axiumites defending a body, and she knew whose it must be. For Raden, she thought: the kind of friend who handed you his shield in the middle of a battle.

"Can you shield me all the way across the platform and up the steps?" she said.

Derset moved beside her and, taking her by the hand, guided her up to the platform—past Six throwing fire, through the remains of the palms and over to the stairs, without looking back. They sprinted side by side. She could hear her breath in her ears as something sailed past her neck—a coin-knife, she realized, as it rolled across a step ahead, and Derset moved behind her, blocking another one with his shield. The third time, she did not flinch. In an hour's length, while women and men were falling without prayer, you became used to death, its formless presence swirling around, waiting for your misstep, your false shot.

They burst through the doors of Rayonnant Palace and into the corridor, now empty. "Why on earth did Raden put them on the third floor?"

"I don't know, my lady. I suppose that dining room must have been the only place the Lyrians weren't checking."

"I hope they can fight well." They were nearly at the top of the staircase. "The battle's turning ugly."

The second floor was just as desolate. She caught her breath, then ran with Derset up the next flight. There was not far to go once they emerged. The third-floor dining room had the advantage of being not far from the stairs, but it also had a blind corner before it. No sooner had they rounded the elaborately furnished bend than they came face to face with soldiers in armor and spiked helmets.

Lysande skidded to a halt, grabbing hold of a statue. The Pericleans rushed forward.

A woman with a chimera on her breastplate grabbed her by the shoulders; another pinned her hands behind her back. She struggled, kicking with all the energy left in her, but the mercenaries forced her arms into place. Another soldier with a star on his armor stepped forward and ran a finger down her cheek. She impelled herself to hold back a wave of fear.

The man's breath gusted against her skin. A grin spread across his face, which was entirely unremarkable: no misshapen ears, no pock-marked cheeks, no extrusive scar; nothing that would have distinguished him from another citizen in a marketplace or city square; and that, in itself, made her heart flip over. It would have been almost comforting to see cruelty written on his skin; something, at least, for her to read. His smile, too, gave nothing away. There was a pause, in which all of the mercenaries looked at someone behind Lysande, and as she struggled, something that Derset had said popped into her mind: *Captain Hartleigh asks to be excused for his temerity, my lady.*

It had never been like Raden to apologize for battle tactics, nor to use a word like *temerity*.

"What should we do with this one?" the man touching Lysande's cheek said, still grinning. "Kill her, or spend a little time with her?"

"We'll take her up to the roof," a voice answered. "Her Majesty wants her alive."

It was a voice she knew all too well. Yet it was not the same voice. The earnest tone, the gentle turn of phrase, the hesitation that guided every suggestion—they were all gone, as if someone had pulled off a silk cover. Lysande twisted her neck as much as she was able.

Lord Derset met her look without a flicker of a reaction. He stood only a foot from her. With a casual movement he unbuttoned the back of his collar and shrugged off his robe, exposing a low-collared doublet. The cloth of the skinbrace was gone. A mark stood out on his bare neck; it was an image she had seen twice since Sarelin's death, yet this third time was worst of all. The imprint of the chimera had blackened the skin.

Lysande could not repress a sharp exhalation.

How useful a high collar must have been.

Derset raised a hand and stilled her captor, who had begun to push her forward. "One moment."

He held an arm out and, with a twist of his hand, sent a jet of flame onto his robe.

The green velvet caught fire and burned on the floor for a minute or so. Derset stood, watching it. The expression on his face was like that of a man who had unshouldered a boulder that he had been carrying for a very long time and was watching it roll away.

When the garment began to smoke, he nodded to the soldiers and walked on.

The group followed him as one. Lysande's captor pushed her down the corridor, toward the stairs, and with a lurch of her stomach she realized that they were going away from the enclosure—past the fourth floor, the fifth, and the sixth, to somewhere higher still. Luca Fontaine's entreaty not to leave the ball alone rang in her head.

It was never Fontaine, she thought. And it was never one of the city-rulers.

A door slammed below her. She felt the end of a sword-hilt in her back, and picked up her pace.

Fourteen

It was not easy to climb seven flights of stairs with her hands behind her back, least of all when she was being bumped over each step, her shins striking the stone. She winced a few times as she struggled up, laboring for breath, but her eyes remained on Derset, his silver-streaked hair glimmering in the torchlight, guiding them to the top.

Had he grown taller after casting off his robe? No—it was just that he was no longer stooping to whisper in her ear or tucking his hands behind his back. He waved the guards forward. Lysande swallowed something that she felt would be best unvoiced.

They stopped at the entrance to the tenth floor. The woman outside the door grasped the hilt of her sword. When she saw Derset, she raised her free hand to her chest.

"Aren't you forgetting something, Hapsley?" Derset said.

The guard looked Lysande over, but could not produce an answer. Derset's gaze did not soften.

"All weapons are to be confiscated and presented to Her Majesty. They're property of the regime now. I thought your captain would've drummed it into that thick skull of yours. Take the blades, and be quick, or I'll take an eye."

Only a few daggers remained in Lysande's sheaths after the battle, and these Hapsley procured, clutching them to her chest. For one protracted moment, Lysande feared that her doublet would be ripped open, the last few weapons exposed, yet the moment passed, and of course, fear was a strange beast: you always imagined that your enemies possessed the insights of your own mind. When Hapsley made to grasp the gold dagger, Derset stepped forward and stretched out his hand.

"I'll take that one. You know she doesn't like to see anything that reminds her of that woman."

He slipped the dagger into the pocket of his trousers, and Lysande bit her lip as she watched it disappear. She reached up, almost unconsciously, to finger the chain around her neck. The texture, the sheen, even the temperature of that fluid silver: she knew them as intimately as a queen knows a crown. Ever since Derset had given the chain to her, she had only taken it off to bathe, and even then, it had remained within her view. Her fingers closed on a few links.

Derset smiled. "Oh, you can keep that," he said. "It was never Sarelin Brey's."

She felt a wave of something molten rise in her throat, and fought it down.

A click of Derset's fingers brought the soldiers through the door and into the corridor, and Lysande's ribs knocked against the doorframe as they pushed her through.

The tenth floor served as a collection of rooms in which Lyrian royalty could venerate the sun—several prayer-rooms, a dining hall with glass walls, and then, largest of all, the observatory, Princess Ariane's chandeliered creation, a tribute to nature at an unnaturally high cost. Derset led them down the corridor to where three people bent over a body. The corpse had been burned so thoroughly that only its head was untouched, and the arms, legs, and torso had turned the color of freshly cut meat; Lysande's stomach heaved, yet she forced her eyes to witness. The molten tide inside her swirled again, mixed with something more violent.

The nearest elemental opened her palm, casting fire onto the corpse's neck. Scowling, the woman looked up as they entered, greasy curtains of auburn hair framing her face. Lysande discerned that her belt was of Axiumite make; the buckle curved, emblazoned with a crown in the style of one of the capital merchants. The woman beside her sported a sapphire-studded sword-belt that could only be Lyrian, gilded and finely wrought. A slender man knelt farthest from Lysande, a bow slung on his back, the Rhimese design giving its wood the appearance

ke and the woman flinched. "Bring me their bodies when you're
e, and I might just forget to mention your negligence to Her Maj-
"

he trio gathered up their weapons, and Lysande wondered at the
tacle of powerful elementals fleeing from the man who had bowed
taken orders from her. Derset grabbed Crake by the arm and
led her his shield. "Give this to some idiot who needs it."

Vithin seconds, Lysande found herself jolted through the next
. Rayonnant Palace's observatory felt even larger than she had
cted—in Castle Sapere, the top-floor viewing room had been
ded by a glass wall, yet this room opened to the air at the far end.
ecting the Lyrian philosophy of connecting the soul to the sun. It
funny how even at a time like this, the scholar in her head would
quiet, bolts of facts snapping into place, reverberating. With the
ness of the night facing her, she faltered. The chandelier above her
led crystal daggers in the torchlight, quavering in the breeze.

et the steel border around the room provided the real air of men-
at least two dozen guards stood shoulder to shoulder along the left
right walls, and as Derset strode in, they straightened and raised
hands to their chests.

t ease," Derset said.

he whole group lowered their hands again. Light glanced off
d helmets and Periclean armor, the bronze plates thicker than
 of the mercenaries who had poured off the second chimera.
y, these soldiers were not fodder for swords. The weapons in their
bore rubies, emeralds, and sapphires, cut in the pear-shaped Peri-
style, and one woman held a dove in her hand. The man with the
ordinary smile stood at the end of the observatory, a vast collec-
of ropes and stirrups sprawled at his feet.

chimera was coming back, Lysande deduced. Either that or a
big enough to carry a half-hundred soldiers would be landing
She felt the tremor in her hands and wished that she had imbibed
a half-dose of the blue mixture. No; that was the thought of a
ling. She tried to resist the current of nervous energy.

was strange: not long ago, Derset had been lying beneath her, his
rs tangled in the blue silk of her bedsheet, leaning into her palms

of two snakes meeting fang to fang. Such a bow bore th
of craftwork, its form carved not only for strength but
look on its owner's face was anything but beautiful.

If only she had the glow of scale to wash the sight
but a tide of gold could have eased this feeling. She f
look again at the corpse's seared flesh.

"Get up," Derset said, as he entered. "All of you. 7
woman, are we, Raquefort?"

Derset walked over to the Lyrian. He poked the cor
with his foot. Lysande recognized Jale's sister Élérie's f
with many cuts, a wet choker of blood around her thro
roiled.

"We were interrogating her," Raquefort said, suller

"Do you think she'll yield some useful informati
other half-hour and she might give us the details of
fenses." Derset turned to the woman with the Axiur
"You should be begging me for mercy, Crake. You to

Lysande's insides were still seething over Derse
forced herself to examine the elementals before her. R
and Rimini . . . she recognized those names, along
She had read them in the captains' letters when she w
formation for *An Ideal Queen*—had she not? "Cral
Pelouse in northwest Lyria." Yes. She had definitely c
And she had noted the three names in the accounts c
she had borrowed from the Academy, among the han
ran elementals the White Queen had managed to recru
two years had passed since the war, only Raquefort, th
looked old enough . . . the other two, surely, must be
of the captains. Did the White Army have its own fam
idea seemed a mockery of the Axium motto, yet in l
White Queen had applied the central idea. *Everythin*

"In a short while, I will be speaking to Her Maje
"And if you think she'll be pleased when she hears l
your time, then you have failed to grasp her characte

"My lord—"

"Go down and kill any of the Councillors left." H

and taking her direction. Had he ever wanted her direction? *I like what you like.* Her mind moved past that, humming along at a frenetic pace. It was as if she had skipped past fear. Shock could be a drug, too—could it not?—and she shepherded her thoughts into order.

Two daggers remained in her doublet. Maybe three, if she had miscalculated. There had to be fifty or so blades among the guards in this room, from longswords to daggers. How long would it take to draw a dagger from her doublet and throw—five seconds, perhaps?

A small table with chairs whose backs were embellished with solid gold suns stood in the middle of the floor, and into one of these garish creations she was pushed, smarting. Derset strode past to the end of the room and looked out into the night, facing the blackness for a few quiet moments. He turned and walked back to take the chair opposite her. "Has the Iron Queen's pet anything to say?"

"I should have guessed. You'd been in the west for years. That should've been a sign," she said, quietly. "Mea Tacitus was moving around in the Periclean States. An envoy to the foreign lands would make the perfect correspondent. Diamond thread on the purse, too." It was all so easy to see, now. Being thrust into a chair and ringed by armed guards provided a dose of lucidity. "You had it made when you were dealing with Royam, of course. The panther—that came from across the sea too—I suppose you met someone who could train it while you were abroad."

"You worked this out in seven flights of stairs?" His voice did not betray anger.

"The high collar and long sleeves, and the skinbrace—a costume for hiding a brand, of course—but you were always so austere, so modest in your behavior. My suspicions were focused on the city-rulers." The words came from her in a stream; she was speaking out of the frenetic energy running through her. Deduction felt easier when it served to dispel craving, to ward off anger—to tie up the frayed ends of his deeds instead. No flicker of reaction passed across Derset's face.

"You were so skillful, planting the seeds to make me suspect Luca," she said. "You made me second-guess everything he did. All those hints and suggestions, which you took back as soon as they'd taken root in my head. I presume the White Queen told you to direct the blame to him, because of his image." Derset's nod came without hesitation. "The clever prince, who planted archers behind tapestries, who kept his strategies veiled in a cloth of ever-changing words. A man whose very blood seemed to grow tongues and speak of conspiracy. She chose her target well."

Derset remained impassive.

"And that queensflower, left at the Valderran table. You distracted half our number by sowing suspicion, stirring up the north and south."

"They do make it easy."

"I see now that I have been blind where my scrutiny was most needed."

If she had not been so busy watching the city-rulers at the banquet, might she have noticed him slip a silent-sword into a cake? If she had not been focused on Luca, Cassia, Jale, and Dante in the box in the Arena, might she have seen some accomplice unlock the door of the wolf cage? She should have been surveying the whole vista, not a small slice of it. And then there was the casual construction of her own humiliation: she had allowed herself to take comfort the only way that she could, aside from drinking scale. Derset had only needed to seize the plum that she dropped into his lap. She tried not to score her palms with her nails. Two daggers, she reminded herself. Five seconds to throw.

"Even failing to kill the Council didn't induce you to give up on Luca, not when you could hire a sword and wash your hands of the blame. I can see why she used you."

"A servant cannot help but follow orders," Derset said.

"That letter you received." She looked into Derset's eyes. "The White Queen coded it with the *Legilium*. A prince might've had a copy lying around, of course, but you knew it by heart—after all, you studied the law. There was no need to lug along a book."

He leaned across the table, resting his hands on the wood. "You of all people understand the importance of planning. I did what I had to do."

She shook her head. Hiding the mixture of self-loathing and fury that was simmering beneath her skin, she looked into his face. "Clever.

You were very clever. Everything was meticulously organized so that you could act quickly, right from the day Sarelin died."

"A glorious day," he said.

It was hard not to flare up, to reach over and slap the satisfaction off his face; but this was not Luca Fontaine. Derset would not enjoy being struck.

With such strain that she could feel her teeth grinding their outer layer, she forced herself to return to the subject.

"Those busts were your doing, too, in the prayer-house. The only bit I can't figure out is the attack on the Grandfleuve . . . those weren't your people, were they?"

He rubbed the chimera brand on his neck with one finger and closed his eyes for a moment. "Usually, I find that it is when one waits in stasis, between enterprises, that luck strikes," he said. "Fear breeds fireballs. In one way, the shameful neglect of our people was a gift."

How keenly she felt that. "You could have let me burn."

"Why not tighten the bond between you and your dear, patient advisor: the man who always listened to your problems? Once you knew he was willing to risk his life for you, you'd trust him in any crisis, surely. True friendship and warmth . . . of many kinds. Don't all scholars crave that?"

It was humiliating to have the last piece nudged into place by the same hand that had designed the puzzle. She fought the quaver in her voice. "And what was it all for? Why do this to Sarelin, to the realm, to me? All those clever moves—I see it's some kind of game, but what are we playing for, Derset?"

"Henrey." Derset pushed his chair out, the legs screeching against the stones, and stood up. "My name is Henrey. Perhaps you've forgotten it; it doesn't glitter quite like Cassia or Dante or Jale. Or Sarelin."

He walked over to the soldier at the end of the line who was holding the dove. The bird cooed into his fingers as he lifted it. The pellets of dark eyes amid the dirty gray feathers regarded Lysande with indifference, and she watched Derset trace a path down the back of its neck with his thumb. Not long ago, she had traced a path down his chest.

"As soon as I send this dove, the White Queen will come."

"I suppose she likes to do her slaughter up close," Lysande said. "The personal touch."

Derset smiled; for the first time, her remarks had prompted some emotion, even if it was only amusement. "To offer you a choice."

A glance at the ropes laid out on the floor told her that there were enough of them to rig the black chimera that had attacked the enclosure first. If it had flown back to its mistress, there was a good chance Derset was not bluffing. Lysande felt her chest tighten.

Derset sat down opposite her again. He stroked the dove's head. As he did, she felt a twitching in her palm—the slightest flicker of an itch. "Do you remember what Her Majesty was called by the populace after the war?" Derset said.

"You mean the White Queen, not the Iron Queen, I presume."

"I mean the only true queen for people like us." His nostrils flared slightly. "You're an elemental. You know who I mean."

Lysande recalled how he had looked at her when she winced in pain on the ship; how he had asked after her health in the palanquin, after she clutched the cushion. And he himself had winced—but not in pain—just hours ago. His hair had been splayed across the Lyrian silk of her pillow as he gasped, smiling, giving in and writhing under her touch. How long ago that seemed. Before the Conquest, time had not been charted in arbitrary numbers of days, Kephir wrote. When enough people felt that their lives had changed, they named a new season: whole decades chosen by emotion, ages streaked with the black ink of grief or suffused with the dye of love.

"Answer the question," Derset said.

"Usurper." She remembered Sarelin's sharp ejaculation of the term, in the palace vault, before she blocked Lysande's view of the woman painted on a crag.

"It's an oily word, *usurper*. Some names wash off with a little effort, like mud, but not that one. You can try to scrub it away, but once it's on, the word stains. Like *bastard*. Or *commoner*." He patted the dove on the head. "The White Queen found that out the hard way. I watched her reputation plummet and plummet until it lay among the base company of thieves and petty murderers. I knew she needed a thinker who could manage her name."

"You." Lysande could not keep the bitterness from her voice.

"Changes are a tricky business." Derset's tone was still hard stone, but there was an edge to it: an urgency that implored her. "You can cut away all the roses in the garden, but you'll prick your fingers on those thorns."

He placed the dove on the table, and as he did so, she saw his hand tremble—a movement so faint that it could almost have been a trick of her mind, yet she knew that she had not imagined it. No one shivered from cold in the Lyrian delta.

It's her, she thought. He's scared of what she'll do to him if he fails.

The map of scars on Welles' face, Six's burned cheek, and Three's white hair . . . they returned to her anew.

"The White Queen wants you, Lysande," Derset said. "Not Dalgëreth, not Chamboise, not Ahl-Hafir, and certainly not Fontaine, the slinking adder. But you, it seems, are different. I can't say why she fixates on the orphan Councillor. Still, if you want to avoid the stain of *usurper*, you need someone to introduce you to all those bleating sheep across the realm . . . and who better than a member of the old regime to make the announcement?"

"You wish me to convey legitimacy upon the White Queen?"

"Think of it as an honor. You will be the herald of our new dynasty."

Of course. It was always a dynasty, with silverbloods: always the family name falling like varnish down the decades, coating everything beneath it. That was what the realm needed, according to the nobility, because nobles had been raised to believe that commoners yearned for them. But she had seen the bone people with her own eyes, had stood before the elementals on the back of the executioner's cart, and knew that what they yearned for was not a dynasty.

Our dynasty, Derset had said.

"You don't have any status in her ranks, you know."

His eyes glistened. "All of us have status, by nature. Elira has always belonged to elementals. We were the ones who ruled here before the Conquest—and Her Majesty means to take the realm back to the beginning of the calendar, Lysande."

"Trying the Conquest all over again but with the winners and losers interchanged. I can't say she lacks ambition. But if she does succeed and uses our neighbors to invade us, what makes you think she'll share this realm with you?"

Derset chuckled. "Oh, Elira is the prize, I'll give you. The homeland. All those climates and the goods they produce will prove useful for our rule. But Bastillonian troops . . . and Royamese mines? Do you really think she means to pick our neighbors up and drop them down again?"

"Sun and stars," Lysande said quietly. There had to be a name for a moment like this, when everything fell into place—*epiphany* did not convey the horror of a chasm opening before your feet, to a place where every piece of light rattled around between walls of solid stone, a place too deep to plummet into. "It's an empire, isn't it?" she said.

Too easy to imagine Bastillón thinking it had made a new ally, only to discover too late who that ally was. All too easy to imagine Royam taking an ambitious line, joining with another to go after Elira's resources and losing its own sovereignty in the process. The neighboring lands would not know they were sowing a disaster. They would stumble, and the White Queen would be there to seize them.

Derset placed a hand on her shoulder. "Good. Now choose."

She drew a deep breath. An empire. It was still sinking into her mind. At times like this, rumination was expensive. But she had a feeling that she held the key to why this was the White Queen's goal. Was it not possible that Mea Brey, in serving her cousin, had nurtured the seeds of martial expansion with a desperate need; that after being overlooked for so long, she had decided never to be forgotten? The aims she pursued, even now, suggested that she *needed* the glorious recognition of becoming Mea Tacitus, the White Queen, instead of Mea Brey.

A desperate need could be a weakness if you learned how to turn it to your advantage. If she strained her mind to the utmost, maybe she could slide her remaining pieces across the board.

"Dole out my support, in public, or be a meal for a chimera," she said, as evenly as she could manage. "As far as I can see, that's not much of a choice."

"You've misunderstood me." Derset stroked the dove again. "The choice is not whether you'll do it. The choice is how you'll do it. Will you appoint her of your own volition—or will you do so under the White Queen's control, your mind in her grip?"

Her mind. What was it Sarelin had said to her, when she escorted her to the target range at Axium Palace for the first time? *I'll teach you to throw daggers if you'll teach me to fling words.* She had never doubted what her real weapon was.

I won't give it up, she thought. And nor will I hand Mea Tacitus her empire. Forget fear, hesitation, and the swordlace vines of possibilities that twisted ahead. Determination pooled in her.

Use logic. There was a reason why the White Queen had chosen her to be the liaison, even if she did not know it. It had sustained her this far.

She stared unflinchingly at Derset, ignoring the strands of hair that had fallen into his eyes—the same way that strands had decorated his brow when she had kissed him the last time, pressing him into the sheets and watching the last remnants of his guard give way. Details molded memories. The length of a sigh or the fall of soft hair gave your past a form, and what could create for you could also unravel you entirely.

"How long do I have?"

"I can allow you a few minutes." Derset was watching her with a hint of melancholy in his expression. "But I suggest you think quickly. The White Queen has waited over twenty years . . . she is renowned for many things, Lysande, but patience is not one."

Lysande felt the itch in her palm again. The sensation passed in less than a second. It could have been a spasm under the skin, a fleeting twitch of the muscle, but surely it was stronger than before.

The warrior Titarch, in the Silver Songs, had journeyed through the dunes until she was captured at a waterhole. She had kept her captors talking, grabbed a sword, and slaughtered them. Titarch, Lysande thought, had not been faced with the choice of trying to reach within her doublet without attracting attention or using a scarcely matured weapon that might kill her if she couldn't get it under control.

"Why are you doing this?" she said. "Even beyond this splintered thing between us, you told me you owed Sarelin everything you had."

"Oh, I owed her what I had, all right," Derset replied, his eyes narrowing. "Seven years in the cultural wasteland of Belága, bending my knee. Twelve years in an outpost by the western wall, making excuses for the exploits of drunken border guards . . . sweating over agreements that would be forgotten when Sarelin Brey changed her mind. Removed from every comfort of Axium, every friend I had, in a job I could never rise from. A third child, with no glory." He gave a harsh laugh. "I doubt she thought of me, between hunting and drinking. After spending my whole childhood studying law, I was pushed out to serve those barbarians as envoy—and your queen made Pelory Mistress of Laws. Pelory!" The utterance of the name was almost a curse. "The woman whose biggest sacrifice for the crown was giving up her gold-stitched doublet!"

She hated Pelory, Lysande thought, remembering the day that Sarelin had agonized over the appointment in her suite, weighing up the talents and shortcomings of each candidate. As she looked at Derset, she recognized the flush in his cheeks.

"When you spoke of her, it was like hearing of a goddess," she said.

"Perhaps I loved her. For half a spring. And still longer than she loved me. Love was a new colt to her; she rode it once and then changed it when she knew its moods. She was never without a fresh mount."

Derset's lip was curling—the first sign of anger since he had burned his robe—and she could see herself scorched like that cloth if Sarelin's name passed through her lips again. It was never really grief, she thought. Not really. Those times he had turned his countenance away from her, he had been hiding this—the kind of rage that had boiled too long—yet she had seen what she herself felt. Had she not written her own pain onto his face?

"It must have taken a lot of skill, to deceive everyone after you joined the White Queen. I have to admire you, despite everything." She dropped her voice to a murmur. "Convincing me for so long. Most people would take years to learn that kind of skill."

"Oh, it was simple." He smiled. "I knew the two words most powerful to an orphan."

"Which are?"

"'My lady.'"

Now she wanted to scream at herself for being so stupid, yet her palm itched again, reminding her what she was aiming at. *Keep talking, like Titarch.*

"The poem you were reading—Inara's sonnet. Wanting to be hunted. Wanting to be pierced by love. Was that in memory of Sarelin, too?"

"I bribed a page-boy to tell me about your chamber in the staff tower, before we met. What you kept there. What you cherished most. He sounded impressed by the sight of your translations; according to the little sneak, you had eight volumes of Inara."

Lysande bit down on an angry retort. "When you responded to my touch," she said, "how much of it was real?"

"How much of anything is real? When we feign at playing a personage from dawn till dusk, how much of the actor becomes the role?"

She shook her head. "I have been a fool."

"Or have I been?" He was not smiling any more. "It began with feigning. That much, I admit."

She drew a shaky breath. "Let us not wander from the point. That point is your decision—which may yet be changed. Look beyond your fury. You know it was ignorance that truly kept the rulers of this realm from reaching out to elementals, Henrey."

"Of course, you would defend the crown. You were raised by a tyrant. Once she walked in starlight for me, too, every step gilded, as firm as the goddess of valor." He looked away, a vein in his forehead pushing outward, as if it might break free of the skin and form an angry spur. "Believe me, I understand why you feel as you do, making excuses for her—I'm sure you've spent your life being told the Iron Queen was good and the White Queen bad, and it's made the brute into an idol for you. But there can be no defense of her kind."

The itch in her palm was growing by the second. She would have given a hundred cadres to rake her nails across and claw at the flesh.

"You're wrong," she said. "I loved Sarelin. She was the only person who ever loved me. In a way, she taught me how to love. But I know some of her deeds were unjust. She shouldn't have let the executions go on. We should have welcomed the hidden people among us and written their freedoms out in ink, not flecked their bodies with the sacred paint of their own blood."

It hurt to say the words. If Sarelin was an idol, the statue had been smashed ever since she understood how Charice could flee from a mob, how a young boy in the desert could wear the face of a skeleton, and how she herself could feel like one of the enemy.

"You must see, though, Henrey," she said, "crushing women and men while we raise elementals is not the answer. Diversity is our strength. Is that not our motto?" She held her expression firmly in place. "And if you think the people need another silverblood enshrining a hierarchy, no matter whether she calls herself Brey or Tacitus . . . then you fail to understand the populace at all."

The fund for the poor, the survey of the realm, the law about vigilantes. They were not final measures but the beginning of a process.

This is where it all pivots.

He stared at her, and she caught a glimpse of the Derset she had known, though it was trapped under something else. He rose from his chair and walked over to her.

"I'll give you one minute to choose," he said, laying a hand on her shoulder. "You gave me your time, after all." The words landed heavily upon her.

The itch in her palm spread and burned with a fury that surprised her, and she grabbed hold of her hand, realizing, too late, that she had not hidden her concern from his view.

"It's not possible," Derset said, his eyes flicking to her palm. "It should take three weeks . . ."

Lysande winced again. Unlike the pains before her transformation, the burning did not seem to be disappearing. *Three weeks.* It had only been nine days since her maturation, as Luca had reminded her. Every soldier in the room was staring at her.

The sound of footsteps echoed outside. A moment later, a Periclean woman burst through the door, panting. Lysande impelled her knees not to quake.

"My lord, Raquefort said to send word. We're losing ground."

"What?" Derset stared.

"The Rhimese. They came out of the gardens. It was like a flood of black. At least three hundred, my lord. And the Axium Guards have been carving up our force—their second group poured out of the palm garden." Lysande realized, with a jolt, that this news meant hope.

"Goddesses below." Derset added a curse Lysande had not imagined he was capable of voicing, and squeezed the dove. "I thought we had the Rhimese and Axiumites trapped."

"They must have moved before the ball. There are too many of them. After Captain Hartleigh fell, that other Axium captain led the whole force forward, calling out Hartleigh's name as a battle cry." The woman directed her gaze down. "There are elementals in their army, too. Two of them. Every time we seem to gain some ground, they shoot fire and air at the chimera."

Showing her pleasure did not seem like the wisest course. So Luca must have lied to her about the number of his guards. Most inconveniently, it seemed, she could not be angry at him now.

And Chidney, rallying the guards in Raden's name. Her heart did not dare to knock against her ribs. She hoped that Litany was watching out for the captain as they fought, shadowing her amidst the tangle of bodies, arrowheads, and gore-flecked steel.

"And the Councillors?" Derset said. "Tell me, did Crake, Raquefort, and that idiot Rimini do their job?"

"They're trying, my lord. But the big Valderran and the blonde boy are fighting side by side, and every time they get near one, the other one steps in to defend." Lysande had an image of Dante and Jale working together to fight off their enemies. It was not a pleasant one for the enemies. Alone, Dante's axe-swinging would have sundered bone and gristle, and alone, Jale's leaping and weaving would have seen fighters cornered, but together . . .

"We can't break the Pyrrhan ranks, either, though Raquefort's doing her best," the messenger said.

Even as Lysande's shoulders tensed, she forced herself not to make a sound.

Derset put the dove down on the table. His hand movements were becoming less and less controlled. "And Fontaine?"

The woman looked down and stammered over her answer for a moment. "My lord," she said, "Fontaine is—"

The next word came out in a gargle. Spit flew from the soldier's lips; her eyes bulged, and an arrowhead protruded from her chest. She staggered, but the cry in her throat did not find its way out.

"Late," a cool voice said.

The woman toppled to the floor. Luca stepped around her body and walked into the observatory, only to be seized by half a dozen guards; his arms were pulled behind his back, his bow snatched, and his quiver of arrows removed from his hand, but he did not attempt to struggle. The Pericleans marched him over and shoved him into the chair opposite Lysande. She saw that his doublet had been smeared with blood across the swathes of red silk. Smoothing down his sleeves, he smiled at her.

Not for the first time, Lysande thought that Luca Fontaine might be a little bit mad.

Several of the captains strode over to Derset and exchanged words. As they talked, Lysande leaned across to Luca. "Three hundred Rhimese archers?" she whispered. "Did you forget to mention those?"

"As I recall, you said you only had a hundred guards. There was at least double that number carving up the Pericleans back there. Interesting arithmetic, no?"

The fiery itching in her palm flared up again, prompting her to wince.

Derset walked back, and the captains dropped back a little to allow him to approach the end of the table, where he loomed over Luca. "Here he is. The clever prince of Rhime."

His eyes flicked from Luca to Lysande after he spoke. He was watching for her reaction, she realized, belatedly, and the look betrayed something more than passing interest.

"Oh dear. Lovers' quarrel?" Luca said.

"We're not—" Lysande began, just as Derset said, "Something like that."

Luca's face was impossible to read. Derset passed Luca's bow to one of the captains, who dropped it on the floor and stamped on it. The woman's boots snapped the frame.

"That little trick of yours with the Bastillonians wasn't bad," Luca said. "Making them think we ambushed them—nothing says 'we're tearing up the agreement' quite like a flaming prince, does it? But if you lose today, you must know, it'll count for nothing. I'll win back Ferago." Luca smiled. "One of my people's already got her hooks into Merez."

Lysande remembered Carletta Freste walking arm in arm with Gabrella Merez. She wanted to groan for missing the importance of the detail.

"Boast all you like. You're an arrogant half-breed." Derset's lip curled again. "You should have stayed in your castle in Rhime or stuck to banditry like your brother. A bastard has no business in ruling."

"Ah." Luca leaned back in his chair. "I'm afraid you're ignoring the difference between my brother and I. Raolo was a bastard by nature, you see, a real venomous, black-livered, ill-natured scraping of a man; whereas I'm just a bastard by name."

"I couldn't care less."

"Perhaps you should. It's odd that you, with all your schemes and tricks, never found the time to give my name some thought. My mother was born in Lyria, you see, and she knew the desert long before she sought work in an eastern castle. She gave me my name. And in ancient Lyrian, Fontaine means . . ."

Lysande remembered walking through the courtyard in Castle Sapere, watching the water flow with no source; standing in front of the water mill that had produced its own light in Luca's castle and wondering how it worked; crouching behind the pavilion at the ball and hearing Carletta Freste say, "Prince Fontaine designed the fountains in the pools." She saw the jets and arcs of water that had put out the chimeran fire in the battle: jets to which Three had refused all claim after they splashed and quenched the flames; and she saw Luca standing by the great fountain under the Lyrian sun, giving her the clue that she had not recognized.

In the ancient Lyrian, it was "fontaine de vivre."

"Water," she said, softly. "*Fontaine* means *water.*"

The blast of liquid caught most of the guards and knocked them over, flooding the room. Derset's legs slipped out from under him, and he grabbed on to the side of the table. Luca blasted the guards again, curving the jet of water around; Lysande had never seen anything like this, even in the weeks since meeting Three. The power of the tide from Luca's palm swept everything in its path.

Vases jumped from their shelves. Glasses smashed on the floor, fracturing into shards, and the screams of the Pericleans cut through the air as they were washed from the observatory. Over the edge and into the blackness they tumbled, flailing as they fell.

"Get back, Prior," Luca shouted.

He took her by the hand and pulled her into the doorway. The touch felt molten, a shock of skin. They both unclasped their fingers. Pausing for less than a breath, he held his arm out and sent out a fresh flood. The wave whipped around the room, aiming for the guards who were clutching the furniture. As he controlled it, his eyes flashed black fire, glinting and flaring. She gaped for a moment, watching his countenance harden, until she realized that some of the Pericleans were copying Derset and grabbing hold of the table.

There was an opportunity here. No one was going to stop her if she moved first, surely. She reached inside her doublet and drew a dagger out, and the blade came smoothly from the pocket, so smoothly, as if it wanted to be free.

"Prior, I won't tell you again! Go to the battle! Tell the others to come up!"

But she was not listening: her eyes were assessing the position of the chandelier.

One throw would be enough if she could hit the half-loosened bolt at the top. She lined up her eye with the target, and her hand with her eye, concentrating hard. No need to dwell on the old chant now— *restrain, constrain, subdue* was a motto for a different woman, a woman who now resided in the past. Lysande's wrist flicked.

The dagger did not fly. It dropped as flames came out crimson-bright from her palm. Her flesh burned fiercely, yet somehow, she felt no pain.

The fire flowed from her without her control; it shot out and sped to the top of the chandelier, and she watched it as if she were watching a spectacle put on by somebody else. For the first time, even the return of her craving could not distract her, the yearning now lowering its head beneath a force of her own making. It curled up, dulled, but not gone. The flames burned with an incandescent luster until the metal had melted through, dissolved, and the whole structure gave a lurch.

Prior, she thought. *Fire. Luca was right. There was no coincidence at all.*

Tiers of pointed crystal dropped onto the table and the floor, spearing whatever they landed on. Screams rose above the roar of water and flames: a guard floundered with a piece of crystal in his neck, collapsing onto a woman in a helmet who had been impaled three times through the back, her body spread-eagled on the floor. Lysande saw mercenaries scramble out of the wreckage, coughing. They were swept by Luca's tide, and only one managed to duck in time: a captain cowered under a half-smashed chair, shouting a curse.

Lysande bent over, gulping down air. The fire that had come out of her hand had left her drained. Her chest ached, and her mind seemed to be going in multiple directions. Looking up, she noticed something moving on her right.

"Look out!" she cried. "Luca!"

Bloodied arms wrapped around Luca's body as Derset tackled the prince to the ground, smacking him into the stone. The two of them rolled over and over. Luca seized Derset by the hair, but Derset twisted free of his grip and slammed Luca bodily against a table leg. Lysande had no time to intervene, nor to regret the accident of using Luca's first name: she dodged a dagger whistling past her head, and looking up, she saw the soldier with the chimera on her breastplate, clutching a longsword, running at her.

The fire would not return. She was pathetically weak, like a fevered patient who had been bedridden for a week, and she fumbled at her doublet.

Still undoing the buttons, she ducked under the woman's arm as she charged. She should have been dead in an instant, but somehow, she was running past. She doubted that she could really reach into her pockets to draw a dagger in time to avoid being slaughtered, and then she remembered Sarelin forcing her to move, telling her to stop thinking. *Be the blade.* Her hand pulled a dagger free, and she positioned it with a firm grip while she counted to three, then whirled around, just in time for it to meet the neck of the soldier coming at her.

The woman stared, her eyes opening wide. Lysande pulled the blade out of her throat. It emerged red.

She lowered her weapon slowly. The woman unfastened her armor and lay on her back, chest heaving. The crest on her doublet gleamed in bronze thread. No—not a crest, but the head of Fortituda, goddess of valor. The same goddess Sarelin had sworn by. The soldier's breathing ceased.

"Prior, if you're going to do me the indignity of rescuing me, now would be a good time," a voice called behind her.

Lysande spun around. Luca and Derset had moved on from wrestling on the floor and were fighting rapier to rapier, so furiously that neither had a chance to cast their element. Perhaps they were emptied and weak, like herself. Luca was slashing quickly, but Derset was no poor swordsman.

"Really, Prior, any time now!"

She sprinted closer to them, summoning all the strength in her body, until she was nearly in a delirium of effort, holding her palm out. No flames coursed through her fingers. Clenching her teeth and endeavoring to imagine her fire, she felt the dead weight of her arms and assessed her odds of throwing another dagger with any accuracy.

Shuffling through all her memories of Sarelin, Lysande searched for something: a piece of wisdom or advice that would guide her; and the gold dagger and gold quill Sarelin had presented her with aligned in her mind. *Blades and words.*

She reached inside the doublet for the quill and found herself probing an empty pocket. It was gone. She reached again. No stem; it was really gone. The fact bounced around her mind, rebounding and rebounding, until she forced herself to move past it.

"Did I ever tell you that I am a third child?" she called out.

Derset had Luca pinned to a wall, their rapiers crossed, but the pair of them looked across at her.

"You said that to me, Henrey, while we stood with the sand of the Arena caking our boots and the crowd baying around us. You offered me a piece of your life, just the right size for me to grasp, memory-hewn. 'You can learn to stand before crowds . . . even to like it.' You added that. I remember how my feet became a little firmer when I heard you say it. Not because I believed your words, but because I could tell you believed in me. I don't think you had a single strategic thought in your head when you put your hand on my shoulder."

"Lysande." Derset's voice wavered, raw.

"And the time you saved me on board the ship." She took a step toward him. He was still standing on the flood-slicked stone, his blade pressed against Luca's. "Those weren't your people attacking us. You didn't know the fire was coming. When you pulled me out of the path of a speeding fireball, you were acting of free will."

He looked as if he was about to speak, but she plowed on.

"Oh, you tried to use it against Luca, later, to drive a wedge between us, but in that moment, you weren't thinking about maneuvers or what the White Queen might do to you, were you? You were listening to that part of yourself that says you care about me every bit as much as I do you. Just as you did that night in Rhime . . ." *When you lay beneath me and made paths through the coppices of my hunger.* "That's why you've stopped fighting to listen to me, now."

The top of Derset's head dipped almost imperceptibly. His hands remained fixed, one on his rapier and one holding Luca's arm, yet for all the strength of his grip there was something softening in his demeanor. She willed herself not to see it.

"You should be at my side," he said. "The way I've been at yours. Don't fight the wave that is coming, Lysande. Let it carry you to higher ground."

"And submerge everyone else?"

"Not everyone. Not a single elemental who doesn't deserve it."

They stood opposite each other, and for a moment there seemed to be nobody else in the room, just Derset and Lysande, the two of them calling to each other in a language that had no letters, no words. They might have been in the Oval again, after everyone else had left, or in her bedchamber, while the fireplace crackled and sparked, and the touch of her lips against his collarbone and his fingertips against her thigh blazed—into something that a fireplace could not have held—the force of his belief in her flaring, nourishing the stalks within her. The world had dissolved, leaving them alone, and the breeze died as she took a step toward him, the air welcoming her.

Derset's rapier scraped as it moved.

Lysande's eyes flicked to Luca. The prince lunged at once, and she could not help but admire how smoothly he took the signal, forcing Derset's blade back an inch or so, both arms pushing Derset's sword-hand down. Derset struck Luca's rapier and sent it flying with a triumphant shout, but Luca held his palm up, almost lazily, and a flood hit Derset in the face, knocking him backward across the shards of crystal and wood and bloodied bodies to the end of the room. He landed against the wall, gasping.

The flash of satisfaction across Luca's face did not escape her.

A slapping of boots sounded and a few seconds later, Litany burst through the doorway. Lysande held up a palm and her attendant skidded to a halt.

She turned back to Derset, in time to see him sit up and scoop something into his hand. It was a ball of gray feathers, Lysande saw, staring as he whispered something to it. At once, she remembered the purpose of the dove.

"Stop him!" she screamed. "He's going to bring the White Queen here!"

Everything seemed to occur at once, across the room, in an odd and contemporaneous balance: Litany drew a dagger; Luca channeled his powers, wincing; and Lysande stumbled forward, her legs as hollow as the rest of her. She could see it all occurring in a motion that had slowed to a crawl, even as something stirred inside her. It rose and sprouted and wrapped its tendrils around her bones, this thing, and it told her that in a second, she could reach the target before any of them.

Derset had tossed the bird into the air, yet it stopped, mid-flap, to dangle like a puppet between acts of a show. She could hear its heart beating inside her head, a quick beat that sped faster by the second, and the thing inside her said that she could stop that drum with her will, could make it silent once and for all.

She looked over to the dove and focused her gaze on its body. The black eyes flickered, and the wings slowed.

All she had to do was stare, hold it in place, and reach out with her mind.

This is dangerous, a voice in her head told her, and another voice replied: *Yes. I know.*

With a hand she could only feel, not see, she reached into the suspended bird's chest. The dove's black eyes darted from side to side. She grasped the heart and squeezed it in her invisible hand. The animal shivered.

In a fraction of a second, she stopped the heartbeat.

The gray ball of feathers plummeted and hit the stone. It did not move after it landed, not even to give a last flap of its wings. Derset rushed over and picked it up, shaking the dove with both hands.

Her whole body was coursing with a thrill. It was charged with some kind of energy, and she reveled in it.

Litany dashed across the floor, kicking a sword over to Lysande, then grabbed Derset's hands and pulled them behind his back. Luca joined her and wrestled Derset around to face Lysande.

"The owner gives a dog its mercy," he said, wrapping one arm around her advisor's neck. "Do you want to give the blow, Prior? Or shall I?"

Of course, Luca expected her to decide, as if she were merely snapping her fingers. Of course, he could do this kind of thing without thinking—without blinking—she knew that he could turn a weapon on someone in the hair-fine breadth of a moment, as he had by the fountain, when the attacker nearly ran him through. And she had seen the bodies swinging at Ferizia, from the arch. But she did not have a childhood in Rhime to prepare her for this circumstance.

She picked up the sword from the floor. It weighed heavily, the kind of blade that some grim warrior would use in a story to enact justice, and she could just see herself holding it up; pretending that taking a life was some kind of duty; teaching the world a lesson.

"No," she said.

This was not a lesson for anyone but herself.

"Prior, I know you love to contradict me at every turn," Luca said. "But now is not the time for mercy."

"I didn't say to let him go."

The sword clattered onto the stone. Everyone turned to her. The thrill was still running through her body.

I killed the dove.

She focused her mind on Derset, in the same way that she had focused on the bird, and within seconds, she could hear his heartbeat.

An ordinary sound, steady; a timekeeper's rhythm. It would be so easy to snuff it out, like the beat of that little, gray, feathered thing.

"Give me one answer. You owe me one honest answer, for all the lies, Henrey. It was you who poisoned Sarelin, wasn't it?"

Silence filled the observatory.

"You're the closest of the White Queen's servants. She wouldn't trust it to anyone but the Umbra, would she?" Lysande said, staring into his eyes. "You'd planned and practiced for years . . . it was your hand that tipped the chimera blood into the jug."

"I told you the day I met you, in the crypt." Derset held her gaze. "There are assassins who know the ways of silence."

"All this time you were working to bring us down, but did you feel any remorse? Just once, for the Council, or for me?"

He nodded, as much as Luca's arm would let him. "For you?" he said. "A great deal."

The look on his face told her all that his words did not. It was infused with the same melancholy she had glimpsed before, when he had asked her to choose whether to join him. It was full of the embraces that had transformed into shared notes, in the music of two bodies entangled in a foreign bedchamber, each of them learning the other's breathing. She tried not to allow her response; tried to blot out the sentiment that swelled.

"And for Sarelin? When you tipped the vial into her medicine, when you unleashed the panther in the forest, did you feel any remorse for the woman who defended the realm?"

"That's a much easier question to answer." His smile returned now. "Never. The brute deserved to die."

She was standing in the forest again with Sarelin, and the queen was sheathing her dagger.

Any soldier can kill something she hates, she heard Sarelin say. *It's only when you kill something you've come to love that you learn how to lead. One day, you'll understand that, Lys.*

The air was fresh on her cheeks, but Sarelin's hands warmed her shoulders.

Then she was standing by the fire in the Painter's Suite and Derset's hands were on her—warm, too, like his words—holding her close to him. He was sitting by her side in the Great Hall as she navigated her way through the conversation, offering hints about the ladies and lords with whom she had never been acquainted. He was lying beneath her, his breath quickening as she ran a single finger along his left hip. He was letting his words melt into a gasp, which in turn became a half-voiced prayer. *That's when I realized: there's more than one kind of queen.* His body pressed against hers, holding her on the deck of the ship, as fire rained over them and struck the wood, and their chests merged into one. Even with smoke around them, he kept her beneath him, shielding her from the flames. Warmth. Nothing but his warmth, and the thump of his heartbeat, fragile and close.

You are her Councillor, appointed on her authority, as a seal presses into wax and marks it out.

His fingers tied the double-woven riding-cloak under her neck. His gaze met hers with new appreciation as she walked toward him at the ball. A smile cracked his face as she attempted a joke about Classical Era homonyms, one night, and though she had not been sure that he understood her pun about lips and speeches, she had known that he was smiling to see her pleased.

Yes, she thought. I understand, Sarelin.

A movement brought her back to the observatory. Litany had picked up the sword, crossed the floor, and was holding it out to her, but she shook her head. Across the wreckage, Luca watched her with all the intensity of his stare.

"There's a dagger in his pocket," she said. "Throw it over here, if you please."

Sarelin's dagger whistled over the floor, and she picked it up and drew it from its sheath. The tip of the blade reflected her face: a determined mask that she scarcely recognized.

"This belonged to the queen of Elira," she said. "She always faced her enemies and looked them in the eye. I want to kill you the way she would've done, Henrey."

There was much less chance of veering off course if she threw quickly enough. The blade spun from her fingers, landed exactly under the rib she wanted, and sank through the doublet. Red blossomed on emerald. She stood, quite still, as Derset began to choke.

A hand nudged her arm. Litany was holding out three daggers, their hilts pointing toward her. Wordlessly, she took them and threw them, one by one, into Derset's chest.

It was curious that she could not feel a sting of pain: nothing but the same energy flowed through her.

She put a hand to her face and wiped her eyes. Her fingers came away dry.

Fifteen

The colors of Lyria encircled the hill in a variegated quilt: here, the swathes of gold sand, and there, the brilliant, coruscating blue of the river, diverging into three paths as it rushed to the sea, while beside the delta, a ring of sandstone buildings teemed with a population twice the size of the capital. Scents of spice, sweat, palm oil, and crushed vanilla leaves mingled. Mosquitoes hovered in clouds, and the sun struck the bald peak, making a blazing crown where Lysande stood.

She unfurled her palm and let the fire sit in the air. The ball of flame wobbled, trembling at the edges. It flickered between almost-blue and almost-orange, and she inhaled and cleared the frustration from her head, watching the fire stabilize with her emotions.

This must have been the place where Oblitara perched, higher than them all, on a rock that afforded no shade. Kicking a stone over the edge, Lysande imagined the great chimera standing on the hill at the end of the Conquest: the queen of hybrid creatures, awaiting death, her scales mirroring the fury of the Lyrian sun.

Footsteps approached. She closed her fist, snuffing the fire out.

"Come on, brooder. They'll be ringing the damned bells any minute," Cassia said.

The palanquin-bearers bumped their way down the stairs. It was hard to avoid looking at Cassia's eye-patch in such a small space. A bronze leopard gleamed on the leather, a badge of color where another woman might have preferred a plain overlay.

As they made their way south, she glimpsed figures through the gap in the curtains, darting into shuttered houses and shops. Black ribbons drooped from door-handles. She remembered Raden: his eyes, still closed by her own fingers, and his body, stretched out inside a coffin barely large enough to hold it; the Axium banner he had kept rolled in his saddle bag, now unfurled by his guards, laid out on his chest. How she had wanted to speak to him, but with the eyes of the Council upon her, she had settled for a whispered farewell. How her heavy feet had dragged her to the next coffin. The man who had served her closest wore a new robe, the dagger-marks on his chest now hidden, the fabric smoothed over; Derset's hair had been brushed back from his face, and in death, he looked like her advisor again.

The surge of anger that she had expected did not come. She had taken out the chain that he had given her, fingering the silver. A pezzo-vita, the Rhimese called the tradition. It had taken some time to select an item to represent the life of the deceased. When she had reached the edge of the coffin, she had stroked the chain one last time before letting it fall onto Derset's chest.

"I wanted to be the first to say goodbye."

Cassia's voice jolted her back. They were passing through the plea-sure quarter of Lyria, weaving through a group of men in near-transparent robes, one of whom followed the palanquin, waving at Cassia and Lysande through the gap in the curtains, his bracelets jin-gling. "I know you've been busy, dispatching doves," the Irriqi said, "but I wanted to check you weren't plunged into despair. You know, after what happened with your—"

"I appreciate it," Lysande said quickly. "I want to thank you, actu-ally. For what you did in the battle. Taking charge. Jabbing your sword into the white chimera's breast while I was kept from the fight. I imag-ine we'd all be cinders if it weren't for you."

Cassia took her hand in hers and clasped it, their fingers interlacing. The Irriqi said nothing, but she maintained the grip. When Lysande looked across and saw the compassion in that one gleaming eye, she was sure that she didn't need to speak either.

For a long time, she had tried to believe that the livea branch would achieve its goal—that after she had breached the peace between them, a friendship could be rekindled. Even as Cassia had seemed to warm to her again, her doubts about the Irriqi's loyalty had returned, worrying at her as an ice-bear worries at a bone. Now, she had finally sent them away, since fighting an army together whilst a chimera scorched bodies around you could heal the deepest rift. She was not the woman now that she had been weeks ago. She knew what she wanted.

The question was: what did Cassia want?

The palanquin lurched, and a scent of decay wafted to Lysande's nostrils. She looked out into a square where a crowd surrounded a pile of bodies. They passed the makeshift pyre and snaked through the alleys that led to the dock, reaching the leaving party. Lysande's gaze swept the small crowd for tufted brows or an aquiline nose, but she saw no trace of Gabrella Merez and knew that she had guessed correctly about the Bastillonians' anger.

Cassia steered her down the middle of the group. "Swift sailing, my friend."

"The same to you, my friend," Lysande said.

Cassia smiled at the term. "For every mile that you put between us, I shall pray to Vindictus to strike any hand that comes near you."

"I should like our hands to grip the same quill, in a happier state of politics."

"Believe me: when I read your message, I had the will to accept the idea, right in the moment. With *that* position? You might have handed me a letter I wrote myself. But all the good will in the world is no substitute for long hours of contemplation, Lysande, even when the matter concerns a friend. What one commits to, one must be sure of."

Lysande searched for the right words and knew that she had them already. "I watched you wave soldiers forward and charge into battle while steel rained around you. I watched your eye bleed, crimson painting your face with a gory majesty. Already I am drafting a poem about it, and I do not lack for images—the lines leap to my quill." She could hear her voice swelling. "Still you kept coming, swinging that sword, no matter how swiftly they ran at you. You did not seem to know you were invincible. Of course, you are right: what one commits to, one must be sure of. And I am sure of you."

"Then we shall speak soon." Cassia's clapped Lysande on the shoulder. "You sound like a woman battle-forged. I promise, you will have my answer to your proposition when we meet in Axium."

They embraced, and Lysande took a long time to let go, noting that

Cassia's grip had the firmness of Sarelin's. The river of grief that traversed her body blended, now, with a rivulet of joy: the way Cassia faced her attackers head-on, the way she slapped her friends on the shoulder, the way she said whatever was on her mind, with neither trepidation nor shame; these things echoed painfully down the corridors of her memory. She was beginning to understand her instinctive liking for Cassia. If Sarelin's life had been written in Pyrrhan ink . . . might it not have looked like this?

She turned away, and walked over to Dante and Jale, noticing that Jale stood as close to Dante as possible. The prince's hand entwined with the First Sword's, earning sharpened stares from northerners and southerners alike, but Jale pretended not to see them, gripping Dante's fingers tighter still.

"Ah," he said as Lysande arrived, appraising her garments with a sigh. "I see my new cloak was not to your taste."

"It was a sumptuous gift, Your Highness. A little too sumptuous for me. As I tied the laces, I could hear Sarelin telling me I looked like a gilded rooster, puffed up to crow." She glanced across to where Litany stood. "Rest assured, my attendant has packed it carefully."

"Oh, good. Do wear it, during that one week of summer you get in Axium."

"If you will do me the favor of keeping this, in return, for your half-week of winter." Of course, Litany had not missed her cue. The heavy velvet unfolded neatly from her attendant's hands, dropping to reveal the full length of the design, the silver embroidery of the name *Chamboise* curling around a crown. Jale clapped, then seized it.

"But this is personalized! True artistry! I shall wear it sooner than winter—when I reach you in Axium, I shall look just like a local soldier, draped in honest Axium cloth."

Lysande privately reflected upon the likelihood of that, before hugging Jale farewell.

As they pulled apart, she noted the moisture in Jale's eyes and considered how light his tone had been, just now—a little too light for someone who had suffered the loss of his own people. "Jale . . ." She searched for words. "Your sister will not be forgotten, I am sure."

"I intend to build a tomb of white marble, with Élérie's likeness on top, sculpted by the best-trained artist in Lyria. The eyes will be especially detailed—they looked like widening orbs, sleek and bright, when she was talking. The people will see her as she was. Whole, and full of spirit." He gave her a small smile. "You are thoughtful, Lysande, and at the risk of repeating my compliment, you listen well. Spare some of that thoughtfulness for yourself. And make some time to listen to your own grief."

They embraced for much longer this time, and Lysande's eyes were wet too when they drew apart again. She turned to Dante. The two of them bowed, and Lysande searched for something to say that would keep the conversation light, at least on the surface.

"I hope some morning will arrive when we sit together and talk of northern fir trees, and the winter lights of Valderos."

"That we shall." Dante stepped closer to her. "May you grieve Captain Hartleigh in your own time. Years have taught me how to grieve my fallen captains. And one must learn. Take solace in knowing that he died the way he lived: defending the jagged crown of Elira with courage."

It was a soldier's tribute, Lysande thought: clear and unembellished. Not the way she would have phrased it, but the way that Raden would have understood.

"May you grieve your own people, too." She laid a hand on Dante's arm. "And take your own solace with whomever you please."

She saw Jale shoot a swift look in her direction.

As she made to join her party, she felt a hand grip her arm. Sun glanced off a bow, the black frame of which was decorated with tiny silver cobras. Lysande tried to affect nonchalance as she turned; by now, she hoped, she was getting better at it. Luca handed the new bow to Malsante and offered her his arm. He was so close that she could hear every syllable, dropped out in that cool voice. "You've been avoiding me. Studiously. I suppose one should expect that from a scholar."

Their last encounter hung between them, so tangible that Lysande could almost grasp it. She felt the scrutiny of his gaze trickling over her, to her boots. "Come to Axium Palace the night before the meeting, Fontaine."

"Very well." He shrugged. "Where will I find you?"

She thought of his arms around her as they danced, his body under hers in the library, his hand blasting a jet of water into Derset's chest, and the way he had looked at her, in the observatory, with his doublet covered in blood.

She thought of how he had raised his palm and sent dozens of guards flailing into the jet-rich depths of the night.

"You won't," she said. "I'll find you."

Now that she could summon fire from her flesh, Lysande would have been satisfied with Litany as her only escort, yet she had a feeling that even if she had been able to explain the situation to her guards, Chidney would not have accepted being parted from Litany's side. The captain hovered around her attendant, somehow managing to stay close to Litany while keeping the soldiers in order, handing Litany a pouch when she needed a drink and offering her an extra cloak. Lysande surrendered to the inevitability of an entourage. They led their horses from the ship and set off into the central scrub, casting a last glance at the Grandfleuve.

The road seemed uneven, but the horses' hooves flew over it. Villages sped past. Lysande saw eyes peeping at her out of the windows of houses, only to disappear again.

A crossroads approached: Axium to the north, Rhime to the east. They were trotting down the Scarlet Road for a few minutes before her mare reached a lump in the road.

"Stop!" Litany shouted, pulling her horse's reins.

As Lysande dismounted and walked over, she saw the lump move. Something sank inside her, but she had seen bodies dripping with blood, by now, and had spilled blood herself, and she gathered herself with only a moment's pause. Clouds hunkered above the treetops. She bent over the form of a soldier, noting the ring in the man's ear and the word in foreign script that hung on a bronze disc around his neck: a word carved in one of the wayfarer scripts from the Periclean States. Rolling up the man's sleeve, she took in the chimera brand on his wrist, black as new ink.

He wheezed, and Lysande's gaze slipped downward. A fish hook had ripped the bottom of the man's stomach, and she repressed a noise of disgust; he could have lain here for days. The hook had driven into the belly, cutting through layers of flesh without causing much blood to leak. Every exhalation had to be an agony.

"A half-death." There was grim recognition in Litany's voice, and Lysande looked up. "I think someone's taken justice into their own hands, after the battle."

Lysande took the mercenary's arms. Wordlessly, Litany took hold of his feet. It required both of their strength to drag the man into the shade of the closest tree, and she gestured to the guards to keep their distance; she considered sending her attendant away when it was done, for experience told her that Litany could keep the guards at bay, but after a lengthy pause, she beckoned Litany closer.

The man's breathing reminded her of a stag Sarelin had killed. A poor shot, unusual for the queen, had left it with a punctured lung, until Sarelin's sword put it out of its misery. A man was not a stag, however. She would not strip the humanity from him, as someone else had sought to do.

"I know a way that might be swift."

The soldier looked up at her. He did not attempt to reply; the nod he gave was so tiny that it might have been a tremor, yet it was enough.

"Councillor, if you would rather I leave—"

"No." She met Litany's eyes, above the dying man. "I need you to see this."

There was a difference between *want* and *need*. You could not comprehend that difference easily, in the inked phrases of a definition; only when you were in the middle of *need* yourself, sinking to your knees in its alluvium, searching the horizon for a figure, any figure, to haul you out of the cloying sediment, did you understand what it meant to be without choice. Nobody merely wanted to be pulled free by a firm hand. Nobody merely *wanted* to be seen.

She thought about how little time she had had to think when she had used her power in front of Luca, Derset, and a room full of mercenaries. Looking down the road, now, she saw only leaves stirring and a few motes of dust dancing in the faint breeze.

It was a danger, of a kind, to spend your life in perpetual shadow—was it not? Did hidden people need to make themselves visible? Was it not an act as fundamental to survival as drinking water, eating bread, and breathing air?

Her gaze locked on Litany's once more. Briefly, she put a finger to her lips.

She dropped to her knees, not touching the man. This was not like moving an element, where she could channel the fire in her veins. The power resided in her head, not her body, and she knew she had to wait. She reached out with her mind.

The pulse came clearly. She felt the *thump-thump*, looked down, saw his eyes widen, and closed her phantom hand around his heart. Without hesitation, she squeezed.

The man gave a wordless cry. Lysande compressed his heart until it burst and his lungs ceased to strain, and she felt his primal self dissolving, disappearing into the air, slipping into translucence while his body fell back against the ground. His head slumped. The pendant slid across his chest and he lay still, the look in his eyes neither pained nor peaceful, but empty of everything.

She stood up, the same energy coursing through her again.

It took a few moments for her to notice the way that Litany was looking at her now, and to read all the shades of emotion in that gaze: awe, fear, respect, concern, and something she could not quite make out. Lysande held out her palm and let a jet of flame flow upward, forming a small fireball, before she closed her palm and snuffed the fire out.

"I'll allow you four questions."

If she had to pick a number, she would pick the number that Sarelin had always used: the number of the goddesses.

Litany rose, facing her. "Have you always been one of them?"

"No. There was a process of transformation, and I discovered it that way. That is why I was laid up in bed, in the palace . . . they call it a maturation."

"So you *were* hiding something!" Litany's exclamation was almost a yelp. "And you went through it alone!"

"Is that another question?"

"No." A smile flitted across Litany's face. "Rather, I would know . . . what is it like, to use such a power?"

There was almost a hunger in her eyes, now. Lysande hesitated.

"There is nothing I can compare it to. Killing with magic is beyond any other act, Litany. It is like itself. That is all."

It is like drinking without raising a wineskin to your lips. It is like swimming without ever holding your breath. It is like kissing a stranger and then pushing a honed rapier into their chest, hilt-deep. It is like waking to the scent of crushed paradisiac after a long storm. It is like the dance of a quill on a perfectly blank sheet of paper. It is like soaring.

"It must feel easy, or hard, to some degree."

"Adroit of you, to use a comment as a question." Lysande tried to whittle down her thoughts. "It feels both easy and hard at once."

Litany cast a look at the mercenary's expressionless face. The mixture of jealousy and curiosity in her glance did not escape Lysande.

"You, and the people who aided us in the battle, and your friend . . . will you ever throw your support behind the White Queen?" Litany's voice trembled slightly.

Lysande knew what it cost her to ask that. She respected the courage of the question, even as something less generous in her resented the implication.

"Anyone I work with is, to the best part of my knowledge, staunchly opposed to her. Listen to me, Litany." She expected to hear her own voice trembling, too, but somehow, it held firm. "Everything I did, when I first took up the Councillor's staff . . . I did it for Sarelin. And with every week that passed, I have learned that that is not enough. It is not easy to learn about the savagery of the woman you loved above all things; but I have learned. I do not find her faultless. If I must remedy her wrongs, though, I will do so for my supporters: for my base." She was speaking too quickly. How did one sound heroic? *Should* one sound heroic? "I mean, for the people who move the elements, and the people who move nothing but sacks of grain. I will knit this populace together." She laid her hand upon Litany's arm. "The White Queen will unravel it until there is nothing left but the hungry points of needles."

She felt the chill of exposure. In speaking of such things, and in using her power of the mind, she had laid herself bare, twice over, and now she waited . . . and waited. So this was what it felt like to be seen.

"I cannot claim to be a true Axiumite heroine, Litany. I have worked in the shadows, sometimes, when I could not work in the light."

Slowly, the girl nodded. "Working in the shadows. That, I know well."

"If we are to continue down this road together, you must accept what I am. You must accept it and support it. In return, I would offer you a greater role, by which I do not only mean money, but a position that everyone recognizes. You shall be my Mistress of Defense, newly created."

Litany placed her hand upon Lysande's. "I accept your nature. Not that it is my right to accept or no. I know you bear no love for the White Queen; I have seen what you risk."

"And the position?"

"It is a lot to consider."

"Then consider it." Lysande patted her hand once and let go. "Give me your answer when you can be sure. I shall appoint no one else in the meantime."

She folded the mercenary's arms across his chest, brushed his sleeves, and turned back to the road. She had barely taken a stride when Litany's voice called after her.

"You owe me a fourth question."

"Catch up, then." Lysande smiled at the ground.

Noiselessly, Litany closed the distance to reach her side. When she spoke again, it was in a much quieter voice. "Did you enjoy . . . releasing him from suffering?"

Lysande swung onto her mare and turned to the road ahead. A nod was all she managed as she glanced across at Litany, but she felt sure that the girl understood.

The palette of Rhimese colors spread over the land again, bright, but not glaring like the desert. The Flavantine could be glimpsed from time to time, meandering between pairs of conical trees or flowing alongside cobbled streets; from hidden alleys and walled gardens, the voices of water murmured. Lysande pressed a hand to her temple as they guided their horses through a town arch. She was not distracted. It was just that the thought of mixing blue flakes, sugar, and water, of heating the ingredients and watching them shiver and melt, listening to the soft fizzing of the liquid, and drinking . . . then feeling the anvil-blows in her chest and the burning of her forehead, before a hard-won taste of oblivion . . . it all prompted a pang to run through her. Every now and then she clutched the reins a little too tightly, and the leather bit into her palm.

The closer they got to Pescarra, the more her thoughts slipped. She noticed the temptations of Pescarra's cheese-sellers without stopping, leading Litany to an inn tucked at the end of an alley where a fig tree spread its branches. Her attendant stood guard outside.

The door on the second floor did not yield. Lysande knocked.

"Who goes there?" a woman said.

"One who brings fire without carrying wood."

The door creaked open and offered a sliver of a burned cheek. A second later, Six pulled it open. "Your aim's getting better, I hope," she said, waving Lysande through.

Lysande could not quite hide her smile. She did not need to ask where to go—there was only one door at the end of the room, and in the next room, a double window greeted her, admitting a deluge of light.

"Ah, Signore Prior." Three looked up from the table, his hair spilling across his shoulders. "Anyone who could resist Pescarran smoked would be an uncouth boor. Have a bite."

He pulled out a chair. She sat, and took a piece of smoked cheese from his plate. The taste was enough to prevent her from speaking. As Six took the chair beside them, Lysande did not miss the glance that passed between the two Shadows members; nor did she miss the small mark on Three's wrist, shining unusually bright against his skin, like a smudge of oil.

Perhaps the Shadows have their own kind of discipline, she thought. Or perhaps he merely got it in the battle.

"I am sorry for your loss, my dear."

The statement caught her in the chest. She had expected a question about the Council or a comment about the battle—something practical and straightforward.

"We were close; I am sure you understand how it can come to be like that. I have tried to reconcile all I knew of Lord Derset with his betrayal."

"Indeed." Three raised an eyebrow. "But I was referring to Captain Hartleigh."

A tide of guilt ran through Lysande, crashing against inner rocks. "Let us make sure Raden did not die in vain, then. Let us meet the White Army's power," she said.

Both of them, Lysande suspected, were now thinking of soldiers dropping from the air, landing wherever the White Queen wished to put them. She tried not to shiver.

"I shall not attempt to conceal what we now know: Chamsak had the eggs." Three shook his head. "We should have guessed, but *a weapon* sounded like some kind of device."

Lysande pictured Six driving back the chimeras with her air, once more. She felt less than triumphant, though, when she remembered the way the golden orbs had regarded her during the battle, the jade eyes, too, locking on to her own.

"Let us speak of strategy in a little while. I have plenty of suggestions." Three leaned back in his chair, his sharp features half-lit by the sun, half in shadow. Lysande was conscious of Six straightening against the wall, and of both their gazes. "There is a woman you will need to work with. Have I mentioned that we have agreed to take on a new member? She insisted upon waiting in the garden. Indeed, she seemed to take a great interest in speaking with you."

The oranges had ripened in the little haven behind the inn. Sunlight poured through the gap in the trees, the branches trimmed just enough that they did not meet, a golden line separating the two halves of the garden. Lysande made her way to the stone bench under one of the trees and sat, facing the woman on the opposite side, watching her companion's fingers peel back the skin of an orange.

"I thought you would have been loath to bargain with them," she said.

Charice looked up from the fruit. "I made my terms. As did you."

"I hear we are to work together," Lysande said. "Did he win you over to the cause? Or did you make the link yourself: the defeat of the White Queen and, in time, with it, a shift to elemental rights?"

"In time. Yes, I can imagine that suits you. You've always had time, inside those palace walls. Perhaps I don't want to wait my turn, though."

Lysande saw the clenching of Charice's jaw, a tiny movement, but significant if you knew how well Charice could dissemble. "Do I have to get on my knees and beg you to stay?"

"I was always the one on my knees. Or have you forgotten?"

"I'm not good at forgetting. There's a talent to it. Sarelin said I was born with a different set of skills, you see." Lysande paused, for just a second. "There must be a way to tackle elemental rights. A strategy. I intend to plan it thoroughly, and to act."

"I suppose I should wrap myself in your promise, for now, and use it as armor?"

Lysande held her gaze. "Will you leave the Shadows as soon as you have joined, then?"

"Not when I'm so looking forward to our next adventure." Charice took a bite of her orange and rose, walking toward Lysande, the fruit still cupped in her palm. Lysande walked to meet her. The two columns of trees cast shadows over them, the light that passed through the gap in the branches throwing Charice's mouth into relief.

"You should understand something," Charice said. "I am bound by no one, and I give myself to no one. Perhaps the Shadows deserve all the medicines and poisons and other things I can bestow, and perhaps you deserve to shape the realm in your own way . . . with all the time you need. But perhaps there is not so much time to spare." She tossed the orange onto the ground. "Perhaps the realm is a garden whose fruit trees droop, and if you do not pluck the fruit now, it will fall, and land where it may."

Lysande took her hand very slowly, folded it, and kissed the fingers. Moving around in a circle, she lifted Charice's hair and kissed her friend on the nape of the neck, the same place she had kissed many times while they lay talking or listening to each other's breathing, their chests rising and falling with the same rhythm. Charice's breathing quickened, but when Lysande came back around to face her, Charice's mouth was a tight seam, offering no entry.

"Are you with me?" Lysande said, offering her arm.

"I see no better option. For now."

"Sometimes I think you will slip into Severelle's middle space, where things are never certain, and stay there forever."

"It sounds tempting. I'll give you that." Charice did not take her arm. "But we can only dream of such places. In life, we must choose."

And bear our choices, Lysande thought, turning slowly and walking away.

Roses lay piled at the fence for Raden, and green ribbons fluttered on the posts, farewelling all the dead. It was a struggle to keep from speaking, and Lysande almost succeeded at hiding her grief as she brought Litany around to the eastern gate of Axium Palace. No sooner had she slipped through than she was shown to the Great Hall, where the ladies and lords formed legions in jewels, armed with questions: Had she a mind to put the court in mourning, or throw a banquet to celebrate the victory? How would Elira defend itself against the White Queen? Were they equipped for the other chimera's return? The advisors did not speak, but their glares did the talking for them. Only Lady Bowbray congratulated Lysande on her "expert management of castles she had never been invited to enter," her lips twisting into a smile. Lysande did not reply.

Hallways hurt, and paths curving through the grounds tugged at her sinews; it was not truly a physical pain but the response of her body to something much deeper than battle-aches. With no foreign places to distract her, no Rhimese castles or Lyrian hills to draw her mind from the hollow inside her, she felt her loss anew. Grief had been waiting, all the time that she had been fighting off a threat. Now it leaped from its corner in her consciousness and sought to push its way out, through her organs, through her very pores. She stopped by the royal suite and felt her body buckle.

It was supposed to be easier. To seal itself with time, until the rawness of bereavement was gone. Even if the damage was still there somewhere deep down, you were meant to feel the softness of a little healing; but if anything, the pain felt sharper upon coming back.

By the lake in the grounds, sitting on the verge of grass, she blinked back a few tears, transported to the morning of her nineteenth gift-day when she had knelt by a tactos-board beside the water and pretended to struggle with Sarelin's queen. I'll never go a day without missing

you, she thought. Even after a thousand days have passed. Even though
you wrote your name across the realm in magical blood.

On the two Sarelins, woman and state, she had clearer opinions
now. They had separated with greater precision.

She waited until Litany had left her for the evening before taking
out the chest, turning the key in the lock. She stood there for a minute,
the sound of her own breath amplified. The sight of all the jars side by
side, uniformly shining, filled with the shade of blue she had imagined
so many times since her maturation, sent a shudder through her as she
opened the lid. She picked up the first jar. The more she tried to slow
her impulse, the more it gathered speed, the desire gyrating inside her.

How many times had Charice warned her, with that pinched look,
you don't know what it's doing to you?

It had been an age since the last dose. That meant she was imbibing
a lot less, really.

She held up the long silver shape of the spoon to the light and measured two spoonfuls of flakes into the vial. Sipping every drop slowly
from her goblet would help her endurance, surely. She had not forgotten what it felt like to drink scale; how her heart threatened to drum
itself out of existence, while the pain melted and ceded to the golden
glow, the physical stimulus and mental calm combining; yet the imprint in her mind gave way now to the real thing, and she reached for
the spoon again. One more.

No question of using night-quartz now. She saw the stone, wrapped
and swaddled in the corner of the chest, and seemed to hear a whisper
of salvation. She ignored it.

Gold raced through the room, just as her heartbeat reached an angry
pace. It swelled and spread, flowing into every corner. Her fingers tensed
on the goblet. Speeding glow: that had never happened with two spoonfuls. Every space was infused with goldenness, every surface glossed
with it, and the *feeling* of gold was not only in every mote of dust but in
her veins. She could feel her stomach twisting and contorting with the
same fury that drove her heart to race, but she ignored it. She held on to
the sensation for as long as she could, leaning against her desk.

Her breath pounded in her ears as she entered Sarelin's chambers,
and in the garden, she lay down upon the grass and looked up,

exhaling slowly. Sarelin had looked up at the same sky before her eyes closed for the last time. There was no voice to respond to her, yet it felt good to put the truth about the bone people directly to Sarelin . . . if she could not demand an explanation, she could challenge her closest friend. She raised the matter of the childhood that Mea Brey had spent serving Sarelin, too: Why had she not been informed? Had the Iron Queen who had carved her way through seven battlefields felt so guilty about her cousin's treatment? What did Sarelin think of Lysande, now, an elemental? Did she approve, or did she recoil? For a dead woman and a live one, they had much to discuss.

Litany found her in the suite, on the second morning, touching the dent in Sarelin's armor where the White Queen's sword had made its mark. It still shocked her, how stealthily Litany could enter a room, leaving even the dust unscattered.

"Twenty-three years."

"I'm sorry?" Lysande said.

"That's how many Queen Sarelin lived before she took the throne." Litany nodded to the dent. "She was barely past youth when the White Army bled the realm. My mother taught me that, before she taught me my prayers."

"Sarelin always said war was what made her a woman." Lysande glanced at the box in the girl's hands. "Have you brought me a gift, Litany?"

"Of a sort. I wanted to return this to you."

Inside, a gold stem shone against the wood. The feather attached to it was spattered with blood, and the writing-tip had been coated until it was entirely covered in crimson; yet it was her quill, undoubtedly, the one Sarelin had given her. Lysande placed it in her palm.

What were the chances? She had given up hope of ever finding it again after it had tumbled from her pocket during her capture. She felt a rush of joy, bolstered by the swirling of gold within her.

"I had the staff of Rayonnant Palace out searching for it as soon as I knew you'd lost it. The dove came this morning."

"A happy answer, and most unlooked-for." Had she imagined Litany's smile?

"I hope it is not the only happy answer I can deliver."

Lysande started. She caught Litany's eye, and the girl smiled openly this time.

"I will be your Mistress of Defense. But on the condition that I may do my work in secret. Some plants only grow in the shadows, while others thrive in the sun: I was not born to be a creature of the light."

Slipping the quill into her pocket, Lysande extended a hand, and they shook, Lysande's grip matching Litany's for firmness, the two of them grinning unashamedly now. They moved in and held each other for far longer than the usual Axiumite embrace. Lysande did not mind at all that she was still beaming when Litany let go.

"Of course, an appointment of such importance should be marked with a gift."

She led the girl to her chamber, smiling at Litany's curiosity, and did not say a word. Once inside, she reached for the object that was resting on the desk and handed it over. A silver dagger sparkled, engraved with the name *LITANY*. "You have beaten me to the giving, it seems," she said. "After all I put you through, from the battle to what happened with Derset. . . . you still find time to salvage my possessions. You really are the only gem I cherish in this glittering world, Litany."

Litany was prevented from being swallowed up entirely by embarrassment by her desire to whip the dagger around. Lysande watched her swinging it. She let Litany sputter out her thanks, only half-listening.

At last, she pulled the quill out of her pocket again, turning it over in her palm. She ran a finger over the pointed end, where the blood was thickest, and felt the coat that had ossified. *A red quill.* There was something curiously fitting about it.

"I could get someone to polish it for you," Litany said, "if you want to use it. The smith can clean it until it shines."

"No." She wrapped her fingers around the tip. "I think I prefer it this way."

Litany folded her arms. It was the same pose Raden had adopted, more than once, when they were talking of pre-Conquest societies or the complexities of ancient linguistics, and she had said something he didn't understand; the same belligerent stance, born of the fond frustration that friends harbored for each other, softened by a smile. The

sight sent a stab of pain through her, but with it came a dart of pleasure, in remembrance.

"Honestly," Litany said. "What are you going to write with a
bloody quill?"

Lysande raised the quill and eyed the girl over the point.

"That remains for me to decide."

The morning of the Councillors' arrival came with a storm of polishing and cooking, and Lysande did not emerge from her chamber while
the staff were working. By the time she left the tower, the palace was a
dark doublet, slashed here and there with the brilliant silver of moonlight.

Her feet slipped over the stone floors. The attendants did not greet
her and even the guards who had once jeered her did not speak; Oxbury, a woman with a thin nose who had always thrown barbs at Lysande, kept her eyes down as Lysande passed the doorway of the wing
where she kept her vigil.

It's mine, Lysande realized, as she took the stairs at a brisk stride.
The palace is mine.

It was a queer thought.

The Rhimese guards on the door to Luca's suite were conversing
with Carletta Freste, but all of them looked up as she approached. One
guard made to block her way.

"Let her through, Taglio. That's Councillor Prior," Freste said.

The woman gawked at Lysande's ink-flecked doublet as she stepped
aside.

Lysande kept her ears attuned as she entered the bedchamber. In
the dim torchlight, she could make out Luca's clothes strewn on the
floor—dark fabrics, red silk, and belts of soft ox-hide, along with quills
poking out of pots, and books piled on the desk. From pamphlets to
thick tomes, some imprinted with seals, and others bound with string
that glinted, she saw such a variety of books that she wondered how he
had transported them all.

A pile on the corner of the desk offered a number of foreign books;
she picked one of these up and read *A Short History of Long Pleasure*

on the spine. Taking in the imprint on the front cover, a tripartite design of bordered scenes, she gazed at the large picture of a woman and man entwined, flanked by a scene of female lovers and another of male lovers, each couple thoroughly occupied—and she dropped the book hastily.

The sound of running water caught her attention. There were no fountains in Axium Palace's suites, yet she could hear splashing. She knocked on the bath-chamber door, but no reply came. The handle gave way. Somehow it did not bother her that she was intruding.

Moving in, she navigated through a wall of mist; jets of water leaped from one end to the other of the long bath, splashing down, then arcing back up again. Steam warmed her neck. Torches burned in brackets on the right wall, flickering. Their glow was not bright enough to illuminate the whole room, and it took her a moment to notice that Luca was sitting in the dry pocket at the end, wearing nothing but his ruby ring.

She froze. He did not appear to have seen her; as he bent forward to mark the parchment that rested against his knees, she examined his profile, from shoulders to toes: not thin enough to be a commoner's, nor bulky enough to be a soldier's. A scholar's, perhaps. On the patch of floor beside him, the shimmering coils of Tiberus' tail wrapped around an ink-pot. The small black stone she had seen him touching in Castle Sapere lay next to the pot.

"Don't try to scamper off, Prior."

The words cut through the steam. She had forgotten about the elemental senses. Putting one hand on the wall, she tiptoed over. "Writing, here?"

"We Rhimese are cold-blooded in every sense. We do our best work in the heat."

As he rolled up the parchment, Lysande sank down onto the floor beside him. The warmth seeped into her legs. "Your family is more cold-blooded than others," she said.

The words hung between them.

"Did you know your brother was using the bone people for target practice in his quest to 'cleanse' the realm? If they'd been elementals or not, it didn't really matter, did it? They were poor enough not to matter."

The question had not been intended, but she was glad to have asked it, all the same.

Luca put down his quill and dropped it into the pot. After a moment, he spoke, softer than before. "You'd have been surprised how Raolo could cover things up. I only found out years after I killed him what he'd been doing in the desert. But I don't think it would have mattered to my father—Raolo shone with the light of burnished gold to the great Prince Marcio Sovrano. My father never tried to scrape the gilt back and see what was underneath. He didn't even mind when his firstborn son decided to murder his bastard brother." At her expression, he chuckled, still softly. "Oh, yes, Prior, Raolo planned it well. Late at night, with a pack of dogs, two guards he had bribed, a bucket of oil, and a firebrand. I'd be cleared from the family line in the most direct way."

"Mercy." Lysande sucked in a breath.

"I don't know if Raolo knew I was elemental. But I have my suspicions. I'm not one for putting trust in prayer, so I made sure Tiberus was awake to alert me—you see, I knew which night they were coming. I had spies among the guards."

Luca picked up the little black stone and held it in his hand, turning it over, moving it from palm to fingers and back, keeping it in motion. She had seen that rotation before. Those dextrous fingers moved over and over, as smooth as the stone's surface, dancing.

He leaned toward her, and she leaned back, averting her eyes; the next inch of skin below his hips had almost come into view.

"Do you ever stop playing with that thing?" She tried to keep her voice light. It did not seem right to acknowledge the intimacy of this conversation.

He held out his palm. "Try it."

She curled her fingers around the stone. Heat shot through her skin. She dropped it, before it could burn her, and Luca took it back from her quickly. "Takes a while to get used to."

"Get used to?" Was he joking?

"I don't mean the heat." Luca's mouth was still curled, but his tone was not flippant. "I mean the pain."

In the pause that followed, Lysande thought of him turning the stone over and over, rotating it between his fingers. She thought of the term *proclivity* for a moment. It seemed to leap out of a dictionary and into her mouth.

"Your gift," she said.

"Oh, yes, Prior; did you bring it?"

"Only out of a desire to know how someone who observes me so closely might be so far off the mark." She drew the black velvet bag from her pocket; the bag that she had kept aside for so long, only picking it up to feel the curves of the object through the material. Now, she pulled the drawstring and shook the rope out, watching it uncoil on the floor. "I know what a binding-rope is, Fontaine. I have seen drawings. And the giver of such a gift is the one who applies it. If you think I will be tied by you . . ."

"The Rhimese tradition is a little different from the Axiumite one, it seems." He smiled faintly. "We only give a binding-rope to a person we hope will do the tying. Do you think I have forgotten that quadruple knot on the package of the line-bloom you gave me, before we ever met?" He slid the black rope along the floor to her. "It was not a present to be used *on* you, Prior. It was a present for you to *use*."

He held out his hand, wrist up. In the reflection of the light from the wet stones, he looked like a painting, the skin over his veins gossamer-fine, an artist's polished work. "One begins here."

"Oh," Lysande said.

"If that's what you like."

She was aware of a hundred powder-keg fuses sparking inside her.

Scooping up his things, Luca began to stand up, and Lysande was suddenly very conscious that he was wearing nothing but his skin. A desire to rush out and let her blood cool overwhelmed her, yet she was sure he would be amused if she did; this was some sort of game to make her blush, or at least, it was a very good strategy. Rising with him, she noticed a few thin lines scored into his back, tapered as if from the end of a whip.

"Gawk all you like, Prior." He didn't even turn. "Scars aren't like Axiumites. They don't embarrass easily."

Lysande was suddenly very busy with her boots, still feeling the

impression of the stone on her fingers as she brushed them down. By
the time she followed him into his chamber, Luca was fastening a robe
of black silk around his waist, knotting the tie.

She wanted to ask him many things: how he felt about killing his
brother; how he had survived all this time as an elemental when he was
surrounded by a court; who his mother had been and where she was
now; how he had acquired those scars. But this was not the time. The
way he was looking at her told her that he had something to ask, too.

"Conspiracy is hungry work," Luca said.

"Are we conspiring, then?"

"I certainly hope so."

He lifted a domed cover from a platter on the table. Upon the silver,
layers of brown-and-white cake formed a block. An amorata, Lysande
realized. Sarelin had ordered one, years ago, when she was in an all-
night meeting with a pretty young lord from the Lynson family. Dotted around this cake were the crimson globes of firettes, a fruit rumored
to taste sharp and sweet at once—she had always struggled to find
them in Axium's markets. Perch had implied, once, that firettes were
not favoured in the capital because they were somewhat . . . sensual, as
a dessert . . . even disreputable.

The heat from the stone had begun to fade. She flexed each of her
fingers.

Luca poured wine into the two goblets on the table and passed one
to her, and they drank in unison. The cake divided smoothly under his
knife. Lysande ate her piece slowly. Many sweet flavors mingled in
each mouthful, and she was determined to taste them all.

As she looked up, she became aware that they were standing side by
side. She smelled the faint scent of orange blossoms, tinged with a bitter edge.

"When you're one of us, Prior, and you have eyes upon you every
day, it's as if you're walking on a pond in winter," Luca said. "The ice
has frozen just enough to venture out. At any moment, it might crack,
and send you plunging down below. So you walk carefully; you take
ginger steps, and if you reach out to hold another's hand, your fate
becomes bound up with theirs. If they fall, you fall. If they make it
across, you do too."

"I'm sure you're going to approach the point at any moment."

"It can't have escaped you that there's never been a chance like this, in modern Elira, with *two* elementals in power." He put his goblet down. "Now that the others know the White Queen is back, with a chimera and who knows what else, they'll look to protect their own people. Cassia will go back to the jungle and reequip her guards from those unfairly large armories. Dante and Jale will be trying to control their cities . . . if they can prize themselves off each other." He took a forkful of cake and paused. "What Elira needs is someone to take charge of the realm."

"You mean to nominate yourself as leader of the Council." Lysande didn't need to phrase it as a question.

"I can stand above the cities and coordinate them, fortify against chimeran fire, and win back King Ferago at the same time. With you to assist me, of course." Luca's stare had intensified. "We're walking on the same ice now, Prior."

"Let me guess. You want me to support your motion to elect a leader?"

"No." He took a sip of wine. "I want you to propose the motion. It'll look better if it comes from you."

Of course. Of course, he had thought it through to the level of practicality.

"Why not propose a Consul, instead of a monarch? It was what rulers elected by their peers called themselves in the Classical Era," she said.

Luca paused, regarding her. "In the Classical tradition, a Consul should have a deputy of great standing. How does it sound: Lysande Prior, my second-in-command?"

Lysande had the odd feeling that they were back at the tactos-board and he was playing a double game—that he had waited, again, to reveal his best move. There were times when it was better not to speak, however, but to pay attention to every word directed your way: to take in every sign, wrung from tone of voice and movement.

"I saw you in the observatory after you killed Derset." Luca laid his hand on hers. "You were shaking like one of those ribbons tied to the gate: trembling. That's when I thought, you deserve better than this. You can step out of the blood and the flames, Prior. Just put your vote behind me. There won't be anyone closer. I'll give you access to all the rare volumes in the Academy." His words were flowing, coursing over her. "It'll be exactly like it was when you worked for Queen Sarelin."

"Not exactly the same, I think." She placed her hand over his and pressed down.

He slid his hand to align beneath hers, palm against palm. She waited to see what he was going to do, until she realized he was waiting for her—that the soft fingers under hers were not a direction but a question. For a moment, she was not sure what she would try.

The ends of her nails dug into the flesh of his palm, marking the skin. His eyes closed. She dug harder, then let go of his hand and put her goblet down. He was only an arm's length away, and she could reach out and push him away; she could tell, by the way he was watching her, eyes open again, that he half-expected her to. It would be intriguing to see what he did if she struck him across the face again, but instead, she leaned across and brought her hand around, and dug her nails into the back of his neck.

This is what Cassia would do, she thought. Not me.

Yet she gripped him by the hair with her other hand, pulled him to her, and pressed her mouth to his. She had begun this in the book-lined room at Rayonnant Palace and she wanted to finish it now. He shuddered. The whole of his body yielded to hers, under her grip, and as she twisted the lock of hair, he breathed a soft "Yes." It was sweeter to Lysande than the amorata's white-and-brown layers. Was this not what she had wanted, deep down: her own desire, reflected and transformed, as in a pane of sheer glass?

When she had run her palm down the warm skin of Derset's back, she had thought to herself, *this is mine*, but now she knew vanity, and she knew desire. Luca did not belong to her. He met her at eye level, every time, in flame or in flood.

She removed her other hand from his neck and ran it across his back, tracing the scars beneath the robe.

The amorata lay on the table beside them, surrounded by the smooth firettes. She detached herself from Luca and picked a firette off the platter.

Circling around to face Luca again, she slipped the fruit into her mouth. The sharp tang of it spread on her tongue, even though she did not take a bite. She walked into Luca without stopping. Why was it so easy to push him into a chair, to wedge her leg between his thighs, to wrap her palm around the side of his soft neck and hold it there?

She waited until his breathing had sped up, then slowly pressed her lips to his. As he opened his mouth, she slid the firette off her tongue and onto his.

He said nothing, but his eyes brightened, and he chewed slowly, keeping his gaze locked on hers. She pulled her mouth away and watched as he swallowed. When she brought her mouth to his again, his breathing mingled with her own, and she tasted the sharpness of the rare fruit, lingering; she lowered herself until she was mostly on top of him and ground his body into the chair-back.

"Don't move." Her whisper carried a weight, a lead-rich quality that manifested in the air.

"I assure you, I haven't the slightest desire to." He looked directly into her eyes. "You could do anything to me, from this position."

"Not quite. I can make a start."

He almost managed to hide his pleased interest. "I assume an education is in order?"

No . . . it was not only interest. He was looking at her with a kind of veneration. *As if I were . . .* what was it, exactly? And then she knew. It felt as if she had always been meant to look down at him, as if she were resting on a throne. His stare had taken on a new expectation. She considered the soft pinkness of the lips that had accepted the firette from her tongue; considered the deliberate way that he had swallowed; then brought her hand up, watched his eyes brighten, and swung her palm down into his cheek.

She had been right about the first time she had slapped him—she knew that at once, for his eyes brightened even more as he inhaled. Their glances met and he said nothing, but she brought her lips to his again. The sharp sweetness of the firette still lingered in his mouth, and the blend of wariness and fascination in his eyes reflected her own. She wanted to believe that she had found it, the other half of a broken mirror, the missing piece that fit opposite her, but she could not allow herself so much hope.

You could shape anything into a match for your own desire, when that desire was rare. You wanted to believe that you heard a note of excitement in a lover's voice; that you glimpsed a signal in another's glance, a flag fluttering in their smile. If you dared to show yourself, you risked losing that imagined signal forever. When you did get a sign, you often lunged at it—after so long without a flag, you were willing to trust the first one to unfurl itself to you. Derset had responded to her. She had believed that he did so out of the same desire, but she had not peeled back the surface of that desire and peered down. *I like what you like.* She would not make that mistake again.

Without hesitation, she shifted her weight entirely onto Luca. He gasped, and she knew that it was not in pain. She felt his fingers curl around her back, and heard his whisper: "Prior."

A waver, in his voice. It sounded real enough. But who could be sure after such a short time? She kissed him again, slipping a hand between his thighs.

It was curious, but she could not quite tell how long the second kiss lasted. Time seemed to ebb away, and yet she was aware of claiming his mouth with her tongue, grasping his neck with her fingers, but pulling away at the end: leaving the promise of a conclusion. Luca's stare fixed on her as she let go.

"You can do that again, you know." He breathed the words against her mouth.

"Kiss you?"

"Hit me." There was a depth to his voice, and she felt something flowing inside her, like ink spilling over the top of a pot. His cheek was pink, so pink where her palm had struck.

"Should I take it that you've decided?" he added.

Lysande smiled. "I think you've identified exactly what the Council needs," she said.

The torchlight dipped and flickered as she walked across the chamber, and she made sure to not to look back as she passed through the door: not to allow him a glimpse of her face.

She tried to breathe as evenly as she could while she stood in her chamber, listening to the buzz from the crowd lining the palace fence. The mingling of voices, deep notes blending with higher, had signaled other events in the past: the gathering for Sarelin's jubilee, or the beginning of a hunt. Did these people hope for another Sarelin now?

"It's strange," Litany said, brushing out the last knot in her hair. "This feels so different from the first time I dressed you in this room."

Everything shifts just a little after you discover your attendant could put you to sleep with a draught from a well-chosen bottle, Lysande thought.

Litany straightened out the silver lock of hair, running her fingers from the top of the deathstruck tress to the very bottom. When she looked up from the queer, glittering strands, Lysande read the question in her eyes.

"Yes," she said. "I will wear it unbound today."

"Your hair looks . . ."

Unnatural. Unseemly. Unworthy of display.

". . . majestic," Litany finished.

Lysande caught her reflection in the mirror.

"Do you have your daggers at the ready?" she said.

"Always."

"Well, then." Lysande smiled. "I think we are ready to spend some time with the populace."

They did not have to wait long for the arrival of a troupe of ushers. The pair of them were surrounded, bowed to, and marched down the stairs with many congratulations on their deeds in Lyria, all of which rang hollowly after the experience of battle. Lysande crossed the grounds to the sound of shouts and cheers that seemed as polished as the palace spires, and just as distant. Ignoring the ushers' remarks about the time, she walked to a spot on the fence and, after a brief hesitation, put her hand through it, touching the palm of a girl in shabby clothing. The girl colored and shrank back while her parents pushed forward to thank Lysande, but after a moment, she dared to fix her eyes upon the Councillor again, and they shared a look: not happy, exactly, but full of promise. Lysande moved along the line, and in a few minutes she had covered a good portion of the crowd, shaking more hands, tapping shoulders, and touching pendants or rings for luck.

The sound died away, but when she bowed and turned to walk back to the palace, it rose again. The Axiumites shouted only one name.

"You're their leader," Litany said. "I mean, you were before, but you really are now."

She took her Mistress of Defense by the arm, squeezing her slightly, and strode into the palace.

A rainbow of colors ringed the Oval, formed by capes and doublets. It was almost a dream to see the Council in one place again, without bodies lying underfoot or sheets of mesh falling from above, and without the smell of blood rising from the ground. She spotted Cassia on her right, lounging with her arms folded, and she winked at the Irriqi as she passed. Ever so subtly, her friend tapped the table twice.

"Here she is at last," Dante said, looking at her from between two captains. "Can we begin?"

"In Axium, when we say 'on the hour,' we mean 'on the hour.'" Lysande bowed to the right as she reached him; the northern gesture of mourning was a little stiff, but she thought she managed the general idea. Dante's gaze softened. He turned his attention to Jale's hair, picking a piece of leaf from the strand on which it had nestled.

Pelory was the last to arrive. Lysande studied Luca as the others discussed chimera sightings, mercenaries, and enemies, her gaze wandering to the expanse of neck that was visible above his collar, and then down. She reproached herself for dwelling on his lips. How it would feel, though, to push a firette onto his tongue again, and watch him swallow . . .

His gaze skipped to her. He did not meet her eyes; he was looking at the hair on the left side of her part, the queer silver lock that now glittered in full view. A smiled tugged the corners of his mouth.

"We haven't discussed experiments for fortifying stone against chimeran fire," Cassia was saying, raising one hand.

Listening to the others argue and sling information back and forth, Lysande was conscious that she owed her life to the Shadows—as did they all—and that it would be folly to betray what Three had told her after her conversation with Charice. Some things took time to change. She pictured herself dealing information as cards from her hand—the possibility of another chimera, Signore Chamsak's weapon-stores, and

Three's plan to buy any remaining eggs, explained briefly to her—and after laying them out on the table, she gathered them up and reshuffled them into her deck. Wondering if there was something she might pass on, she ran over her last conversation with Derset in her head.

Her Majesty means to take this realm back to the beginning of the calendar. The remark had remained in her mind, yet she did not feel it was the right time to share it. In fact, she was not entirely sure what Derset had meant.

The smack of Dante's fist hitting the table made her jump.

"We should make an example to them," the First Sword said. "That chimera's the White Queen's symbol; I say we cut it up or burn it."

Lysande had already guessed that the court of Valderos would be demanding to destroy any remains of the chimera before their citizens; all too easily, she could picture the parched crowds thirsting for revenge.

"Time will bring wisdom. Only tyrants rush into burning and slicing, regardless of whether it is flesh, fur, or scales. Let patience rule first," Jale said.

Dante looked quickly at him. "Are you sure you wish to keep the body?"

"I could persuade you of the benefits to science. If you would let me make my case in private, that is."

"I fear that your case in private would always sway my hand."

"If the two of you are done batting your eyelashes for now," Cassia said, leaning back in her chair, "I, for one, will not have Lyria sitting on its golden haunches, holding up progress. I will take the chimera, and we will examine it in Pyrrha."

"Oh, certainly. And I suppose we should all let you walk away with a source of untapped knowledge, should we?" Luca said. "Shall I remind you that the Academy is the only place equipped to examine such an animal?"

With another smack on the table, Dante intervened, this time arguing that no one should touch the chimera. Cassia's replies grew ever more belligerent. Lysande looked past the end of the table and caught Pelory's eye. She nodded ever so slightly.

"If you please, Your Highnesses," Pelory cried, producing a volume that no one seemed prepared for.

Jale and Cassia paused in the middle of trading insults.

"Perhaps we should address the question of a leader."

Lysande rose, aware of her cheeks heating but determined to keep the flush from them.

The advisors, captains, and followers were staring. She had expected this, and she expected a challenge, too: the reiteration of her words in the Pavilion, the order her memory was too well-trained to forget. *You will rule together until the White Queen is dead or imprisoned and Elira is secure.*

Every head in the room was turned in her direction. She wished Sarelin could have seen her now. City-rulers and nobles waiting for her next move, and she was no longer brittle, nor unwilling; she simply had no guarantee that this plan would work.

"It is our duty to see the realm through this struggle," she said, "and that is why I propose—not a monarch, but a leader of the Council. Someone must coordinate our tactics, oversee five armies, and deal with the foreign lands. We might call them our Consul." She looked around. "It was what rulers elected by their peers called themselves in the Classical Era."

Silence continued to cloak the table. Luca pushed out his chair and stood up. Lysande saw a few hands hover over hilts.

"I nominate Prince Fontaine," she said.

A sudden brawl of voices: a dozen different speakers clashed with each other; the room filled with exclamation, yet no sentence could be heard except in part, as if a troupe of poets were competing to grind each other down. The noblewomen beside Jale shouted something about a plot, while several people insisted that there had been an agreement made between Axium and Rhime, and the Pyrrhans flung their objections through it all. Eventually, Luca leaped up onto his chair.

The speech was everything Lysande had expected. "Are you not aware that there have been thirty-four attempts on my life since I was crowned prince? Eighteen attempts at poisoning, nine attempts at stabbing, three attempts at shooting, two lunges with a garotte, one sabotaged saddle, and one strategic use of a mad dog." He looked around the table. "You need a leader who can survive anything, if you want the realm to survive."

"So we should vote for a ruler who is constantly under siege from the populace?" Dante folded his arms.

"Every ruler is constantly under siege from the populace. The question is whether they know it." Luca smiled. "And whether they are ready. How prepared do you think we will need to be for the White Queen's next attack, Dalgëreth? Will it take a week? A few months? Or a lifetime of understanding the minds of murderers?"

"And you have been studying the minds of murderers since you were a boy, I take it?"

"Naturally. I grew up in Rhime."

Cassia took over from Dante in interrogating Luca, bombarding him with questions about strategy. While Luca described his commitment to defending the cities and hinted at funds tucked away in the vaults of Castle Sapere, he returned most often to the benefits of having a single leader: the freedom it afforded the others to tend to their own domains.

"You will soon find a great advantage in running your cities in person, as you used to. No one likes a mob breaking down their palace walls." Luca assumed an expression of concern. "Are you really willing to believe that in your absence, nothing will go wrong?"

She could see Dante nodding, and Jale ruminating, tapping his rings against the table. Luca was correct, last night, she thought. They're worried.

She watched the lines of Luca's torso as he gestured, and thought of how he had gasped, softly, hungrily, and utterly without control, when she shifted her body onto him.

Luca sat down, and Pelory called for any other nominations. After a moment, Cassia rose, pushing back her chair with a scrape of wood. Lysande felt her breath hitch.

"I nominate Councillor Prior," Cassia said.

Lysande stood. She was aware of Luca's lips parting as he stared at her. This time, Pelory had to raise her voice incrementally until the room accepted her order to be silent; Cassia tapped her chest with her fist, over her heart. Lysande felt taller at once.

"Let me lay out my promise," Lysande said, loudly, before Luca could speak. "Prince Fontaine has made many good suggestions, and I cannot claim his experience. Yet I claim a powerful motivation. It was my advisor, Lord Derset, who led us to this pass, and I swear to you that I will atone for what he did." She drew a piece of parchment from her pocket and unfolded it. "Where Prince Fontaine offers broad promises, I have a specific plan."

"Goddesses below," she heard Lord Malsante whisper to Carletta Freste. "Did His Highness know about this?"

"If he did, I'm a Lyrian dancer," Freste muttered.

Lysande had expected her hands to be trembling. They were not. She let her gaze pass from face to face, feeling the weight of the silence, holding it for as long as she dared. Across the table, she saw Luca's jaw tighten, his face elegant and crossed by anger.

She got it all out, thankfully: the need to improve the conditions for the poor, ensuring that they were well fed and gaining many more soldiers in the process. Her recent law banning vigilante attacks and her Leveling Fund needed to be declared, too. There were protests, of course, but she spoke firmly. Next, she outlined the need to use their best minds to defend against the chimera, making use of their inventions and harnessing the talent of the Academy, with Pyrrhan inventors involved too. Then the need to embark on a course of diplomacy with Royam ("*Royam?*" Dante cried), whose people and leaders had, for much of Eliran history, been wantonly overlooked, as well as the need to repair relations with Bastillón immediately. Lysande let them know in a clear voice that she had compiled all the references to Royamese customs from the palace library. It was too soon, perhaps, to say anything about elementals, though she wanted to, with a fierce yearning; a beat tapped in her consciousness, a drum warning her to hold back, and she reminded herself to keep marching at her own pace.

Finally, she declared her intention to recover all books on magic and all accounts of the White War, beginning with those in the Academy. The spluttering and glaring from the Rhimese did not surprise her.

"Is there anything else you'd like to tick off your list?" Luca said.

In the corner of her vision, she caught sight of Cassia's poorly suppressed smile. She wanted to grin back. You could bargain with allies, but with friends . . . with friends, you pledged yourself. You gave, and you hoped.

"I thank you for reminding me, Prince Fontaine. In fact, I mean to declare my intention to appoint Cassia Ahl-Hafir as an official Mistress of Chimeran Knowledge."

"Mistress of—is this a joke?"

"Far from it. She will be responsible for investigating their biology, their mentality, their capabilities. Without knowledge, we have no hope of defense. Indeed, Prince Fontaine," for Luca had begun to interrupt again, "without someone to gather facts about chimeras, how could I lay the right foundations to defend Elira? I would be rushing to seize power without a strategy. Not that I accuse you of any such thing, you understand."

Voices clamored as the Councillors argued, and for a while, Lysande watched them. She let the discussion ebb and flow. When she was ready, she cleared her throat and looked around the table.

"I am but a scholar, and Prince Fontaine is . . . well, a prince. But as a scholar, I know how to marshal facts and rule ideas. You know me as one who trained under Queen Sarelin. Let us not forget that before Axium Palace, I lived many years in a public orphanage. The people do not forget it, I promise you. When war draws near, they will lack courage, and who better to restore their valor than one whom they can relate to—one whose unpolished name they chant?"

"Is that another quote from the Silver Songs, Councillor?" Jale asked.

"No." She cobbled a smile together. "I wrote that line myself."

Amid the flurry of whispers that broke out in the Oval, Pelory managed to get over to her. Lysande and Luca were to leave the room immediately, Pelory insisted, while the rest of the Council considered the matter. Luca was escorted out with her, and Pelory shooed away the attendants who had stuck their heads out from doors.

Lysande walked to the painting of Queen Montfolk. The crown that nestled in the queen's hands dominated the corridor, shining in the dim light, its paint brighter than the matte paint which covered the rest of the canvas. Lysande stood on the right side of the portrait. After a moment, Luca joined her, standing on the left of the crown.

"How bold of you," he said.

"A prince once told me that I should be bolder when I jump. He said a horse would never do as I bid if I asked it politely." Lysande could still remember the moment she had stood beside him, perched on a cliff, the white stone buildings of Rhime laid out before them.

"Very clever, those ideas about helping the poor—or is that using them?" He shook his head. "I could've protected you, Prior."

"Perhaps you failed to grasp why I was trembling in the observatory. You see, I was shocked, but not because I threw my daggers into Derset." She had wanted to say this to him before, in his suite, only she had not been able to find the words. They were arriving now. "The only thing more shocking than murdering someone is discovering that you don't feel shocked at all. Or weak. Or horrified. Or any of those things you're supposed to feel. I could have killed him again, Fontaine, sunk my blade into him again and again, until there were no places left to pierce." She looked into his eyes. "So you see, I have no need for protection—from you or from anyone else."

For a long time, he held her stare, and she could not tell what he was thinking, though she had the impression that he was seeing her for the very first time.

"I learned a saying, here in Axium, as a child." She did not drop her gaze. "*Restrain, constrain, subdue.* We had to chant it in the orphanage, every day, to remind us not to speak too loudly, nor to step across any lines. I confess, I believed that every child in Axium learned it. I heard the blacksmith's daughter say it to her mother on one of my trips to the city. But after I moved to the palace, I never heard a silverblood repeat that phrase—not a single noble, nor an advisor, nor the queen. I came to wonder if they had ever been taught it at all."

"That would certainly fit with their official motto."

"*Everything in its place.* Oh, yes, they all know that one." She smiled, just a little. "When people have been showing you for years that you are not part of their group, then why should you borrow their words? Mottos are not goddess-given. People wrote them. It seems to me that a different kind of leader needs . . . new words."

The door swung open and Pelory called their names. In the doorway, Lysande paused. She placed a hand on Luca's throat and held it there, feeling the pulse. He stiffened.

The talk ceased as they entered the Oval again. It did not seem right to take their seats, with everyone staring at them, so they stood in front of the table. Lysande glimpsed Litany at the end, and she saw the girl's hand slip instinctively to her dagger-belt.

Dante cast his vote first. "The more time spent running a city, the better one is at running a country. It stands to reason." He shot a glance at Jale. "Whatever my personal thoughts, I must defer to experience."

"Are you voting for me, Dalgëreth?" Luca sounded delighted.

"I hope I do not come to regret it."

Lysande exerted all the effort she could to remain impassive. She inhaled, feeling the last vestiges of the golden glow. If she could take three spoonfuls of scale right now, perhaps the gold would speed through the room once more and enter her veins. She would stand as a tower: ready for a siege.

Cassia rose and declared her support for Councillor Prior. ("Now, there's a surprise," Luca remarked.) Lysande caught her friend's eye and they exchanged grins, Lysande mouthing the word *chimeras* across the table.

Jale, however, announced that he was going to abstain. While Pelory checked the rules, Lysande waited, trying to ignore the whispering.

"It appears there's a rule. Where all leaders of the cities are called to vote on one issue, anyone may abstain if she or he finds it impossible to reach a decision," Pelory said.

"Well, there you are. Simply impossible for me, I'm afraid," Jale said.

"A split vote. Perhaps we could have two Consuls," Pelory said at last. "But as to how authority over the city-states would be split . . . without a precedent, the division is opaque . . ."

You mean you don't have even the scrap of an idea, Lysande thought.

Dante called to one of his captains, who rummaged in a bag and unrolled a cloth. A stitched map of Elira confronted them. Lysande was suddenly reminded of the size of the land and the size of what she could be taking on; people always defined a country by its common characteristics of terrain and culture, but in fact, it was the differences between cities and towns, between one group of people's beliefs and another, that constituted a realm. As she watched, Dante ran his finger down the middle, dividing the west side from the east, his fingertip stopping at the Grandfleuve.

"Lyria's territory is vast," Luca mused. "We *could* divide it between the two of us."

"I should like the northern half," Lysande said. "Where the bone people live. As Consul, my first act will be to take them under my authority and protection, by law."

"Can we just reforge legal tradition like that?" Pelory said.

"I will melt it down myself, if I must." Lysande met her gaze.

Luca shot Lysande a cutting stare. It was the last question to settle, however, and after bows had been made and hands shaken, Lysande and Luca agreed to have a draft of terms drawn up. Dante drew his sword and carved the map in two. The Oval erupted into applause and comment, guards and nobles swarming to the divided cloth, Pelory muttering something about the possibility of sewing the map back together with merchants' thread when they could avail themselves of a skilled artisan. Jale thanked Lysande and whispered something about the bone people that she did not catch.

Pelory escorted the pair of them out, and Lysande hastened to keep up with her as they marched down the corridor. Her own body seemed warmer than usual, her chest hotter, but she kept the excitement running through her from showing on her face. It had worked. Unbelievably, it had worked. No silverblood had blocked her plan.

She had no notion where they were going. She needed a few minutes, a few breaths, to catch up with what had just happened, and the staff lining the walls seemed to feel similarly, peering after them. A pair of guards sprang apart at the entrance to the fifth floor. Lysande and Luca made their way along the corridor until Pelory waved them over to the largest window in the palace. The crowd spread out along the fence below, rows of people in emerald-hued caps and homespun shirts, talking and pointing.

"I anticipated that after the meeting, the populace would be waiting for you," Pelory said, with a glance at Lysande. "We all need something to celebrate."

She nodded, observing the crowd for a moment.

"I took the liberty of decorating the western balcony. In case you'd like me to lead you to a place where you might make an appearance," Pelory said.

Clever. Put yourself in front of the populace as queenmaker, she thought. She laid a hand on Pelory's shoulder. "You've earned it. Still, don't forget to remind the people that it was Captain Hartleigh who gave his life for them. They should be conscious of who they owe their thanks to, after all."

She gestured to the corridor ahead, and Pelory led the way, walking less ebulliently now. Luca fell into step with Lysande. He did not smile, but nor were his eyes flashing with their dark fire; he was looking at the portraits of poets, captains, and nobles, shining from silver frames on the walls.

As they neared a family tree of the Breys, he slowed. "The orphan and the bastard," he murmured. "I did say it has a ring to it."

"Sounds like a pair of thieves."

"Perhaps that's what we are." He stared at the tree. "Thieves."

They stood, confronting the chart for a moment. A black patch covered the place where the name of Sarelin Brey's second cousin should have been. It had been sewn on with many small stitches. She felt sure that Luca had noticed it.

"Since we're to share responsibility, I wish to be clear, Fontaine. Don't think for a moment that I'm going to sit back and assist you while you make the decisions."

"Oh, I wouldn't expect that, Prior. Not from a Consul of the realm like you."

"The last Consul was stabbed to death in her courtroom." Lysande's gaze lingered on the chart. "By a group of twelve silverbloods."

Silence answered her. She looked across to see Luca gazing thoughtfully at the black patch.

Rounding the corner of the corridor, they came out onto a balcony. Over the top of the silver and emerald ribbons tied to the rail, Lysande made out a sea of upturned faces. She did not attempt to still the nerves coursing through her. When you faced a sea, you could slink back onto the shore, or you could swim into the currents and ride them as they formed peaks, breaking and foaming, carrying you to a place where you might struggle to float.

Freste and Malsante were waiting for Luca on the left side of the balcony, holding his bow and his cobra, and on the right side, Litany beamed, clutching Lysande's dagger-belt in one hand.

The breeze blew with bitter intensity, but they did not wait long until Pelory walked out below and said something to the crowd. Cheers swelled and the words *Fontaine*, *Prior*, and *Elira* drifted up over the rail.

"Perhaps, Consuls," Pelory said, returning to them, "if you were to raise your most prized weapon, the people might look to the future with courage."

Luca turned to where Freste and Malsante were waiting. He placed Tiberus on his shoulder and took his bow—the new instrument, long and black and embellished with cobras—and brandishing it, he looked out at the human sea. A wave of applause washed over him.

Litany held out the hilt of Lysande's gold dagger. Lysande examined it, gazing at the blade Sarelin had given her. She thought of the words she had spoken to Derset across a table striped by torchlight, about a woman familiar and yet reborn to her.

After a final glance, she slid the dagger into its sheath.

"Not that one," she said.

Litany proffered the dagger-belt, but Lysande shook her head and reached into her doublet pocket. Her fingers closed around something slender.

"That?" Litany asked, eyeing the item as she pulled it out. "Will it do?"

The red-tipped quill gleamed in Lysande's palm. Its coating felt cool.

Yes, she thought. It will do nicely.

She lifted the quill and waved to the crowd, surveying the rows of faces. A ripple of something potent and unspoken ran through her. As she looked across at Luca, their eyes locked, and something crackled in the air. The drumming of her name came back at her, louder and louder, with all the rhythmic certainty of a legion's march.

With her hand raised, she let it spread.

Acknowledgments

This book owes its biggest debt to my brother John, whose kindness and ceaseless support helped me to start, continue, and finish *The Councillor*. John gave feedback on every chapter, even when he was inundated with his own work. His belief in me was matched only by his generosity in taking time to carefully consider my writing. Although he died before this novel was published, his advice and insight stay with me—as does his boundless love. John, I did this for you.

I owe deep gratitude to my parents, Jennifer and John, who have helped me immensely. Ever since they read me *Macbeth* in the bathtub as a baby, they have been encouraging me to follow my creativity. Their belief in the value of education and their many practical acts of help have been a constant gift to me. Thank you for supporting me no matter what.

An enormous thank you to my agent Julie Crisp for taking on this novel and believing in it. I am grateful for her hard work across a multiplicity of tasks, and for her enthusiasm in championing *The Councillor* throughout its journey to publication.

A huge thank you to Leah Spann, my editor at DAW, for taking this book on and offering thoughtful and constructive advice. Thank you for pushing me to refine the book further while staying true to the essence of my writing.

Thank you to all the team at DAW who were involved with the production of this book, or helped it along its journey in any way. It takes a village to create a book, and I appreciate the work you do. Thank you to Joshua Starr for guiding me through the copy-edits, and to copy-editor Richard Shealy who clearly devoted time to detail in reviewing my work. Thank you also to Adam Auerbach for the beautiful cover he created, which feels true to this novel.

Thanks to Lucy Neave and Kate Flaherty for backing my work and for their guidance and support from start to finish of my thesis. Lucy went above and beyond her duty to read my novel several times and provide feedback, even after I had graduated—a truly generous supervisor, she deserves an award.

I am grateful to all the English teachers and lecturers who encouraged me. To Kate McColl, Yvette Arnott, and Adrian Caesar: thank you for your belief in my work.

There are too many friends to thank for their support of this book's journey. I am grateful to every one of them. To those who engaged with me about literature, fantasy, and stories: thank you for making me think and for boosting my spirits.

My gratitude goes to the other writers who have supported me on this journey by giving feedback and swapping work. My deep thanks to Rosamund Taylor, poet extraordinaire, perceptive thinker, and caring friend. Thank you to Sam Hawke for answering so many questions and being generous from the start. Thank you to the other novelists who've shared their experiences of writing and publishing with me.

To all the writers who have inspired me, from the classical period through to the present, thank you for the fire of your words.

Finally, thank you to Angshuman, who loves and supports me exactly as I am.